"I'm James Carson," he said, his voice low and soft, silkily malicious. He was close behind her, twisting her arm behind her back. She could feel his breath on her neck as he said, "Get in the car. Your car. *Now*."

Sobbing, she obeyed. She felt him beside her now—and felt something hard on her upper thigh. It was a knife blade.

He groped for the keys, then the Toyota's starter whirred; the engine caught, roared. Using one hand, Carson put the car in reverse and backed expertly down the driveway.

"Now," he said, "we close the gate and we lock it. And then we go inside—" He nodded to the cabin. "And we talk. Right?" The last word was almost a whisper. It was a lover's question, spoken as a lover might speak: softly, intimately. As he said it, she felt the point of the knife press gently.

It was a lover's touch—delicate—yet knowing, probing, promising....

SPELLBINDER

by

Collin Wilcox

FAWCETT GOLD MEDAL • NEW YORK

SPELLBINDER

Copyright © 1981 Collin Wilcox

Published by Fawcett Gold Medal Books, a unit of CBS Publications, the Consumer Publishing Division of CBS Inc.

ISBN: 0-449-14436-4

Printed in the United States of America

First Fawcett Gold Medal printing: October 1981

10 9 8 7 6 5 4 3 2 1

Prologue

AS HE WATCHES the four TV monitors, the director's fingers move delicately from the second camera switch to the fourth, ready to cut from the choir to a heads-and-shoulders, three-quarters shot of a young woman in the audience, lips parted, eyes fervent, chin lifted. Berger, on four, has been doing faces for eight shows. His eye is sharpening.

"Hold it, Berger. You're coming up."

In the earphones, Berger's voice acknowledges: "Coming up. Roger."

The delicate fingers hover over the fourth switch. These split seconds are the moments that make directors, or break them. Will she hold the pose? The note of the choir swells as the second chorus begins. Timed earlier, each chorus takes seventy seconds. Figure forty seconds for the rapt young woman, figure thirty seconds for the end of the song, on camera two.

The fingers descend, touch the switch. Over the number four monitor, a red light glows. Across America and Canada next Sunday, the anonymous woman's face from the audience will fill the faithful's TV screens. Will she blink? Burp? Scratch her nose?

It's a crap shoot, an all-or-nothing gamble: the reason directors perspire. And change jobs, statistically every twenty-seven months. And pop bennies. And worse.

But there's always the tape—the editor—the scissors. Of this thirty seconds, only twenty will show next Sunday. Margin for error, thirty percent. It's a generous figure, a model for the industry. On The Hour, no expense is spared.

"Come in closer, Powell. Back to you in thirty seconds."

On camera two, Powell is already refocusing. "Thirty seconds. Roger." Powell is quick, but uninspired. His strength is backgrounds, not people.

"Warnecke, come to the curtain, for Holloway."

On camera one, Warnecke moves to focus on the floor-to-ceiling draperies, iridescent gold. The drapes have just been installed at a cost of eighty thousand dollars. Did the gates of heaven shimmer so bright?

"Ten seconds, Powell. Mark."

"Ten seconds. Mark."

"A little closer. Let's see their teeth. Center on Rosemary."

"A little closer. Roger." On the second monitor, the choir draws a deep breath in unison. Eyes are cast up. Bosoms swell against gauzy bodices, loosely cut, according to orders. The third chorus is beginning.

Eyes moving between the clock and the monitors, the director's fingers are poised above the camera-two switch. On number four, the young woman looks as if she's seen a vision. Her job is almost finished. She hasn't scratched, hasn't seen the camera focused on her. Twenty-five good seconds—twenty-seven—thirty. Home free.

The fingers touch the camera-two switch. For thirty seconds, it's Powell's show. The director turns up the sound, hears the last strains of "Listening to the Lord." Words and music composed by Holloway's son. Or so the faithful are told.

On camera one, Warnecke is steady on the curtain. Thirty seconds. Twenty. Ten. The curtain moves. Holloway is in place: Polonius, behind the arras.

One swordthrust, and millions would lose a messiah. The director would lose a job: fifty-five thousand, last year.

"You've got it, Powell."

"Roger."

Head bowed over his old leather prayer book—a gift from his Daddy—Austin Holloway strides gravely toward center stage. Behind him, monitored by camera three, close circuited, the choir executes their slow shift to stage right. Katherine, the mother messiah, is moving on satin-slippered feet from the wings to stage left. Her attendants, once more, have not failed the faithful. Eighty minutes into the program, and Katherine Holloway is still sober, still functioning. Soon she'll be taken home to bed and bottle. Remorselessly, artlessly, the closed circuit camera tracks her. On camera three, big brother watches.

On camera one, Holloway is cut off at the waist, just below Daddy's old leather prayer book. Behind him, tracked by camera three, The Son, Elton, moves to stand beside The Mother. Sixty-five thousand pairs of eyes in the Temple can see them.

So they turn to each other, smile with a brief, false brightness and then hold hands.

Mother and son...

Madonna and child...

One of them a drunk, the other a treacherous, bad-tempered liar, on probation for reckless driving. Original charge: felony hit and run. One of his victims will never walk again. The Ferrari was totaled. Twenty-seven thousand dollars, a mass of blood-spattered wreckage.

On camera one, Holloway slowly raises his hand. The "final words" will now begin: words to live through the week by. Sometimes the final words take less than three minutes. Sometimes they take as much as fifteen, and once a full half hour. Anything more than five minutes means monumental cutting and editing problems.

And, today, Holloway has hinted at something special. Translation: something longer, more ponderous. More pompous. During the past week, perhaps, God has called. Person to person.

"Hold it, Warnecke. Don't come in till I tell you."

"Roger."

Jaw set, eyes-of-a-prophet blue and steady, noble forehead freshly powdered, tinted hairpiece firmly set, Holloway lets the measured seconds pass. His timing has never been better. Berger has him from the left, in perfect profile, medium close-up. Powell is on the right, too far away. Still too timid.

The words begin: slow, solemn, expertly paced. The faithful stir in their seats, hopeful of a high. They're already hooked. With his first few words, Holloway has "gripped their hearts," a favorite phrase. Today, despite rumors of bad health, Holloway is in top form. Obviously, he's winding up for a major effort, pacing himself for something special. Minimum, this speech will run five minutes. Maybe more. Among the choir, feet are subtly shifting. They know, too.

"Come in, Powell. Slow."

"Slow. Roger."

"Berger, go hunting. We've got time."

"Roger." Camera four wanders out into the audience. Without being told, Berger is hunting old, wrinkled faces. They pay the bills, the old ones. For them, heaven is a necessity. Heaven and natural-acting laxatives. And Fixident, too, for dentures.

Ninety seconds into the final words, the director moves both camera one and camera two in close—slowly, smoothly.

Reverently, one hopes. To keep the job—the fifty-five thousand, with bonuses this year—the cameras must move as if angels guided them. It was a Holloway axiom—spoken first in white-hot anger, later refined, finally catechized.

But Berger is Jewish: a mustachioed angel with a girlfriend in West Venice. Elton The Son had once objected to the mustache. But not to the girl.

Berger has found an old woman weeping as she watches. Fade to Berger—hold ten seconds, with Holloway's voice over. Then superimpose Holloway, then come to Holloway alone, face and shoulders. The voice is rising now, coming on strong. Soon he'll throw the show off balance, sure enough. On camera three, Elton and Katherine exchange a resigned look. They know. The old man has the bit in his teeth. Warnecke, meanwhile, has slipped the cross filters on camera one. On cue, he can make stars out of the spotlights, more perfect than the star of Bethlehem.

But not now. Not until the final moments of the final words, now nowhere in sight. If the camera leaves Holloway for long, displeasure comes quickly at the videotaping immediately to follow. The final words are sacred—and Holloway's vengeance is swift and sure. Fifty-five thousand, farewell.

Suddenly, unexpectedly, Holloway raises his arms in heavenly supplication—and reveals dark crescents of sweat staining each blue polyester armpit.

But it's all right.

If Jesus bled on the cross, Holloway can sweat on camera.

The director smiles at his dials.

The manager sits behind a small plate-glass window set high in the Temple's west wall, facing the stage. Loudspeakers are close beside him, one on either wall of the small viewing booth. A single TV monitor is before him. A spiral-bound notebook lies open on a narrow shelf beneath the window. With the blunt end of a Bic ball-point pen, in time with the choir's tempo, the manager taps on the shelf. Half the notebook's page is covered with his small, precise handwriting. Because he can get more on each page, the manager uses a fine-point Bic.

Now he reverses the pen, writes *Hips. Tits.* on the next empty line. The notation above reads, *Flow, Temp. N.G.*

It's Elton's doing, he knows: the with-it, hard-rock beat of the hymn, the hip-swinging, tit-tempting choir, eight white girls, four black. At age thirty-two, Elton is making his move. Steadily, cleverly, he's shaping The Hour in his own image. It's takeover time, and Elton is ready. One more Holloway heart attack, and Elton will inherit. His grandfather died face down in sawdust, surrounded by the faithful, wailing and rending their clothing. His father could die the same way, with his clip microphone crashing into the polished surface of the stage: an earthquake of sound in the Temple's huge speakers. Instantly Mitchell, the bodyguard, would spring to the stage from his seat in the first row. Mitchell's four somberly dressed assistants would be close behind him, doing the job they'd been drilled to do. While Holloway's soul ascended, Mitchell and his men would protect the corpse. Elton, meanwhile, would advance with head bowed, step measured. During his passage from the wings to center stage where his father sprawled, Elton would take on substance, dignity, gravity. The short trip would invest him with everything he needed, everything the faithful required. Picking up Daddy's prayer book, holding it high, Elton would preach over the corpse. All the rating records would topple, reruns thrown in.

The manager blinks the scene below back into focus. The choir's last chorus is almost finished. At stage left, Holloway touches the curtain, a cue. He's ready. Sick or well, he's ready. The show will go on. Never mind last week's ominous electrocardiogram. Never mind the twitching left eye, the mouth that sags at the corners and distorts to the left when fatigue confounds him. Never mind the terrible pallor, then the grotesque flush. For those problems, cameras have filters, soft-focus devices. Makeup men have their potions. But whatever afflictions can't be filtered out or covered up could be a plus. In the service of Christ, a messiah must sometimes seem to suffer. Thus, without his craggy features, Billy Graham might never have made it. So let Holloway sweat. Let him twitch. Let the lines and creases show, and the mouth sag at the corners. Just don't let him die. Not yet. Not before Elton makes another mistake with another Ferrari.

Did Daddy sweat and twitch and palpitate in the weeks and months before the sawdust chips ground into his face that summer night in Muncie, Indiana?

Eyes piously raised, the chorus hits the last note, holds it, lingers lovingly with it, then lets it slowly die. Their workweek is finished.

The curtain stirs. Holloway's foot appears, the black shoe

brilliantly polished, the ties tassled. A hand follows—an arm—the full figure, clad in blue doubleknit polyester, white shirt gleaming, wide tie too boldly patterned.

If the grandfather wore a flamboyant frock coat and black string tie, the son would wear doubleknit. And the grandson, too, waiting in the wings with his mother, diaphanously clad in pale pink gauze, crisscrossed at the bosom, trailing as she walks—unsteadily.

As the final words begin, the manager's eyes circle the audience, making a ritual calculation. A slip of paper on the shelf beside the spiral notebook is inscribed with the figure 63,400, the attendance tally. The month is October, the seventeenth day. Most of the faithful have just been paid. October is a promising month, with no vacations to strain family budgets. No taxes due. No Christmas presents, or Easter clothing. In Washington, credit is loosening, inflating the economy in an election year. Therefore, beneath the 63,400, the manager notes $42,000. It's his estimate of the take. For twenty-two years, each time Holloway has preached, the manager has estimated the take. At first, his estimates were wild, usually too high. Now, he comes closer than a computer.

His eyes wander to the man standing alone in the center of the stage. Almost imperceptibly during the last minute, the houselights have gone dim. Three beams of light hold Holloway in their soft golden glow—all on cue.

The final words are beginning.

When the manager had first brought in a lighting expert, Holloway had objected. The spotlights and the footlights bothered him. He wanted to see his audience—to communicate with them, he said. Wanted to feel them. Touch them. But the TV crews needed lights. And, slowly, the manager had introduced the special effects, the dramatic highlights. As Holloway lost touch with the faithful, he became rich and famous: the first successful TV evangelist.

In spite of himself.

In spite of his canvas-and-sawdust background, his down-home delivery, his simplistic, jingoistic appeals. In spite of an alcoholic wife, a ruthless son, a disaffected daughter—and, somewhere, an illegitimate child.

With his family life a disaster, Holloway still manages to appear the devoted husband and father. For an evangelist, it is essential. On stage, evangelism is a family matter. Unlike politicians, there are no divorced evangelists.

From the loudspeakers, the final words are continuing,

running too long. Although their sense is lost among the manager's thoughts, their import is clear: Holloway is building up to something big. Some surprise for all of them, he'd promised, the audience and staff alike. When the introduction is finished and the meat begins, the manager's attention will focus on the words, not the rhythm of their mesmerizing cadence. Holloway is in fine form—in perfect control, as usual. Sixty-three thousand souls believe him. Sixty-three thousand, plus one. Because Holloway, himself, still believes. At age sixty-three, he's been preaching for more than fifty years. He's cheated and swindled and raved at his enemies and fornicated with the faithful. But his vision of God remains clear and concise: and old man with a flowing white beard, eyes that never blink and a stomach that never sags. Holloway's evocation of God is as natural and spontaneous and often as truculent as a small boy's my-father-can-lick-your-father boast. They are a team, Holloway and God. A successful team, capitalized in the millions.

Thanks mostly to the manager.

Now he finally tunes his attention to the words coming over the loudspeakers. The meat, he knows, is coming up:

"Every one of you in this great Temple," Holloway is intoning, "and everyone at home, watching this service on their television sets, surrounded by their family, they all know how I came to the service of God. They all know how God first called to my Daddy, and told him to go out among the people and bring God's word to everyone who wanted to listen. They all know how my daddy started preaching the gospel in a vacant lot. Yes, friends—a vacant lot, in Peoria, Illinois. Finally, after years of serving the Lord, and raising a family, and saving every cent he could from the collections on Sunday, my Daddy scraped together enough money to buy a tent. It wasn't a big tent, friends. But it was a holy tent. It was a consecrated place. It wasn't consecrated by any bishop, or any pope, or anyone else who wore fancy robes, and preached from a fancy pulpit. No—" Holloway's voice begins to tremble. As he lifts his eyes toward heaven, he blinks against tears. The manager glances quickly at the monitor. Yes, the cameraman caught the tears.

"No," Holloway is saying huskily, "that tent wasn't consecrated by any of the princes of the church. They didn't know it existed. And they didn't care, either. But it was consecrated by the people. It was consecrated by the people who came there every Sunday, and knelt down in the sawdust and prayed with my Daddy for their eternal salvation, and life everlasting. It was consecrated by the little people—the ordinary people. They never earned much money, these people. And they never wore fancy clothes, either. Why, I can remember, as a boy, seeing them come in overalls, walking all the way into town from their farms, miles away. And I can remember something else, too. I can remember that, when I was eight years old, I began passing the collection plate. And I remember seeing those people—those simple, wonderful people—digging down in their worn pockets and dropping whatever they could into the collection plate, to help my Daddy do God's work."

Eyes still raised, Holloway pauses, as if to control himself. He drops his eyes to the prayer book he holds in both hands before him. Then, in a low, solemn voice:

"My Daddy died when I was only nineteen years old. He died under the canvas top the people had bought for him. He was preaching God's word when he died. He was doing God's work, just like he'd always done. Healthy or sick, rich or poor, hungry or not, my Daddy was doing what he'd always done. He was praying for sinners, trying to light their way to glory.

"By that time, I'd already been preaching for eight years, friends. Yes—" Holloway nods out toward his audience, invisible to him as he stands in the glare of the three golden shafts of light. "Yes, friends, I began preaching when I was eleven years old. But it wasn't until I was nineteen years old that I began my ministry. It wasn't until my Daddy laid down God's burden. Because when he laid down his burden and ascended to heaven, I knew that my time had come. The burden was mine. And I accepted it—accepted the challenge to do God's work, even though I wasn't truly a man yet.

"So I started preaching in that old, patched canvas tent of my Daddy's. But then, just a few years later, the Lord showed me a better way to preach. I was still very young, still very inexperienced. I had a lot to learn, friends. I had a whole lot to learn. But I could feel the Lord's hand on my shoulder, offering guidance. I could hear His voice in my ear. He was telling me that He wanted me to reach thousands of people with my ministry, not just hundreds. And He showed me how to do it. Yes, the Lord showed me the way. He opened my eyes, friends, to the miracle of radio. He made me understand how the very essence of His work is trying to reach more people—more souls, aching to be made whole, and be led out of the darkness and into the light of Christ's own salvation. He made me understand that the words of Jesus Christ are like a pebble thrown into a pool—a pool of life everlasting. Rings of ripples spread out from the spot where that pebble hit the water, and those ripples never stop. They didn't stop with the Apostles, even though they only spoke to a handful of people at a time. They didn't stop with my Daddy, who could only speak to a few hundred people, under that canvas tent. And, friends, those ripples didn't stop with me, either.

"And so, in 1936, I preached my first sermon on radio. And, praise God, more and more people listened, and believed, and prayed with us. They knelt down beside their radios, and we prayed together. The ripples of Christ's own teaching were spreading wider.

"And then, of course, there came God's own ultimate miracle—television. And it was then that God touched my shoulder again. He told me to take my wonderful wife Katherine and my young son Elton, and He told us to come here to Los Angeles, the home of television. He made me understand that if radio could work one miracle in His service, then television could work a thousand miracles. That was twenty-eight years ago, friends—in 1950. And I don't mind telling you—I don't mind admitting to you—that I was shaking in my soul the first time I preached a sermon in front of a TV camera. Because I was awed by it. I'm *still* awed by it." As he speaks, Holloway turns to face the camera, eye to eye. Confessing: "Because I knew—I was convinced—that the camera's eye is all-seeing. It never blinks—and it never lies, either. I knew that the TV, God's own miracle, would test me sorely. And I prayed to God Almighty that I could pass that test, and that people would believe me. I prayed that the Lord would allow me to bring His words to millions throughout the world, face to face, as Christ first brought the words from heaven down to earth."

Now Holloway pauses. His eyes fall to the prayer book. Beyond the footlights, the audience is still. When Holloway raises his eyes again to the camera, he speaks softly, humbly:

"Yes," he says, "I prayed for help, and for guidance. And God answered my prayers. Because within five years—five short years—we were able to build this Temple. We built this magnificent Temple the way my Daddy erected his poor, patched old canvas tent. We built it with your help, friends. With your help, and your dollars. And with God's own guidance.

"But the erection of the Temple wasn't the end of our struggle. It wasn't the end of our mission. It wasn't the end of God's plan for us. No, friends, that was only the beginning—only the first circle in that ring of ripples everlasting on the great pool of life. This Temple is only made of wood and glass and concrete and steel. It's a temporal thing—a thing of the world, and not of the spirit. And God knows that, friends. Because His wishes are clear. I can still feel His hand on my shoulder. I can still hear His voice. I can still hear His command. It's just as clear as it was many years ago, when I was nineteen years old, and taking up my Daddy's work. That command is just as clear and as strong as the TV picture that comes from this Temple to your home, God's own miracle.

"And that command was—" A long, solemn pause. Holloway stares straight into the camera. Then: "That command was, 'Reach out to others. Widen the ripples of Christ's teachings. Use God's electronic miracle to help bring the message of eternal salvation to every person in every home in every village on earth.' And if those homes don't have TV sets, if they don't have radio sets—and many of them didn't, and still don't, friends—then our command was equally clear. We were to supply those radio sets, and those TV sets.

"And so, with God's guidance, we made our plans. We planned our campaign as carefully as any general ever planned for any battle, or any war. We drew up our battle plans, and then we carried them out. We would start humbly, we decided, just as Christ started. We would go into a remote village, and we would find the largest public building, and we would supply it with radios, and TV sets. We would start humbly, but we would finish triumphantly, God willing. Using the miracle of electronics—God's own ultimate miracle—we would take Christ's message to all the world.

"And that, friends, is just what we did. We did it with your help, just as we built this Temple with your help. We went first to Chile, in 1961. We took radios and television sets into the towns and the hamlets of that poor, primitive country, and we gave them to the people. Some of those trips were made on horseback, friends, with radios strapped to the backs of burros. Some of our people rode through dangerous jungles, risking life and limb for God. But they achieved their goals. They accomplished their missions. They delivered their holy cargo.

"And then, after we'd done that, we went to Santiago, and we rented their soccer stadium there. We brought the choir, and we brought Pastor Bob and Sister Teresa, and all the other people you've come to know and love and depend on for your own weekly walks with God. And we brought our TV cameras, and our transmitters, and our technicians, too. And then, friends, we had ourselves a good, old-fashioned prayer meeting. It was the same kind of a meeting we'd have if we went to Joliet, Illinois, or Little Rock, Arkansas, or St. Petersburg, down in Florida. And I remember, friends—" The voice trembles. In the monitor, looking again straight into the camera, Holloway's eyes are misted with memory.

"I remember that when I asked who it was that would come down the aisle to repent his sins and take the Lord Jesus Christ for his savior, why, the first person to come down the aisle of that mammoth soccer stadium was his honor the mayor of Santiago. And he was crying, friends. He was crying like a child, unashamed. And his hands were stretched up to heaven, reaching out. And he was only the first of hundreds, friends. Only the first of three hundred and eighteen souls, to be exact, who declared for Christ that day."

A long, heavy pause. Then:

"And the most miraculous thing about it was, friends—" Holloway shakes his head, overwhelmed. "The most miraculous thing of all, was that God's work was done that day with an interpreter. Except for the first sentence, I didn't speak a word of Spanish. And the audience, they didn't speak English, of course. But that didn't matter. It didn't matter one single bit. Because God spoke through me directly to the hearts of those poor, simple people. He spoke, and they understood. And they believed. And they made their decisions for Christ. All three hundred and eighteen of them, following their mayor down the aisle of that soccer stadium.

"That was in 1961, like I said. Then, in 1965, we took our ministry out to the Philippines, and we reached out to touch the natives there. Next came Africa, in 1972. When we told you that we wanted to buy a river steamer, and outfit it, and sail it down the Nile under God's banner, to work for Christ among the natives of Africa, you heeded our call. We told you we needed a half million dollars. Yes—" A slow, grave nod. The beautifully barbered head remains momentarily bowed. Intently, the manager looks at the line where Holloway's hairpiece meets his natural hair. The joining is almost imperceptible.

"Yes, the mission to Africa was our most ambitious crusade for Christ. We wanted to go directly into the heart of that dark, savage land. And we needed your help. We needed money. Lots of money—a half million dollars, just to start. Just to get the boat, and to get it into the water.

"So we asked you for the money we needed. Just like, so many years ago, my Daddy asked those poor, humble folk in Peoria for help to buy his tent. And you responded, friends. In only six months, you sent us *more* than a half million dollars. We bought our steamer, and we named it the *Sister Katherine,* after my helpmate and partner in the service of God for so many years. We sailed the *Sister Katherine* down the Nile, and we talked to the natives. And they listened, and they understood. And they believed.

"That was in 1972. And the *Sister Katherine* is still at work, plying those dangerous waters in the service of the Lord.

"But that was six years ago. This is 1978. Our missions in South America, and in the Philippines, and in the heart of Africa are still steadily winning victories for the Lord— still expanding those circles that the Apostles started, so long ago, when Jesus first cast that holy pebble of His gospel into the great pool of life.

"But what victories, you may ask, are we planning for the future? You may ask whether we've decided that we've done enough—that we've decided to let others fight God's battles, bringing His word to the world's unbelievers."

Another ponderous pause, as Holloway looks out beyond the footlights. Then: "If some of you have asked yourselves that question, then I'm ready today with your answer. Yes, my friends, today I'm ready." The voice is enobled by a deep, fervent tremolo. "Today—now—I'm ready to reveal to you that, during these last six years, we've been planning our greatest victory for Christ. Because I'm ready to reveal to you, here and now, before this audience and in front of these all-seeing TV cameras, that our battle plans have been drawn. And, with God's hand still on my shoulder, I am determined to take our crusade for Christ to the most populous nation on earth."

In the silence, a murmur runs through the audience like a hum of high voltage electricity.

"Yes, my friends—" He looks hard into the camera—the commander now, taking his place at the head of his legions. Almost unnoticed, the strains of "Onward, Christian Soldiers" have begun, played on the organ. "Yes, my friends. With your blessings—with your help—I will take Christ's

16

holy word into the People's Republic of China—the most populous country on earth, where nine hundred million human souls live and work and raise their children without knowledge of the one true God, or the teachings of Jesus Christ, His Son."

The manager blinks, shakes his head admiringly. Writes neatly on the pad:

TOTAL WAR.

One

EYES CLOSED, Austin Holloway slumped against the marble shower stall, letting the coarse spray beat hard on his chest. Outside the stall, his blue suit had been taken away. Bath slippers, shorts, casual slacks and a terrycloth robe had been laid out on a bench, together with the leather-bound prayer book and his alligator wallet. In the hallway outside, discreetly on guard, Mitchell waited for him to finish showering. Down the hallway, in the conference room that adjoined the Temple's public rooms, the Council waited for the video taping session to begin.

Instant replay . . .

As football teams profited by videotape, so did The Hour. God's work used any tools.

With an effort, Holloway pushed himself away from the smooth, wet marble. Still with his eyes closed, he stepped closer to the shower stream, letting its full force strike his face. Water could help. Water could cleanse the body, restore the spirits, make the mind whole again.

But not now. Not today.

Today, his legs were dead weight. His arms hung heavy at his sides. Pain throbbed across his chest and down each arm, like cat claws raking the flesh of a helpless enemy. Behind closed lids, his eyes burned. He could feel his heart laboring. Its uneven rhythm was working against itself; its work was going badly. Daily, now, he felt the pain. According to the electrocardiogram, the heart was failing him. After sixty-three years of service, doing a good job, the heart was finally running down.

If he willed it, he could die. If there was really a God up there, waiting for him, he could arrange a meeting. He was convinced of it. Eyes closed, shutting out the world, he could move backward until he felt the wet marble against his back. Then, carefully, he could lower himself until he sat on the tiled floor, head hanging low in the stream of water. Sitting like that, gracelessly, he would will his heart to stop, setting his soul free. He wouldn't say a prayer before dying, either. He wouldn't beg, wouldn't try to strike one last bargain. He would simply die. Water would wash away the excrement released when his bladder and his sphincter relaxed. When they found him, he would be cleansed. More than that, maybe he couldn't ask.

Mitchell would find him.

Discreetly, Mitchell would tap at the bathroom door—as he'd tapped before, over so many years, at so many different doors for so many different reasons. In Chile, stricken with diarrhea, writhing on his bed in a blur of stomach-heaving pain, he'd heard Mitchell's early morning knock on his bedroom door, and had been marvelously comforted. Mitchell would help him. Mitchell had always helped him. Whatever he required, Mitchell would do. In Denver, years ago, thrust deep into the flesh of a woman named Stella, he'd heard Mitchell's warning knock on the door of her hotel room— then heard the sound of fighting from the corridor outside. Mitchell had knocked her husband unconscious, allowing Holloway to escape. The next day, in a plain white envelope, he'd given Mitchell a hundred-dollar bill. Silently. With thanks.

In Tallahassee, Mitchell had taken a knife thrust intended for him. Bleeding from a stomach wound, Mitchell had drawn his revolver and killed the assailant with a single shot. Then he'd collapsed on the sidewalk, murmured his mother's name and fainted. He'd been on the operating table for three hours, in the hospital for five weeks. But, as soon as he could walk, Mitchell was back on guard: a somber, hulking presence, with him wherever he went. For more than twenty years, Mitchell had taken care of him better than a son could take care of a father.

So, today, it would be fitting that Mitchell would find him.

Mitchell would enter the bathroom, turn off the water, lift him and carry him next door to his small bedroom. Mitchell would lay him out carefully on the bed, and close his dead eyes. Mitchell would fold his arms across his chest, and then discreetly cover his lower body with a blanket.

And then, quietly and privately, Mitchell would cry for him.

Mitchell wouldn't raise his voice, or rend his clothing, or

protest God's final judgement. No one would ever know that Mitchell had cried for him.

Yet, among all the others, only Mitchell's anguish would be real. The rest of them—Katherine and Elton and Denise among the family, and Flournoy, his manager—all of them would gaze upon his dead body and secretly rejoice. Katherine would finally have her revenge. Elton would have his chance. Denise would have her freedom from the guilt she felt, forsaking him.

And Flournoy, with his thirty percent of Austin Holloway Enterprises, would finally have the opportunity he sought: to do battle with Elton, may the best man win.

All of them—each one of them—had betrayed him. Katherine had denied him her body, forcing him to risk disease and discovery and disgrace. Elton and Denise had denied him the love of children for a father. And Flournoy had denied him loyalty. Flournoy was the Cassius in his council, the serpent slithering in the grass, silent and venomous. Flournoy watched. And waited. And secretly schemed.

Holloway leaned away from the torrent of water still cascading over him, head to toe. He opened his eyes, shook out the water, reached forward and turned off the shower. During the last few minutes, imagining his own death scene, the pain in his chest and arms had lessened. Miraculously, the water had helped. His heart was calmer now, his thoughts more ordered. He was ready to watch himself on the video screen as he proclaimed his last, his greatest crusade.

Today, the show should be something special.

He watched his video image grow smaller as the camera drew back from the stage. The choir came into the screen on the left. His wife and his son, holding hands, were smiling into the camera from the right. Superimpose the starred spotlights, then one rapt middle-aged face in the audience, then himself, close up. He was looking full at the camera, his eyes serious, his mouth firm, his jaw squared, his chin lifted. He was in command.

Then cut to a longshot. And then the stars. And then the audience solemnly attending him. And once more himself, lips moving soundlessly—praying for them, they thought. And then the longshot.

And, finally, fade.

Had the image of himself seemed somehow smaller than last week's image? Was it the blue suit, diminishing him?

Or had he mysteriously lost substance since last week?

He'd told them, in the final words, that the camera saw everything—God's miracle, the all-seeing eye: remorseless, omnipotent, inevitably revealing the truth, harm whom it may.

Was he, then, the camera's victim?

He cleared his throat as he swiveled to face the Council, seated in their appointed order around the conference table: Elton on his right, Flournoy on his left. Cowperthwaite, the director, sat on Elton's right. Weston—Pastor Bob—sat on Flournoy's left. Next came Reynolds, the publicist. Below Reynolds, in order of descending rank, sat the music director and the Temple's floor manager. At the foot of the table, still dressed in her white satin gown, Sister Teresa sat like a bloated toad, complacently watching him. Last week, Columbia had offered her an album contract: *Sister Teresa Sings the Spirituals.* The news had made both *Variety* and the *Hollywood Reporter,* page one. *Time* had interviewed her, too.

They were waiting for him to speak first. As always. And, as always, he turned to Weston. For a moment he stared at the familiar face: broad and seamed, with a low forehead, a spectacular thatch of thick white hair and eyebrows to match. The friendly blue eyes were surrounded by an intricate network of deep, folksy crinkles. At age twenty-two, Bob Weston had killed an Arkansas sharecropper with a shovel, and had spent fifteen years on a chain gang. Today, seventy-one years old, he looked like a prophet. And acted like one, too. In all of evangelism, there wasn't a better warmup man than Pastor Bob. He could cry one moment and stomp the next. He could bellow like Jove on a mountain top, hurling thunderbolts with both hands. When Pastor Bob turned over a congregation, the faithful were soft of eye and sweaty around the collar. If evangelism named an all-star team, Bob Weston would be everyone's second choice.

"What'd you think, Bob?"

Weston reflectively tapped his cigar ash into a crystal ashtray. "China, you mean?"

"That's what I mean."

"What do the Chinese say? Will they let us in?"

"Why wouldn't they? They're letting in everyone else."

Somberly, Weston nodded, puffing thoughtfully at his cigar. At her end of the table, Teresa flapped a hand at the smoke and frowned.

"If it works, it'd make history," Weston said. "No one else

has ever thought of it, so far as I know. Much less done it."

"Maybe there's a reason," Elton said. His heavy face, prematurely jowly, sagged skeptically as he spoke. His dark brown eyes, inherited from his mother, had narrowed. As always, Elton gave away nothing. Elton would await developments, keeping his options open, calculating his chances for gain—cutting his down-side risks. He'd always been devious, even as a child. Instead of snatching candy from his sister, Elton would discover where she'd hidden it, biding his time. He'd always had a plan.

"There've been missionaries in China for years," Teresa announced. When she spoke, even casually, her voice had a coloratura's fullness and form. Everything Teresa said had the ring of authority, real or imagined. "Fifty, a hundred years ago. At least."

"We're not talking about missionaries," Flournoy said softly. "And, besides, the Communists aren't exactly pro–Christian." He looked straight ahead as he said it, giving no offense. Flournoy preferred to avoid arguments—so long as he got his way in the end. If Weston was carved from seamed, weathered wood, Flournoy was fashioned of thin, cruel steel.

For the first time, Cowperthwaite spoke: "Do they have TV in China? Consumer TV, for the public? Is it widespread?"

"Not really," Flournoy said, still speaking softly. Now his gray eyes, cold as ice, remained fixed on the small spiral notebook that lay open on the table before him. At the end of the table, Teresa moved in her chair, shifting her massive buttocks for a better purchase. The signs were clear: a confrontation was coming, Teresa vs. Flournoy. Teresa would bluster and blow, running up and down the scale. Flournoy, with his slim, elegant dagger poised, would watch for his chance. Teresa would never feel the thrust. She always thought she won.

Holloway rose heavily to his feet, leaned forward and pressed the "off" button on the small console that controlled the tape recorder. Still standing, arms braced wide on the table before him, he remained for a moment with head silently bowed, compelling their attention. Then, slowly raising his head, he looked at them each in turn before he began to speak:

"I'm sixty-three years old. I've got more money than I'll ever be able to spend. When I was a boy, I had to sleep with my brother until I was twelve years old. In the winter, we

22

had to pile overcoats on our bed, to keep warm. And, winter or summer, we had to use an outhouse. We were almost the only family in town that didn't have indoor plumbing.

"Now I've got a house that has ten bedrooms and six bathrooms and a private projection room in the basement. I'm rich, and I'm famous. My name is in the papers, sometimes in the headlines. I've been to the White House. Every Sunday, coast to coast, I preach for the people. I preach, and they listen. And we both profit.

"But all of that isn't really important. It's nice. It feels good. I like to read about myself in the newspapers. I'd be a hypocrite if I denied it. But it's not *really* important. What *is* important—what's vitally important, to me—is the sure, certain knowledge that, ever since I was a young man, I've had the capacity—the God-given ability—to do whatever it is that I decide to do.

"Now, to you, that might seem like a vain, shallow boast. And maybe it *is* a boast. But it's also the truth. I wanted to build this Temple. I asked the people for money enough to do the job, and they gave it to me. I asked for money to go to Chile, and to the Philipines, and into Africa. And the money came—with some to spare, for all of us. Consequently, there isn't anyone here who isn't a whole lot richer than he was when he first came with me.

"Yet, over the years, around this table here, there've been doubts. When we started the dial-a-prayer program, some of you thought we'd lose money on it. And we did lose money, for a while. We lost almost a million dollars before we got the bugs worked out, and got it showing a profit. The same was true of everything else we tried: the recorded sermons, and the book program, and the regional Bible school franchises. They all cost us money, to get them started. But within a year, they were all *making* money. Every one of them. But they were all a risk, going in. At first, each and every one of those programs started off in the red, like any business venture does, getting started. But eventually they worked. They showed us a profit. And, what's more, they're *still* showing us a profit. Every single one of them.

"Now, let's look at Chile, and the Philipines, and Africa. And China, too—" As he spoke, he pushed himself away from the table, and sank down in his chair. Suddenly his knees were trembling. And, across his chest and down each arm, the pain was beginning: a persistent, ominous presence, come back to claim him. He paused, blinked, waited for the pain to pass its first cruel crest. In a moment it would recede. The pain was his constant companion. He knew its habits; he could calculate the malevolence of its mood, and therefore its intention. They lived as one, inseparable. Constant enemies, sharing the same death struggle.

Finally he could speak in the same slow, solemn voice he'd always used, talking business around this table:

"When you think about Chile and the Philipines and Africa," he said, "you'll realize that they're different from the other things we do. They're different in one very important, very fundamental respect." He paused, looked at them each in turn, then said, "If you'll think about it, you'll realize that the difference is—" Another short pause, the last one, for final emphasis. "The difference is that, with these crusades, we don't lose money. They're not like the book program, or the dial-a-prayer program, or even the franchises. Because they don't require any risk capital—not one red cent. We simply make the appeal, and see what kind of a response we get. When we've got enough money to start, we start. If it does well—if the money keeps coming—we expand the program. If it doesn't go as hoped, we chop it off. And, of course—" He permitted himself a small smile. During that session, it would be the first and the last time he would smile.

"Of course, if it does *very* well—much better than expected—why, then, we declare a dividend."

Around the table, one at a time, he looked into their faces, and saw his small smile answered.

It was settled, then. The Council had decided.

He reached forward, switched on the tape recorder, and asked for discussion.

Two

LYING ON TOP of the covers, Denise lifted a bare foot, closed one eye, sighting, and moved her big toe until it covered first her father's face, then her brother and her mother, holding hands for the camera, stage left. From the small portable TV set her father's voice rang with righteous fervor, evoking God the Father and Jesus the Son, proclaiming a new crusade aimed at some unsuspecting race of contented non–Christians. This time, he planned the invasion and conquest of China, his most ambitious scam to date. The faithful, rapt in their seats and ripe for the plucking, stared with mindless adoration at the man in the doubleknit suit, wired for sound, wearing a real-hair toupee and cufflinks presented to him in the Oval Office.

As the voice faded and the music swelled and The Hour came to an end, she remembered the day he'd come home from Washington, wearing the cufflinks. He'd arrived in a chauffeured limousine. She'd been in an upstairs window when the black limousine turned into the circular driveway. She'd been gazing out across the low, odious layer of hazy yellow smog that had covered the Los Angeles basin like poison gas settling down on some vast battlefield. The year had been 1969. She'd been nineteen; her father had been in his middle fifties. Because he admired the President, and supported the Viet Nam war, her father had been summoned to Washington to pick up his reward: a presidential handclasp, a hand-lettered scroll and the cufflinks, gracefully inscribed. Because of the prestigious occasion, the satrap Council had rubberstamped her father's decision to charter a Lear jet for the trip to Washington. He'd debated taking the whole family: the mother, the daughter, the son. But, at the appointed time for departure, the mother had been too drunk to stand. And the daughter, protesting the war, had deliberately waited until the last moment, then announced,

25

wickedly, she remembered, that she wouldn't go to the White House unless she could spit in the President's face.

So the father and son—the king and crown prince—had embarked for Washington, escorted by a handful of barons and dukes. And Sister Teresa, with her Valkyrie's body, her sock-it-to-'em style and her beehive hairdo, towering one layer higher than usual for the occasion.

The ceremony in the Oval Office had rated almost five minutes on the local TV newscast. But, despite the best efforts of Clifton Reynolds, her father's flack, the item hadn't made the network news. For that small favor, she'd been grateful.

Flying home from Washington, Elton had ordered the pilots to circle the Grand Canyon, so he could take pictures. The delay, he'd calculated, had cost two hundred dollars.

She lowered her foot, swung her legs over the edge of the bed and crossed the small bedroom to switch off the television set. From the kitchen came the clatter of crockery counterpointed by the sound of cool jazz. Listening to FM, Peter was making breakfast. Eggs scrambled with green onions and sautéed chicken livers, he'd promised. His specialty.

Wearing a shorty nightgown and bikini bottoms, she turned to the window, looking across the rooftops to her own personal patch of San Francisco Bay, blue and sparkling this morning. The Oakland hills were purple in the background, with a scattered fleece of clouds clinging to the crests. In the foreground, huge cylinders of gas storage tanks combined with mantislike shipyard cranes to make a montage that could have come from a Diego Rivera mural. Overhead, a pair of jet fighters flew low over the Bay Bridge, coasting down for a landing at the Alameda Naval Air Base, across the Bay.

"Two minute warning," Peter called.

"Two minutes," she repeated. She pushed the bedroom door closed, slipped off the shorty nightgown and stepped before the full-length mirror. Feet together, arms at her sides, she took the inventory: eyes a little too small and close set, nose a little too uptilted, chin a trifle too sharp. At best, it was a heart-shaped face—at worst, an asymmetrical triangle. But the honey-colored hair falling naturally to her shoulders softened some of the angles, and the arch of dark blond eyebrows beneath a broad forehead was certainly a plus. With only a trace of makeup, the flare of the eyebrows balanced the close-set eyes. Altogether, it was a B-minus face. Sometimes, when she was rested and happy and working well, she rated the face a "B."

The slope of her shoulders was marginal, but her breasts were acceptable, round and still firm, with small nipples centered on the swell. Her waist was narrow, with only the suggestion of a midriff bulge. But her hips were a little too wide, especially seen full front. And, from the same view, her thighs were a little too skimpy, a little too hollow on the inside curve.

"One minute."

"I hear you." Quickly she took a maroon sweatshirt from the chair beside the bed, slipped it over her head, finger-combed her hair, then reached for her blue jeans, hanging on the same chair. After breakfast, she would shower and put on fresh clothes.

In the kitchen, Peter was pouring orange juice into stem glasses. English muffins were stacked on a plate in the center of the table, buttered and steaming. He hadn't told her about the muffins, or the strawberry jam beside them. He'd bought both at the corner store, along with the Sunday paper.

She kissed him on the tip of his left ear, quickly stroked his Sunday-stubbled cheek and slipped into her chair, reaching for the paper. According to their custom, she would read the comics and the magazine section and the supplements while he read the main news section, the sports and the business sections, and the editorials. Then they would switch. Across the table, he was spreading strawberry jam on an English muffin.

"What's with the Hour of Power?" he asked. "Did I hear him say he's planning to convert the Chinese hordes to the blessings of Christianity—with 'Onward, Christian Soldiers' playing in the background, for good measure?"

"It's not the Hour of Power. I keep telling you that. The Hour of Power is someone else's." She tasted the first forkful of scrambled eggs and livers. "This is delicious. Better than last Sunday's."

He smiled at her, then turned to the newspaper, folding the front news section and propping it against the pitcher of orange juice. He was wearing a Japanese karate coat she'd given him for Christmas. Held together only with a belt, the heavily quilted coat was opened down to the waist. The hair of his chest and torso, exposed by the coat's V almost to his naval, was thick and dark and curly, almost a caveman's pelt. With his dark, longish hair uncombed and his face unshaven for the day and his eyes a dark, snapping brown beneath a thick bar of eyebrows, he could have been an Italian peasant, called in from the fields and incongruously dressed in the quilted white coat—perhaps to tryst with the honey-haired foreign visitor, overbred and neurotic, sexually unfulfilled, come from another country to meet him secretly, her forbidden lover. The place could be a villa that she'd taken for the year, her retreat from the constraints of her other life, a secret from him. She might be a young Englishwoman, upper middle class, trapped by marriage and convention—and by two beautiful, loving children, a boy and a girl. The time would be the years between the two World Wars—D. H. Lawrence's era. And the heroine, too, would be Lawrence's: previously unawakened and incomplete, made whole by the erotic love she shared with this dark, intense, exciting man.

His looks fitted the fantasy, and so did the family name, Giannini. And so did his ancestry: Southern Italian, and proud of it.

"Whose is the Hour of Power?" he asked.

"The Reverend Schuller's, I think. He's really a reverend, too. Ordained and everything. He started out in Los Angeles, giving services in drive-in movie theaters."

"At night?"

"No," she answered. "During the day. Sunday."

"Does his flock sit in their cars and eat popcorn and listen through loudspeakers hooked to the windows?"

"That's right." She leafed through the *California Living* supplement, skimming a story on hang gliding. Suspended in the sky, with cliffs and hills for a background, the multicolored gliders were perfect: bright, adventurous shapes, man-made, each a brilliant geometric contrast to nature's bright blue of the sky, and the soft, green growth of the seaside cliffs, and the rolling white of the surf breaking against the massive black rocks of the shore.

"Drive-in movies, and drive-in banks, and drive-in, plug-in campgrounds. And now drive-in churches." He shook his head, drank coffee, banged the mug down on the oak-slab table. "Taking communion in the family car, probably with the windows rolled up and the air conditioning on, is the perfect symbol of this society, you know that? And then there's your father, who's got the gall to think that a pop evangelist can teach the Chinese something. Someone should tell him that the Chinese had a culture and a religion while our forefathers were still scratching fleas."

She put the *California Living* section aside and helped herself to an English muffin. "I'd be interested to see you debate my father sometime."

He snorted. "To have a debate—an intelligent debate—you've got to have some common ground. And I doubt that we could find much common ground."

"You might be surprised. He's a charlatan, but he's no dummy. He's no monster, either. He believes what he's saying, I've decided."

"You didn't always think so."

"I know," she answered slowly. "People change, though."

"Is that why you've been tuning him in, the past few Sundays?"

Spreading the muffin with strawberry jam, she considered. Then: "I'm not sure. Maybe it's because I'm twenty-eight years old. I can't stay mad at him forever. And, besides, I find myself thinking about my mother lately."

Across the table, his mouth came to a thoughtful set as he watched her for a moment before saying, "Worrying about her. Is that what you mean?"

She shrugged. "I suppose it is. She's fifty-six years old. She's been drinking for a long, long time. I—" She hesitated, bit into the muffin, sipped her coffee, looked thoughtfully beyond him. Pepper, Peter's dignified standard poodle, lying on the kitchen floor, caught her eye and amiably twitched his tail. "I think about her, that's all. I wonder about her."

"You should call her, then. Or write her."

Still staring at Pepper, she didn't reply. Peter was letting the silence lengthen, sharing it with her. It was characteristic of him. One minute he could be bombastic, the next minute pensive. And always, no matter how loudly he pounded the table, he was attuned to her mood.

"How long has it been, since you've seen her?" he asked quietly.

"Five years, at least."

"She calls you on your birthday and at Christmas."

"You said 'seen.'" She realized that the correction had been sharper than she'd intended. She glanced at him, searching for a reaction. Whenever they talked about her parents, the conversation often veered, lost its balance, sometimes tipped toward quiet contention. Neither of them wanted it to happen. But it did.

Peter could sense what she was thinking. She could see it in his eyes. She could feel it. She watched him decide, deliberately, to turn his attention to his newspaper. That done, he pitched his voice to a neutral note as he asked, "Does your father know we're living together?"

"How could he know? It's only been two years." Again, she heard herself speaking too sharply.

"Still—" Eyes on the newspaper, he turned a page, patted it into position, then said, "Still, I get the feeling that your father—" He hesitated, choosing the right phrase. "I get the feeling that he has an intelligence network." A small smile followed before he said, "Or maybe he's rented time on God's computer."

Ruefully she nodded over her own part of the paper, the *This World* section. "Sometimes I get the same feeling," she said softly.

Eating, drinking, reading, they let another silence lengthen. This was an easy, companionable silence, smoothing over the small, subtle tension. Yet Peter's question, never asked in so many words, remained unanswered: Why, during the last few months, had she switched on The Hour with increasing frequency? Was it because she wanted to see her mother—wanted to reach out to her, however imperfectly? Or was it more complicated than that? For years, she couldn't bear to watch The Hour. She couldn't bear to be in the same room with the sound of her father's voice, couldn't bear to see him strut and posture for the cameras. She couldn't bear to hear him evoke God as casually as an iron-hatted, ward-heeling politician at the turn of the century might have evoked his Tammany boss.

Yet now—lately—she found herself planning how best to watch The Hour without giving offense to Peter.

At best, it was a manifestation of maturity, an effort to put her past life into perspective, the better to get on with her present life, and therefore the future.

At worst, it was intellectual backsliding. For eight long, hard years, since she left the Beverly Hills mansion three days before her twentieth birthday, she'd managed to live her own life—sometimes for the better, often for the worse. She'd made the ritual runaway's mistakes, and each time she'd paid the full price. She'd confused the muzziness marijuana offered with the balm of inner peace. She'd confused the searing, kaleidoscopic visions of LSD with what she thought the artist could see, and the poet could feel. She'd confused the heedless, headlong rush of sex with the true excitement of love.

And, finally, she'd confused her father with the devil. She'd blamed him for everything bad that happened to her, past and present. It had been, she knew, a cop-out. Because Austin Holloway wasn't evil. He was vain, and heedless, and over-bearing. He was venal, too. But he wasn't the devil.

Through her thoughts, she heard Peter's voice:

"Did you really appear on The Hour when you were a kid?"

Slowly, gravely, she nodded, looking at him over the rim of her coffee cup. "Just as soon as I could walk, and was out of diapers. My brother and I used to sing along with the children's choir. Except that neither of us could carry a tune. So we just mouthed the words. Once my mother caught me singing, and she pinched me."

He frowned, puzzled. "I thought your brother sang, though. That's what he does, doesn't he? Sing? With his duck's ass hairdo, and his teeth, and his pelvis, even."

"He learned. He was coached for years. Under some of the best voice teachers in the country."

"Jesus, you must have been hot stuff in your prepubescent peer group, if you were on TV every Sunday."

Hearing him say it, she felt her eyes drawn inexorably away from him. It was an involuntary reaction, self-protective. She didn't want him to see the pain the offhand remark had evoked. Because, suddenly, the terrible loneliness and desperate disassociation of those years came rushing back: the Shirley Temple syndrome, someone had called it. Like a stereotypical child movie star, she'd found herself an unwilling passenger on an emotional roller coaster ride, strapped helplessly in her seat, alternately titillated and terrified, yet unable to get off. She'd been unable to recognize herself, unable to determine for herself who she was, or how she felt. It was something for others to decide: her father, or Flournoy, or the choir director—her teachers, or her classmates, or a playmate, whenever she found one.

Again, she heard Peter's voice:

"...through?"

"Wh-what?" Still struggling against the remembered tears, she blinked as she looked at him, confused.

"Are you through with the *This World*? I'm ready to trade, if you are." He was smiling at her as he spoke.

Silently, over the coffee and orange juice, they traded sections of the newspaper.

Three

AT THE END of the corridor Carson saw Gallagher sitting at his small metal desk. Gallagher's metal chair was tipped back against the green-painted cement wall. His uniform cap was cocked high on his head, revealing a fringe of iron gray hair. Gallagher was a big man with a massive paunch and powerfully sloping shoulders. Beneath the uniform cap, his thick hair had been cropped close to his skull. Under the hair, the skull was dented and scarred. Gallagher's face was squared off, with a heavy jaw, a misshapen nose and small eyes sunk deep beneath prominent brow ridges. Gallagher claimed he'd boxed professionally when he was a young man. But Carson knew the boast was probably false. Many of the men inside, both inmates and guards, claimed to have been fighters. On either side, it was a lie that came cheap. If it could save one hit, anytime, it showed a profit.

"What's with you, Carson?" Gallagher grunted. "This is two Sundays in a row, if I'm not mistaken."

"Is there room?" He nodded to the closed door of the day room.

"You're the last one, as a matter of fact. Twelve is the limit." Gallagher moved his hand toward the thick metal door. "Go on in. The door's unlocked. Just remember, asshole, you come out one at a time. Anyone that doesn't—" Gallagher tapped the butt of his walnut baton, holstered at his side. A year ago, Gallagher had used the stick to kill an inmate with a single blow to the base of the skull.

As long as Gallagher had the stick, it didn't matter whether he'd ever boxed or not. With the stick, Gallagher was a certified killer.

"They're watching those religious shows until noon, at least. You know that?" Asking the question, Gallagher lowered his chair to all four legs. He'd decided to talk. Sundays were quiet; Gallagher was bored.

"I know."

"You one of those? Jesus freaks?"

"No."

"Then why're you watching?"

He shrugged.

"To me, you don't look like someone that's got religion," Gallagher said amiably. "To me, you look like a plain freak. Not a Jesus freak. Just a plain freak." Suddenly Gallagher guffawed. He was enjoying himself—passing the time.

Once more, he shrugged, moving a step closer to the door.

"How soon you getting your time?" Gallagher asked idly.

"Ten days."

"That's why you got religion, then. You're bucking for low time." Contemptuously, Gallagher blew out his scar-thickened lips. "Am I right?"

Eyes lowered, helpless, he shrugged.

"*Answer* me, asshole," Gallagher barked suddenly. "I ask you a question, you answer me."

"I—yeah. I guess you're right." He kept his eyes centered on the guard's chest. Of all the guards in the institution, Gallagher was the most unpredictable, the most dangerous. Carson had been in the yard when Gallagher had used the stick. There'd been a fight—a quick, vicious fight between two lovers. Gallagher had cocked the stick, stepped in quickly and swung all in one motion. He'd moved on his toes, lightly and delicately. Like a ballet dancer. The inmate—Farwell—had dropped in his tracks, twitched for a moment, then lay still, staring up at the sky. Blood had begun to trickle slowly from his nose, and each ear. Three days later, Carson had heard two guards discussing the killing. The problem, they'd said, was that Gallagher carried a weighted baton. And you couldn't calculate the force of the blow, using a weighted baton.

Still he stood before the small metal desk, waiting. Gallagher wasn't finished with him.

"What're you in for, anyhow?" the guard asked.

Still with his eyes centered on the broad, beefy chest, he cleared his throat. "Sodomy."

Again, Gallagher blew out his thick lips. "You're one of those, eh? Not that I had to be told. All I got to do is look at you, to tell. What'd you do, anyhow?" Now Gallagher's lips twisted into a leering smile. "Tell me about it."

"Well, there—" Again, he cleared his throat. "There was

33

this girl. She lived around the corner from me, and she kept—you know—asking for it."

The distorted smile widened. "I don't think I ever heard one of you kinks come right out and admit that it was your idea. It's always that someone talks you into it. What'd you do to her, anyhow?"

"Well, I just—you know—we just—"

"How old was she, anyhow? Tell me that, before you tell me how you gave it to her. Tell me a little something about her. Describe her."

"I—I don't remember how old she was. I—"

"Bullshit, you don't remember. You remember everything about it. You know how old she was, and what she wore and what she said and how she felt. There isn't anything about it that you don't remember. You think about it all the time. Every day, and every night, with your meat in your hand, you think about it. So tell me." Suddenly the bogus smile was gone. The guard's eyes were hard and ugly: two dark, malevolent agates beneath brows whitened and mottled by ancient scars.

"She was—twelve."

"And how old were you?" Asking the question, Gallagher's voice had roughened. Resting side by side on the table, his knob-knuckled hands began to clench into fists. The agate eyes were smouldering now, like coals snatched straight from hell.

"I was—twenty."

"All right—" Slowly, deliberately, the guard unclenched one fist, gesturing. "All right. Now tell me how you did it to her. And tell me the truth, goddammit. Because all I got to do is pull your file, you know. And then, if you lied to me, so help me, I'll..."

Suddenly a bell jangled: the small telephone hung on the green concrete wall. Angrily motioning for him to remain, Gallagher snatched the receiver from its hook.

"Station thirty-four. Gallagher speaking."

Stealing a direct look, Carson saw the guard's eyes narrow dangerously as he listened, pressing the receiver hard against his ear. Finally he grated, "Yessir, that's right. But..."

From the phone, Carson could hear a sharp, staccato voice, interrupting. Suddenly Gallagher's eyes shot him directly. Angrily, Gallagher was waving at the day-room door, gesturing for him to go inside.

First looking through the small, wire-reinforced window,

he pushed open the heavy door. Eleven men sat on a mismatched collection of plastic-covered sofas and chairs. Some of them were reading magazines taken from racks bolted to the concrete walls. Others watched a nineteen-inch color TV set, also bolted to the wall. There were only three color TV sets in the institution, one for each of the three day rooms. Only trustees and inmates with fewer than thirty days left to serve were allowed in the day rooms. The other inmates watched TV on black and white sets located in the cell block corridors, controlled by the guards.

In this room—day room C—the TV was controlled by a group of four trustees: Massingale, Davis, Gaumer and Haskell. Of the four, only Haskell was white. Each Sunday morning, until noon, Massingale, Gaumer and Davis insisted that the TV be tuned first to the Austin Holloway Hour, then to Oral Roberts. Early in their sentences, all together, the three men had taken decisions for Christ, born again.

Of all the men in the room, only Massingale and Gaumer were attentively watching the Austin Holloway Hour. Davis and Haskell were playing knock poker, betting a cigarette on each knock, two cigarettes if the player who knocked got beaten. The others were reading, or talking quietly. One of the inmates was frowning over a jigsaw puzzle.

Carson took a copy of *Argosy* from the rack, sat on one end of a blue plastic sofa and braced his feet against a large linoleum-topped coffee table.

"Hey, man," Massingale said softly, "get your fucking feet off the fucking furniture, you mind?"

Without looking at the hulking black man, he lowered his feet to the floor. If Gallagher had lied about being a boxer, Massingale had told the truth. In Massingale's cell, Scotchtaped to the wall, a clipping from the *Newark Times* showed him with his gloved hands raised in victory, smiling into the camera.

Because Massingale was a heavy timer, in for murder, and because Carson was a kink, Massingale continued to abuse him, calling him obscene names, registering his contempt. As required, Carson listened with eyes lowered, staring at the magazine. If he talked back—even if he frowned—Massingale would find him in the yard, later. A shuffle of feet, a single lightning jab, and Massingale's huge fist would crash into his stomach. While Massingale strolled away, others would step quickly forward, supporting him until he could stand. If he vomited on one of them, the process would be repeated a few days later: a different attacker, same result.

While Massingale cursed him, quietly and earnestly, it would be better not to turn the magazine's pages.

Finally finished, but still glowering, Massingale turned toward the TV, moving his head from side to side, keeping time to the rhythm of a finger-snapping, hip-swaying, bright-smiling choir, swinging a spiritual. With the *Argosy* open across his lap, Carson looked at the singers: eight white girls, four black, each one looking straight at the camera, selling themselves, selling the song. Selling Jesus, God and, waiting his turn in his bright blue suit, smiling at the choir like an overweight, overage whoremaster, Austin Holloway, too.

Every Sunday, his mother watched the Austin Holloway Hour. It was the only thing in her life that she could focus on—that could claim her full attention. Everything else had fallen away from her, lost forever.

The choir was in its last chorus, voices rising, arms linked, swaying in slow, sappy unison. Beside him, Massingale was turning to Gaumer, muttering something about the black girl on the right. Answering, smiling broadly, Gaumer was elaborately licking his blue-black lips. Tall and thin, stoop-shouldered and hollow-chested, narrow across the torso, Gaumer had started out as a finger-snapping, jive-talking New Orleans pimp—and ended controlling heroin in the city's black ghetto. On the outside, Gaumer was still important. So, inside, he was one of the men to see. Between them, the brains and the muscle, Gaumer and Massingale ran cell block C.

Now Holloway was beginning his sermon. Carson watched for a moment, then dropped his eyes again to the magazine. When the choir came on again, he would look. To himself, he smiled. If he wrote to Holloway, maybe the black girl on the right would send him an autographed picture of herself. He could pass it on to Gaumer, a farewell gift. When he got out, in ten more days, Gaumer might help him.

Ten more days...

On his two hands, he could count them. Five days from now, he'd only need one hand. And five days after that, he'd go into the administration building and pick up his clothing: the checked sports coat and the gray trousers and the white shirt that he'd worn during his trial. He'd put on the clothes, and take the twenty-five dollars in cash, and wait for them to drive him to the bus station, where they'd buy him a ticket. Three hours later, he'd be in Darlington. Home.

Home...

What did it mean, that word? For him, what would it mean? Did it mean his mother's dark, dank little house with mice in the walls and rats underneath and roaches mashed on the kitchen floor? Did it mean a rooming house on Prince Street, behind the bus station? In Darlington, everyone knew him. They all knew, and they wouldn't forget. Everywhere, eyes would follow him. Just as eyes followed his mother, wherever she went.

Now, at that moment, muttering and gesturing, she was watching Austin Holloway. For her, Austin Holloway was God come down to earth, talking just to her, privately, every Sunday. When Holloway told her to do it, she dropped to her knees, placed her hand on the TV set and prayed. When she prayed, she cried. And when she cried her face became a wet, paint-streaked mask: a madwoman's mask, from Halloween. Because every Sunday morning before she turned on the Austin Holloway Hour, she went into the bathroom, and locked the door, and painted her face with lipstick and mascara and bright red rouge. So when she cried for God, on Holloway's command, all the paint dissolved. After The Hour was finished, she staggered into her bedroom, sobbing, and locked the door. Her sheets and pillow cases were always filthy, stained black and red from the makeup.

His eyes wandered back to Holloway, speaking directly into the camera now. In Darlington, on her knees beside the TV, his mother raised her grotesque face up to heaven.

Maybe.

Or maybe not.

He hadn't heard from her for more than six months. Why? And why were they paroling him to his Uncle Julian, not to his mother? Uncle Julian had arranged for the job that all parolees must have. Why? During the last six months, only Uncle Julian had written him. Not his mother. Why? For him, beyond the prison's walls, it was as if only one person existed.

Why?

On the TV, Holloway was finishing his spiel. Massingale was getting to his feet, changing channels. Oral Roberts was next. Turning the magazine's pages faster now, Carson had come to the back section of *Argosy,* filled with small ads arranged in catalogue style. Some of the ads promised more money, others more muscle. Courses in TV repair and burglar-alarm installation were offered, along with pamphlets on raising earthworms, and mushrooms, and chinchillas for profit.

When he'd been a boy, twelve years old, he'd wanted to send away for a book that promised to make him stronger. The book had cost five dollars. When he asked his mother for the money, she refused. Her check hadn't come, she'd said. The check was late. But he'd known she was lying. Always, by the fifth of every month, the check came. When he was still very small, five or six years old, he'd learned to recognize the envelope: plain white, with an Arizona postmark and no return address. For him, the envelope was magic. Because when it came, it made his mother a different person. Sometimes, when the check came, his mother would smile—actually smile. Her eyes would clear, and seem to really see him. And that was magic.

When he'd asked her for the five dollars, it had been the middle of the month—the twelfth, or the fifteenth. He'd known she'd gotten the check, and had already taken it to the bank, and had cashed it. She'd had the check, but hadn't admitted it. She'd lied to him. So, a dollar at a time, patiently, he'd taken the money from her purse. That was magic, too. Because, after that, he always had money.

When he slipped that first dollar from his mother's purse, he'd been aware of a small, intense tremor of fear, followed by a rush of exhilaration when the purse was closed and he was safe. Over the years, as the jobs got riskier and the money got better, it was always the same for him. The fear never lessened, but neither did the high that followed. The two went together—first the fear, then the exhilaration. Without the first, the second wasn't possible.

He closed the copy of *Argosy*, rose from the couch, returned the magazine to the rack and stood for a moment watching the TV. The scene was the campus of Oral Roberts University. A group of carefree girls crossed the campus, laughing and talking. An appreciative murmur went through the day room.

At that moment, his mother lay across her bed, sobbing. Her goblin's face, streaked black and red, was buried in the filthy sheets.

Why did she do it, every Sunday?

And why was he there, watching as she watched—remembering?

During the last four years, he'd hardly thought of her, except to wonder fleetingly when she would die, and release him.

Yet now, watching the TV and wondering, suddenly, whether his mother might be dead, he realized that a tremor was beginning, deep inside him. It was the same tremor he'd experienced when he'd stolen that first dollar from his mother's purse, so long ago.

Four

WITH BOTH FEET on the blue circle that spotted her for the cameras, Katherine Holloway stood with hands clasped, chin lifted, eyes wide—smiling at a point just beneath camera two. To her right, alone on center stage, her husband had turned directly to the front, squarely facing camera one, suspended above the pulpit. Alone among them all, Austin was the only one allowed to look directly into the cameras. It was Austin's first principle.

In the wings, the director was holding up one finger. The show had one minute to run.

In one minute, for this week, it would be all over, and she would soon be home. Soon her car would be turning into the circular driveway. She would wait for the car door to be opened before she alighted. It was another of Austin's principles. Nodding and smiling to Susan, who would open the front door for her, she would enter the house. Without haste, climbing slowly in her organdy dress, holding her long skirt gathered before her like a duchess rising step by regal step above her subjects, she would gracefully ascend the staircase to her bedroom. Moments later, with the door closed safely behind her, she would be alone.

One more week—seven more days—would have passed. Gone forever—days and hours passed dust unto dust, slipped somewhere far behind her, lost forever.

Someday, alone in her bedroom, she would cry for all the lost hours and all the forgotten days.

Because even a duchess cried. Secretly. Alone.

But now she must smile at her husband as he raised his right hand high in final benediction, left hand lifting Daddy's old leather prayer book for a better camera angle. She could feel her smile widening—wonderfully, radiantly widening. Her smile was her best, most photogenic feature. Everyone said so. Even Austin. On TV next Sunday, wearing the new

40

organdy dress, she would see herself as others saw her. On tape, rebroadcast, millions would see her. Paying millions.

Millions upon millions, blessed dollars. Riches upon riches, dust unto dust. All to Austin's glory. His voice was rising now, saving the sinners who paid for the pleasure. She glanced quickly at the small red light glowing beneath the lens of the nearest camera. Soon—in seconds—the light would wink out, releasing her.

Until next week.

Seven days.

Alone.

She heard her husband's voice rise, saw his arm raise one last time, watched him hold the pose.

Until, at last, the red light winked out.

Austin was free, too.

Slowly, slowly, she let the smile fade graciously away. Now a half turn to her right, take three steps, hesitate as Austin turns toward her, offering his left arm, as gracefully as a princeling, escorting his lady. He was smiling into her eyes. Head lifted, she was answering his smile as she took his arm, doing a dainty dancing-school pirouette.

For more than thirty years, once a week, they'd smiled at each other like this.

Had they smiled when they'd lain together in the bedroom darkness, coupled, conceiving their children? She couldn't remember.

Did she care?

She couldn't remember.

Ahead, at the parting of the golden curtains, Elton was waiting for them. Elton, too, had learned to smile. He'd become rich, these last few years, smiling and singing.

In San Francisco next week, Denise might smile. To Denise, watching the family on TV, it would all be a joke.

Dust unto dust.

Now she was smiling at Elton, her firstborn. For eighteen hours, she'd labored to birth him. It had been a breech birth— the first of countless agonies he'd caused her.

Taller than his father, Elton was smiling down at her. His arm, too, was crooked. Six steps separated them. Five. Four. Now, in unison, arms linked, they pivoted in platoon front, smiling a last time out toward the footlights. In front of them, on cue, Elton's three children—"the grandkids"—bowed and curtsied, herded fondly by their mother, also smiling.

And then, left turn, they were filing through the curtains. Finished for the week. Free.

And instantly, the backstage furies surrounded them. Mitchell, unsmiling, was ready with the white towel and white terrycloth robe, for Austin. Flournoy, always watchful, revealed nothing behind his courtier's oily smile. Cowperthwaite, as always, congratulated them. Later, he would complain about cues and timing and lighting. Elton's own lackey, newly hired, waited for his master, grinning, proffering towel and robe. Like his father, the son had his own shower. Austin preached, Elton sang. So they both perspired.

But for those who only smiled for the camera—for the wives—there would be no showers. Instead, Elton's wife would herd the three "grandkids" into the waiting Lincoln. One of the children, Amy, had a fever. Already Amy was wailing, complaining of her cold. But on camera, Amy had been a hit. Because Amy, with her dimples, was the fairest of them all.

Walking behind her daughter-in-law and her three grandchildren, Katherine reached out to touch Amy's shoulder. Without looking around, Amy pulled sharply away from her. Carrie, Elton's wife, didn't turn. As Katherine fell back, Carrie and the three children were suddenly surrounded by a polite phalanx of cheerful, efficient assistants, each one plucking at the children, chattering their congratulations and ritual compliments.

As if on cue, Katherine felt a touch on her arm, just above the left elbow. It was a jailer's touch, cold and firm.

"You were wonderful, Mrs. Holloway. Perfectly radiant. And the new dress, it's perfect."

It was another Sunday morning ritual.

"Thank you, Miss Fletcher." As she said it, she felt the pressure of Miss Fletcher's grip subtly tighten as they turned toward the door opening onto the enclosed driveway that led from the Temple's underground garage. Now they were walking toward the door together. A dozen faces beamed at her, nodding and smiling. They were strangers' faces, without names. Every Sunday she saw them, smiling. But they would always be strangers.

One of them opened the door. Beyond the door, her Mercedes waited. Jack Calder stood beside the car. Jack was smiling, too. But Jack's smile was real. Among them all, Jack was her only real friend. He was her jailer. But he was also her friend.

"How'd it go, Mrs. Holloway? Good turnout?" As he asked the question, still cheerfully smiling, Jack opened the car's rear door for her.

"Yes, Jack. It was a good turnout. Thank you."

Inside the car, sunk deep in its glove-leather seat, she sighed softly, letting her eyes close. In less than thirty minutes she would be in her own room, safe. In the armoire beside her vanity, it would be waiting.

Breathing deeply, she stood for a moment with her back against the bedroom door. Today, the climb up the long spiral staircase had tired her. She could feel her heart beating hard: a small, throbbing animal, struggling inside her breast, trapped and frightened. Always, now, her heart beat hard when she climbed the stairs. Her breath came short. Sometimes multicolored spots danced before her eyes. Was this how Austin felt? If he did, then finally they'd found something to share: the ominous sound of time's wingèd chariot, inexorably hurrying near.

Did Austin fear his appointment in Samaria?

Did she?

No, she didn't. Lately, the void waiting beyond seemed to invite her. Sometimes she could almost hear voices from the past, calling to her.

Yet she was only fifty-six. Austin was only sixty-three. For both of them, death should still be years ahead.

Without realizing it, she'd allowed her eyes to close. When she'd been a very young child, she'd always closed her eyes when she wished for a present, or when a rush of happiness suddenly overwhelmed her, sometimes leaving her weak and trembling. Somehow, when she closed her eyes, she could commune more closely with the pleasure she felt.

And then, slowly, she would allow her eyes to open—as they were opening now. She was looking at her bed, with its ruffled canopy, damask spread, its elaborately embroidered pillow slips. She loved her bed. She loved the feel of its satin sheets against her skin. In bed, she always felt safe.

Now her gaze rested on a bookcase filled with mementos: her favorite books, her grandmother's Bible, her mother's collection of Dresden dolls, the framed snapshots of the children. She'd always preferred snapshots of Elton and Denise, rather than studio photographs. Children were meant to laugh and play and squint up at the sun, not pose for formal photographs.

Next she let her eye fall on the chaise, with its small sidetable and its floor lamp with the pleated silk shade. The chaise was covered in flowered chintz, matching a loveseat set against the far wall.

On the table beside the chaise, in the center of a small silver tray, a glass had been placed. The glass was cut crystal, and sparkled in the sunshine that came through the criss-crossed organdy curtains.

Every Sunday this same glass waited for her. It was a ritual. An offering, she sometimes thought.

Once more she allowed her gaze to circle the large, sunny room: first the bed, then the chaise and the loveseat—finally the vanity with its bench and, close beside it, the delicately carved French provincial armoire, where she kept her most treasured possessions. The room—these things—defined her life. Its four walls protected her.

Because, beyond this room, demons waited.

Pushing herself away from the door and slipping off her silk sandals, she walked across the thick woolen rug toward the vanity. The feel of the thick, luxuriant wool on her stockinged feet suddenly evoked a teen-age memory. She'd fled to the privacy of her room after her father had forbidden her to act in a class play, because the play was immoral. That night, she'd cried herself to sleep, the first of many times.

As if to inflame the wound, her eyes fell on a snapshot of her father, slipped under the glass top of her vanity. He'd been a tall, good-looking man, secretly vain. All her life, her mother had been grateful that he'd married her.

But her mother's life had been short, only thirty-five years. A week before Katherine's ninth birthday, her mother had killed herself with sleeping pills. In her coffin, her mother had looked prettier than she'd ever looked in life.

She trailed an idle finger across the glass as she turned finally to the armoire.

It was inside the armoire, on the bottom shelf. Waiting for her.

So, moving with grave deliberation, as ceremoniously as Austin might move for the camera, blessing the penitents, she opened the armoire's door.

As always, it had been placed precisely in the center of the bottom shelf.

And, as always, she began to tremble as she reached with

both hands for the bottle. It was the same secret, tremulous pleasure that had always overwhelmed her, ever since childhood. Sometimes the trembling made her sob. She'd never known why.

Five

HOLLOWAY STOOD with his back to his desk, staring out across Prospect Park toward the improbably small, isolated cluster of skyscrapers that marked downtown Los Angeles. Except for the skyscrapers, miniatures in the distance, the city was flat and featureless, sprawling low and gray beneath an obscene yellow stratum of smog and smoke.

Forty years ago, he'd come to town with a single valise, a postal money order made out to himself for six hundred dollars and a letter from the manager of a local radio station. He'd been twenty-three years old, green as grass. The station manager had immediately tied him up for twenty-six weeks at a hundred twenty-five dollars a week—a fortune, he'd thought.

Three years later, in the spring of '41, the same radio station had begged him to take a thousand dollars a week, week-to-week, no strings attached. He'd been twenty-six years old when they'd made the offer, and the world was bright with promise. He'd just bought his first tabernacle, a decrepit I.O.O.F. hall in Pasadena. He'd owned a twin-six Packard touring sedan, his third Packard in two years. His Malibu apartment had looked out over the ocean. Every Wednesday, after prayer meeting, Marie Thatcher had come to his apartment in her own car. Thirty-three years old, twice divorced, Marie had taught him the art of love. He'd been a virgin until age twenty-two, when the wife of a Baptist minister had taken him to her husband's vestry, and kissed him, and put his hand on her breast. Then, smiling dreamily, she'd stood in front of a moonlit window, undressing. Making love, he'd had a momentary vision of heaven splitting open before him, a thundering golden cleft between two pearlescent halves, spilling forth pleasure that had carried him soaring far beyond himself, free forever.

The woman had never let him make love to her again.

Later—much later—he'd learned that she took neurotic pleasure in taking men to her husband's vestry. Any man, any time. But never the same man twice.

That first time, he'd felt weak with release, utterly surfeited. But it wasn't until he'd known Marie Thatcher that he'd truly experienced the full rush of sexual love. With Marie, he'd learned what love could mean. For him, there would never be another woman like her. He'd wanted to marry her. Many times, he'd asked her. But she would never agree to marriage, saying that her past would ruin him. Finally, one Saturday, he'd gotten a letter from her. She was leaving for St. Louis, she'd said. She was going to marry a high school sweetheart, a man who'd just inherited a wholesale heating oil business. It would be her third marriage.

Two months later, he'd met Katherine. She'd been nineteen years old, and had auditioned for a vacancy in his choir. She'd looked at him like Mary Magdalene must have looked at Jesus, her brilliant blue eyes moist with wonderment, rapt with adoration.

A year later, in 1942, they'd married. The wedding had been staged by Floyd Mangrun, who later directed the second unit of Ben Hur. After the ceremony, with Katherine at his side, he'd preached his first hour-long radio sermon. Price, five thousand dollars. He'd never felt so fulfilled, so completely confident of his destiny.

Behind him, a buzzer sounded. Reluctantly, he turned away from the window. The time for reverie had passed. Flournoy was waiting.

He slipped on his jacket, smoothed down his hair in front of the mirror and sat behind his desk. Now he pressed the intercom switch.

"Yes?"

"Are you ready for Mr. Flournoy, sir?"

"Send him in, Marge."

"Mr. Elton Holloway would like to see you, too."

"Regarding what?"

"He didn't say, sir."

He glanced at his gold desk clock, a Christmas present from Billy Graham.

"Give us a half hour. Then send Elton and Cowperthwaite and Reynolds in. Mr. Flournoy will stay. We'll be discussing China."

"Yessir."

Moments later, the tall walnut door to the outer office

swung open. Flournoy strode into the office without closing the door behind him. As always, Flournoy wore a conservative suit, an immaculate white shirt and a small-figured silk tie. His shoes, as always, were a gleaming black. At age forty-four, slightly balding, Flournoy was as slim as a matador. His eyes were as watchful and dangerous as a hired assassin's. He never raised his voice—never revealed either anger or pleasure. Flournoy was a machine: completely efficient, utterly cold.

As Flournoy took an armchair facing the desk, the secretary tentatively smiled as she quietly closed the door. She'd always been a little frightened of Flournoy.

"What can I do for you, Austin?"

He allowed a long, deliberate moment to pass as he stared into Flournoy's unrevealing gray eyes. Finally he said, "CBS called me last night, at home. They want to do a *Sixty Minutes* segment on me."

Typically, Flournoy didn't respond directly. Instead, giving himself time, he said, "How'd they get your number?"

Holloway smiled. "They have their sources, I imagine."

Now Flournoy was ready with his response: "Is it about your China initiative?" Since Sunday, Flournoy had consistently referred to the China mission as an "initiative." Signifying, perhaps, that Flournoy thought the idea smacked more of statecraft than evangelism. Of course, no one had ventured to ask Flournoy for an explanation.

Once more, Holloway smiled—then nodded. "Yes. They're interested. Very interested."

"What'd you tell them?"

"I said I'd call them today. Naturally, I wanted to tell you about it."

Flournoy nodded over the tips of his fingers, allowing a long, deliberate moment to pass before he said, "I'm glad you did, Austin. Very glad. Because, to be perfectly candid, I have grave doubts about China. And this offer from *Sixty Minutes* might just confirm what I've been thinking."

"I don't follow you." With an effort, Holloway hitched himself up straighter in his chair, lifting himself a little higher than Flournoy. Dropping his voice to a lower, graver note, he said, "What're you getting at?"

"What I'm getting at, Austin, is that the *Sixty Minutes* crew are headhunters. You know it as well as I do. And I'm afraid—very afraid—that they'll try to make you look silly."

"They're going to be talking about the China Crusade."

It was the first time he'd used the phrase, and he paused a meaningful moment, to emphasize the name he'd chosen. Finally he said, "They're interested in the idea. It's caught on, in just three days. And this is a golden opportunity to get some publicity. Free publicity, coast to coast."

Now it was Flournoy's turn to pause. Then, elaborately patient, he said softly, "Austin, I'm sure you recall your last, ah, appearance on *Sixty Minutes*. They were out for your scalp. And they damn near got it, too."

"That was two years ago. This is a new crew. I know. I checked. And besides, I don't quite agree with you, Howard. It was a dogfight, yes. But I don't think I came off second best, necessarily."

"But that's exactly my point. Second best or first best, we don't need another dogfight on network television."

"This business is built on publicity, Howard. You know it as well as I do. Our people, when they see the interviewer trying to do a job on me, they'll get mad. They'll give the network hell. And, like as not, they'll send us a check, to show they're with us. Believe me. I've seen it happen. And, besides, don't forget the old saying: 'I don't care what you say about me, just so long as you spell my name right.'"

Raising one hand in a gesture of tightly controlled impatience, Flournoy said, "All right, let's let that go for a minute. Let's talk about this China thing."

"The China Crusade, you mean."

Inclining his head in a condescending little nod, Flournoy said, "The China Crusade. Right." His voice was edged with displeasure at being prompted. But, still, he'd said it—called the mission by its new name. Satisfied, Holloway relaxed in his chair, waiting for the rest of it:

"I didn't say anything at the Council meeting on Sunday," Flournoy began. "I didn't want to oppose you in public. But the fact is that I have doubts about the whole idea. What concerns me, Austin—and I'm going to be brutally honest about this—is that I frankly wonder whether you've got the stamina for something like this. Never mind whether it's a good idea. That's a separate question. I'm talking about your health. Your heart, specifically."

"It's not my heart that you're worried about, Howard. It's the profit picture. That's all that concerns you." Locking his eyes with Flournoy's, he spoke quietly, coldly.

Flournoy didn't reply—didn't flinch—didn't drop his eyes. "Am I right?"

Flournoy raised his elegantly tailored shoulders, disdainfully shrugging. "If you want to put it like that, Austin, then my answer is obvious. Without you, we don't have a profit picture. So it amounts to the same thing, really."

"Well, now—" Smiling, he settled back in the chair, hands spread wide on the walnut desk top. "I'm glad to hear you say it. And, to be generous—and also accurate—I'll be the first one to admit that, without your expert help over these last ten years, the profit picture wouldn't be half what it is now. Maybe not a tenth of it, for all I know. But, still, you're missing one essential point, Howard." He paused, drawing a deep, experimental breath. Today, the small demon inside his chest had been quiet. Breathing was easier. So, without overextending himself, he could take a few moments to enjoy Flournoy's admission that he was indispensable. He could afford to sermonize:

"The point you're missing," he said, "is precisely the one I tried to make on Sunday. Which is to say, Howard, that this ministry and myself are inseparable. We're one and the same. The ministry is me, and I the ministry. Which is to say that my ministry is an extension of me. That fact—that *truth*—should be self-evident to you, Howard. Because it's certainly evident to almost everyone else.

"Now, I take it as kindly meant, when you express your concern for my health. You don't want me to die. Not now. And, God knows, I don't want to die. Between you and me, the prospect terrifies me. But just because I don't want to die, that doesn't mean that, every year, I don't want to do more than I did the year before. Because, believe me, I do. I'm a famous man, Howard. I don't say that boastfully. I say it to explain what moves me to do what I do. Because people become famous—in America, at least—precisely because the more they get, the more they want. Not too long ago, if you remember, I had my picture on the cover of *Newsweek*. And you probably thought I was pleased. And I *was* pleased, too—for about one whole minute. And then I started wondering about *Time* and *U. S. News*.

"So now we come to the China Crusade. And you're doubtless saying—like so many inside the organization are probably saying—that I'm crazy to take on a challenge like that with a bad heart. And, just on the bald evidence—on logic—I'd certainly have to agree with you. But the problem is, Howard, that you miss the essential point. Which is, Howard, that I've just about run out of worlds to conquer. At first, getting the faithful to send in their dollar bills was a challenge. And building this Temple—raising the money—that was a challenge. The Philippines and Africa—sure, they were gratifying. But I'd no sooner done it, than it paled on me. And besides, there's no trick to evangelizing backward people. All you do is pass out trinkets with the prayer books—and then write it all off against profits from America. But the Chinese, that's a different matter. The Chinese are smart. And they're tough, too. They're worthy adversaries.

"So that's the reason for the China Crusade, Howard," he said, dropping his voice and smiling across the desk in genial conclusion. "It may kill me. And I may fail. Both things are possible. But also, I may succeed. I may pull off something that nobody's ever done before. And that, Howard, is what it's all about. That's what makes me go. That's why I'm famous—and intend to become still *more* famous."

"If the Chinese go for it," Flournoy said, "it'll be because they've figured how to turn a profit. As you say, they're smart. And tough."

Holloway smiled. "Just so they *do* go for it. Which they will." He lowered his voice to a richer, more confidential note. "Just so *Time* covers it. That's the essential point."

Flournoy's thin lips stirred in a pale facsimile of an answering smile. He shrugged, saying quietly, "I can't argue with you, Austin. And I can't fault you, either. You want to go to China, I'm with you. We'll do it. However, since we're being frank about your health—since *you're* being frank, which I appreciate—I'd like to ask a question."

"What's going to happen after I die. Is that the question?"

Deliberately, Flournoy nodded. "That's the question, Austin."

"Well," he answered, "the plain truth is that I'm damned if I know. I've got seventy percent of the stock, as you know, and you've got the rest. When I die, Katherine gets thirty percent. Which gives you and Elton equal shares."

"Thank you. I appreciate that. I really do. But that's not what I'm asking."

"I know that's not what you're asking. You're asking who's going to stand up in front of the cameras. And the answer is, I just plain don't know. It'll be either Elton or Teresa—or maybe Bob, for all I know." He spread his hands wide across the desk. It was a rich, eloquent, truth-laden gesture—of TV quality, no doubt. When his heart behaved, the magic came easily, as gracefully as ever. "It's up to the faithful, really—

the people who send in the dollars. In the end, they'll decide. Not me."

"That's bullshit, Austin. And you know it. You tell the faithful how to feel. And *what* to feel."

Amiably, he smiled. "Maybe."

"For God's sake, put Elton in front of the camera. Now. Bring him along. The Hour's always had a family motif. That's its trademark. If Elton doesn't succeed you, it'll be like trying to sell Coca Cola without the logo. It just won't work."

He smiled—a lazily teasing smile. "I consider that very selfless of you, Howard. Because, if Elton takes over, it's an even bet he'd fire you."

"That may be," Flournoy answered evenly. "I'd lose my salary. But I'd still have thirty percent of a going concern. I'd happily take my chances. I can always get another job."

"If Teresa takes over, you might have both."

Again Flournoy's lips twisted mirthlessly. "You've never liked Elton much. Have you?"

Instead of answering, Holloway turned to the intercom, asking: "Is Elton out there, Marge?"

"Yessir. But—" As she hesitated, Holloway sensed tension in her voice. "But Mr. Mitchell's here, too, sir. He'd like to see you. It's—" Once more, she hesitated. Then: "It's important, he said."

"Send them both in." As he waited for the tall walnut door to swing open, he exchanged a puzzled frown with Flournoy. Unless it was a matter of life or death—his death—Mitchell wouldn't intrude. Mitchell would wait to be summoned.

Wearing a khaki safari shirt that bulged over a fast-growing paunch, Elton entered the office first. Pointedly, Holloway frowned at the shirt and flared slacks. Dressed so casually, Elton thought he was asserting his in-the-family prerogative. But, instead, he was revealing—once again—his insensitivity to accepted procedures within the organization.

Walking close behind, Mitchell appeared, his stolid, broadshouldered, blue-suited presence a reassuring contrast. At age fifty, Mitchell was totally dedicated, totally loyal. Like his squared-off, heavily muscled body, Mitchell's face was sternly sculpted of heavy, durable material. Elton's face was also broad and heavy. But the material was puffy and flaccid, without strength or substance.

Yet, because his name was Holloway, Elton was entitled to sit in one of the two comfortable leather armchairs placed directly in front of the desk, for principals. Mitchell, as expected, pulled a smaller straightback chair up to the desk—and waited, patiently, for recognition.

Immediately, Holloway turned to Mitchell.

"What is it, Lloyd?"

Mitchell cast a brief, regretful glance at Elton and Fournoy before he turned earnestly in his chair, facing Holloway directly.

"It's Mrs. Holloway," he said quietly. "She's been in an accident."

Reacting involuntarily, Flournoy snapped, "What kind of an accident?"

Still with his eyes fixed implacably on Holloway, Mitchell said, "It's a traffic accident."

Holloway felt himself sag suddenly back in his chair. For years, she'd been with him. Drunk or sober, in sickness or in health, she'd never missed a performance. The Hour was a family affair—Flournoy's words. Without the family—without Katherine and Elton and Carrie and the three much-publicized grandkids, all of them a team, The Hour would lose credibility, lose impact.

The queen mother, a columnist had once called Katherine. Always serene. Always smiling. She'd always been perfect for the part.

Weak, vulnerable Katherine—a helpless drunk. For a bottle a day, she served faithfully and well.

"Is she—" Elton licked at full, slack lips. "Is she hurt?" Suddenly Elton's eyes shown, as if he might cry.

"No," Mitchell answered steadily, still speaking to Holloway. "No, she's not hurt. What happened, you see—well, it was a terrible coincidence, I guess you'd say. Or, more like it, several coincidences. There were just two people in the house, when there should've been three, besides Mrs. Holloway. Calder was taking the Cadillac for gas, and he didn't tell Susan. He didn't expect to be gone long—and he wasn't. But then Miss Fletcher had a dental appointment, downtown. She told Susan she was going. And, before she left, Miss Fletcher looked in on Mrs. Holloway, and saw she was sleeping. She—Miss Fletcher—didn't plan to be gone longer than an hour. But then, Susan decided to go to the store for some spices, or something. She thought Calder was in the garage, working. She thought she saw him through the garage window, she claims. She also claims that she tried to reach him on the intercom, and couldn't—which made her think something was wrong with the intercom. So she decided to run out to the store. She wasn't gone for more than a few minutes.

"But, anyhow—" Mitchell sighed heavily. "Anyhow, Mrs. Holloway apparently got out of bed. She, ah—" Mitchell shifted uncomfortably in the chair. Resting on either knee, his hands clenched as he said, "She apparently didn't have any more, ah, gin left. And Miss Fletcher doesn't give her another bottle until five o'clock, as I understand it—just before dinner. And all this happened just a little after two. So, anyhow—" Mitchell cleared his throat, and lifted his bulldog chin, as if to accept a blow. "Anyhow, Mrs. Holloway apparently got the keys to the silver Mercedes from the board in the garage, and she got in the car, and she drove down to the shopping center, off Montecito, where there's a liquor store. And—" Now Mitchell slowly shook his head as he doggedly continued: "And, when she was in the parking lot, she apparently took a wrong turn. Someone blasted her with a horn, and she got rattled, I guess. So, without looking behind her, she put the car in reverse, and stepped down on the gas, hard. There was a woman behind her, with two little kids—two girls, three and five years old. And—" Mitchell blinked regretfully, shaking his head. "And all three of them are in the hospital. One of the girls—the older one—has a skull fracture, and she's unconscious. The other one—the youngest one—has internal injuries."

"Where's Mrs. Holloway?" Flournoy asked sharply.

"At police headquarters," Mitchell answered, for the first time looking at Flournoy directly. "Hollywood division. I have a friend there. He called me, as soon as he saw her come in. She hadn't been booked when he called. And, just a few seconds later, Miss Fletcher called me."

"Why the hell did she call you?" Flournoy asked. "Why didn't she call me? Or Austin, for Christ's sake?"

"Because," Mitchell answered stolidly, "Miss Fletcher didn't know what happened, when she called me. She only knew that Mrs. Holloway was missing."

"In other words," Flournoy mused, "it'll probably be some time before we'll be notified officially. There're procedures the police follow—red tape." As he spoke, he tugged sharply at his right earlobe. It was the only sign of stress that Flournoy ever revealed.

"That goes for the reporters, too," Elton offered. "They probably don't know, either."

"Don't bet on it." Flournoy was standing now. His legs

were braced, his head held aggressively high. With the situation assessed, he'd made his decision and was ready to act. Watching him, Holloway realized that his heart was hammering. The demon had come awake, threatening to kill him where he sat helplessly gripping the arms of his chair, as if it were his only refuge. Around him, the room was tilting precariously. Multicolored spots were everywhere, madly dancing.

"You stay here with your father, Elton," Flournoy ordered. "Don't take any calls, except from me." Without waiting for a reply, Flournoy turned to Mitchell. "You come with me, Lloyd."

Not moving, Mitchell questioned Holloway with his dark, steady eyes.

With great effort, Holloway nodded. Whatever else happened, he must let Flournoy leave—before Flournoy discovered that the demon within him had awakened.

Because, surely, Flournoy and the demon would ultimately join together. It was inevitable.

Six

FASTENING THE TOP BUTTON of the suede jacket, Denise
tucked her chin down into the soft woolen scarf she'd twisted
twice around her neck and thrown back across her shoulder.
She'd crocheted two matching scarfs during the month before
Christmas, and put them both under their small Christmas
tree. Unwrapping the present, Peter had teased her about
the matching scarfs, accusing her of a his-and-her motorcycle
jacket mentality. But then he'd kissed her—tenderly, yet
fervently. She'd been sitting on the floor, unwrapping a
gaudy, overpriced present from Elton. She'd put the present
aside and kissed Peter back, hard. Moments later, they were
making love on the floor, amid the crackling confusion of
discarded Christmas wrappings. It had been a wild, wonderful
meeting. Whatever happened between them, now or in the
future, she would always remember that Christmas morning.

"How come you never wear your scarf?" she asked.

"I wear it all the time. When it's cold."

"It's cold tonight."

"Tonight, yes. But not when we left the city."

She looked up into the night sky. Low clouds were scudding
across an almost full moon, high in a star-spangled sky. They
were walking on a narrow gravel path that twisted down a
hillside to the parking area shared by a half dozen houses
built high on a Mill Valley hill that overlooked San Francisco
Bay and the city beyond. One of the glass-and-redwood houses
belonged to Ann and Cyrus Wade. Of all their friends, they
felt most at ease with Ann and Cy. Whenever the two couples
got together, they'd always shared something special. Yet,
during the entire evening they'd just spent together, before
and after dinner, conversation had lagged. Their normally
easy, confident ambience had somehow eluded them.

As he so often did, Peter articulated her thoughts:

"That wasn't much of an evening. The food was great. But everything else was off. Just a little off."

"I know. I was just thinking the same thing."

For a moment they walked in silence down the steep, gravel-slippery path. A month ago, after a party, Peter had slipped and fallen on this same path—hard.

"Cy and I had lunch a couple of weeks ago," Peter offered. "He said that Ann wants to get pregnant. He's not so sure he likes the idea. I'll bet that was the problem, tonight. I'll bet they're fighting about it."

"Once they had a baby, Cy would love it."

"I'm not so sure," he answered. "Cy's very self-centered, you know. And he's determined, too. Very, very determined. First and foremost, he thinks of himself as a conceptual artist. That's his self-image, and he's deadly serious about it. Everything else—being a husband, being a father—that comes second, with Cy."

Like you, she was tempted to say, teasing him. But, to Peter, his determination to succeed as a film writer wasn't a joking matter. It was a lesson she'd learned early in their relationship—and always forgot, to her sorrow. Peter was thirty years old, and time was beginning to torment him. For thirty-two hours a week, from ten at night to six in the morning, he worked on the docks, loading cargo. Thirty hours a week, to the hour, he spent writing scripts. In the two years they'd been together, Hollywood had called twice. Both times, his enthusiasm and blind faith had been pitifully, ruthlessly betrayed by glib shoestring producers who promised to make Peter rich and famous—provided he'd agree to give them a year's option on the script for almost nothing. The second time it happened, he'd vowed to give it all up. But, the next day, he'd come home from the docks, as usual, at six-thirty A.M. And, as usual, he'd started writing at seven, stopping only to make a pot of coffee. If she was home, she never disturbed him until eleven o'clock, when he went to bed. On the days he didn't work on the docks, he wrote eight hours a day. It was a long, discouraging struggle. And, at age thirty, the outcome was still in doubt. Peter never admitted to discouragement. But she could sense the doubts he sometimes felt in the small things he said—and didn't say.

So, instead of teasing him, she decided to say, "Ann's determined. If she wants a baby, I'm willing to bet that, this time next year, they'll have a baby."

For several long, gravel-crunching strides, they walked in

silence. Without looking at him, she could sense that, for Peter, it was a somber silence. So she wasn't surprised when he quietly said, "What about you, Denise? Ever think about a baby?"

It was, she knew, a tricky question—a loaded question, despite Peter's effort to speak casually, without inflection.

"Everyone thinks about babies." It was a careful-sounding answer. Too careful, maybe. As she spoke, she stole a look at him. Hands thrust deep into the pockets of his favorite blue pea coat, shoulders hunched, head bowed, he was looking down at the pathway at his feet. She couldn't see his face. But she could feel him frowning.

"You're twenty-eight years old. That's about the time most women think about babies, put up or shut up."

Now she, too, was staring down at the pathway directly in front of her. She knew that the evening had made Peter gloomy; she knew he might be bordering on one of his black moods. And she knew, therefore, that she should change the subject.

Instead, though, she heard herself saying, "Are we talking about Ann and Cy—or us?" As she said it, they turned the last corner. The parking lot lay ahead. In unison, the rhythm of their walking had slowed. It was as if, by common consent, they'd agreed that this conversation couldn't be interrupted. Before they got into the car, they must finish it.

Beside her, still walking with his head down, she heard him sigh. "I've got one kid, Denise. Every time I see him, it tears me up. I just couldn't face that again."

"You couldn't face another failed marriage. Isn't that what you're saying? It's not that you don't love David. It's because you love him too much that you're reluctant to have more children."

"Yeah," he answered heavily, "maybe that's what I'm saying. And when I hear myself say it, I realize that I'm talking about me, not you. I mean—" He broke off. Glancing at him quickly, she saw him shaking his head. It was a dogged, mutely defeated mannerism. In the pale glow from the parking lot's overhead light standards, she saw his face. His expression was somber, saddened. Whenever Peter talked about his son, she could always see anguish, deep in his eyes.

"I mean," he said finally, "I'm being selfish. I know it. I *realize* it."

Standing beside Peter's battered pickup now, she waited for him to unlock the door on her side.

"Let's talk about it later," she said softly. "In bed."

Suddenly he guffawed: a spontaneous eruption of strong, simple, Italian-style humor.

"Are you saying that we should make a baby? Tonight? Just do it, without further philosophizing?"

She dug her elbow sharply into his hard, flat stomach. "I'm saying that some things are better talked about in bed, that's all. Like babies. Now come on—open the door. I'm cold."

As she opened the apartment door, the phone was ringing.

"Christ," Peter said, looking at his watch as he switched on a living room lamp and crossed quickly to the phone. "It's after midnight." Then, curtly: "Hello. Who's this?"

Bolting the door, she turned toward Peter, standing beside the sofa, phone in hand. As he listened, she saw his thick black eyebrows raise sharply. Peter was surprised—genuinely surprised. It didn't often happen. Now he covered the mouthpiece, saying softly, "It's for you. It's someone named Flournoy. He says that your father wants to talk to you, for God's sake."

"My *father?*" As she said it, she felt herself go suddenly hollow at the center. It was her mother. Something had happened to her mother. She knew it. She could feel it.

Slowly, reluctantly, she took the phone from Peter.

"Hello? Dad?"

"Hello, Denise. I'm sorry to be calling so late. How are you, Denise?"

"I'm fine, Dad. What's wrong?"

"It's your mother, Denise. This afternoon, she—" He hesitated. It was, she knew, a pause calculated for effect. Automatically, instinctively, he was building the suspense. His voice lowered to a more somber, more dramatic note as he continued: "She left the house when she wasn't supposed to, alone. She got the Mercedes, and drove to a shopping center. She was—she'd been drinking, and she had an accident. A bad accident."

"She's hurt."

Hurt...

Or dead?

She was mutely searching Peter's face, looking for strength enough to survive the next few moments.

"No, Denise. She's not hurt. She's fine. But she hit a young mother and two children—backed into them, by mistake. The

59

children are hurt. Badly hurt. One of them is in a coma. She—she might not live, Denise." As he said it, his voice caught. It was another orator's trick—wasn't it?

"How are you, Dad? How's your—" She paused, deciding to say, "How's your health?"

Instead of *How's your heart?*

"I'm fine, Denise. Just fine, thank you." It was an almost pitifully formal reply. Except for the obligatory Christmas phone call, they hadn't spoken for more than two years. They were strangers now. Total strangers. She could hear it in his voice. And he could hear it, too. Whatever his faults, he'd always been perceptive, always sharply tuned to even the smallest, most subtle nuance.

"Is Mother—" Once more she paused. "Is she in—in jail?" As she said it, she looked again at Peter. He stood in the doorway of the living room, frowning worriedly as he looked at her. She covered the phone, saying quickly: "It's a traffic accident. Mother was drunk, and hit a little girl."

"No, she's not in jail," her father was saying. "We managed to get a quick hearing, and had the matter put over. I don't understand the legalities of it. But she's here now, Denise. And she's upset. Very upset. She's asking for you. That's all she can think about, or talk about—just you. Just seeing you."

"Do you want me to come down there? Is that what you want?" She said it slowly, regretfully. She was conscious of the dull, leaden dread she felt, asking the question.

Could she do it?

Could she return to the house that held so many bitter memories? Could she face her father, whom she couldn't respect? And Elton, whom she'd never liked? Could she watch her mother suffer, killing herself as she tried to dull her pain?

No, she couldn't do it.

Suddenly the thought of entering the Holloway mansion and facing the huge spiral staircase that led up to her old room was more than she could bear. Even for her mother, as much a victim as she was, she couldn't do it. The effort of breaking away had cost her too much. Going back would risk it all. And, as she sought Peter's eyes once more, she saw him almost imperceptibly shaking his head—pleading with her, please, don't risk it. For her sake. And his sake, too.

"No, Denise. That's not what I was thinking." As he said it, she could hear calculation come into his voice. And instantly, before he said it, she knew what he wanted of her:

"I was thinking," the deep, rich voice continued, "that it would be better if she came there for a while. To you."

To get her away from the reporters, Dad, she should retort. *To save your skin—your hypocritical hide, goddamn you.*

But instead, dully—she was repeating: "To me?"

"Yes, Denise. Can you take her in, for a week or so?"

"Dad, I—"

"She's all packed, Denise. I've taken that liberty. All day—all evening—we've been trying to reach you. During that time, your mother's come to believe that she's going up there, to San Francisco—that you'll take her in, Denise. I just couldn't bear to tell her differently. I didn't have the heart."

"You should have talked to me first." She spoke quietly, coldly, as she searched Peter's face for some solution—some way out. Peter was helplessly shrugging, unable to put the conversation's pieces together, listening only to her. So, abruptly, she put her hand over the receiver. Saying: "He wants me to take her in. Here. *Now.* What'll we do?"

Striding quickly to her side, Peter said, "Do whatever you want—whatever you have to do. I can go to Mendocino for a while. You decide."

Still searching Peter's face, she spoke into the phone: "Let me talk to Mother, Dad."

"Denise—" The single word was a rich, rolling tremolo, eloquently evoking his deep regret. Now he was performing—doing what he did best. All the stops were out. "Denise, I'm afraid she can't come to the phone. She's, ah, indisposed. You know what I mean."

"You mean she's drunk. You got her drunk. You gave her more than she could handle. Didn't you?"

"Denise—"

"Didn't you?"

For a long moment, the phone buzzed as her father fell silent. Then, speaking softly and reproachfully, he said, "I can't argue with you, Denise. I—I'm not up to it. All I can tell you is what I've said already—that your mother is terribly, terribly unhappy. She's afraid that she might be a murderer, Denise. She's shocked. Terribly shocked, and terribly afraid. And she wants to see you. That's all I can tell you. I've got to go now, Denise. I've got to lie down, and rest. I'm going to let you talk to Howard. You can tell him your decision. Goodnight, Denise. God bless you." The phone clicked dead. He'd left her hanging. He'd left her to struggle alone with whatever guilt he'd decided to lay on her, as he'd done so often in the past. And all in God's name, with God's benediction. Whatever he did—whomever he harmed—the blasphemous old bastard always evoked God. All her life, she'd never displeased her father directly. It was always God to whom she must answer.

Again, the phone clicked.

"Denise? Are you there?" It was Flournoy, his voice as cold and metallic as a computer's. God, how she hated him.

God God God

Blasphemy Blasphemy Blasphemy

"How bad is my mother?"

"She's gone to pieces, Denise. All she can talk about is you."

"I'm not sure I believe you."

"That's your choice."

As always, he was one move ahead of her.

"You want to get her out of town, that's all. Away from the reporters. Out of harm's way, so she can't embarrass you. That's what this is all about. Isn't it?" She realized that her voice was rising, half hysterically. She was laying it all on Flournoy: all the frustration her father had left her with, and all the sudden, searing hatred she felt for him.

"If that was it," Flournoy was saying coldly, "we'd simply send her to a sanitarium. We'd have Miss Fletcher take her to a sanitarium. That would be safer, you know. Much safer, for us."

And, of course, he was right.

So, sinking suddenly onto the couch, she surrendered: "All right. Send her up."

"Thank you, Denise. You're doing the right thing. She and Mitchell will be there early tomorrow morning. He'll help you—give you anything you need."

"Money, you mean."

Silence. Then, politely thanking her again, Flournoy broke the connection.

"God—*damn.*" She slammed down the phone in its cradle, hard.

Seven

SHIFTING THE BROWN PAPER BAG to his left hand, Carson dropped fifteen cents into the fare box and turned toward the rear of the bus.

"Hey, buddy." It was the bus driver's voice, behind him. Aware that nearby passengers were staring, he turned back to face the driver.

"It's twenty-five cents, you mind?"

"I—I'm sorry. I—thought it was fifteen."

"The sign says twenty-five." As the bus lurched forward, the driver jabbed a finger toward black letters stenciled on the bulkhead over the windshield.

"I've been away."

"For two years?" the driver jeered. "That's how long it's been since it was fifteen cents."

Not replying, he walked past the rows of smugly staring passengers. Already, it was starting. Less than a half hour back in town, and already eyes were following him—watchful, hostile eyes.

He tossed the bag on an empty seat and slid in beside it.

The wrinkled paper bag was all he had—the paper bag, plus the twenty-five dollars they'd given him at the institution, plus the clothes he was wearing: a jacket, slacks, a shirt and a tie. They were the same clothes he'd worn at his trial, the same clothes he'd worn when he entered prison, four years ago.

He'd always been careful about his clothes. He'd always studied the ads, to memorize the latest styles. His mother had sent him a newspaper clipping, written about his trial. The reporter had described him as "the dapper defendant." He still had the clipping, carefully Scotch-taped along its cracked-open creases.

The dapper defendant...

He settled lower into his seat, allowing his eyes to lose

focus as Darlington's familiar landmarks slid by beyond the grimy windows beside him.

It was only the beginning, that cracked, yellowed clipping. Because it was inevitable—absolutely inevitable—that other reporters would write other stories about him. Someday he would be famous. He would be rich, and powerful—and therefore famous. He was an exceptional person. Therefore, he'd made exceptional plans for himself—plans that only he, a gifted person, could carry out. Every day during the last four years, he'd refined the plans, testing and retesting, calculating and recalculating. With his superior IQ—near genius, the prison psychiatrist told him—he'd been able to plan his future, step by step. Nothing had been left out—nothing left to chance.

His mother was the key—the first key—that would open the first lock that held the first door closed and barred against him. Because, since he'd been a small boy, listening to her wild, incoherent ramblings, he'd heard her say that he was the remarkable son of a remarkable father: a rich and powerful man, famous throughout the world. He'd always known she was half mad, so he'd always assumed that his rich, powerful father had been a creature of her demented imagination. But, during the past four years, imprisoned with his thoughts and memories, he'd come to realize that there was a consistency to her descriptions of his father.

His father wasn't a figment of his mother's imagination.

His father was real. He existed.

And the money existed, too—his father's riches. The envelopes that arrived each month were the proof.

He swung down from the bus and stood on the curb, looking up and down the block. In four years, nothing had changed except for the worse. The houses were even smaller and more dingy than he'd remembered. The yards were unkempt, littered with the remnants of discarded playthings and broken-down cars. Overhead, the late afternoon sky was low and threatening, promising rain before nightfall. The air was heavy and oppressive. In a nearby house, a child was screaming. Now a woman's voice bawled out, adding her frenzied shouts to the din.

He was home.

All his life, he'd lived here, imprisoned.

He crossed the street, angling toward the small, one-story house where his mother lived. For a moment he didn't recognize the house. She'd had it painted: an apple green with darker green trim, and white window sash. And then he remembered: a year ago, his Uncle Julian had written that he was having the house painted and the roof repaired.

As Carson came closer to the house, he began to notice details. The window shades were half drawn, all to a uniform height above the sill. Advertising circulars littered the small front porch. The grass around the house was ankle high.

He mounted the two wooden steps to the porch, and felt behind a doorstop, where a key was kept hidden. The key was gone. Still stooped, he heard a nearby window slide open. It was a sound that had dogged him throughout his childhood. Because, inevitably, the sound of a high, shrill voice would follow the sound of the opening window:

"James! James Carson!"

It was Mrs. Kerrigan, who'd always hated him. Turning, he saw her large, florid face framed in the open window of her dining room.

"You're home, I see."

It was an accusation, harsh and spiteful. For a long, silent moment he stood staring at her. Could she see the contempt in his eyes—the loathing he felt for her? He hoped so.

"Are you looking for your mother?"

"Yes."

"Well—" Her gap-toothed smile was malevolent as she crossed her fat forearms on the windowsill. He knew that mannerism. She was complacently settling herself to enjoy the effect of what she was about to say:

"Well, your mother ain't here. About six months ago, they took her away to the asylum. Or maybe it was seven months ago, now. I forget."

As he pressed the bell button, a low angry muttering of thunder sounded from the west, where ominous tiers of purple clouds lay heavy on the horizon. Almost immediately, a second rumble followed the first. To himself, he smiled. In high school English, in Miss Farnsworth's class, he'd learned about Shakespeare's use of sympathetic nature, when an angry nature reflected the dire deeds of men. So it was appropriate that thunder should sound as he pressed his Uncle Julian's bell button. Because, sooner or later, dire deeds would follow.

From inside, he heard the sound of footsteps: light, quick footsteps. A small, white hand flicked aside the lace curtains covering the beveled glass of the tall, deeply carved door.

Through the gap in the curtains he saw the narrow, anxious face of Barbara Carson, his cousin. He smiled at her, and nodded a greeting. The curtain suddenly fell back into place; the face disappeared. He knew that she could still see him through the curtain. So he kept smiling.

Finally the curtain parted again.

"My father isn't home. He won't be home for another half hour, at least."

"Well, let me in. I can't wait out here."

Slowly, reluctantly, she was shaking her head. "I'm not supposed to, James. I'm not supposed to let anyone inside, until Daddy gets home."

"Where's your mother?"

"She's in Charleston. Grandma's sick. Mom's taking care of her."

"Well, let me in, Barbara. I've just got back. And your father's *responsible* for me. Just like he's responsible for you. So let me in."

"Responsible?"

"That's right. Responsible."

"He didn't tell me about it. I didn't even know you were coming."

"He probably didn't know when I'd be here. Not exactly. Now let me *in*, Barbara."

Once more, the curtain fell. But now he heard a night chain rattling. Cautiously, uncertainly, the door swung open. Everything Barbara did was uncertain. She was frightened of everything. She was a mouse—a nothing.

But he remembered to smile again. "Thank you." He walked past her, into the large, high-ceilinged living room that opened off the entry hall to the left. Uncle Julian lived in a restored Victorian house, one of Darlington's historical landmarks. Uncle Julian was a grain broker who also dealt in real estate. Still not fifty, with a handsome wife and a spectacular house, Uncle Julian was one of Darlington's most prominent citizens. When Julian Carson walked down the street, people smiled and nodded. Julian Carson was important. So, to his face, no one mentioned his sister—or his nephew.

He tossed the brown paper sack on a tufted, red velvet sofa, and sat beside it. The bag was wrinkled and torn. Soon his possessions would fall out—his comb and his toothbrush, what the officials called his "personal effects." Somehow the image of his personal effects exposed in his uncle's house seemed an obscenity.

Barbara edged onto a small, straightback chair, facing him with her knees pressed together, hands anxiously clasped in her lap. She was fourteen years old, just developing. Her body was slight, but finely formed. She was wearing tight-fitting white slacks that clung to her thighs, and dove deep into the cleft of her crotch. A red sweater revealed small, budding breasts.

When she'd said she wasn't expecting him, she'd been telling the truth. Because, dressed as she was, she'd never have let him see her. Not Barbara. Not if she remembered the time she'd let him touch her, so long ago.

"You're fourteen," he said. "Fourteen years old."

She nodded—a single small, grave inclination of her head. Her hair was blond, long and finespun. A twist of red ribbon held the hair at the nape of her neck, pulled smooth over her head. Her hair would be silky and smooth, soft to the touch. Soft, and exciting. When she lifted her head, he saw her swallowing. Her throat was thin, delicately modeled, exquisitely layered and muscled.

Beneath his hand, her throat would feel like a wild bird, fluttering and wildly beating, struggling to escape. But, captured, birds couldn't fly. So, crushed to death, they died. Pressed hard against his, he would feel her body buck and shudder: a doomed, desperate bird. Dying.

"You've grown, since I saw you."

Once more, she nodded.

He let his eyes linger on her, watching a sudden flush stain the pale flesh of her face. Finally, softly, he said, "Say something to me, Barbara. Don't just nod. Say something."

"I—" She licked at her lips. "I don't—don't know what you want me to say. My father won't be home for a half hour or so. I've already told you that."

"Did Uncle Julian tell you I was—getting out?"

"He—yes, he did. But he didn't say when. And my grandmother, she's been so sick, lately, that—" She left it unfinished. Once more, her eyes fell away from his. In her lap, her hand still twisted. She was afraid of him—afraid of being there with him, alone. Watching her, he felt his genitals tightening. Beneath his clothes, he was suddenly perspiring. His throat had gone dry. It was, he knew, the first sign—the first warning.

But she mustn't know—mustn't suspect. Not now. Not here.

So, again—still—he was smiling as he said, "Your house is beautiful, Barbara. You've done a lot, since I was here the last time."

She nodded. Then, with obvious effort, she said, "Thank you."

"Don't you know my name?"

"Yes. It—it's James."

Still smiling, he gently prodded: "Cousin James. That's what you used to call me, when you were smaller. Do you remember?"

"I—yes—I..."

From the hallway, he heard the sound of a key turning in a lock. Instantly, she was on her feet, fleeing into the hall. He heard the sound of the front door closing, followed by the sound of hushed, anxious voices. A silence followed. Then Uncle Julian stood in the open archway to the living room. Behind him, Barbara was silently fleeing down the hallway—gone.

"As I understood it," Julian Carson was saying, "you weren't to've arrived until next week. Tuesday, to be exact."

On his feet, facing his uncle squarely, he shook his head. "I don't know. They just told me to go, and gave me a bus ticket. So that's what I did. I left."

"How long have you been in Darlington?" Julian's voice was brisk, clipped. His eyes were hard. They were watchful eyes. Hostile eyes. The eyes of the enemy.

"About an hour."

"Did you go home? To your house?"

"Yes. Mrs. Kerrigan—the neighbor—said that my mother's in an asylum." He was satisfied with his voice—calm, cool. In control.

"It's not an asylum," his uncle answered curtly. "It's a sanitarium. A very good sanitarium, in fact."

"Is it expensive?" His voice was still calm. He was still in control. Perfect control.

For a moment, Julian didn't reply. Suddenly his eyes were guarded. Finally, cautiously, he said, "Yes, it's expensive. Very expensive, in fact. But she's got to be there, no question. No question at all. She's a sick woman. A very sick woman." Then, quickly, Julian raised his wrist, glancing at his gleaming gold watch. To steal the watch would be wonderful: a wild, dizzying rush of pure pleasure.

"Listen, James," his uncle was saying, "I've just got time to shower and shave before I've got to go out. It's business. Let's see—" Still looking at the gold watch, Julian frowned. "Today is Thursday. You've got a job at the Chevron car wash, down on Bagley. It's all set. Everything's arranged. But it doesn't start until Monday. Are you staying at home?"

"I don't have a key. The door's locked."

"Yes. Well—" He reached into his jacket pocket, for a long alligator wallet. "Well, I don't have time to look for the key. Not now. So why don't you take this—" He extended three twenty-dollar bills. He held them gingerly, as if to avoid the contamination of finger-to-finger contact. "Take this, and get yourself a room downtown. Get yourself settled. Give me a call over the weekend. We'll get together, and I'll fill you in on what's happened."

"Where's my mother? What sanitarium?"

Glancing again at the watch, Julian said, "It's the Prospect Sanitarium, out north of town. But I'm not sure you should see her, James. That is, I'm not sure it'll do much good, for you to see her."

"I'd like to see her, though, Uncle Julian. I've got some business to talk about. Important business."

His uncle's small, narrow-set eyes came suspiciously alive. "Business? What kind of business?"

He paused a moment. Then, speaking in the same slow, calm voice, he said, "Money, Uncle Julian. I need money."

"Well—" Julian's round, smooth cheeks puffed out. He was a short, fat man with a round face and thick, stubby arms and legs. Once Carson had seen him swimming. His round white body had looked like a big, bloated frog.

"Well, you'll have money, James. I mean, I'll give you some—a stake, to start. Then, if you work hard, you won't have anything to worry about. Nothing at all."

"Still, I'd like to see her."

"Yes. Well, that's only natural, I suppose." Fussily, Julian nodded. "And there's no harm, I guess. But now, I've got to go. Call me over the weekend, James. We'll get together. Maybe you can come over for dinner."

But, as he picked up the wrinkled brown bag and walked past his uncle to the front door, he knew there'd never be a dinner invitation. He could see it in his uncle's eyes.

Eight

AT THE DOOR, she heard a knock. It was the jailer, coming for her. Or was it the devil, rattling the gates of hell? Or an angel, striking a golden gong?

Or her mother, coming to punish her—to flay her with a whip until her legs ran red?

Again it came: three short, sharp blows on the white wooden panel. It was a signal. So she could be ready.

So, quickly, she moved back until her back found the wall. Then, eyes still on the door, fingertips light against the wall on either side of her body, she moved to her right—two steps, three steps. The fingertips were her eyes. Because the eyes must look, mustn't leave the door.

One more step. The fourth step. It could have been the title of a song—of a poem set to music, played by a fiddling fool.

One more step—the final step. She'd found the corner. Without eyes, she'd found the corner. It was the place of power, her secret triangle. Kings had crowns and pyramids. Clowns had wands and waggles. But she'd found her corner.

As, slowly, the door opened.

As, slowly, she was sliding down the wall to the floor. Crouched. Ready. Watching.

Yes, it was the devil. The costume could change, and the face could smile. And the walk and the talk and drop and dangle and drabble could sniggle and slide...

But never the dross-downer.

And never the snake's eyes, or the vermin mouth, with pointed teeth behind red-painted lips. Moving now. Talking. And smiling, too. Saying:

"You have a visitor, Mrs. Carson. Your son. James."

But if the devil had knocked, then the son wasn't Christ's. Because where Christ could come, no devil dared ever walk.

And none could the son come. Never more.

The son

The son

And none could ever believer deceiver receiver the son from the Christ dramble.

But—yes—it was the son. The sound of his voice was the same. And the face-shape and color of hair, brown, with eyes the same, so crystal cruel. Christ's eyes.

Because Christ had been cruel, too. Ripping and tearing into her, to give her the son with the crystal eyes...

...the crystal-cruel eyes.

"Hello, Mother. I'm back."

Yes, he was back. No one else could speak in that soft, dead voice. So he was back.

So she must remain crouched, protected. Especially from him. Her mother had bloodied her legs. But he had bloodied her soul.

Too.

Too many times.

Too too many times.

"Talk to me, Mother. I want you to talk to me."

From outside, she heard the distant roll-wooly loudsounds of an airplane above, somewhere far in the sky beyond.

And that was her answer. She could open her mouth and the engine sound of distant thunder could speak for her. Magic.

Magic.

But to believe it might make her cry.

Why? *Why?*

Alone in the corner, crouched down, she heard her thunder-voice answering him. And, yes, she was crying. Because her face was wet beneath her eyes. Her fingers told her so.

She could remember that song: a Sunday school song, every stanza ending: *Because the Bible tells me so.*

Which began, really: *Because her fingers told her so.*

THE BIBLE TOLD HER SO.

But why was she crying? Because now she remembered the first part:

Yes, Jesus loves me

Yes, Jesus loves me.

And so, because Jesus had loved her, the son was there. In this room, standing over her. Saying: "Talk to me, goddammit."

Cruelly. Cruelly.

So now she must scream. Nothing. Anything. Something. But scream. *Now*.

"Goddammit, shut up."

She could see his hands, drawing back.

"Shut up."

She heard the words through a sudden crash, flesh against flesh, bone on bone. Blinding her.

"Shut up, I said."

And now, with his angel's face close to hers, she could hear him say, "I want the money. Those envelopes. They're mine, now. They're for me."

But did he love her?

Or had love gone with the sound of thunder, rolling off across the sky to leave her without the voice she'd found?

"Does Julian have it? Is that it? Uncle Julian—does he have the money? Do the envelopes go to him now?"

How could she answer? With the thunder gone, nothing was left for her. No voice. No hope.

"Just nod, goddammit. Or shake your head. One or the other. Or else—" The hand came back. That hard, heavy hand, so cruel for an angel's.

"Is that it?"

Now the room was moving up and down, keeping time to her head, nodding. And, finally, with her head bowed, she heard the sound of footsteps departing.

So, softly, while she stared down at the small drops of blood on the floor, she could cry.

Nine

HE DRAPED the damp, heavy cloth over the wire drying line, and reached in the hopper for two more cloths, one for each hand. Glancing over his shoulder, he saw a green Buick station wagon emerging from the strips of heavy canvas that hung across the exit. Blasts of steamy air rippled the canvas. "Dragon's breath," they called it. And the wail of machinery was the dragon's voice, a constant, angry roar.

A black teen-ager—Willard—sprang into the Buick, started the car and drove it to the right of the wide concrete driveway. The Buick's owner, a slim woman wearing fifty-dollar denims and a hundred-dollar bush jacket, advanced toward the car, raising her wrist to look at her watch. She was late. Wearing her expensive clothes, driving her new Buick, the whole world waited for her. Anything she wanted, she could get. It was plain in every movement of her body, every line of her clothing.

For today—his third day on the job—this car was his last.

The Buick dived as Willard set the parking brake. Before the driver's door had slammed, Junior Frazer was wiping at the car's roof, on the right side. Frazer's side was always the right. The left side was his.

"Hey, man—come on. Let's *do* it, Jimmy." Frazer's strong, velvet-brown arms curved and corded as his two drying rags swept across the gleaming green metal. Frazer was eighteen years old. He'd never had a full-time job before. Pleasure was plain in every move he made, every quick, deft switch of his twin drying cloths.

"Come on, Jimmy, let's dry this mother *off.*"

In all his life, except when he was very young, no one had called him "Jimmy."

Now he was leaning against the car's left door, sweeping his own rags across the roof. Some of the roof on his side was already dry.

73

Thank you, Junior Frazer, you dumb black bastard with one tooth missing in front.

Thank you, Junior Frazer, you big-lipped black ape.

As he began on the hood, Junior was already on the trunk, and now moving around toward the left rear fender. Apes were good workers. They'd been bred for work like this.

Junior and Jimmy. The perfect team. Master and slave.

Behind him the conveyor clanked and the canvas strips blew open again as another car emerged from the dryer—a white Lincoln, with a gleaming black top.

But not his. Some other slave's. Not his.

He turned away, draped the two cloths over the drying wire, and strode to the time clock.

In all his life, he'd never punched a time clock. Not until now, his twenty-sixth year.

A small slip of paper was clipped to the time card:

> *See me before you go home.*
> *Krober*

Through the plate-glass window of the office, he saw Krober waiting for him. The master, waiting for the slave.

He slid the card into the clock, waited for the mechanism to click, slid the card back into the rack. Slid the slip of paper into his pocket—turned the knob and opened the plate-glass door of the manager's office.

Krober was a tall man with a narrow face, unhappy eyes and a knife scar across one cheek. Two years ago, the car wash had been robbed. Krober had been cut across the cheek and stomach. He'd been left for dead, he said, on the floor of the office.

"You wanted to see me?"

"Yeah, Carson, I did." Krober pushed himself back in his chair, bracing both hands on the edge of his chipped steel desk. He sighed once, deeply and regretfully, before he said, "I'm afraid you're just not working out, Carson. I'm sorry. Real sorry. I've known your uncle for years, from the lodge. And I'd like to help. But we got quotas here, you know. Performance figures. And if somebody doesn't keep to his quota, then the others complain. And that's what's been happening. There've been complaints. Several." As he spoke, Krober kept his eyes fixed on the desk in front of him.

"The nigras, you mean. They complain."

Krober raised his bony shoulders, unhappily shrugging.

74

"When do I get paid?"

"Come by tomorrow. About three. I'll have it for you then. I'm sorry, Carson. And tell your uncle about the quotas, you mind? Tell him it's nothing personal. Which it isn't. Nothing personal at all."

Without speaking, he turned and left the office, carefully closing the door behind him.

Insects were already chirping in the gathering dusk as he mounted the two stairs to Uncle Julian's front porch. Inside the big house, lights shone from all the downstairs windows. In the large living room, to the left, lamplight filtered through heavy velvet drapes, fringed in gold. The light made the velvet glow, a deep rich red.

He pressed the bell button. Almost immediately, he heard footsteps approaching: hard, heavy footsteps. Uncle Julian was coming. As the door swung open, he realized that he'd stepped back into the shadow of a pillar. He saw Julian's eyes momentarily narrow, staring into the gathering darkness. Then, as he stepped forward, he saw his uncle's eyes widen as displeasure replaced puzzlement.

"Oh—James."

The disapproval so plain in the two words said it all. Yes, Krober had called Uncle Julian. Yes, Uncle Julian was angry.

"Come in, James." It was a reluctant, resigned invitation. Stepping back, his uncle held the door open. "Come into the study. There, on the right. The closed door. Yes, that's right."

He opened the door, found the light switch, flicked it. The room was small, its walls lined on two sides with bookshelves. The books came from a book club, his uncle had once told him, one book a month. The room's only furnishings were two leather armchairs, a leather-topped walnut desk and a smaller chair placed behind the desk. A miniature grandfather's clock stood on the desk, together with two identically framed pictures. The pictures were enlarged snapshots of Uncle Julian and his family.

"Sit down, James." Behind him, Uncle Julian's voice was heavy and slow, expressing a deep, ponderous regret. As he sank into one of the two armchairs, he heard the door close: a solid, somber sound, like a cell door closing. Now his uncle was rounding the desk, sitting down to face him squarely. Uncle Julian was dressed in a sports jacket and sports shirt. An ornamental cord secured by a small sliding medallion. It was an Elks medallion. So, tonight, Uncle Julian—a past president—was going to the Elks club. Carson glanced at the miniature grandfather's clock. The time was eight-thirty. What was the night's entertainment at the Elks club? Was it a smoker?

Smoothing his sparse hair over his round, shining skull with one pudgy hand, Uncle Julian was slowly, ponderously shaking his head.

"I was afraid of this, James. I was afraid this would happen."

"It was the nigras. There's almost all nigras working there. They complained about me. Because I'm white."

Somberly regretful, his uncle sighed: a deep, disapproving sigh. Appeal denied.

"That's not what Henry Krober said."

"Then Henry Krober is a liar."

"What?"

"I said Krober is a liar, if he says the nigras didn't complain about me. Because they did."

"Henry Krober said you weren't doing the job. He said you worked too slow."

"That's what the nigras said. He believes the nigras because he wants to keep them working for him. That's because he doesn't have to pay them anything. Just like he didn't pay me anything."

"Now, see here, James—" It was the beginning of a hard-voiced, hard-eyed warning. Sympathy denied. Understanding denied. Blood-tie denied. Always, his uncle had been on the other side, an enemy.

"It's not a fit job for a white man, washing cars." As he said it, he saw Uncle Julian's face suddenly flush. The close-set eyes contracted. The small, pursed mouth came set, suddenly hard and angry.

Always, when his temper rose, Julian's voice sunk to a soft, silky note, deadly as the sound of a slithering snake:

"You're a paroled convict, James. You're lucky to get any job. Any job at all."

"Am I supposed to work with niggers?"

"If I say so, then that's what you're supposed to do. And, in the meantime, I'll thank you not to call Henry Krober a liar. You might not be aware of it, but he's a lodge brother of mine."

He raised his head until his eyes were level with his uncle's, coldly staring. Let him see it all—the hatred he felt, and the determination. Let him see all the angry years, and

76

all the silent vows of vengeance. Let him realize—now—that this was the moment everything between them changed.

In the silence, he heard the miniature clock ticking. He could hear the sound of his uncle's breath coming harder.

Until he saw the narrow-set pig eyes falter, steady, then falter again—and finally fall.

So now, speaking in a low, deliberate voice, tightly controlled, he could say what he'd come to say:

"I saw my mother, Sunday."

A long, watchful moment of silence followed. Then, still snake-soft: "Your mother's crazy, James."

"She said you're taking her money. The money she gets every month. The checks." His voice, too, was ominously soft. Again their eyes locked. And now, deep inside his uncle's eyes, he saw the first flicker of fear beginning.

So, to conceal it, the other man's voice suddenly rose, bullying him now:

"Your mother's crazy. You can't believe anything she says. Nothing."

"She's not getting those checks. They wouldn't let her have them. So you must be getting them. You're the only one."

Now he could see momentary uncertainty in his uncle's eyes—followed by calm, cold calculation. They were talking about money, Julian's specialty. So Julian's voice dropped to a deeper, more confident note as he said, "Those checks don't have anything to do with you. They're for your mother, to keep her. And I'm keeping her now. I'm responsible for her, just like I'm responsible for you. So they're my checks now. I've got her power of attorney. They've got nothing to do with you. Nothing at all."

"They're to keep me, too. My mother, and me. Now she doesn't need them. But I do."

"What the hell you talking about, she doesn't need them? She needs them more than ever, boy. And you'd better remember it."

"Don't call me 'boy,' Uncle Julian."

"Well, then you'd better start talking sense."

Now the old, easy bluster had come back in Julian's voice. The flicker of fearful uncertainty had died.

So, quietly, he said: "Where does she get those checks, Uncle Julian? Where do they come from?"

"They come from a bank. That's all I know—and that's the truth. They come from the National City Bank, in New York, once a month. And that's all I know about them."

"You know who sends them, though."

"Like hell I do. They're cashier checks."

"Then you know why they're sent."

"What'd you mean, 'why'?"

"I mean that you know who told the bank to send the checks. You know who gave the money to the bank."

Another moment of cold-eyed calculation. Then, cautiously: "What makes you think I know?"

"Because I can see it in your face, Uncle Julian."

"You can—" A quick, outraged moment of silence. Then, suddenly, a loud bray of laughter. Forced. Faked.

"You can see it in my *face*? Is that what you said?" It was almost a merry question, incredulously querulous.

But, still, forced. Faked.

"That's what I said, Uncle Julian." He could clearly hear his own voice. He was speaking calmly. Coldly. He was in control.

"Well, then—" Sudden fury sharpened his uncle's eyes, pinpoints of hatred now. "Well, then, if that's what you said, boy, then I think you'd better just stop one little goddamn minute to remember that it only takes one word from me, and you're back in jail. Just one word. You hear me, boy?" Julian's breathing was harsh and ragged. His face was pasty pale.

"Don't call me—"

Suddenly his uncle was on his feet. Shouting: "I'll call you anything I want to, you little bastard. Because that's what you are. You're a bastard. And those checks, they come from your father. He's a very rich, very well-known man, your father. But if anyone ever finds out his name, then those checks stop. Which would mean that your mother would go into an insane asylum—a *state* insane asylum, where she'd be treated like an animal, which is maybe where she belongs. But, just so you understand where I stand—*boy*—I'll tell you, right out, that I don't want her in a state asylum for one very simple reason. And that reason—*boy*—is that it wouldn't look good for me to have a sister there. Now—" Balefully blinking, mouth working furiously, still breathing harsh and hard, Julian said, "Now, that's the truth. That's the whole goddamn truth. Your mother is the worst thing that ever happened to me. The worst day of my life was when she came back to Darlington carrying you in her belly. She came back with you in her belly and a trunkful of some kind of holy roller pamphlets and some money in her pocket book, and

78

she rang my bell. And ever since then—*boy*—my life hasn't been worth shit. So now—" A trembling forefinger pointed to the door. "So now—*boy*—I'll thank you to get the hell out of here. And don't ever come back again. Not until you're asked. And that'll be never, I promise you."

Ten

CARSON SLIPPED the prybar between the door and the frame, gripped the doorknob with his left hand and pressed with his right hand against the bar as he turned the knob. The door shifted, cracked, but still held fast. Had someone installed a bolt on the inside? Uncle Julian?

He glanced over his shoulder as he shifted his feet, working the bar deeper into its slot. Now he leaned with his full weight against the bar. A sudden shift, a sharp splintering, and the door sprang free. As he stepped quickly into the dark hallway he turned, looked out into the street. Except for a car turning the Maple Street corner, nothing stirred. Closing the door, he slipped the prybar down inside the front of his pants, looped its cord around his belt and carefully knotted the cord. From his hip pocket he withdrew a penlight. Holding the penlight close to his palm, he pressed the switch. Yes, the tiny circle of light was bright; the batteries were strong.

He was ready.

Three quick steps took him to the doorway of the small living room. Pale light from the streetlamp outside fell on the familiar shapes: the couch, the armchair, the two straightback chairs, the small coffee table placed in front of the couch. Except for the TV, predictably missing, nothing had changed. Even the odor was the same: musty and rank, the smell of misery—and madness.

He'd always hated it. Standing in the open doorway of the room, listening, he could hear the lost, lonely echo of her sobs, and her shouts, and the small, strange sounds she made in the night, struggling with her demons.

Slowly, he turned away. His bedroom was next to hers. The door of his room was closed. As he turned the knob and pushed the door open, he felt his own demons stirring. The familiar shadow-shapes that crouched in the darkness could have followed him from prison, ready once more to conspire with his memories. With their tops swept clean by some mysterious hand, the desk and the bureau were strange, squared-off sentinels, waiting and watching. The bookshelves were empty. His pictures and posters had been taken from the walls.

It was a stranger's room, worse than a cell.

Shifting the penlight to his left hand, he drew a knife from his hip pocket. A snap, and the blade came alive in his hand, gleaming in the darkness. He moved to the bed, standing for a moment motionless beside it, looking down.

Then, suddenly, he struck—once, twice, three times. Short, savage slashes ripped open the mattress where his head could have been—his heart—his genitals. Each sweep of the blade—each twisting, tearing slash—could have torn his body open, leaving him alone in the darkness, lying dead in the blood and the excrement that would soak the mattress around him.

It was the waking part of a dream he'd often had, lying helpless on the bed, pinioned, while someone with his face—his knife—killed him.

He held the knife before him now, turning the blade to reflect the pale rectangle of night light from the window.

He'd bought the knife tonight, after leaving his uncle. For more than a week—for nine days—he'd thought about a knife, remembering how a knife would feel in his hand—remembering how it could flash in the darkness—remembering how blood could gleam on the silvery blade.

And remembering, too, that possession of the knife could send him back to prison.

For nine days, deciding whether to get the knife, he'd been incomplete.

But never again.

Never, never again.

His thumb touched the knife's locking slide. The blade disappeared into the handle. Its magic was sheathed, releasing him. So, moving smoothly now, he returned the knife to his pocket and stepped out into the hallway. The stranger's room was behind him. Gone.

So, swiftly, he walked to the big hall closet, empty now. Because she'd once locked him in the closet, he couldn't close the door. But, tonight, it was a meaningless problem. Because he was reaching above his head, firmly pulling on a length of rope suspended from the ceiling. One long, firm pull, and the spring-release staircase came down, extending itself as it dropped to the floor at his feet.

Six steps took him to the attic, smelling sour and stuffy. But there were no demons here—only dirt and dust.

No demons, and no danger.

The trunk was against the far wall, where he knew the pale beam of the flashlight would find it. The trunk was unlocked, as he'd expected. With the penlight held in his teeth he used both hands to raise the old-fashioned curved lid. Rusty hinges creaked, feebly protesting.

Long ago, wearing a bandana wrapped around his head, pretending to be a pirate, he'd raised this same curved lid. He'd peered into the same musty, mysterious interior with the same sense of forbidden adventure and anxious, tremulous excitement that he felt now.

His fingers had slightly trembled then—as they were trembling now.

His breath had come in short, shallow gasps; his mouth had been dry—then, and now.

The trunk's top tray contained the well-remembered collection of cheap, sentimental junk: old photographs, yellowed playbills, a beaded purse she'd carried to her first dance, bits of broken jewelry and faded mementos from her childhood. Carefully, he lifted the tray and set it softly on the floor beside the trunk. He knew what he wanted—knew where to find it.

The dark interior of the trunk held a tangled skein of gauzy, sequined theatrical costumes, each one a memento of a play in which she'd appeared. Long ago, he'd climbed the retracting stairway to find her crouched beside the trunk, surrounded by the costumes. She'd been dressed in one of the costumes. Her face had been made up for the theater: eyes and mouth enlarged, cheeks darkened, nostrils deepened. But she hadn't used a mirror, and her face looked as if she wore a grotesque mask that had slipped. When she saw him, she began to cry. In the cramped, airless attic, he'd smelled the strong odor of alcohol. He'd never smelled the odor before, never seen her drunk before.

Quickly, he dipped into the flimsy costumes, trailing their random lengths of satin and gauze from impatient fingers. Soon the costumes were strewn around him, raising clouds of dust.

If she'd poked her head up into the attic now, as he'd done so long ago, she would find him crouched down beside the trunk with the costumes surrounding him—just as he'd found her.

An old fur coat, bedraggled as a dead cat, lay at the very bottom of the trunk. He hurled the coat away from him...

...and lifted out the scrapbook.

The pages riffling beneath his anxious fingers were just as he'd remembered them: the baby on its blanket, the little girl in the ruffled dress, the teen-ager on stage in her first play, the face in the gospel choir, posing in front of a microphone.

And, finally, an 8x10 studio photo of the young woman standing raptly beside an older man. The man was posing in front of a TV camera. His eyes were cast reverently up toward heaven. His right hand was raised high in a gesture of grand supplication. The words, *For Mary, with God's love and mine, Austin Holloway,* were written in fading ink across the bottom of the photograph.

The rest of the scrapbook, page after page, was filled with newsclippings, all about Austin Holloway.

Turning back, playing the penlight's beam more closely on the 8x10 photo, he could make out a date written by Holloway in the lower left-hand corner of the photograph:

September 3, 1951.

Less than a year before he'd been born.

Raising his head slowly to window level, he looked inside the garage. Yes, the Buick was gone. Uncle Julian was still at the Elks club. The time was a little after ten. Time remaining, at least an hour. More than enough.

Crouched beneath the line of a hedge that ran along the property line, he moved cautiously toward the house, his feet silent on the thick lawn. Uncle Julian was proud of his lawns. The gardener came at least once a week, all through the year.

As he came closer to the house, he heard the sound of a neighbor's dog barking. Insects buzzed in the grass at his feet. The distant muttering roar of a jet airliner came from somewhere in the northern sky. The horizon to the east was lightening. The moon was about to rise.

The screen door to the back porch was open, as he'd expected. In Darlington, proud householders often boasted that, in their town, doors need never be locked.

Gently, he tried the back door. The knob turned; the door swung slowly open.

Uncle Julian would boast no more.

As he stepped across the threshold into the darkened kitchen, he felt his stomach shift. His genitals were tightening. His breath was coming faster. His throat was dry.

Here, in this house he hated, windows were lighted. From somewhere upstairs he could hear the sound of music and voices, followed by tinny laughter. A TV was playing, or a radio. Barbara was upstairs. He could sense her presence.

The house was alive.

And he was alive, too.

For four years, locked away, he'd been dead. But now, advancing down the dark hallway toward his uncle's dining room, he'd come alive. Finally, fully alive.

The dining room was dark, deserted.

The living room, too, was dark. Ahead, on the right, light came through an archway that opened on a small parlor, across the hallway from the living room. As he moved to the wall beside the archway, he was aware that his right hand had slid into his hip pocket. He held the knife in his hand. He hadn't heard the click, but he knew the blade had sprung out, locked and ready.

With his back flattened against the hallway's flocked velvet wallpaper, he was inching toward the archway. He held the knife in his right hand, delicately probing ahead, as deadly as a snake's tongue. Behind him, the fingertips of his left hand slid lightly over the velvet flocking.

Until, beyond the final inch, he could see into the parlor...
...empty.

Instantly, he turned to face the carved walnut door to his uncle's study, diagonally across the hallway. The door was closed; the crack beneath the door was dark. Three short, light steps took him to the door. His left hand was on the embossed brass knob, turning it. Soundlessly, the door swung open. He was inside the study, with the door safely closed behind.

Standing in the darkened room, he could clearly hear the remembered echo of his uncle's voice, furiously lashing him:

"That's what you are. You're a bastard."

He could clearly remember his uncle's eyes, too. He could clearly see the hatred, and the old, easy contempt. It was the memory of those eyes that had brought him here.

His uncle's eyes, and all the others. Always, he could see them. Awake or asleep, they would never release him.

His footsteps were noiseless on the thick carpet as he moved around the desk. The only sound was the ticking of the miniature grandfather's clock. With the knife in his right hand, he trailed the fingers of his left hand gently over the leather desk top, finally to rest on the clock. He lifted the clock, placed it on the floor, placed his right foot lightly on the clock. Then, slowly, he shifted his weight to his right foot until he heard a cracking, and felt the clock flatten under his foot.

Behind the desk now, he felt for the twin knobs of the desk's center drawer. The drawer was stuck—or locked. With the knife gripped in his teeth, he used both hands to pull at the knobs. Yes, the drawer was locked.

Confirming that, yes, it was here that Uncle Julian kept his valuables.

He placed the knife on the desk top, withdrew the penlight from his pocket and shone the slender beam on the line where the drawer joined the desk. Yes, there was enough room for his prybar. He placed the penlight beside the knife, neatly aligned. His fingers moved to the cord knotted around his belt. He could...

The door was opening.

Dressed in a sheer nightgown, backlit by the light from the parlor across the hallway, Barbara stood in the open doorway.

He was around the desk. His left hand crashed into the base of her throat. As she staggered back, sagging against the wall, he kicked the door closed. She was struggling to keep her footing, trying to push herself away from the wall. In the dim light from the window behind the desk, he could see her eyes, wide with terror. Her mouth was coming open; her throat was convulsing.

"Don't scream, Barbara," he said softly, moving forward until the point of the knife touched her chest between the swell of her small, pubescent breasts. "Don't scream, or I'll slit you up the front. I promise."

"*James.*" Her voice was almost inaudible. Then, in a breathless rush: "*James.*"

"That's loud enough, Barbara." He raised his left hand, pointing to an armchair. It was the same chair his uncle had gestured him to so contemptuously, on Thursday afternoon.

"Sit down." As he said it, he gestured with the knife toward the chair. It was a delicate, elegant gesture, just right. Her eyes were fixed on the knife. She was fascinated, helpless. "Sit down, Barbara," he repeated softly.

"James. Please. I..."

down, Barbara. Or you'll bleed. I promise you, you'll ~~bleed.~~

With a sudden desperate, awkward rush of arms and legs akimbo, she lurched into the chair. The skirt of her nightgown drew taut across slim white thighs. Small breasts strained against the flimsy fabric of the nightgown. Standing over her now, he leaned forward to reach across her shoulder for the penlight, still on the desk. The movement brought his genitals into contact with her shoulder. Instantly, the warm rush of sensation leaped up from his groin to his solar plexus, then to his throat, tight and dry. It was almost a physical pain, leaving him momentarily helpless. He felt her shrink away from him. He turned the penlight on her face, and pressed the switch. Yes, her eyes were wild, fixed on his face. She was terrified, visibly trembling.

So it was beginning. In this small room, where her father had called him a bastard, their game was beginning.

But slowly—slowly.

The small, round spot of white light was moving, beginning its delicate dance. First, playfully, the circle moved down to her throat, where he saw a small droplet of blood. Smiling, he placed the knife on the desk, out of her reach. With his right forefinger, he touched the spot of blood. He held the finger in front of her eyes, for her to see. Then, still smiling, he lifted the finger to his lips, licking the fingertip. From deep in her throat, he heard a retching sound.

Yes, the game had begun. Soon he must unbuckle his belt, unfasten his pants. He must—

From behind him came a metal-on-metal sound, followed by a faint stirring of air.

"Daddy. Help me."

The door was flung wide, crashing back against a wall. Light from the hallway flooded the study. Head down, shouting a garbled obscenity, Julian was charging toward the far wall, lined with books. Suddenly the small room was filled with shouting, dangerously loud. As he sprang toward his uncle, knife ready, he felt his foot strike something solid. He was tripping, falling. It was her legs, tangled between his. Rolling free, up on his knees now, he saw his uncle clawing wildly behind a row of books, sending books crashing to the floor. Now his feet were under him, braced. With the knife held low, he lunged again toward the stocky figure of his uncle, still tearing at the bookcase. One slash, one thrust, and Julian would fall.

But, as he rounded the desk, his uncle was pivoting to face him. A gun gleamed in his uncle's pudgy hand. He saw the barrel come up, aimed squarely at his chest. He saw a forefinger tightening on the trigger...

...felt himself falter in midstride, heard himself screaming, begging...

...saw the finger fully tightened on the trigger, knuckle-whitened. The finger clamped again on the trigger—unclamped—clamped. Now his uncle lifted the pistol, staring at it with round, outraged eyes. It was a .45 automatic, army style. The hammer was sunk into the receiver, uncocked.

As he stepped forward, he realized that he was wildly laughing. Uncle Julian was still staring at the pistol, furious—impotent.

He balanced himself, swung his right leg, crashed his right foot deep into his uncle's crotch. Still holding the pistol, his uncle sunk suddenly to his knees, gently exhaling, sorrowfully shaking his head.

Carson slipped the penlight into his left pocket, slipped the knife into his right pocket, reached down with both hands to contemptuously wrench the automatic free.

"You forgot to cock it, Uncle Julian," he whispered. "You have to cock it. Like this." Two small metallic clicks, deliberately spaced, filled the room. Except for the clicking of the hammer and the harsh, uneven sound of their breathing, the room was quiet.

Still on his knees, holding his crotch, head hanging helplessly, his uncle spoke thickly, indistinctly:

"You'll pay for this."

"No, Uncle Julian. I won't pay. You'll pay. You and Barbara. You'll both pay."

With great effort, Julian raised his head. Gasping: "You'll go back to prison. I promise."

Finger on the trigger of the automatic, he aimed the gun at his uncle's forehead. "If I go to prison," he said softly, "it might as well be for murder, Uncle Julian."

Still huddled in the armchair, clutching herself with desperate hands locked around thin forearms, Barbara suddenly began sobbing. He moved the pistol until the muzzle was centered on her chest.

"Be quiet, Barbara. Or I'll kill you. I swear to God. I'll kill you."

The desperate hands darted to her mouth. But her chest heaved convulsively, forcing the sound of dry, racking sobs between her fingers. Suddenly she closed her eyes, as if in prayer. Relaxing the pressure of his finger on the trigger, he touched one of her breasts with the muzzle of the gun. She started, pulled back. Then, eyes still closed, she began to shake her head. Slowly. Hopelessly.

Whatever he wanted to do, he could do.

Caressing the small, firm breast a second time with the gun barrel, he felt the warm, urgent warmth suddenly return, suffusing his genitals.

"Stop it, you goddamn pervert." His uncle's voice was stronger now, suddenly furious. So, slowly, he turned the gun again on his uncle. Julian was crouched on his knees: a lineman ready to spring forward, punishing the opponents. His small eyes were watchful and alert, clear of pain. Dangerous.

"Sit back, Uncle," he said. "Sit back on the floor, flat on your ass."

"You goddamn—"

He stepped forward, swung his arm, felt the heavy gun barrel strike bone, high on his uncle's temple. Behind him, Barbara screamed. His uncle's hand came up to his temple. Blood smeared the white, sausage-thick fingers. Blood stained the expensive doubleknit jacket, the gleaming white shirt, the impeccable tie.

"Oh—*ah*." Still holding his head, Julian suddenly sat flat on the floor beside the desk, legs splayed wide, eyes round and shocked, curiously innocent. He could have been an oversized child, injured in a playground game.

One blow, and Uncle Julian had collapsed, no longer angry—no longer dangerous.

Drawing back the gun for another blow, he turned toward the girl. "You want one, too, Barbara? Is that the only way I can stop your fucking noise?"

With her hands still tight around her mouth, staring at him over white-knuckled fingers, she helplessly shook her head, choking on dry, racking sobs.

"Then shut up, Barbara," he said, his head bent close to hers. "Shut your fucking mouth." He spoke softly, intimately. With their heads so close together, they could have been lovers.

A final gasp, then a tremulous silence. Her terrified eyes were on the gun, helplessly fascinated.

"Please, James." It was his uncle's voice, brokenly pleading. "Please. Not her."

Turning, he smiled as he looked down at his uncle. Sitting

shoulder-hunched, eyes vague and sick with pain and shock, his uncle's bluster had turned to blubbering, bleating terror.

So—finally—his time had come:

"Take out your wallet, Uncle Julian. Toss it over."

"Yes. All right. Yes."

Fumbling in his haste to please—still pressing one hand to his bloody head—Uncle Julian reached with his free hand awkwardly in his hip pocket, withdrawing the wallet. It was the alligator wallet, thick and promising. He reached forward and took the wallet, nodding his mocking thanks. Holding the gun with his right hand, still aimed at his uncle, he used his left hand to open the wallet. It was an elaborate wallet, with separate sections for money, and papers, and credit cards. The money compartment bulged with tens and twenties. A plastic accordian-style file held a dozen credit cards: gas cards, bank cards, an American Express card, department-store cards. He folded the wallet, thrust it in his pocket.

"Now the car keys, Uncle Julian. Hand them over, please. Slow and easy."

Another fumbling search yielded a jingling keyring. Nodding again, he pocketed the keys, saying:

"Where's the rest of your money, Uncle Julian? Where do you keep it?"

"There's no more. Honest to God, that's all there is—just what you see, in the wallet. Take it, for God's sake. Take it, and go. Take the car, too. Anything."

"I will, Uncle Julian. I certainly will. But before I do, I'm going to tell you my plans. Would you like to hear my plans?"

"I could have a skull fracture. Just go. Get out of here, for God's sake. Go."

"So you can call the police, as soon as I'm gone. Is that it, Uncle Julian?"

Holding his bloody head in both hands now, his uncle silently shook his head.

"Look at me, when I talk to you, Uncle Julian." He was satisfied with his voice: deadly soft, silkily menacing. In all his life, except for the girls, he'd never spoken to his victim. To the men with the money or the women with the jewels, asleep in their darkened houses, he'd always been faceless, without substance. They'd never known his name. Not until now—here.

"I said, look at me, Uncle Julian." Still soft. Still silky. Just right. Finally, just right.

Obediently, Uncle Julian raised his head, letting his blood-smeared hands fall helplessly to the floor beside him. Beaten. Finally, totally beaten.

"I'm going to take your credit cards and your car," he said, "and I'm going out to California." He paused, watching for some response: some small twitch of the facial muscles, some flicker of the eye, signifying recognition.

And—yes—he saw it: the pig eyes blinked, faltering. The blood-clotted lips tightened, weakly protesting.

"I'm going to find my father."

Helplessly, his uncle could only stare, hopelessly shaking his head.

"I'm going to find him, and I'm going to get what's coming to me. Every dollar, for every minute of my life. And then, Uncle Julian, I'll send back your credit cards. Maybe I'll even send your money back, too, if you're good, and don't call the police."

"I won't call the police."

"I hope you won't, Uncle Julian. Because—now—I won't hurt you anymore. And I won't hurt Barbara, either. Not now. Not this time. But I swear to God, Uncle, that if you call the police and get me put back inside, I'll kill you when I get out. I'll kill both of you. I'll torture you, and then I'll kill you."

Dumbly, the splay-legged man could only nod.

"If they put me back inside, it won't be for more than five or six years. That's all the time you'll have to live, either of you. And then I'll come back here, to Darlington. I know you'll be here. You're too rich to move, Uncle. So I'll find you, when I get out. And I'll kill you. Do you understand?"

A slow, heavy nod of the blood-matted head.

"Do you believe me?"

Another nod.

"All right. Good. Then I guess I'll leave." He turned, walked to the door, then turned back. "Just to make sure, Uncle Julian—just to double-check—tell me his name. Tell me my father's name."

The bloody lips parted. Then, croaking: "Austin Holloway."

"Austin Holloway. Yes." He smiled, nodded, and left the room, softly closing the door as he went.

Eleven

HOLLOWAY WATCHED Flournoy slowly, regretfully shake his head as he used a manicured forefinger to push the contract away from him, toward the center of the long walnut conference table.

"I'm sorry, Austin. I wish I could say I'm enthusiastic about this. But the fact is that you're giving away everything. You've got no leverage at all, according to that contract. You can't even see the video tape before the show airs, much less edit it."

Seated across the table, Clifton Reynolds frowned. "The reason for that," Reynolds said, "is that *Sixty Minutes* has more clout than it had the last time they interviewed Austin. A *lot* more clout. So, naturally, they want more control. When we first did the show, they needed us as much as we needed them. Maybe more. Now it's different. I'd venture to say they get a thousand requests a week for interviews."

"That's not the point," Flournoy retorted. "The point is—the *only* point is—are they going to help us, or hurt us? Apparently you're convinced they're going to help us. But I'm not so sure."

Reynolds shrugged. "There's no guarantee, with *Sixty Minutes*. I thought you understood that." As he spoke, he looked toward Holloway, subtly appealing the point.

"What Clifton means," Holloway said, speaking to Flournoy, "is that it's up to me. It's a contract, one man pitted against the other, may the best man win. It'll be a debate, Howard. A great debate."

Flournoy sat silently for a moment, his severely drawn face typically unreadable as he considered his response. Then, speaking with slow, measured emphasis, he warned: "It's *not* a debate, though. It's an inquisition."

"You're wrong, Howard," Holloway answered. "It isn't an inquisition. It's a gamble. A high-stakes gamble."

Ruefully snorting, Flournoy flicked at the contract with an impatient finger. "On that," he said heavily, "we can agree. The question is whether it's a gamble worth taking."

"And you say no. That's your vote." Holloway spoke in a calm, measured voice. Preparing to veto Flournoy's objections, he must be judicious, tolerantly benign. So, as he spoke, he smiled.

Flournoy nodded curtly. "If you put it like that, then—yes—that's my vote."

Also nodding—still smiling—Holloway turned to Reynolds. "What about you, Clifton? How do you vote?" Asking the question, Holloway watched his publicity chief steal a quick, covert glance at Flournoy. The two were remarkably similar: lean and hungry men, cold-eyed disciples of the Great God Success, Mammon in modern dress. If Caesar had his Cassius and his Brutus, then Austin Holloway must surely have Flournoy and Reynolds.

Because, most certainly, they served him faithfully only so long as his words and his images generated the money by which they measured their success—Flournoy with his stock portfolio, Reynolds with his expensive tastes in women, and cars, and sailboats and clothes.

After a final look of subtle defiance cast at his counterpart across the table, Reynolds said quietly, "I agree with you, Austin. It's a gamble. But I say let's do it. Let's take the chance."

Holloway paused a last long, grave moment, as if deciding how to break the tie. Then, finally, he nodded. It was a bogus bit of business, calculated to save Flournoy's face. Now, gravely, he leaned forward and drew the contract to him, at the same time taking a golden desk pen from its crystal holder, placed at his right hand especially for this small ceremony. He turned to the last page, signed quickly, then pushed the contract toward Flournoy.

"You set it up, Howard. They want to get on with it, I'm told. They've waited for two weeks, to see how much interest the China Crusade is generating. Now they're ready to go. As I understand it, Clayton Brill himself will do the interview."

"Clayton Brill!" Pleasantly surprised, Reynolds nodded, smugly pleased. "Wonderful."

Ignoring the remark, still speaking to Flournoy, Holloway said, "They were talking about tomorrow afternoon. Here, in my office. If so, it's agreeable to me. Tell them that I'll only wax eloquent on the subject of the China Crusade. Which is, as I said, what interests them. And tell them also that my schedule doesn't permit more than just the one time slot, at just the one place—my office. Be sure and stress that."

Gathering the contract together, coldly ignoring Reynolds' smug self-satisfaction, Flournoy said, "Why just your office?"

"Because," Holloway answered, "that's the big thing I learned the last time they interviewed me. They got me unsettled, moving me all around, hither and thither, with them calling the shots, and us just going along, willy-nilly. It got me off balance, and I never quite got my equilibrium—never quite got my feet under me, so to speak. This time, it'll be different." Careful to include both men equally in his smile, he lifted his hands in easy, graceful benediction. "I'll promise you, here and now, that it'll be different this time. You'll see."

"I'm not quite sure I understand your question, sir." As if puzzled, Holloway frowned down at the desk, at the same time stealing a glance at the small glass-and-gold desk clock, the gift from Billy Graham. They'd been talking for more than an hour. The final tape would edit down to eighteen minutes, according to the contract. Yet Clayton Brill showed no signs of winding down. With the door closed and the lights glaring, the office was stifling, even though the air conditioning had been running constantly. Under his shirt, Holloway could feel sweat stick on his skin. His arms were aching. His chest was tightening. His heart was protesting, rousing the demon within, his constant enemy.

"Let me rephrase the question, then," Clayton Brill said, smiling as he slightly lifted his chin, presenting his profile for camera one. "What I'd like to know, Mr. Holloway, is precisely how this, ah, crusade will be organized. Will it be a media blitz of the kind you use so successfully in America? Or will it be a grass roots effort, similar to your efforts in Africa? In other words, the question I'm asking is how you view your, ah—" A short, ironic pause. Then: "—your, ah, marketing problem, in China." As he spoke, Brill's easy smile twisted to a subtle smirk.

Once more, Holloway dropped his eyes to the desk. The time for their final efforts had come—the contest's last, decisive phase. So far, they'd fought to a draw. But now, perhaps sensing that his opponent was tiring, Brill was coming on stronger. His smile was more obviously malicious, his Ivy

League voice was more plainly derisive. In the final minutes, Brill was trying for a knockout.

Lifting his own chin, Holloway let a moment of silence pass while he stared straight into Brill's clear blue eyes. Then, beginning slowly, pitching his voice to a deep, solemn register, he said, "In the first place, sir, I should like to take the liberty of correcting your choice of words, if I may." Still staring into his opponent's eyes, he let another moment of silence gravely pass. It was a ritual pause, a prelude to his final effort, winner take all. In response, acknowledging the challenge, Brill mockingly inclined his head in courtly acceptance, then raised his eyes once more to camera level. Now the other man was projecting an air of faintly amused contempt.

"When you say 'marketing problem,'" he continued, "you give the impression that we're engaged in some kind of a public relations effort, instead of a crusade to spread the teachings of Christ throughout the world. 'Media blitz,' I'm sorry to say, conveys the same impression. But the fact is— the *truth* is, Mr. Brill—that missionary work has been going forward in China for hundreds and hundreds of years. Many, many men and women of all the Christian faiths have united to bring the word of God to the Chinese. And their efforts have been successful. There are millions of Chinese Christians. But that's not enough, Mr. Brill. We want *hundreds* of millions. *God* wants hundreds of millions of Christians. He wants a world full of Christians, Mr. Brill. And that's the reason God gave us the wisdom to create the electronic miracle of TV, of which we, right this moment, are availing ourselves. Because God knows, Mr. Brill, just as you and I know—and all the millions who are seeing us, right now— we all know that, until we succeed in our efforts to make the whole world Christian, we'll never be free from wars, and pestilence, and starvation. Because wars are caused by the have-nots in this world. Wars are caused by the undernourished, underpaid masses of men and women without hope, who covet what Christians have. And that's the reason, Mr. Brill, that God has commanded me to take His word to the far corners of the world, including China. And that is why—" He turned toward camera one, staring solemnly into the lens, "That is why I shall obey His command."

With the small, sardonic smile still teasing the corners of his mouth, Brill said, "I'm not precisely sure that I agree with your view of history, Mr. Holloway. If I remember correctly, World War II was started by Germany and Japan. I'd hardly call them undernourished nations."

"I wouldn't either, Mr. Brill. But I *would* call them Godless nations. Nazism was a heathen, pagan creed whose first mission was to destroy the Christian church in Germany. And Japan, of course, is Shinto."

As if he were tolerantly amused, Clayton Brill smiled. "That's probably something of an oversimplification, Mr. Holloway. As I read history, it seems to me that—"

"If I may interrupt you, sir, I should like to state that, yes, it's probably an oversimplification. You're right. Because that's my job, Mr. Brill. That's the work the Lord has marked out for me. I try to make things simple, so that ordinary people can understand what it is that God means them to understand. I try to help ordinary people find faith and strength and dignity.

"You, on the other hand, have chosen to make things more complicated. Your trade is asking questions, Mr. Brill. You ask the questions, and you leave others—like me—to help ordinary, everyday people find the answers."

For a moment Clayton Brill sat motionless, still with his chin lifted, still posing for the camera. Then, slowly, he began to smile—a wry, good-humored twisting of his handsome mouth. He turned to the director, and drew a forefinger across his throat. The director repeated the gesture, and a moment later the small red lights under the three cameras winked out. The big white TV lights mercifully died.

Letting himself sink slowly back into his leather armchair, Holloway closed his eyes and brought his hands up to his temples. Thank God, it was ended. Thank God and thank Clayton Brill. In the sudden bustling babble of voices, he heard Brill speaking again. Opening his eyes with great effort, he saw the commentator still smiling. It was an off-camera smile, genially amused.

"In the vernacular, Mr. Holloway, you are something else. Honest to God, I've crossed swords with some of the greatest orators around, but there isn't one that can top you. I mean it. I'm a fan." Now the other man paused as his expression turned quizzical, his smile more familiar, man-to-man. "I would like to know, though—between us—whether you really believe all that—that stuff."

Gathering himself, pushing himself more securely straight in his chair, he decided not to return the smile. Instead, speaking slowly and somberly, he said, "Thank you, Mr. Brill. I'm a fan of yours, too. If I can help it, I never miss *Sixty Minutes*. Even though—" Now he permitted a small smile, calculated for its gentle smugness. "Even though you broadcast on Sunday."

As he spoke, he saw Elton, Flournoy and Reynolds pushing through the press of technicians and equipment that crowded the office. Once more he closed his eyes, sinking back in his chair. With the battle done, and the laurels won, his faithful squires were coming to bear him from the field.

"I've got to admit," Flournoy said, "that I was wrong. You did it, Austin. You beat him at his own game. If they air at least part of that last segment, we've got a winner."

"This afternoon," Reynolds said, "I'll call Brill's producer. I'll tell him that we're expecting them to air at least part of the last segment, and that I'm sending him a letter to that effect. There are FCC regulations governing proportional content, and if they don't run at least part of the segment, I think we'd have something actionable."

"Don't get their backs up, though," Flournoy cautioned. "Don't mention the FCC. Not directly."

Impatiently, Reynolds shook his head. "Naturally. But, nevertheless, the implication is there."

"I thought," Elton said, "that Clayton Brill actually seemed very nice. Very generous, really, there at the end. Didn't you, Dad?"

Holloway sat silently, staring at his son's heavily jowled moon face with its eyes like raisins pressed into white, pudgy dough. For someone so devious and so suspicious, Elton could sometimes be naive. Stupid, and naive.

For a moment Holloway didn't reply, but instead sat staring at the ruins of the lunch they'd finished. Finally, sighing as he propped his elbows on the table, he said quietly, "Brill's a professional, Elton. Just like me. He gives credit for a job well done—just like me. But that doesn't mean that he wouldn't've chopped me up into little bitty pieces, if he could have pulled it off. He was out for my scalp, no question. And I suppose he might lift it yet, depending on how they edit the tape."

"Maybe they'll let us see the final cut," Reynolds said, pushing himself away from the table. "I'm going to make that call now, I think, rather than wait. If they decide to air it this Sunday, which is a possibility, they've probably already seen the video tape." Standing now, he nodded to Holloway. "As soon as I get something, I'll get back to you, Austin. Where'll you be?"

"In my office, for a couple of hours."

"Shall I leave a message with Marge, then?"

"Leave the message," Holloway said, "in case I'm taking a nap. Which is what I intend to do."

Fatuously, Reynolds nodded. "Good idea. After that performance, you should rest. A well-deserved rest, I might add." He nodded again, smiled a little too brightly, and turned to the door of the executive dining room.

"I'd better go, too," Elton said, also rising. "I'm auditioning a new group, for a guest shot. They're all black, right out of the Deep South. Their lead singer has a voice like Diana Ross—and looks to match."

"Just make sure they're not too hot," Holloway cautioned. "We've got to strike a balance, remember. We want to appeal to the young people, without stirring the old people up. That's important. It's vital, in fact."

"And if you think you want to use them," Flournoy said, "be sure to tell them that we choose their costumes. *That's* important, too."

Annoyed, Elton frowned. "Of course. Naturally." He turned and abruptly left the dining room. Slowly, Holloway allowed his head to sink in his hands, eyes closed. Across the table, he could hear Flournoy shifting in his chair. It was easy to imagine Flournoy's expression: watchful, calculating, concerned. Because every time his heart faltered—every time he allowed himself to reveal the exhaustion that could so suddenly overcome him—Flournoy saw his own future cloud over.

Now he heard Flournoy softly, tentatively clear his throat. Flournoy had lingered until they were alone because he had something on his mind—something that, to Flournoy, was important. Meaning, probably, that some financial decision must be made.

"Austin? Are you feeling all right?"

Meaning, did he feel up to discussing business.

He drew a deep breath, opened his eyes and raised his head. "I'm just tired, that's all. I'm all right. What is it?"

"I—ah—" Flournoy momentarily hesitated, deciding how to make his point. Then, speaking crisply and decisively, he said, "I wanted to talk to you about something that's been bothering Mitchell. Did he talk to you about it?"

"What's bothering him? Is it money? Does he want a raise?"

Flournoy permitted himself a small, frosty smile. "No, it's not money. I'm sure you could pay Mitchell nothing whatever, and he'd still be working for you."

"Is it Katherine?"

"No."

"What is it, then?"

"Well—" Flournoy frowned. "Well, it's probably nothing. Probably nothing at all. Which is the reason I decided to sit on it, until after this *Sixty Minutes* thing was over."

"What is it, Howard?" he asked quietly. "Never mind the preamble. Just tell me what it is."

"Well, it seems that there's someone who's been—harassing us."

"Harassing us?"

"Yes. It started three days ago, Mitchell says. It seems that there's a man—a young man, Mitchell thinks, judging by his voice—who's been calling three or four times a day, demanding to see you. Or, at least, talk to you."

"It doesn't sound like a problem. People are always trying to see me. You should know that."

"I *do* know that. But usually they want to kiss the hem of the robe." Plainly pleased with his metaphor, Flournoy smiled again. Then: "But this is different, according to Mitchell. And I agree. The last time he called—just this morning—Mitchell put him through to me." As he spoke, Flournoy drew a miniature cassette player from his attaché case and placed it on the table. "Since I was forewarned, I was able to record the conversation. Do you want to hear it?"

Aware of a sudden emptiness in his solar plexus, Holloway realized that he was unconsciously bracing himself against the table, leaning away from the cassette player, as if the machine could harm him.

Because, in truth, the machine might menace him. In the modern world, constantly monitored, danger was first perceived by electronic devices. First came the beep, then the disembodied voice from a tape. Then the fear began—as it was beginning now.

With an effort, he nodded, then gestured across the table. "Go ahead. Play it."

Momentarily Flournoy hesitated, as if the response concerned him. Then, diffidently, he pressed a button. A whirring began, followed by Flournoy's voice:

"Hello?"

"Hello. Who's this?"

"This is Howard Flournoy. Who am I talking to, please?"

"My name doesn't matter, Mr. Flournoy. I could give you a name, but it wouldn't be the right one. So why bother?"

"Just as you like. What can I do for you?"

"I want to talk with Austin Holloway. I understand that you can arrange that."

"Possibly. But first I have to know why you want to talk to him."

"It's a private matter. A very private matter."

"If you won't leave your name, and you won't state your business, you can't expect me to help you. Mr. Holloway is a very famous man. And he's a very busy man. People are constantly trying to get through to him. If we let it happen, Mr. Holloway wouldn't have time for anything else."

A brief silence. Then: "The information I have is worth a lot of money to Mr. Holloway. A *lot* of money. Tell him that. And tell him that, when he knows what the information is, he'll be glad I didn't talk to anyone but him. Understand?"

Another silence, longer this time. Finally: "What you're really saying is that you're trying to blackmail Mr. Holloway. This is a blackmail attempt. Am I right?"

"Yes, Mr. Flournoy, that's exactly right. You've got it."

"Are you aware that you're committing a crime?"

"Yes, Mr. Flournoy. I'm aware of that."

"It doesn't bother you—doesn't concern you?"

"No, Mr. Flournoy it doesn't. Not at all."

"Then you're a fool."

"No, Mr. Flournoy. You're the fool, if you don't take this seriously, and tell Mr. Holloway to talk with me. Because my patience is running out."

"How should he get in touch with you?"

"He can't get in touch with me. I'll call you, tomorrow. And you'll put me through to Holloway—or else."

"You'll have to give me a name—something that I can pass on to Aus—to Mr. Holloway. Otherwise, you're simply wasting your time and mine."

Another silence. Then, softly, the voice said, "Just tell him that James will be calling."

The line clicked dead.

Holloway watched Flournoy lean forward, switch off the cassette player and return it to his attaché case. During the half minute of silence, Flournoy kept his eyes averted. It was

99

a characteristically diplomatic touch, the product of all the years they'd spent facing each other across so many different tables, in so many different rooms. Flournoy was, after all, an employee. Should it become necessary, he must allow his employer to save face—to compose himself in the face of adversity, or even defeat, without scrutiny from a subordinate.

And—now—it was necessary.

Finally, speaking in a flat, noncommittal voice, Flournoy said, "What'd you make of it? Do you know any James?"

"No," Holloway answered slowly, staring off across the walnut-paneled dining room. "No, I don't."

"In that case," Flournoy said, "there's probably nothing to it. Still—" He hesitated, thoughtfully frowning. "Still, I've got to confess that it made me a little uneasy, talking to him. It seemed as if—" Once more, he hesitated, frowning as he searched for the phrase. "It seemed as if he was very—purposeful. Very determined." As he spoke, his eyes ventured into direct contact. He was probing now. Testing.

With an effort, Holloway pushed himself away from the table, positioned his feet beneath him and slowly stood up, gripping the edge of the table with both hands. Immediately, the room lurched, steadied momentarily, then began to slowly slip away from him. He blinked, shook his head, blinked again. Slowly, the room began to right itself.

"Austin. Are you all right?" Flournoy, too, was standing. Staring at him. Frankly worried.

"I'm all right. But I think I'm going to lie down. Send Mitchell in to me in my office, will you? Tell him to come right in, by the side door. He's got a key." As he spoke, he looked at the door that led from the dining room to the hallway. The distance was perhaps twenty feet from the table to the door. Once in the hallway, he must walk fifty feet, at least, to his office.

Total distance, seventy feet.

Suddenly it seemed an impossible journey—a trial that no man should be forced to endure.

Yet, because of its very impossibility, it was a challenge that, win or lose, he must accept. Now. Immediately. Just as soon as he could stand steadily, without clutching the table for support.

Twelve

HE LAY with his eyes closed, hands folded across his chest. Beneath his clasped hands, his heart was quiet and steady, each pulse measuring the moments of his life, one beat at a time.

Moment to moment—beat after beat. It was everyone's fate. It was the way everyone must pass from life to death—from the void before birth to the eternity that lay beyond. Listening to his own heart ticking out the time that was left. Wondering. Waiting.

Unconsciously, he'd assumed the position of eternal repose—the position in which, someday, they would lay him out in his casket.

One beat—two beats—three.

Sometimes, at night, he lay with his finger on the pulse at his throat, counting...

Wondering.

Waiting.

How would they plan his funeral? Lord Mountbatten, before he died, had meticulously planned his own ceremony, down to the smallest detail. It hadn't been a state funeral. Not quite. Yet crowned heads from all over Europe had paid their respects. Prince Charles had eulogized his favorite uncle—Uncle Dickie, according to the tabloids.

In years past, state funerals had been important diplomatic functions. After the final rites, the Hapsburgs and the Hohenzollerns and the Romanoffs, all of them related, would gather together privately, taking the opportunity to size each other up, deciding who looked infirm, and might be the next to die. So that, upon returning to their separate kingdoms, they might begin plotting how to profit from the next death among them.

Just as, at his own funeral, the pretenders to the empire he'd created would gather to mourn—and then retire to plot and scheme, secretly sharpening their daggers behind the rustle of medieval draperies as each rival eyed the others—

A knock sounded on the outside door. It was Mitchell's knock: heavy, measured, reassuring. He levered himself upright on the couch, waited until the room steadied, then said, "Come in, Lloyd."

Wearing his usual dark blue suit, black shoes and pale blue shirt with a plain tie, Mitchell entered the room, closed the door behind him, tested the lock, then advanced to a chair that faced the couch. He sat with his feet flat on the floor, his big-knuckled hands resting on each knee, clenched into loose fists. At age fifty-six, with his squared-off face and his unrevealing, uncompromising eyes, Mitchell could have been a Roman centurion, implacably awaiting orders.

"Is there anything about this caller—James—that you didn't tell Flournoy?"

Mitchell slid his huge hand inside his coat, withdrawing a sheet of paper, neatly folded into quarters. Holding the sheet of paper in his hand, still folded, he said, "The calls started three days ago. At first, I didn't think anything about them. By the second day, though—after three or four calls— I started to wonder.

"Then, the night of the second day, I got a report that someone—a man—was seen loitering around your house, approximately eleven o'clock to midnight. All we got was a general description—slim, brown hair, probably in his twenties. Still, I didn't think much about it. There wasn't any attempt made to enter the premises. And, as you know, we don't like to discourage people who want to see you in person—if that's all they want.

"But then, last night, Bursten said that the same man tried to force the rear gate. Or, at least, he apparently did enough to the gate to trip an alarm, which could've been a matter of just slipping something metallic inside the jam. Again, it didn't seem like anything very serious. It's happened before. Many times.

"But, to double-check, Bursten called the local police station, and they put it out to the sector car. The car was only a block away, so they cruised past—just in time to see someone answering the prowler's description getting into a car. It was a green Datsun—" Mitchell unfolded the paper, reading: "License number CVC916, registered to Hertz, in Los Angeles—and rented by a Mr. Julian Carson, of Darlington,

North Carolina." Mitchell refolded the paper, returned it to his pocket and resumed his previous position, saying: "Does that name mean anything to you?"

"Yes," Holloway answered slowly. "Yes, Lloyd, it does."

Silently—stolidly—Mitchell waited, still sitting as before: a big, broad-shouldered man in an ill-fitting blue suit, erect in the chair, attentively listening, alert to everything that passed between them, spoken or unspoken. Still awaiting orders.

"How long has it been, Lloyd, that we've been together? How many years?"

"Twenty-four years," Mitchell answered quietly. "Twenty-four years in December."

Holloway nodded. "Yes, I remember. You started working for me on December first. And, on Christmas, you had dinner with us. Do you remember?"

Impassively, Mitchell nodded. "I remember."

For a moment Holloway sat silently, looking into the other man's eyes. In all those twenty-four years, he'd never known what Mitchell was thinking, or feeling. He could predict what Mitchell would do, but he never knew why. He knew very little about Mitchell's life, only that he'd been raised an orphan, had been an infantry sergeant in World War II and later had worked as a policeman. He'd been married during the war and then divorced. Somewhere he had a son. Two or three times a year, usually on a Saturday night, Mitchell locked himself in his small apartment over the garage and drank. Monday mornings, his face pale and his eyes bloodshot, he would report for duty as usual. In the trash on those Monday mornings, the maids sometimes reported finding five empty whiskey bottles—which they added to the empty gin bottles taken from Katherine's suite, one bottle a day.

For twenty-four years—almost a quarter of a century—he'd entrusted his life to this man, with perfect confidence. Yet, during all those years, they'd always been strangers. It was a paradox. He trusted a man he'd never really known. He spent more time with Mitchell than with any other person on earth. From the very first—from that first Christmas dinner—Mitchell had been included in their family group: a silent, mysterious presence. From the first, the children had accepted Mitchell. They'd been tiny, then—Denise had been four, and Elton had been eight. In those early years, they'd reacted to Mitchell almost as if he'd been a contemporary of theirs: a playmate who never played, yet who understood their games. Perhaps the children understood intuitively that they were safe with Mitchell. Like a watchdog, he would always protect them, regardless of the danger to himself.

"Twenty-four years," Holloway said heavily, repeating his own thought aloud. "I don't know that I've ever thanked you for everything you've done for me, Lloyd. Not *really* thanked you. I've paid you—salaries, and bonuses. I've often thought I should pay you more. I remember asking you, from time to time, if you needed more money. But you never did."

"That's right," Mitchell said. Repeating: "I never did."

"I can remember paying you," Holloway said again. "But I don't remember thanking you."

"You've thanked me. You've thanked me often. Many times."

Aware that his head was heavy, Holloway nodded. "Good. That's good. Because I wouldn't want you to think, Lloyd—never would I want you to think, even for a moment—that I didn't appreciate everything you've done for me. Because I do appreciate it. And, more than that, I realize—I've *always* realized—that, really, you're the only one I've got around me, here, that I can trust. Do you realize that?"

For a long, silent moment Mitchell didn't respond, either by word or gesture. Then, almost reluctantly, he gravely nodded. Nothing more: just one simple inclination of his big, grizzled head.

"The reason I'm telling you all this—" Holloway said, speaking with slow, deliberate emphasis, "the reason I want you to understand that you're the only one I can trust, is that I'm about to tell you something that no one else knows. Or, at least, no one *here* knows—no one in the Temple, and no one in my family, either."

Once more, Mitchell nodded—stolidly waiting.

"Twenty-seven years ago," he said, "I met a woman named Mary Carson. She was just a girl, really—just nineteen years old. We were doing The Hour from Raleigh, and we were in town one week, as I remember. Mary was a real believer—an old-fashioned, down South fundamentalist, the kind you never see these days—and almost never saw even then. She was stagestruck and she was—well—she thought I was Jesus Christ come down to earth, I'd have to say. The only problem was, she was a little crazy. At first, it seemed as if she was just crazy for the love of God. But later—well—" He gestured with an open palm, pushing the memory aside. "That's another story.

"In any case, when she heard I was coming to Raleigh, she told her folks she was going to see me—that she was going for the whole week. She was going to hear me preach, and she was going to sing for me, too, in the hope that there'd be a place for her in the choir. Well, her parents said no. *They* were fundamentalists, too—real Bible thumpers, and no mistake. They were both of them very old to be the parents of a nineteen-year-old girl. Sixty, at least. They'd gotten married late—waiting for permission from the Lord, according to Mary. But then, again according to Mary, they apparently neglected to get permission from the Lord to have a child. So that, when Mary was born, they figured she was sin incarnate, and she must be purified. Which is to say that her life was just pure hell. Everything she ever did that was wrong, it was God's judgement visited on her parents, to punish them for the sin of conceiving her. And, apparently, she could never do anything right.

"So, anyhow, when she felt she was called to Raleigh, her parents felt just the opposite. They saw Raleigh as both Sodom and Gomorrah. So when she insisted, they threw her out of the house. That didn't deter her, though. She was determined to hear me preach.

"Well, she arrived in Raleigh with a cardboard suitcase, and her Sunday dress, and the most angelic smile you ever saw—plus three dollars and forty cents, exactly. And I can tell you—" He paused, momentarily lost in memory. "I can tell you, Lloyd, she was beautiful. I mean, everything about her was perfection. Absolute perfection. She was beautiful all over, if you know what I mean.

"Well, I won't go into all the details, except to say that I enfolded her to my bosom, so to speak. And she—well—she accepted me with an innocence that was absolutely awesome. So—" He paused again, once more remembering the week in Raleigh, twenty-seven years ago. Then, in a clearer, brisker voice: "So—very shortly—I realized that I had a problem on my hands. You know what I mean. You ought to know, if anyone in the world does. In a manner of speaking, it was like having a tiger by the tail. I couldn't let her go. I simply couldn't, never mind the risk. But I couldn't hold on, either. Or, at least, I couldn't bring her back to Los Angeles. That would've been just plain foolhardy.

"So, finally, I struck a compromise. I found her a job singing in a tabernacle in Raleigh. Or, to be more accurate, I, ah, subsidized her. And, of course, in the months to come, I found business, in Raleigh. I was, in a word, obsessed by her. It was the first time it had happened to me—at the age of thirty-six." He broke off, letting his eyes wander across the room. Even now, twenty-seven years later, he could still see her: a creamy body lying on a moonlit bed, her pale hair a halo around her head, her pink-nippled breasts rising to his caress, her flaxen pubes an eager mound, lifted to receive him.

"Of course," he said finally, speaking in a low, soft voice, "she became pregnant. I tried to tell her about birth control, but I knew it was no use. I couldn't tell anyone else to tell her, because then the secret would be out. And, worse yet, I couldn't simply do the intelligent thing—break it off, arrange for the tabernacle to fire her, and hope that she got back home. I was obsessed, as I said. So, when she told me she was pregnant, I did the next best thing. I suggested an abortion. But she wouldn't do it. I never thought she would. So—" He shrugged. "So she had the child. A boy. She named him James."

Speaking quietly, in a voice that was without inflection, revealing nothing, Mitchell asked, "What's he like, this James? What's his background?"

"That," Holloway said, "is the problem. James Carson is a criminal—a vicious, sadistic degenerate, according to my information."

"Have you ever seen him?"

"No. I haven't seen him, and he hasn't seen me, to my knowledge. Up until now, as far as I know, he didn't know I existed. His mother took him to Darlington, North Carolina, soon after he was born. She had an older brother there— Julian Carson. All these years, I sent both of them money. I sent Mary money to keep her child—and to keep her quiet. And I sent Julian a like amount, to make *sure* she kept quiet. He was my insurance, I thought.

"But, four years ago, James went to prison. And less than a year ago, his mother finally went over the edge. She's completely insane, and she's institutionalized. About a month ago, I heard from Julian that James was being paroled. So—" He gestured with a heavy, hopeless hand. "So, in one sense, I was expecting this."

"Do you think he's dangerous?"

"Yes," Holloway answered reluctantly. "Yes, I think he probably is dangerous."

"Then we should get him arrested."

"It's not that simple, Lloyd. The fact that he's here means that he knows he's my child. And if it ever comes out that I have an illegitimate child—a *degenerate* illegitimate child who's an ex-convict, with a mother who's crazy—I'm afraid I'd be in trouble. Deep trouble."

"I'm not so sure," Mitchell answered thoughtfully. "A lot of things are hushed up. They're whispered about, but they're never made public—like Kennedy's love affairs, for instance. There's a kind of gentlemen's agreement, not to smear public figures."

Holloway nodded. "That's right. That's very true. Which is precisely why all this has never been a problem. Certainly, over the years, there've been suspicions about me and Mary—and about me and other women, too, as far as that goes. As you well know. But that's exactly the point, Lloyd. As long as everything's done quietly, there's no problem. There're whispers, but nothing more. But let something appear on the public record—an arrest, for instance, that would connect me and James—and all bets would be off. I'd be finished. I'm not saying that everything would collapse around our ears. Probably it wouldn't. God knows, Aimee Semple McPherson weathered many a storm. But, at the very least, I'd have to keep a low profile, and simply ride it out. Which would mean, sure as anything, that the China Crusade would die a-borning. And that, I won't tolerate."

"What's to be done, then?"

"I don't know," Holloway answered slowly. "I'm sorry to say, I don't know."

"Maybe all he wants is money. If he doesn't want too much, it might work out. I think I should meet with him, and size him up. He might take a hundred thousand dollars, and go on his way."

"Somehow I doubt that. Blackmailers, you know, always want more. They keep coming back."

Mitchell lifted his massive shoulders, shrugging. "Let him come back, then. As long as he stays away from you, and keeps quiet, and doesn't ask for too much, where's the harm? After all, you've been paying him, in a manner of speaking, for years."

"I suppose," Holloway answered thoughtfully, "that you could be right." He sat silently for a moment, considering.

Then, decisively, he nodded. "You *are* right, Lloyd. As always. How do you suppose that we handle it?"

"I take it," Mitchell said, "that Flournoy doesn't know any of this."

"I've already told you, Lloyd, that you're the only one who knows the whole story. Howard knows about the calls, of course. But that's all."

"Does he know that blackmail's involved?"

"Yes," Holloway admitted. "And that's what concerns me. I don't want him to know about Mary and James. I don't want him to have that knowledge—that leverage."

"I don't see why you say that. As nearly as I can see, Flournoy knows everything about you and your operation. He's loyal."

"Howard is loyal as long as it suits his purposes, Lloyd. But I'm getting old. I'm sick. One of these days, I'm going to die. And Howard is thinking ahead. So is Elton. And Teresa. And God knows who else. What we've got here, Lloyd, is an immensely profitable organization—and it's all built around me. That'll change, someday, and nobody knows it better than Howard. He's an ambitious man, Lloyd. And evangelism is a big, big business. Oral Roberts has his university. Armstrong has his real estate, and his jets. The Southwest Christian Network has its own communications satellite, and they're talking about putting another one up. That's a lot of money—a lot of power. And that's what Howard wants. Money, and power."

"But—"

"Howard wants to call the shots. He'd like to have his man—or woman—up there in front of the cameras, Sunday morning. He'd like to see me retire. He wants an orderly transition of power, you might say—provided he comes out on top. And that's the reason I'd just as soon he doesn't know the whole story, where James is concerned."

Mitchell frowned. "It might be hard, to keep him in the dark. It might be impossible."

"Maybe. But we can try."

"We might be able to go around him. James wants to talk to you, directly. If you're willing to do that—" He let the question linger.

Reluctantly, Holloway shook his head, at the same time tapping his chest. "I can't do it, Lloyd. I just can't take the risk, with this heart of mine. I'd be afraid."

For a long moment Mitchell sat silently, eyes somber,

mouth thoughtfully set. Finally he said, "Maybe you should retire. If you retired, the whole problem would vanish. Maybe it's time."

"Maybe you're right," Holloway answered softly. "But, right or wrong, I just can't do it. Maybe it's something to do with my past—my heritage. My Daddy died with his face in the sawdust. Maybe that's the way I'm destined to go, too."

In response, Mitchell was gravely nodding.

Yes, he understood.

Thirteen

DENISE PUT the plastic shopping basket on the counter, and looked at her list. Except for scallions, she'd gotten everything. Mr. Byrnes was out of scallions. She balled up the list and tossed it into a cardboard box behind the counter, that Mr. Byrnes used for trash. For as long as she'd lived in the neighborhood—more than two years—Mr. Byrnes had used the same "Old Grandad" box for his trash.

At the counter, a tall, unhealthy-looking teen-ager with sallow skin and an advanced case of acne was trying to persuade Mr. Byrnes that he needed a six-pack of beer for his mother. Flattening a crumpled note on the counter with a grimy palm, he complained: "But that's my mother's signature, Mr. Byrnes. You *know* it's her signature."

"On the contrary, Charlie," Mr. Byrnes said, glancing briefly at the note. "The fact is, I know it's *not* her signature."

"But, Jesus, you haven't even looked at the signature, for God's sake." The thin voice rose to a high, aggrieved note, cracked, and fell. The boy's Adam's apple bobbed indignantly.

"That's correct, Charlie," Mr. Byrnes answered equably, "I haven't looked at it. The reason being, your mom already told me that she's not writing any more notes for beer. Or, for that matter, for anything else. Now, if that's all you wanted, then I'd better wait on Denise, here."

"*Shit.*" The teen-ager snatched up the note, jammed it into his hip pocket, and stalked out of the small grocery store. Watching him go, Mr. Byrnes slowly, regretfully shook his head. "Charlie is a bad apple," he said quietly. "I've known him since he was six years old, when his father took off with a secretary, for God's sake. His mother works hard, to try and raise Charlie. She's a good woman. But Charlie, he's breaking her heart. And it's going to get worse, not better. It's obvious."

"I agree with you."

"You know Charlie?"

"No, but I believe you."

"Yeah." Mr. Byrnes gave a final shake of his head, then emptied her basket on the counter, and began ringing up her purchases on an old-fashioned cash register. At age sixty-three, he was a short, compactly made man, totally bald, with quick shrewd eyes and a paunch as round and solid as a medicine ball. He walked with a rolling, bandy-legged swagger, and talked with a brusque, salty directness, both the result of years spent on the docks, working as a stevedore. A year ago, when two knife-wielding heroin addicts tried to rob him, Mr. Byrnes used the cut-down baseball bat that he kept under the counter to break one of the hoodlum's collar bones. The other hoodlum had run—with Mr. Byrnes in hot pursuit. Peter heard the shouts, and ran out into the street to join the chase. When Mr. Byrnes had been forced to stop running, winded, Peter had taken up the baseball bat, finally cornering the hoodlum in a parking lot, holding him at bay until the police arrived. Ever since, Mr. Byrnes and Peter had been friends. At least once a week, after the store was closed, the two men emptied a bottle of red wine in the store-room, telling stories of the docks.

"You don't have any scallions in the refrigerator, do you?" Denise asked.

"Sorry. I won't have any until tomorrow. Anything else?"

"No, thanks."

"Eleven forty-five, please."

She put twelve dollars on the counter, and dropped the change into her coin purse. With her purchases bagged, Mr. Byrnes pushed the brown paper sack across the counter. "Where's Peter, anyhow? It's been a week, at least, since I've seen him."

"He's up in Mendocino. He's taking some time off from work, to write."

"Is that where he's got his cabin? Mendocino?"

"Yes."

He looked at her thoughtfully for a moment before he decided to ask: "How's Peter doing, anyhow, with his writing?"

She shrugged. "It's a tough business, Mr. Byrnes. Considering the time he's been trying—really trying—I think he's done as well as most. But—still—it's tough."

Mr. Byrnes nodded. "I can see that. I mean, if it was easy—

just writing TV scripts, and sending them in, and getting paid—then everyone'd be doing it. Right?"

She smiled—wistfully, she knew. It had been eight days since Peter had left. She missed hearing him around the apartment—missed feeling him beside her in the night. She missed the touch of his hands, caressing her naked body.

"Peter's smart, though," Mr. Byrnes was saying. "He's got class, you know? Not polish, especially—not sophistication, or anything like that. But he's—" He waved a short, muscular arm. "He's got things on his mind, you know? He's a thinker. And people like that, they should do something with what they're thinking and feeling. Otherwise, it's a waste."

Once more she smiled, pleased. "I agree with you, Mr. Byrnes. I agree completely."

"You've got class, too," he announced. He spoke matter-of-factly, almost reluctantly. As if to demonstrate that he was speaking seriously, not frivolously.

"Thank you."

Reinforcing his serious intent, he nodded sternly. "You're welcome." He let a beat pass, then said, "Did I ever tell you that I knew Eric Hoffer, when I was working on the docks?"

"No. But Peter told me. Were you friends?"

"I can't say we were ever friends. He kept pretty much to himself. He was always thinking, you know? Just like Peter. But, on the other hand, I knew Eric as well as anyone, I guess."

"Did he talk about his philosophy?"

Mr. Byrnes shook his head. "Not really. I mean, he didn't talk philosophically, or anything like that. But, every once in a while, if you got him started, he'd talk about politics, and how people lived. And, mostly, how they *should* live. He's got very strong opinions, I can tell you that. *Very* strong opinions."

"Well—" She reached for the groceries. "I'd better be going."

But, before she lifted the sack, he said, "That must be your mother, that was with you in the car yesterday."

"Yes, that's right."

"A fine-looking woman." He smiled. "It runs in the family, Denise. There's a resemblance. No fooling."

"Thank you."

"She's—ah—staying with you when Peter's away writing. Is that it?"

"Yes." She lifted the sack. "Something like that."

"Well, when Peter calls, say hello for me, will you?"

"I wish he could, Mr. Byrnes. But there isn't any phone in the cabin. There isn't even any electricity."

"Oh. Well—" Once more, he smiled. "Well, then, we'll both of us'll have to wait, until he comes home."

She returned the smile, nodded, and walked to the door. As she turned back to close the door, she saw Mr. Byrnes watching her. He was frowning, as if he were worried. Was it because Peter was gone, and Mr. Byrnes didn't like to see her alone?

Or was it because of the bottle of gin she carried—her mother's ration for the day?

"Tonight," she said, "I'll do the dishes. You go into the living room, Mother. Relax."

Her mother put up a hand. "No. *You* relax, Denise. You did them last night. And, besides, it's been years since I've done dishes. I *like* to do them. Really." As she said it, she smiled—too brightly. Across the table, dressed in a Chinese silk housecoat, with pearls at her throat and red silk slippers on her feet, her mother could have been costumed for a Noel Coward play. Every hair was in place. Her makeup was flawless. As she lifted her coffee cup, diamond rings caught the light, flashing blue-white. The dialogue, too, could have come from a drawing room comedy: stilted and mannered. Communicating nothing. Saying nothing, really.

Mothers and daughters—eternal strangers, someone had said.

Sunk in one of his dark moods, Peter had once said that, at bottom, everyone was a stranger. Each man and each woman went through life alone, he'd said, sentenced to a lifetime of solitude. She'd protested the point. Sometimes, with Peter held close and precious, inside her—soaring far beyond herself in wordless ecstasy—she felt that, really, they were one. Yet, even as he held her, she hadn't told him what she'd been thinking—thus proving his point. And then she'd...

"...doing any work," her mother was saying.

She blinked her eyes back into focus, turning toward her mother. "I'm sorry, Mother. What'd you say?"

"You were wool gathering, weren't you?" her mother said brightly. "You were always a wool gatherer, even when you were young. Always a daydreamer." She nodded over the reminiscence, her meticulously painted lips curved in a fixed, false smile. Now she sipped her coffee, and placed her cup carefully in her saucer. At the beginning of the meal, she'd fumbled with her silverware, and slurred her speech. Now, though, her speech was clearer, her gestures more controlled. It was all part of an inexorable routine that had emerged during their eight days together. Her mother would sleep until ten, then spend the next two hours bathing, dressing, and applying her makeup. After a light lunch, her mother watched *Days of Our Lives*—her only indulgence, she always said. Apparently the TV program marked the end of her self-imposed period of daily abstinence. Because, immediately afterward, her mother began finding excuses to go into the kitchen, where the gin bottle was kept, in the cupboard. By that time, the bottle had been opened, but the contents remained untouched. It was Denise's job to open the bottle. Each of them must play her assigned role in this daily farce—this exercise in an elaborate ritual of deceit. The bottle must always be open, perhaps because access implied acceptance. Or resignation. Or despair.

Throughout the afternoon, the gin would slowly disappear, as if consumed by some invisible visitor. As the hours between *Days of Our Lives* and dinner passed, her mother's laughter trilled higher, her voice warbled more loudly, more fatuously. Her movements became steadily less precise, more pathetic—until dinnertime finally arrived, a reprieve for both of them. Her mother never drank during meals, not even wine. So the food helped, temporarily soaking up the gin. During dinner, they could manage polite conversation, both of them able to counterfeit an interest in what the other was saying—as she was doing now:

"What'd you say?" she repeated. "About work?"

"I was saying that I haven't seen you doing any work, since I've been here. When do you take your pictures?"

"I'm taking the week off."

"Now, Denise—" Her mother raised her hand, prettily shaking a manicured forefinger over the remains of her dinner. "Now, I absolutely forbid you to change your routine because I'm here. You're a very busy person. I know that. I *realize* that. You're a successful photographer. And I'm proud of you, for that. And your father is proud of you, too. Very, very proud."

Looking at her mother's face with its makeup applied in layers, like a mummer's mask worn to conceal an abiding

114

misery beneath, she let a long moment pass before she decided to say, "Is he?"

"Is he what?"

"Is he proud of me?"

"Why—" Her mother frowned, puzzled. "Why, yes. Of course. He's always been proud of you. Ever since you were a little girl, he's been proud of you." A brief, reproachful pause followed. Then, solemnly: "You know that, Denise."

Another moment of silence passed while she looked at her mother. Did she really believe it? Dressed in her make-believe party clothing, smiling her make-believe smile, did her mother really believe that they were one big, happy family? Was that the bogus boon gin conferred? Had years of living from one drink to the next made her mother believe that her father loved them?

Suddenly she must know.

She must find out the truth.

But slowly—slowly:

"Is Dad proud of Elton, too?"

"Why, yes." Now her mother was fluttering her eyes: a Southern belle impersonation, lacking only the coyly simpering smile behind the fluttering fan. "Yes, of course he's proud of Elton. Why, Elton is doing wonders, on The Hour. He's the musical director, you know. He's been musical director for almost two years."

"That doesn't necessarily mean that Dad's proud of him, though. It could just mean that Elton's thirty-two years old. He's been a soloist since he was eight. That's a long time, without a promotion."

The simpering mask suddenly began to slip. The fake smile faltered, and finally faded, as if her makeup had softened, and might soon begin to dissolve, leaving her face naked, defenseless.

"If you don't think your father's proud of Elton, Denise, then you surely must not look at The Hour every Sunday. You must not see how he smiles at Elton, and compliments him, right on camera."

"Mother, that's—" She broke off, by force of will lowering her voice before she said quietly, "That's make-believe, Mother. That's show biz. It's all done for the camera—for syndication. For *money,* for God's sake. Sure, I watch The Hour. Lately, as a matter of fact, I've been watching it almost every Sunday, for reasons I don't understand myself. But I don't see pride, when Dad beams down on Elton, and Carrie, and the 'grandkids.' I—Christ—I see dollar signs. He's posing for the camera. That—that's what he *does*. That's his *business*."

"Denise, you sound as if you hate your father. Really hate him." Her mother spoke in a low, hushed voice, fearful of what she was saying.

"I don't hate him, Mother. But I don't respect him, either. How can I, when I see what he's done to you?"

As she said it, she saw her mother wince. The false light faded from her eyes, replaced by a stricken shadow. In the silence that followed, she saw her mother's eyes flee to the door, involuntarily seeking escape. It was the kitchen door, not the door to the hallway. Now her mother was losing control of her mouth. The brightly painted lips began to tremble.

She'd done it.

After eight days, she'd finally done it: stripped her mother of all her elaborately constructed pretenses—all her weak, pitiful defenses.

Why?

Was it revenge for some half-remembered wrong? Simple sadism? Something else?

Her mother sat with her hands clasped before her on the table, fingers intertwined. Her eyes were downcast, fixed helplessly on her writhing hands. When she finally spoke, it was in a low, indistinct voice:

"You've always been hard, Denise. You're strong—but you're hard. You don't understand weakness. Maybe you can't forgive weakness."

"Mother, I—"

"Elton's weak. And, when he was younger, he could be mean. But he's not hard. He doesn't judge people."

"Mother, I'm not judging you. I—if anything—I'm judging Dad."

"You're blaming your father for my—" She broke off, once more letting her furtive glance flick toward the kitchen door. Then: "You're blaming him for my—problem. But that's not fair, Denise. It's not right."

"My God, Mother, you're more of a Christian than he is. Do you realize that? Because, for sure, *he* blames you for your problem."

Your problem.

It was as close as either of them had gotten to admitting that, yes, her mother was an alcoholic.

This, then, was why Alcoholics Anonymous started their litany with the statment that, yes, they were alcoholics.

But what of *her* problem? Was she really unsympathetic, unable to understand weakness in others, and therefore unable to forgive them their faults?

Forgive us our trespasses, as we forgive those who trespass against us.

As always, the Bible said it better—more concisely, with more flair, more punch, more style.

"Do you want me to go home, Denise? Is that what you want?" With her eyes still fastened helplessly on her twisting fingers, Katherine spoke in a voice hardly more than a whisper.

She sighed: a long, deep exhalation, infinitely regretful. Yes, she wanted her mother to go home. Desperately. Yes, she wanted Peter to come back from Mendocino, and take her to bed, and make love to her. Desperately.

But, because she wanted it so desperately, she couldn't say it. So, instead, she sighed again. "Not now, Mother. Not right now. I want you to stay. I really do. And, besides, it—it's important, that you stay here. For a while, at least. Excuse me, please." She pushed her chair back, got up from the table and walked down the hallway to the bathroom. As she opened the bathroom door, she heard the kitchen door opening.

Fourteen

HE DROPPED THE DIME in the slot, waited for the ringing to begin, then looked carefully at his watch. The minute hand showed fourteen minutes past the hour, with the sweep second hand ticking toward the "6."

At seventeen minutes past the hour, exactly, he would leave the phone booth and step into the sidewalk crowds outside, on the Sunset Strip. Instantly, he would disappear.

"Good morning. This is the Temple of Today."

"I'd like Mr. Flournoy, please. Mr. Howard Flournoy."

"Yessir. Who shall I say is calling, please?"

"Tell him James is calling. He knows me."

"Yessir. Just a moment, sir."

Forty seconds later, with the second hand on "3," the line clicked.

"Hello?"

"Hello, Mr. Flournoy. This is James. I want to speak to Mr. Holloway."

From the other end came the sound of a sharp, exasperated sigh. Then: "I'm sorry—James." The hesitation was pointed, plainly contemptuous. "I told Mr. Holloway about our, ah, conversation. But he won't be able to speak to you."

"He doesn't want to speak to me, you mean."

No reply.

"He'd be saving himself a lot of trouble, if he'd talk to me."

"And *you'd* be saving yourself a lot of trouble if you didn't call any more. Believe me."

The second hand was at "8." One minute and ten seconds had passed.

"If Austin Holloway won't speak to me, then this is the last time I'll call."

"I think that's very wise."

"I'll be writing him a letter. I'm going to write the letter this afternoon, and I'm going to mail it tonight. It'll be addressed to Austin Holloway, and I'd advise you to pay very close attention to it. Because he owes me money, and I intend to collect it. He owes me a *lot* of money, and the letter will tell him how he's got to pay it. How, and when. This is Friday. You'll have the letter by Monday, at the latest. And you'll just have a few hours to get the money together. So I'd advise you to be looking for the letter, very goddamn carefully."

The second hand was touching "7." Less than a minute remained.

For a long moment, quietly crackling, the line was silent. Then: "You'll be arrested for this, James. You'll be arrested, and sent to prison. Think about it."

"All right. I'll think about it. Meanwhile, suppose you think about getting together a half million dollars, in small bills. Nothing larger than fifties, please."

Another silence. With his forefinger on the receiver hook, he watched the second hand tick past "4," past "5." When it touched "6," he broke the connection.

He switched on the overhead light, unfolded the letter and placed it on the top of the bureau. It read:

> *Austin Holloway:*
>   *Get together $500,000 in old bills, no more than $50.00 each. Put them in a brown paper bag, and have them ready by Tuesday. You will be called at the Temple of Today. I will tell you how to make delivery. You must do it, personally. If the police arrest me, they will learn about my mother and me. This is money you owe me. If you do not pay it, or if I find out that the police are looking for me, I will kill you.*
>   *And that, father dear, is a promise.*
>
> *James*

He read it again, smiled down at the letter, then smiled at himself in the mirror. If the police ever found the typewriter, one chance in a million, they would never connect it to him.

He slipped the letter into the envelope, sealed it, and glanced at his watch. It was time.

The mailbox was ahead: a squat, blue shape seen through a moving forest of crisscrossing legs and arms and bodies that passed each other on the sidewalk, the Sunset Strip's parade of the living dead. A jungle of prostitutes and pimps and hustlers, each one eyeing the other, looking for an easy score. In the glare of neon storefront lights and sodium vapor streetlights overhead, their faces were hollow-eyed masks, subhuman. They could have been animals on parade: barnyard animals, marching along the sidewalk toward the slaughter house. Dead already.

As he came closer to the mailbox, he moved to his right, at the same time glancing at his watch. The time was ten minutes after nine. The last mail pickup was nine-thirty. His timing was perfect.

He broke stride, stopped, pulled open the door of the mailbox and dropped the letter inside. As the envelope left his fingers and the door clanged shut, he was aware of a surge of elation, almost as if a physical weight had left him.

In prison, he'd once read in a magazine that a scientist had measured a man before he died, and then immediately afterward. The man had weighed less after death. The conclusion: yes, there was a soul.

So it was possible that something had left his body as the door clanged shut. It wasn't his immortal soul, though. It was the weight of memory: twenty-six years of second-class living, all of it behind him now.

As he allowed the passersby to close in around him, he let himself remember the message: *Get together $500,000 in old bills, no more than $50.*

A half million dollars...

His. In a few days, all his.

Today was Friday. Tomorrow, he would make his plans for Tuesday, move by move, minute by minute. Everything would be calculated, down to the smallest detail. He would write down the plans—but cryptically, so no one could translate them. "X" would mean Holloway, "Y" would be the drop site. And "Z" would be the money. Already he'd decided that, no matter how vehemently Flournoy might protest, "X" must deliver "Z" to "Y." It would be his insurance. Because, with Holloway held hostage, threatened with certain death if anything went wrong, the police would never dare move against him.

It would be a reunion: father and son, reunited after twenty-six years.

At the thought, he realized that his hand had closed around the butt of Uncle Julian's .45, thrust in his belt. During the five days since he'd left Darlington, the gun had been a part of him: warmed by his body, constantly within reach of his hand. If the weight of his soul was in doubt, the weight of the gun was a fact. Never again would he be without a gun. It was a guarantee—a lifetime guarantee, of power, and freedom, and all the money he'd ever need.

Ahead of him, a flurry of violence erupted: shouts, a flailing of arms, obscenities screamed in high, shrill voices. Quick as a school of fish sensing danger, the sidewalk crowd came suddenly alive, watchful, tense. Some of those walking around him drew closer to the fight. Others shied away, fearful of the crowd's straining bodies and the hot, avid eyes, looking for trouble. Jostling began. The violence was a contagion spreading instantly in all directions: a sudden fever of the blood, random and wild.

He allowed himself to be carried along the sidewalk to the center: two women fighting in the gutter, locked together, rolling half under the wide, gleaming grill of a Cadillac. Blood streaked both their faces, one black, one white. Painted fingernails, crooked into claws, tore at flesh, hair, clothing.

Two whores, fighting it out.

As he drew closer, straining to see, he felt the close-pressed crowd suddenly shift: a silent, instinctive movement. The beast sensed danger. Following the slant of eyes and the twist of bodies, he saw a black and white police car angling across the street, blocking traffic. The car braked to a stop scarcely a foot from the fighting women. Two doors opened. Two policemen stepped in unison to the pavement, both of them carrying nightsticks. As a rumble of angry protest began, the two policemen advanced with businesslike precision, eyes front, still moving in perfect unison. Now they bent double, knotted their hands in the women's hair, one bleached blond, one black. Brutally, using nightsticks jammed across the throat, the policemen forced the two apart, both men on their knees in the street. Screaming "Motherfucker," the black whore suddenly kicked: a bare brown leg, its silver-slippered foot striking the other woman's crotch. Another police car was arriving, and another. In seconds, both women were spread-eagled on the pavement, pinioned by a half dozen swearing policemen, their knees jammed into backs, thighs, crotches. The women lay with their heads flat on concrete stained with their blood.

And still they screamed: as wild as animals, and just as dangerous.

He stepped back, joining the sullen, surging crowd as it

moved away. Behind him, the screams continued. As he walked, he was aware of a constriction in his throat, an excitement in his genitals, a shortness of breath. The sight of the two fighting women, wild with fury, had left him tight and anxious—as hung up and strung out as a junkie, aching for a fix.

It was a dangerous feeling—a time for caution. Because control was essential. Control was everything. Between now and then—between today and Tuesday—he must be the master, not the slave.

And yet, walking with the crowd, the bubble of stomach-tightened, groin-aching excitement continued to grow, as palpable as something physical inside him, demanding release.

At the corner, waiting for the traffic light to change, he looked back. One of the police cars was leaving. It was all over. It was—

"Hey, man."

He turned. A man of about thirty, short and stocky, wearing a fringed leather jacket and a planter-style broad-brimmed straw hat stood close beside him. Beneath the leather jacket, the stranger's deeply muscled chest was bare, its pelt of thick, black hair crisscrossed by the rawhide laces that secured the jacket. Beneath the wide brim of the hat, his face was in shadow. Only his eyes were visible: two pale points of glinting reflected light, sunk deep beneath heavy brows.

"Hey, where're you going?"

Standing motionless, he didn't reply. This was the wrong time to talk to anyone—the wrong time and the wrong place. Yet, except for the phone call earlier in the day, he hadn't spoken to anyone but the counter girl at a Burger King. So the stranger offered some small contact with the life that flowed close around him.

Still standing motionless, with the passersby jostling him as they crossed the street, he allowed the traffic light to turn green, then amber, then red—waiting for the stranger to speak:

"Those two fucking hookers," the stranger said. "Christ, they're fucking animals. That Rosie—the black one—she gets shot up, she'll take anyone on. Last time, she took on a guy and goddamn near killed him. She kicked him in the balls, and then when she got him down she jammed her fucking spike heel into his face. He's lucky he didn't lose an eye. Gwen, she doesn't know how lucky she is the fuzz came by.

I tell you, she'd be dead by now, if the fuzz hadn't come. And I mean, dead."

Remembering the fight, he felt something at his core subtly shift. The dryness had returned to his throat. Once more, his genitals were tightening, swelling against the tightness of his pants.

Clearing his throat, he said, "You know them, then. Those two."

The stranger's thick lips parted in a slow smile, revealing a pale gleam of uneven teeth. "I know *of* them. Which is as much as I want to know. Except that they say Rosie—the black one—she does things to you that you never forget. That's if you like dark meat. Which, personally, I don't. It's probably my middle-class upbringing." The thick lips twisted into a smile. "Some things never change."

"I guess not." The traffic light had gone from green to yellow to red again. It was time to go back to his room, lock the door, make his plans.

"Hey—ah—" The stranger came a step closer, lowering his voice. "If you want to score something, maybe I can help you. I'm not—you know—connected, or anything. But I know people that know people. There's always a little extra something around. You know what I mean?"

"No, thanks. I'm not into that."

"Oh, yeah?" Now the smile widened purposefully. "Well, what *are* you into?"

He didn't reply. In the silence that passed between them, the noise of the traffic and the confusion of voices around them seemed louder, more strident. Finally the stranger spoke again, this time in a softer, more speculative voice:

"I guess you're from out of town, eh?"

He nodded. "That's right." He let a moment pass before he decided to smile. "Why? Does it show?"

The stranger's shoulders raised in a slow, noncommittal shrug. "A little." Then, after another short, calculating pause: "What're you looking for, then, if you don't want to score anything?"

"I'm not looking for anything. I'm just walking, that's all."

"Walking, eh?" The purposeful smile returning, twisting slowly into a lopsided leer. "You're a health nut. Is that it?"

"Let's just say I like to look. You know—like going to the zoo."

The smile faded—then returned, wider now. "Hey—yeah. Right. That's right on. It's a fucking zoo down here. I mean, it's a real zoo. I mean, I'm from Spokane myself. And there's animals here that they never *heard* of in Spokane." The stranger took another step closer. Speaking in a low, confidential voice, he said, "What about a girl? You want to meet a girl? I know a couple that you wouldn't believe. I mean, they're something else. They tell everyone they're sisters. Which maybe they are, who knows? Anyhow, one of them's about twenty-one, I guess. And the other one, she's about fifteen. No shit. She's fifteen. And, man, she'll turn you inside out, guaranteed."

He glanced at the traffic light, once more just turning from amber to red.

If the light had been green, he would have turned away from the stranger and walked across the street.

But the light was red. It was an omen: a toss of the coin, heads or tails. In his billfold, he carried two hundred dollars, borrowed on Julian's American Express card. At his belt, he could feel the gun, pressing into his stomach.

Fifteen years old...

Aloud, he said, "Fifteen?"

A short, vehement nod. "That's right. I swear to God. Maybe she's fourteen, for all I know. Listen—" Now the smile was easier, more confident. "Listen, what's your name, anyhow?"

"James."

"Well, listen, James, if you want to meet her, I'll tell you how it works. You give me a twenty, and I'll put you together with her. She'll take two twenties. Forty. And I guarantee, you'll never regret it. *Never.*"

"Ten for you and twenty for her."

"No way. I'll take the ten, because you're from out of town, and everything—like me. But she gets thirty. I could tell you different. I could take the ten, and tell you she'd maybe take twenty—and then I could split. But I don't do that. I mean, I'm around here all the time, you know. This is my turf, you might say. And, next time I see you, I want to be able to do a little something more for you, you know?"

"What is it? Is it a whore house?"

"Hell, no. It's just Gracie. That's her name. Just Gracie, and her big sister."

"I don't want her sister." As he spoke, he reached for his billfold. "Just Gracie."

"Right. Just Gracie." The stranger smiled as he took the

ten-dollar bill. "Just Gracie. She's enough. Believe me, she's enough. You'll see."

"You want to take off your clothes, or what?" She stood with her back to the closed door, looking him over. It was a slow, thorough scrutiny—head to toe, then back again.

Lying on the bed, he returned the slow stare. "You like what you see?"

"Sure. Great. You're a regular picture postcard." She pushed herself away from the door, and advanced toward the bed. She wore skin-tight jeans and a tank top. Her feet were bare. Her hair was thick and dark, and hung to her shoulders in lank, unkempt coils. Her body was slim and boyish, with small breasts, lean buttocks and long, tapering thighs. Around her left ankle she wore a fine golden chain.

He sat up in the bed, moving back until his back touched the wall. Sitting erect, he crossed his ankles. Beneath the short leather jacket he wore—bought with the American Express card—he touched the butt of the .45 automatic.

"I'll stay dressed," he said softly. "You get undressed."

Standing at the foot of the bed, facing him, she smiled. Her face was triangular, with broad cheekbones and a narrow chin. Her forehead was broad, her nose short and stubby. Her mouth was small and petulant. Beneath dark, flaring eyebrows, her eyes were small and dull, set close together. It was a closed, sullen face, street-wise and suspicious.

The small mouth curved into a bad imitation of a sensuous smile. "You just want to look, or what?"

"For thirty dollars, I want to do more than look."

She smiled again, ducking her head in a quick nod of agreement. It was an awkward movement, more a teen-ager's mannerism than a hooker's. But, when she raised her head, her eyes were hard and steady. Hooker's eyes.

She peeled off the tank top, dangled it for a moment from one finger as a stripper might, then dropped it languidly on the room's only chair. Her meager breasts were conical, as small and pointed as sow's dugs, with the nipples hanging down. Her arms and shoulders were thin and angular; her torso was narrow and sallow: rib-slatted, hollow-chested. A track of angry red needle marks ran up the inside of both her scrawny arms.

Now she straightened, facing him as she unbuttoned the jeans, one slow button at a time. She was naked under the jeans, and the V of her parted fly revealed the dark brown hair of her pubes. With the last button unfastened, she hooked her thumbs in the waistband and pulled the jeans down over her hips. When the jeans fell to the floor, circling her feet, she scissor-stepped backward. She stood with her arms slack at her sides, legs together, facing him. Her hips and her legs, like her torso, were thin and angular, with bones showing through unhealthy-looking yellowish-white skin. Now her mouth twisted slowly, falsely smiling. But her eyes were narrowed, watching him closely.

"I don't see thirty dollars there."

The false smile widened. "Honey, it's not what you see here. It's what I do there—" She pointed to the bed. Then, tentatively: "Or am I just supposed to stand here? Is that what you want me to do?" As she said it, she shifted her narrow, bony hips, trying for a more provocative pose.

"I still don't see thirty dollars." He lowered his feet to the floor, at the same time sitting erect on the edge of the bed, turned to face her. He saw her smile fade. Her small jaw came set. Her eyes hardened.

"It's thirty dollars," she said. "That's what it is. Thirty dollars." Once more, she forced the false smile. "You'll see, honey. Believe me, you'll see."

On his feet now, turned to face her from a distance of six feet, he slowly, deliberately shook his head. "No," he said softly. "No."

Instantly, the smile disappeared. Her head came forward, her chin pugnaciously upthrust. Her eyes suddenly blazed. At her sides, small fists clenched.

She was a fighter, then. A scuffler.

So it was working.

As planned. Chapter, paragraph, verse. As if he'd written the script, and she was acting out the lines, it was working.

He took a slow, measured step toward her. Distance remaining, four feet. He saw her eyes falter, saw her step back. But her voice was high and strident, defiant as she spoke:

"Listen, asshole. You want trouble, that's what you get. Jerry, he's right outside the door. All I got to do is yell."

Yes. Yes. Chapter and verse.

"Who's Jerry?"

"He's the one that brought you. And all I got to do is yell. Just one yell, that's all it takes."

It was time to smile. And to say, softly, "No, don't yell."

"Well, then—" Irresolutely, she lifted her right hand in

a quick, angry gesture. "Well then, cut out all this shit. Do what you came to do, and pay. And then leave."

"You want me to do what I came to do. Is that it?" He was satisfied with his voice: soft, conversational. Almost friendly sounding. Just right.

"Well, Christ, of course I do. I mean, I don't get paid for talking, you know. For that, go to the goddamn library, or somewhere. Just do it, and pay. Like I said. And then leave."

Another step. An arm's length separated them now. A half step more, and he could touch her. Looking into her eyes now, he saw a small furtive flicker of fear beginning.

Yes. *Yes.*

Reaching out with his right hand, he touched her nipples—first the right nipple, then the left. Another half step, and he could circle her waist with his left hand, centered on the small of her back. When he tightened his grip, drawing her closer, he could feel the brush of her pubic hair. Responding, his genitals were straining to touch her—to rip into her. Beneath the probing fingertips of his right hand, her nipples were hardening. Against his face, he could feel her breath hot and musky.

Now, slowly, he allowed the fingers of his right hand to climb her body, one finger at a time, delicately walking her flesh. At the base of her throat, above the collar bone, with his thumb on one side of her throat and his forefinger on the other side, he tightened his hand, whispering:

"If you want that money, you've got to fight me for it."

He saw the flicker of fear leap into a flame, felt her body suddenly convulse, straining against the arm that held her close against him. Instantly, he clamped thumb and forefinger together, forcing her head back—choking off her cry. Her body came alive: taut with fear, suddenly twisting violently, wild and writhing. Between his fingers, her breath was rattling in her throat. Her pelvis was crushed against him as his thrust began. Inches from his, her eyes bulged with terror. Against his leather jacket, he felt her fists flailing.

Yes. Yes. Yes.

Between his thighs, he felt her legs thrashing. Her head was thrown back, neck arched, throat exposed. A final step, and her head crashed against the wall. Now her eyes were glazing, losing focus. In his throat, his own breath was rattling. The time was closer—

Closer

With her buttocks jammed against the wall, trapped, her

body was an animal's, thrashing against his body, straining against his thrusts—faster, harder, racing the dying light in her eyes, racing the—

Something thudded behind him, followed by a crash, a shout, a sudden scurry of feet. Whirling to face the danger, he dropped to a crouch. The man—Jerry—stood in the open doorway, his right hand fumbling under the fringed leather jacket. Bellowing:

"What the fuck—?"

Beside him, the girl was slumping to the floor, snuffling, coughing, trying to speak. Helpless. No threat. Advancing now, eyes suddenly as watchful as a jungle cat's, Jerry drew his hand clear of his jacket. A single sharp click, and a blade leaped in his hand. Springing back, James felt for the butt of the .45 at his belt, found it, drew the pistol. With his thumb, he pulled back the hammer, then released the safety. From Uncle Julian, he'd learned his lesson.

"Drop it. Drop the goddamn knife."

Slowly, Jerry straightened. Beneath the broad brim of the planter's straw hat, he stared at the gun. His eyes were narrowed, unafraid. Calculating. And, therefore, dangerous.

"Drop it." As he spoke, he moved to his right, away from both of them. On the floor close to the wall, legs spread wide and arms hanging helplessly, still coughing, the girl was trying to speak. Still harmless. In the doorway behind the man, an oblong of darkness, a face appeared—then faded back into the dark. There was the real danger: that face, disappearing. Going for help.

So he must go—get out. He must leave them behind: the naked whore and her pimp, pleasure unfulfilled.

"Drop it."

This time, the knife clattered on the cracked linoleum of the floor. Jerry was straightening from his fighting stance, holding out his hands, palms upturned. Smiling. Afraid, but smiling. Smart.

"Be cool, man," Jerry was saying, speaking in a soft, whining voice. "Be cool. You want to leave—" Cautiously, one hand moved invitingly toward the open door. "Then leave."

"Who's out there?"

"Nobody's out there."

"You're a goddamn liar."

Now the hands spread wide apart, the palms once more innocently upturned. "All right. So there's someone out there. If there is, I don't know about it."

"Move over there. Beside her." He gestured with the gun. *"Quick."*

"Yeah. Right." One step at a time, the pimp moved to stand beside the whore, still sitting on the floor, helpless.

Stooping, he picked up the knife, hefted it once, then threw it at the other man's feet.

"Pick it up."

"Wh—?" The other's eyes were puzzled now.

"Pick it *up*." As he spoke, he glanced at the doorway, still empty. With the gun trained on the pimp, he moved to the opposite wall, half hidden from sight behind the opened door.

Helplessly, the pimp stooped, picked up the knife, then slowly straightened.

"Now cut her."

"Wh-what?" The pimp's eyes were round. Disbelieving. *"What?"*

"I said, cut her. Let me see her bleed."

"What the fuck you—"

"I said, *cut* her. *Do* it. Or I'll kill you."

"Jesus Christ," the pimp breathed, turning toward the girl. "Jesus Christ." The girl was crouched beside him now, on her hands and knees, head hanging down between her bony shoulders, sobbing for breath.

"Do it. You've got two seconds. Just two."

Moving slowly and woodenly, as if he were drugged, the pimp moved the slim, gleaming blade toward the girl's shoulder. Momentarily his hand faltered. Then, responding to a sudden menacing jerk of the .45, he drew the blade across the sallow white skin of her shoulder. A line of bright red blood followed the knife.

As the blood began to run down the white skin of her back, he heard laughter begin: a thin, unsteady laugh, almost lost in the sound of the whore's screams.

It was a stranger's laugh—strange, yet eerily familiar.

Because it was his voice. His laughter.

Fifteen

CONSCIOUS OF THE NECESSITY to control himself, whatever the cost, Holloway kept his eyes lowered to his desk, rereading the letter. On the other side of the desk, sitting with his legs crossed, trouser creases aligned, gleaming white cuffs adjusted to a precise inch beyond the sleeves of his jacket, Flournoy sat watching—waiting. Wondering.

"Here's the envelope," Flournoy said, quietly leaning forward in his chair to slide a plain white envelope across the desk.

As he'd expected, the end of the envelope had been neatly clipped off on the side that carried the stamp. It was routine, part of established mailroom procedure. At least once a week, contributions came into the mailroom with no return address except that scrawled on the envelope. Most of the contributions—and most of the mail—came addressed directly to him. So, unless they were marked "very, very personal," a pre-arranged code, all letters sent to him were opened in the mailroom.

Still bent over the letter, he cleared his throat. "Who all's seen this, would you say?"

He heard Flournoy sigh: a sharp, impatient exhalation. Flournoy hated imprecision—hated surprises.

"One of the mailroom clerks," Flournoy answered. "And the supervisor. And Priscilla, in my office."

"Which supervisor?" As he said it, he finally ventured to raise his eyes. Across the desk, as expected, Flournoy looked as calm and calculating as if he were sitting in on a Council meeting, discussing fiscal planning.

"Julie Smith."

"Did she say anything?"

Flournoy shrugged. "She didn't say anything particular, just passed it on. Julie and Priscilla evaluated it, of course. That's part of their jobs—part of the routine." He let a long, meaningful beat pass before he said quietly, "What's it mean, Austin? What's it all about?"

Instead of answering the question, he asked, "Did you know this would happen—that this was coming?"

"Well—" Flournoy gestured sharply, impatiently. "Well, yes, I did, as a matter of fact. That is, I knew he was sending the letter. Or, at least, I knew he *said* he was sending a letter. He called Friday, and told me what he intended to do. I thought that, actually, the situation might be improving— that he would turn out to be just another crank letter writer— of which, as you know, we get hundreds, every year. So I decided to simply wait and see what happened. Of course, I knew there was an element of risk—that one of the mail-room girls would see more than she was supposed to see. But the only way to eliminate the risk would be to monitor all the mail addressed to you—which would be impossible, given the volume we're handling. But, at the same time—" He gestured to the letter, frowning. "At the same time, I didn't expect anything like that." Still frowning—still patently displeased at the unpredictable, untidy turn of events—he asked again, "What's he talking about, Austin? What's that last line mean—'father dear'?"

"It means," Holloway answered, speaking slowly and deliberately, "that he's probably my son."

"Christ." Because he so seldom swore, Flournoy's single short expletive made the problem seem more dire, more dangerous.

Holloway sighed. "Precisely." As he spoke, he realized that, unconsciously, he'd pushed the letter across the desk, toward Flournoy. Subconsciously, then, he wanted Flournoy to handle it. Flournoy, or anyone else—anyone with sufficient strength, and determination. And, yes, sufficient ruthlessness. Because, undeniably, there was a mortal threat in the letter. So ruthless measures must be taken. Now. Quickly. Before more damage was done.

As if to accept the challenge, Flournoy picked up the letter, rereading it. The shrewd, thoughtful frown had returned, casting the manager's thin, almost patrician face into its habitual expression: closed and cold, revealing nothing. Finally, looking up, he said, "How old is he?"

"He's twenty-six years old."

"Do you think he's dangerous?"

"Yes," Holloway answered heavily. "Yes, I think he's dangerous." As he said it, he felt the room tilt on its axis, then begin a slow, unsteady sideways slide. It was a sensation that, lately, had become sickeningly familiar. His strength had suddenly ebbed, sapped by the letter's malevolence. He realized that he'd slumped back in his chair. Momentarily, his eyes had closed. He hadn't been aware that it had happened—not until the room suddenly disappeared. Drawing a deep breath, he forced his eyes open, forced himself to sit straighter in the chair.

"Today's Monday," Flournoy was saying quietly. He gestured to the letter. "He's going to call tomorrow, that's certain. We've got to decide what to do."

"I'll call Mitchell in. He knows about it—the whole story." He reached out his right hand toward the phone. His fingers were trembling. Suddenly the hand seemed thin and palsied: blue-veined and brown-blotched, an old man's claw.

"How long has Mitchell known?" the other man made no effort to conceal his annoyance at the thought of being the second to know, not the first.

"Since Friday." He lifted the phone and pressed the intercom button. With only minimal effort, he could summon a rich, resonant voice. Saying: "Ask Mitchell to come in, please, Marge."

"Yessir. Right away. Your daughter called, about ten minutes ago. You said to hold your calls, so I said you'd call her back."

Denise. Calling, certainly, about Katherine. His daughter's patience had run out; she'd come to the end of her endurance. She'd called over the weekend, to warn him that it would happen. Now she was serving final notice. It was understandable, inevitable. For Denise, freedom was everything.

Aware that an answer was required, he said, "Did Denise say what was—troubling her?"

"No, sir. But she said she'd wait for your call."

"Yes. All right. Send Mitchell in. I'll talk to her in a half hour."

As if he'd been waiting just outside, Mitchell appeared almost immediately, sitting in his accustomed straightback chair, thus subtly acknowledging the difference in status between him and Flournoy, at his ease in one of the office's two deep-tufted armchairs, placed to face the desk. Wordlessly, Flournoy passed the letter to Mitchell. Watching Mitchell read the letter, slowly and methodically, Holloway looked carefully at the security chief's face, searching for some hint of a reaction. Had Mitchell expected it? Was he prepared for it—prepared to act, protecting him?

Yes. Resolution was plain in Mitchell's calm, thoughtful gaze—in the set of his jaw—in the slow, purposeful flexing of his big-knuckled fist as he read the letter a second time. Whatever must be done, Mitchell could do.

But what choices did he have? What action could he take?

Now Mitchell put the letter aside and turned to Flournoy, who began an ill-tempered summary of the letter's probable significance. Patiently, Mitchell listened to Flournoy's tense, staccato sentences. Occasionally, Mitchell made short responses. Listening to the two men talk, Holloway let his gaze wander to the phone. He must remember to call Denise. It had been two weeks, since Katherine left. Police reports had been made. Lawyers had talked to lawyers. Sums of money had been proposed, considered, finally accepted. Payoffs had been made on street corners, at airports, in hotel lobbies. The reporters had come to the mansion and gone, assigned to other stories by editors whose cooperation had been discreetly solicited. The little girl, paralyzed, had been forgotten by the public. Her parents, set for life, were adjusting. In addition to all the high-level financial maneuvering, Flournoy had arranged for the parents to pick up a new car. The gift, totally unexpected, had been an inspiration. In matters of diplomacy, Flournoy's touch was light and delicate, superb.

But, in the matter of James Carson, Flournoy's talent could fall short. Something in the letter suggested that a heavier, harder hand was required.

Mitchell's hand.

Now Flournoy was turning to him. His manner was brusque, decisive. Once again Flournoy was in command.

"We've got to try and handle it ourselves," Flournoy said. "We've got to exhaust every possibility. That's obvious. We can't assume that the problem will go away—that he'll get tired of asking. Which means that we've got to meet with him. Face to face."

"What'll we tell him?" Mitchell asked. "What'll we say?"

"We'll say," Flournoy answered, "that he can have, say, a hundred thousand dollars. Period. No more."

Mitchell frowned. "What if he wants more?"

"We'll tell him there isn't any more—that, if he persists, we'll call the police."

Holloway shook his head. "No. Not the police."

Flournoy gestured impatiently. "We don't have to actually

do it. But we want him to *think* we're going to do it, to put pressure on him, Hopefully, we can establish a bargaining situation. He says he wants a half million dollars. That's probably an opening position. We'll make a counter offer. Then we'll bargain—on the theory that, the more he talks, the less dangerous he becomes. Which is, I think, sound strategy, psychologically speaking."

Dubiously, Mitchell shook his head. Pointing to the letter, he said, "The way I read that, I think he wants more than money."

Annoyed, Flournoy spoke sharply; "How do you mean, 'more'? He doesn't say anything about more."

"I think he does," Mitchell said mildly. "He says that he wants to deal with Mr. Holloway personally. To me, that indicates that, in addition to the actual money, he wants to humiliate Mr. Holloway. Maybe he even—" The security chief hesitated. "Maybe he might even intend to harm Mr. Holloway."

"Well," Flournoy said sharply, "it won't come to that, believe me. Because he's not going to see Austin. That's nonnegotiable. For one thing—" He glanced at Holloway, momentarily apologetic. "For one thing, Austin's health doesn't permit it."

"What if he insists, though?" Mitchell asked quietly.

"If he insists," Flournoy said, "then he loses. We call the police. Until he's caught, we'll keep Austin secure. Under wraps, so to speak. If necessary, we'll use a rerun on Sunday. We'll say it's got something to do with the China Crusade. We'll suggest some secret negotiations with the Chinese." Thinking about it, Flournoy nodded, plainly pleased with the strategy. "Actually," he said thoughtfully, "it could work out to be a plus." He nodded again, more decisively this time. "It could be a definite plus, if it's handled right. You know—" He turned to Holloway. "We could suggest a parallel between the secret diplomacy that preceded Nixon's visit to China."

Slowly, Holloway shook his head. "We can't tell the police, Howard. We can threaten to do it. But we can't actually do it."

"But—" Flournoy sawed the air with a sharp, impatient wave of his hand. "But we don't have a choice. If he won't be reasonable—if, in fact, he's dangerous—then we've *got* to call the police."

"If he's arrested," Holloway said, "and it comes out that

he's my—" He paused, reluctant to put it into words for the first time. "—that's he's my illegitimate son, then it's all over. Everything. It'll be a matter of public record. And I'll be finished. We'll *all* be finished."

"I don't agree," Flournoy retorted. "There might be a scandal, yes. Or, more like it, a *breath* of scandal. But these things can be handled."

"How?" Mitchell asked, staring steadily at the other man. Mitchell's broad, muscle-bunched face was impassive. His eyes were opaque, revealing nothing. But the question remained: a hard, uncompromising monosyllable, challenging Flournoy to respond.

"At the moment," Flournoy said acidly, "I can't answer that. After all, I've only known about this—this new development for a few minutes." He turned to Holloway, asking: "Is your name on the birth certificate as the father?"

"No. That was part of the deal. The father is listed as unknown. Julian—her brother—worked out the details. Which is how he got on the payroll, all these years."

"Well, then—" For the first time, Flournoy smiled: a tight, mirthless twisting of his lips, leaving his eyes still cold and calculating. "Well, then, our move is obvious. If he's arrested, and tries to smear you, then we finesse the issue. Which, to evoke Nixon again, is what happened in Watergate. Or, rather, *didn't* happen. Instead of covering up, Nixon should simply have admitted that something silly happened. The whole problem would have been defused."

"This isn't exactly something silly," Mitchell said mildly.

"I'm not *saying* it's something silly," Flournoy countered sharply, staring coldly at the other man. "I'm simply saying that there are parallels."

"What kind of parallels?" Unblinking, Mitchell spoke in the same mild, quiet voice, implacably insistent.

"Never mind the goddamn—" Angrily, Flournoy broke off. "Never mind the parallels. All I'm saying is that we should meet the problem head on. We could say, for instance, that the woman was already pregnant when she first met Austin, and that she asked Austin for help. He was touched by her plight, and offered to help her support her child. After all, as I understand it, the woman's insane. So she lacks credibility. Even if she contests the story, which seems doubtful, she won't be believed. And her brother, by the sound of it, can be bought. He probably *has* been bought, already. That just leaves James Carson—a criminal." Flournoy spread his hands. "And who's going to believe a criminal, if there's nothing substantive to confirm his story?"

"The problem with that plan," Holloway said quietly, "is that I've sent her hundreds of thousands of dollars, during the past twenty-seven years. That's a fact. And facts speak louder than words, in matters like this. Especially in the newspapers."

"But the money can't be traced."

"It can't be *readily* traced. But it can probably be traced if the bank records were subpoenaed."

"Well," Flournoy retorted defensively, "I'm not saying it's a perfect solution. After all, we've got a difficult situation on our hands, no question. But it's a possible solution. It's one line of attack. And a good line, I think."

For a long moment the three sat silently, each man staring off in a different direction, thinking. Finally Mitchell cleared his throat. "The best thing that could happen," he said softly, "is that the police would catch up with him—and kill him."

Sixteen

SITTING with his head resting against the back of his tall, leather desk chair, eyes half closed, Holloway watched Mitchell and Flournoy exchange a quick, appraising glance of mutual speculation and evaluation. In the silence that followed, it was clear that, after all the words and all the planning, Mitchell had summed up the sense of the meeting: a payoff might solve the problem, but something more permanent—death—would be a more desirable solution.

As the silence lengthened, neither the manager nor the security chief had looked at Holloway. It was an instinctive reaction—and a proper one. In the Vatican, certain temporal problems required solutions that must be undertaken without the Pope's knowledge.

In the Temple of Today, over the years, similar problems had been encountered—and would be encountered again. Machinery had been created to handle the solutions. If the Pope had his Vatican guard, Holloway had Mitchell and his staff: five big, tough, gun-carrying thugs, each one dressed in a blue business suit, their uniform. And, in addition, he had Flournoy, the fixer. If Mitchell made a mess, Flournoy would clean it up.

For now, then, the conference had served its purpose. The problem had been defined, and the alternatives discussed: the checkbook solution and the solution by force. Next, Flournoy and Mitchell would discuss ways and means. When their plans were complete, Flournoy would make his report.

So, for now, it was time to call a recess.

"If you gentlemen will excuse me," Holloway said, "I must call Denise."

As he said it, Mitchell rose from his chair, saying: "I'll see whether there've been any more calls." As he spoke, he turned to Flournoy. "Shall we talk later?"

Still seated, Flournoy nodded. It was another of his prerogatives that, in any meeting, Flournoy was the last to leave: the principal baron, remaining behind in the throne room for a few final words.

"Definitely," Flournoy said. "I'll come to your office."

"Good." Mitchell nodded to Holloway and turned toward the door. On the parquet floor, his footsteps were noiseless. The big, broad-shouldered man was incredibly light on his feet.

Flournoy waited for the door to close, then said, "Of course, the police aren't going to kill him for us, desirable though that would be. However, if we agree on a price, and if Mitchell delivers the money, he might be lucky enough to get his hands on Carson. If that happened, and he gave Carson the beating of his life, we might not have any more trouble with him."

On cue, Holloway shook his head. "I don't think—"

"I'm no authority on violence," Flournoy put in smoothly, deftly interrupting. "Quite the opposite," he added, his fastidious smirk implying that he disapproved of anything so elemental, and therefore so uncontrollable. "However, I've always understood that people change, after a beating. Especially if they know that the next beating will be worse—and the one after that worse yet. Et cetera, et cetera."

Holloway waved a hand in a gesture that projected both resignation and tacit agreement. The Pope, in similar circumstances, would offer his ring, casting his eyes demurely up toward heaven.

Also on cue, Flournoy changed the subject: "Did Denise say anything about Katherine when she talked to Marge?"

"No. But she phoned over the weekend and I gather that she's just about run out of patience. Which, of course, is understandable. I expect she's calling to say that she's had enough. It's been two weeks now. What'd you think? Is it safe to bring Katherine back?"

"I think," Flournoy said, "that, definitely, The Hour could use her, next Sunday. The mail is starting to show that she's being missed. People don't realize that she hasn't actually spoken more than a few words at a time for years, you know. To some of the old timers, she's important—symbolically, at least. You know—the symbol of motherhood, and the family. And I don't have to tell you that, statistically, most of the money comes from the fifty- to seventy-year-old group."

"I wasn't speaking about The Hour. I was speaking about Katherine's—legal problems."

"Things are settling down very nicely," Flournoy said. "We have a waiver from the girl's parents."

Approvingly, Holloway nodded. "That was a good move, Howard. A very good move."

Gravely, Flournoy inclined his beautifully barbered head: thick brown hair, graying in distinguished streaks at the temples. "Thank you."

"There won't be any problem with her parents, then."

"None," Flournoy answered confidently.

"What about the press?"

Flournoy considered the question, saying finally, "If we keep Katherine away from the reporters—absolutely away—I don't think there'll be a problem."

"So you think I should bring her home."

Obviously unwilling to commit himself completely, playing the percentages, Flournoy gave a deprecatory shrug. "There're no guarantees, of course. However, provided we make *very* sure she's kept under constant surveillance. I think we're safe. And, obviously, she's got to come home sometime."

"All right." He looked at the phone. "I'll call Denise and tell her that—"

The phone rang. Exchanging a look of uneasy surprise with his manager, Holloway eyed the phone. Had he neglected to have his calls held? Whether he'd remembered or not, Marge should know better than to interrupt them.

Unless—

After another look, this time one of apprehension, he picked up the receiver.

"Yes?"

"Mr. Holloway—" It was Marge, her voice deeply apologetic. "I'm *very* sorry to interrupt you. But it's Denise again. I should have told you before, but she wasn't calling from her home. And so she's been waiting at a neighborhood store—a grocery store, for you to call back. I'm very sorry, sir. I should have mentioned it before. But I thought—" She let it go unfinished, plainly flustered by her own temerity.

"It's quite all right, Marge. There's no problem—no problem at all. Put her on, please."

And, a moment later, Denise was saying, "Dad?"

"Yes, Denise. I'm sorry to have inconvenienced you, dear. I thought you were phoning from home. It was a misunderstanding on my part. I'm sorry."

"Actually," she said, "it was my fault. I just gave the number. I should have filled Marge in."

"Is there anything wrong, Denise?"

"Well—" He heard her pause, collecting her thoughts. She'd always done that, even as a child. Denise considered before she spoke. Unlike Elton, who'd never acquired a knack for reflection.

"Well," she said, "there's nothing *wrong*, exactly. It's just that—well—I've had it. And Mother's had it, too. We're—lately, the past few days—we're getting on each other's nerves. And then, now—today—everything came apart. I—I feel badly about it. And I realize that it's my fault. Or, anyhow, most of it. But the fact is that I just can't—" Despairingly, she let it go unfinished.

"Denise, it's all right. It's been two weeks. I understand. I'll make arrangements for her to come home, as soon as you like." As he spoke, his glance crossed Flournoy's. Still seated, Flournoy nodded toward the door, mutely asking whether he should leave the office. Shaking his head in response, Holloway spoke again into the phone: "I'll get hold of Elton, and a security man. They'll make arrangements, and Elton will call you. Is that all right?"

"It's all right with me, Dad. But I don't think Mother's going to like it."

Aware of a quick, foreboding tightness in his chest, he let a beat pass before he asked: "Why do you say that, Denise?"

"Well, it's—" Once more she hesitated. Then: "It's hard to explain. But, if I had to guess, I'd say that Mother had a kind of a crisis here, today. Actually, I've seen it coming for days. Two days, at least. As nearly as I can explain it—or speculate about it—she came up here with the idea that I was her last hope. She seemed to feel that she and I could—" A brief, sharp sigh, infinitely regretful. Then: "That she and I could find each other again, maybe. I think she felt, at least subconsciously, that when I took her in, I was accepting her—that we'd somehow restored the mother–daughter relationship we used to have, years ago, before she—she started to drink, and before I—grew up. And then, when she realized that it wasn't going to happen—that, really, nothing had changed—she started to feel rejected, I guess. Or insecure. Or just plain desperate. Maybe the thought of what she did—of that crippled child—is having a delayed effect. I don't know. But I do know that she needs help. She needs reassurance—lots of

140

reassurance. Or love. Or whatever you want to call it. She—"

"Denise. What're you trying to say?"

He heard her draw another breath—another long, deep sigh, filled with a daughter's remorse. "What I'm trying to say, Dad, is that she wants you. She wants to see you. Now. Here."

"There? But that's—" Involuntarily, he looked at Flournoy. "That's impossible. I've got some very—" He broke off. Whatever he said to her now, it would be wrong. Hopelessly, abysmally wrong.

How had it happened? How had his world turned suddenly so sour? Was it age? Illness? Fate?

And how, suddenly, had it all come down to a single point in time? How had it happened that both his bastard son and his drunken wife, two nemeses, should demand their separate pounds of flesh: instant payment on debts that might, admittedly, have been accruing for decades?

On the other end of the phone line, his daughter was waiting for an answer. His wife was waiting, too—waiting for him to come to San Francisco, and pretend to heal her, perpetuating the myth of a love that had somehow sustained their marriage, keeping its fiction intact so that, every Sunday, they could smile for the cameras.

While somewhere in Los Angeles, James Carson waited for tomorrow, when he would call and make his demand for blood money.

Tomorrow...

Into the phone he said, "Just a minute, Denise." Then, with his palm covering the phone, he spoke to Flournoy: "Katherine wants me to come up there, to San Francisco. Immediately. Apparently she had some kind of a breakdown."

Flournoy frowned, displeased. "A breakdown? Is it serious?"

"I'm not sure. It sounds like it could be serious."

Flournoy's frown faded, replaced by a reflective pursing of his mouth and a look of thoughtful speculation in his eyes. "Maybe you should go," he said. "Maybe you should take Elton, and a couple of security men, and fly up and get her. You could do it tomorrow. You could leave early in the morning, and come back tomorrow night. By that time—" Flournoy spread his hands. "By that time, we may have a resolution of this other matter. And while we're taking care of it, down here, it might be just as well if you were out of town."

"Yes—" He nodded in slow, thoughtful agreement. If Mitchell were successful tomorrow in punishing Carson, it might be better—more prudent—to be out of town. He nodded again, more decisively. Then, uncovering the phone, he said, "I'll be there tomorrow, Denise. Before noon. Tell your mother, will you?"

He could hear an almost palpable relief in his daughter's voice as she said, "Tomorrow. That's wonderful, Dad. I'll tell her. Thank you."

Answering, he lowered his voice to a deeper note, pronouncing benediction: "You're welcome, Denise. You're very welcome."

Seventeen

HE WATCHED the blond girl slip the credit card and the sales voucher into the computer. Now she was attentively waiting, pen poised, while the machine began a series of preliminary clicks. The next seconds would be critical. If the card had been reported stolen—if Uncle Julian had betrayed him—he would probably first see it in her face: a flicker of the eye, a momentary tightening of the mouth as she glanced furtively toward him.

Another series of clicks. And, still, the girl's broad, flat face registered nothing. It was a bovine face—a German peasant's face, with its thick, flaxen hair and large, heavy jaw. Quickly, he glanced over his shoulder toward the nearest exit. Beyond the exit, an airport security guard stood beside a baggage rack, talking to a tall, stoop-shouldered skycap.

A final series of clicks, and the machine ejected the card and the voucher. The blond girl wrote on the voucher, smiled at him, and passed the voucher across the counter.

Uncle Julian had cooperated.

He signed the voucher, passed it back to her, then watched her eyes discreetly drop to the card and the voucher, comparing signatures. Now she smiled again, a trifle more cordially this time, and returned the credit card to him. The second copy of the voucher came next, for him to keep.

"You didn't like the Datsun?" she asked.

"I like it, all right. But I need something a little bigger. Besides, I've always liked Fords."

She nodded and gave him a set of keys. "If you'll just go through there—" She pointed to a door marked Hertz— "they'll get your car for you. I hope you like your Ford. And thank you for thinking of Hertz."

He parked the Ford behind a white Volkswagen. With the engine still running, he moved across to the passenger's seat and looked down the sidewalk toward the huge iron gate that marked the entrance to the Holloway estate. Yes, the angle was perfect. He could see the gates without being seen himself. He switched off the engine, turned off the lights and settled low in the passenger seat. The time was fifteen minutes after nine. Being careful to slide down in the seat when the sector car drove past, usually at thirty-minute intervals, he would wait until midnight, watching the entrance for any signs of unusual activity, especially police cars, with their telltale antennas and their grim, stolid passengers, always watchful. Tonight, he wouldn't get out of the car, wouldn't risk another brush with Holloway's security men, some of them apparently posted on the outside perimeter of the eight-foot wall that surrounded the property.

Was Holloway inside? Or was he still at his office? Were they collecting the money, counting out the bills in neat stacks, then placing the stacks in the brown paper bag?

Or were they at police headquarters, making their plans for tomorrow? Were they—?

Behind him, headlights were coming, curving into the dark, deserted street. As the lights came closer, he lowered himself slowly in the seat. The car was abreast of him. Cautiously, he raised his head. It was a large, expensive car: a Cadillac, or a Lincoln. Not a police car. And, as he watched, the car swept past the gates without slowing down.

Once more, the darkness and the silence returned. The street was narrow and winding, lined on both sides with trees that grew down to the sidewalks. Only four gates interrupted the dark line of tall trees. In Beverly Hills, the rich valued their privacy—and paid for it handsomely.

Another car was coming from the opposite direction. Before he could shrink down in the seat, headlights shown suddenly in his windshield. Immobilized, he sat staring straight ahead. The car was slowing as it came closer. As the headlight glare passed, he could see lights and a siren mounted on the car's roof. Directly opposite now, the police car was slowing, almost stopping. In the driver's window, a small metallic tube gleamed. A flashlight flared, catching him full in the face. He started—blinked—then smiled into the blinding glare. For a long, breathless moment the flashlight beam held him helpless. Still smiling, he nodded—once, twice.

If Holloway had alerted the police, they would question him.

If they hadn't been alerted, they would shine him and then move on.

Still smiling into the light, he unbuttoned his jacket and drew the .45 from his waistband. The pit of his stomach was clenching: a hollow knot of fear and trembling, suddenly nauseous. Behind the fixed smile, his throat suddenly clenched closed. With his right thumb, he drew back the pistol's hammer: two clicks, incredibly loud in the silence. If they came for him, one on either side of the car, he would—

Darkness returned, as suddenly as the flashlight had flared. The patrol car was moving slowly forward, safely past him now. With trembling fingers, using both hands, he eased off the hammer and returned the .45 to his waistband, fumbling awkwardly as he buttoned his jacket.

In another half hour they would return. They would—

Behind him, more headlights appeared.

Was it the police car, returning from the opposite direction? Had they checked by radio with Holloway's security men? Had they learned of the letter?

If it was the same car, he couldn't slide down in the seat. He must sit as before, innocently turning his head toward the passing lights, pretending nothing more than casual curiosity.

The headlights were passing, revealing a Lincoln sedan. The car was slowing, turning toward the Holloway gate. Had the occupants seen him—recognized him? At the thought, he touched the ignition keys. If they got out of the car and came back toward him, he would start the engine and pull away. There would be enough time to do it safely, convincingly.

The gates were swinging ponderously open as a man emerged from the shadows inside the grounds. As the Lincoln moved through the gates, the man peered inside the car, nodded politely and stepped back.

The police didn't drive Lincolns. And neither did the FBI, probably. And, besides, the driver was obviously known to the guard. Otherwise, plain clothesman or not, the driver would have been questioned.

Perhaps the son—Elton—drove this Lincoln. Perhaps the father and mother and son were inside the mansion now, conferring—deciding that, yes, they must pay the half million dollars.

After all, they might reason, it would all be in the family.

Smiling, he settled deeper in the seat.

By tomorrow at this time, he would be on an airplane to

New York. He'd already bought the ticket—courtesy of Uncle Julian. At his feet, in a canvas bag he'd already bought— courtesy of Uncle Julian—he would be carrying a half million dollars in small, used bills, none larger than a fifty.

Tomorrow...

He'd memorized his schedule, hour by hour, minute by minute.

By seven A.M., he'd be at the airport, complaining to Hertz about the Ford. He'd get another car—a Chevrolet, or a Buick. Or, perhaps, he would rent a Cadillac, to blend better with Beverly Hills. At the thought, he smiled again. This time, a tittering sound escaped. He was nervous, then. It was understandable. Completely understandable.

An hour later, by eight o'clock, he'd be back at his post, watching the Holloway gate for any sign that the police had been called. His appearance would be different. For the first time since arriving in Los Angeles, he would be wearing a business suit—courtesy of Uncle Julian—and even an establishment hat. As insurance, tonight he would dye his hair a darker brown. He already had the dye, purchased two days ago.

He would wait until Holloway left in the chauffeur-driven Cadillac, bound for the Temple of Today. Still watching the mansion, he would allow a half hour to pass. Then he would drive to a nearby shopping center. Using a pay phone—one of several at the shopping center—he would call the Temple of Today, and ask for Holloway. Of course, the one that answered—Flournoy—would try to stall, possibly so the call could be traced. If—when—that happened, he would be ready with a reply. If Holloway didn't talk to him, he'd say, then all bets were off. A half million dollars couldn't square the debt, he'd say, if Holloway wouldn't talk to him.

If Holloway wouldn't talk to him—wouldn't agree to his conditions for delivery of the money—then nothing could save him. Mere money wouldn't be enough, after that.

Only death would be enough—Holloway's death: a public sacrifice, on nationwide TV.

Eighteen

AS HE DREW BACK the sleeve of his jacket to check the time, he realized that his fingers were trembling. Beneath the expensive shirt, sweat soaked his armpits. At the pit of his stomach, he was helplessly quivering.

Time: 8:30 A.M.

Twenty minutes earlier, a police patrol car had passed. Just moments ago, another police car had come by: a different car, carrying two different policemen.

Ten minutes ago a foreign sports car had entered the Holloway grounds. It had been a Ferrari, or a Maserati. A single man had been inside the sports car, possibly Elton Holloway. Moments later, a blue Chrysler had appeared. Two men had been in the Chrysler, both dressed in conservative blue suits. The men had exchanged familiar nods of greeting with the guard at the gate.

The players were taking their places. Soon the game would begin: a millionaire evangelist on one side, with hundreds of helpers and supporters, in uniform and out—all of them pitted against one man.

Numerically, the odds favored Holloway.

Yet, without doubt, the advantage was his.

One man with a gun could topple empires, begin wars, change the course of history. Oswald had done it. And James Earl Ray. And John Wilkes Booth. The three men had changed the world.

And, now, James Carson.

Time: 8:45 A.M.

Time for Holloway to leave for the Temple of Today. On each of the five mornings he had stationed himself outside the gates, watching. Holloway's limousine had swept through the gates precisely at 8:45. Ten minutes later, it arrived at the Temple.

Holloway's routine never varied.

And so, today, it must still be.

Because, without the players in place, the game couldn't begin. Without Holloway in the Temple, there could be no phone call.

Or could there?

Should there?

Yes. The game must begin, with or without Holloway. He'd told them he would call. So he must call, with his instructions. They must realize that he would keep his promises. They must realize that his threats were real: a guarantee that vengeance would follow—and, finally, death. So, with fingers still trembling, he twisted the ignition key, starting the engine. He would—

The gates were swinging open.

But, instead of Holloway's black Cadillac limousine, the blue Chrysler was nosing out into the street. Four men were inside the car: the two men dressed in blue were riding in front. Another man was on the far side, in back. And Austin Holloway, also in back, was on the near side, closest to him.

It was a change: a dangerous, deadly change.

He watched the Chrysler brake for a passing gardener's truck. Now, with the truck gone, the Chrysler was turning left, toward him.

Not right, in the direction of the Temple.

But left, toward him.

It was another change—another break in the routine. Was Holloway escaping—putting himself out of harm's way?

Or was it a trap?

In seconds, he must decide—must act.

Sitting rigidly, one hand still on the ignition switch, he kept his head immobilized, faced straight toward the front. In that position, he must wait while the Chrysler passed him—while, as the seconds ticked away, he must decide what to do. He must act.

Now the Chrysler was turning into the road's first curve—gone.

He revved the engine, put the car in gear and began a U turn.

Two cars ahead, the Chrysler was signaling for a right turn—a change of freeway lanes. Looking in the mirror, without signaling, he also changed lanes. Overhead, the sign coming up read "Airport Exit, 1 Mile."

His victim was escaping. Running.

Without Holloway, he had no hostage. No protection. It was the one possibility he'd overlooked: that Holloway would try to leave town. Meanwhile, in Los Angeles, Flournoy and the others would set their traps for him.

Ahead, the Chrysler was changing lanes again—committed, now, to the airport turnoff.

He waited for a red pickup to pass on his right, then swung into the inside lane. Also committed. As he drove, he looked in the mirror. Were they following? Who? How many? Where were they?

Now the Chrysler was turning off. Two cars were between them, a sports car and a sedan. Quickly, he glanced at his watch. The time was twenty minutes after nine. In the pit of his stomach, the trembling had begun again. Suddenly he was alone, without a plan—fighting all of them, his unseen enemies. All his life, they'd surrounded him: evil, leering faces, with hatred in their eyes, their mouths furiously twisted, laughing, screaming, taunting him. And his mother, too. Time without end. Malice without mercy. Screaming. Striking out at him. Hurting him.

Killing him.

Killing him.

Suddenly his eyes were stinging. Tears blurred the shapes of the cars ahead. He blinked, shook his head, wiped his eyes with the back of his hand. It was a shameful gesture, fugitive from childhood. The fear, too, came from his childhood. And the hatred. And—now—the determination. Never again would he fear them. Because Holloway would set him free. Holloway's life, or his death. Both would set him free.

Blinking again, he saw the Chrysler signaling for another turn: "United. TWA. Pan Am."

Pan Am—The International Airline.

His victim would escape. And without Holloway, there was no hope. No hostage. No freedom from the fear. Nothing.

So, looking back over his shoulder, he signaled for the same turn. Wherever Holloway went, he would follow.

Like father, like son.

The thought produced a quick, treacherous burble of tittering laughter. He clamped his jaw, caught his tongue between his teeth. The momentary pain cut short the laughter. It was an old trick, one he'd learned long ago, hot prowling. Everything threatened him. Even his own laughter.

The Chrysler was drawing up at the curb opposite the door marked "United." His car, too, was turning toward the same curb, stopping behind the Chrysler. It was as if the car had driven itself, stopped itself. Ahead, the front door of the Chrysler was opening. One of the men dressed in blue was getting out, holding open the rear door. Elton Holloway was stepping to the sidewalk—followed, moments later, by Austin Holloway. The man in blue closed the rear door. Now, leaning into the car, he spoke to the driver, nodded, spoke again. Already Elton and Austin were moving toward one of the doors marked "United." Austin Holloway's footsteps were slow and shuffling, uncertain. But when Elton took his elbow, the older man pulled sharply away. At the curb, the man dressed in blue was closing the Chrysler's front passenger door, stepping back as the car moved away. Now the man in blue walked briskly toward the United door. Already, Elton and Austin Holloway were inside the terminal.

Snatching the keys from the ignition, he swung open the driver's door and stepped out of the car. A nearby policeman was frowning, watching him closely. So he must play-act, pretending an emergency. He looked at the policeman, pointed urgently toward the terminal and made for the United door, trotting. Behind him now, the policeman was shouting something. But he mustn't stop—couldn't stop. Because, through the glass doors, he could see Elton and Austin moving away from him, toward his left. So, even if they towed the car, he must leave it behind.

Inside the terminal now, he stepped quickly out of line with the policeman's outraged stare, then stopped. Elton and Austin were still moving toward the left. But their progress was slow, the younger man adjusting his pace to the measured shuffle of the older man. To his right, the man dressed in blue was walking toward the United ticket counter.

Elton and Austin Holloway were going to the passengers' concourse. The man dressed in blue would pick up the tickets.

Tickets to where?

To his right, the man in the blue suit was taking his place at the end of a long line of people who waited patiently in a cordoned area that extended the full length of the United counter. Each person waited his turn, then went to one of a half dozen ticket clerks. So he would have no chance to take his place behind the man, listen while the man bought the tickets, then buy a ticket to the same city.

No chance...

To his left, Elton and Austin were approaching the end of

the United baggage counter. In moments, they would turn down the concourse—lost from his view.

Should he let them go?

Should he return to his car, face the policeman's anger, drive to a highway phone booth and make his call to the Temple?

Or should he persist, stalking Holloway to wherever he might flee? If he did—if he succeeded—Holloway would realize that escape was impossible. He would realize that he must pay—and pay—

—or else die.

He realized that he was moving, walking to his left, after Holloway and Elton. He wasn't aware that the decision had been made—wasn't aware that he was committed. He only knew that he had no choice. He must do what he was doing.

Ahead, the two men were turning down a concourse marked "United gates 44–52, TWA gates 53–56." The concourse was enormous: a long, squared-off cavern with dark-tinted windows on either side and a movable sidewalk in the center. Now Holloway and his son were stepping on the movable conveyor belt. On either side of the belt, other passengers were walking unassisted. Some of them moved leisurely, slower than the belt. Others, in a hurry, walked faster. He quickened his pace, walking beside the belt, gaining on the Holloways. Far down the concourse, the belt ended at a barrier formed by two arches and a counter...

...*the metal detectors*.

He realized that he'd suddenly stopped walking. Numbly aware of the travelers jostling past him, he stood with his hand inside his jacket, curled around the butt of the .45. In his pocket, he could feel the shape of the switchblade knife.

Ahead, the two men were almost off the movable sidewalk, about to join the line waiting at the metal detectors.

He moved to the glass wall, clear of the pedestrian jostle. Had he just passed storage lockers? Yes. Looking back, he saw them: a bank of rectangular steel doors, across the concourse and up toward the entrance to the ticket lobby. Opposing the passenger flow, half running, half walking, he dodged his way back to the lockers, looking for one with a key, an empty one. As he looked, he searched for coins in his pockets: two quarters, according to the sign. In the whole bank of lockers, only one was vacant, on the top tier. But how could he get the big automatic inside without being seen? Nearby he saw an overflowing refuse bin filled with candy wrappers, soft-drink cans and discarded newspapers. He stepped to the bin, took out a wrinkled newspaper, stepped back to the lockers. Standing close to the empty locker, glancing quickly in either direction, he withdrew the .45, folded it in the newspaper and slipped it into the locker, along with the knife. He deposited two quarters, took the locker key, put it in his pocket and began running toward the metal detector. Ahead of him, the Holloways had disappeared, already passed through the detector, and were now blocked from his view by others waiting in line. Breathing hard, he took his place at the end of the line.

When would the plane leave?

Where would it go?

How much time would he have to discover its destination, return to the lobby, buy a ticket and return here, to the spot where he now stood?

He looked back over his shoulder, searching the crowd for the man in the blue suit. How many minutes had passed since they'd entered the terminal? How far had the man gotten in the ticket line? He looked at his watch.

Time: 9:35.

The day that would change his life was almost two hours old. After today, nothing would be the same. Already, he was a different person. After only an hour, he had changed. He was in charge—in command. For the first time in his life, others feared him, scurrying before him like small, frightened animals trying to escape his vengeance. Back at the Temple, waiting for his call, they were trembling with fearful apprehension. In front of him, Austin Holloway, famous throughout the world, was vainly trying to run from him—and not succeeding. The old man couldn't move at more than a slow walk.

Father dear, old and sick. No longer could he run. No longer would others fear him. The king was almost dead.

Dying, dying, finally dead.

Yes, if he willed it, dead. Millions would mourn the fallen king. And all because of one man's power, one man's control.

His power. *His* control.

Only one passenger remained in front of him: a tall, teen-age girl wearing tight jeans and something that looked like a Mexican serape thrown over her shoulders. Her hair was long and blond, falling around her shoulders like golden flax, incredibly fine.

She was walking ahead—passing through the detector. The attendant was beckoning to him, smiling. Was he smiling in return? He didn't know, couldn't be sure. But, moments later, he was passing the attendant, passing the two policemen standing guard.

Free.

Trotting again, he came to the first gate, 44. The area was deserted. But the next gate, 45, was crowded. Drawing up, breathing hard, he stopped just inside the entrance, scanning the waiting faces. The faces were all blank: faces already dead, waiting their turn to cross into hell. Some of the faces were hidden behind a wall. He moved to his right—

—and saw them: the father and the son, sitting directly in front of the loading counter. Above the counter, on an illuminated screen, he read:

Flight #812, Los Angeles to San Francisco

Departing 9:55   On Time.

Turning away, careful that they didn't see him, he began running back the way he'd come.

Nineteen

STANDING IN THE HALLWAY outside the closed door of her bedroom, she held her breath, listening. From inside she heard the unmistakable sound of a deep, sad sigh. Then, equally unmistakable, she heard the sound of a suitcase lock snapping shut.

Had her mother finished packing?

Was their mutual agony almost ended?

Soon her father and her brother would arrive. After an hour spent exchanging meaningless pleasantries, her father and her brother and her mother would leave, followed by the omnipresent bodyguard, always keeping his discreet, carefully calculated distance.

Like any other potentate—like any other corporate figurehead or political tyrant—her father's retinue was elaborately structured. Everyone who served Austin Holloway knew his place, and kept to it. Otherwise, he—or she—was replaced.

In the family, the same rules applied—and the same penalties were exacted. Except that, in the family, replacement by dismissal was impossible. So, instead, the royal favor was withdrawn, de facto excommunication. Soon the excommunicate's soul began to shrivel, like a shrunken head, fugitive from some ancient voodoo rite. With the soul so shrunken, the body's disintegration was inevitable. But the wasting away was a slow, subtle process, at first readable only in a downward deflection of the eyes, or a dullness of the voice, or a discouraged cast to the mouth. Yet, once begun, the process was irreversible, and eventually physical manifestations emerged. In the case of Elton, a telltale puffiness was beginning to bloat both his face and his waistline. After thirty-two years, the secret of Elton's debaucheries was showing.

In the case of her mother, the malignancy was more advanced, plain for all to see in the perpetual pain etched into the lines around her mouth, and in the sorrow so stark in her eyes. Her mother's final decline was close at hand. Someday soon, her mother's liver would fail. It would all be over.

And, finally, there was her own case. Denise Holloway, age twenty-eight. Unmarried. Childless. A lonely woman who secretly despised her family. Because it was all that remained to her, she fiercely cherished her own independence—and just as fiercely fought for it. Yet, ultimately, it was a meaningless victory. Because, as Peter had once said, people were meant to live two by two.

Peter...

As soon as her family left, she would throw some things in a suitcase, and water the plants, and set the timers, and ask Mr. Byrnes at the grocery store to watch their stoop for circulars and newspapers. An hour later, she would be on the road to Mendocino. Four hours later, she would arrive at the cabin. By that time, it would be dark. The windows of the cabin would be glowing soft and golden, lit by the kerosene lamps inside. Peter would see her headlights coming through the trees long before he could see the car and recognize it. With Pepper beside him, he would be standing on the porch, waiting and watching—and frowning. In Mendocino, at night, visitors could mean trouble.

But then he would recognize her car. In one bound he would leap from the porch to the ground, following Pepper, already barking and frisking around her car. She would switch off the headlights, switch off the engine and get out of the car. In the darkness, they would hold each other close, saying little, letting the small urgent movements of their bodies seek each other out—exploring, rising, stroking, accepting. At first, their movements would be tender, almost tentative. But, as passion rose, their bodies would begin moving together with one strong, single purpose. Until, with their arms tight around each other, they would go inside, to bed.

Two by two...

Inside the bedroom, she heard soft, hesitant footsteps approaching the door. Silently, she stepped back—one step, two steps. Now the doorknob was turning, the door was opening. Dressed in a beautifully cut sharkskin traveling suit and wearing a sheer silk scarf at her throat, her mother stood in the open doorway, both hands clutching a small beige handbag. Her hair was meticulously coiffed, piled high on her head in elegant chestnut coils. Her feet were together, her chin was lifted. She was smiling: a fixed, mechanical smile, betrayed by eyes that were too bright—too vulnerable. If she were wearing an organdy gown instead of the sharkskin suit, and clutching a Bible instead of the purse, she could have been on stage, smiling fixedly into the TV camera as The Hour approached its finale.

"You look wonderful, Mother. Your hair is perfect. Beautiful."

Most of the morning, her mother had been working on her hair.

"Thank you, dear." Her mother nodded: a quick, artificial inclination of the head that left the hairdo undisturbed.

"Why don't you go into the living room? I'll bring in your suitcases."

"Yes—" Again, the careful nod. "Yes, I will. Thank you."

Walking with slow, wooden deliberation, still moving as if she were on camera, her mother was making her way down the hallway toward the living room—and the kitchen. Denise stepped into her bedroom, where she'd helped her mother put her two suitcases on the bed, open. Now the suitcases were closed and locked. She stood for a moment in the narrow space between the bureau and the bed—her bed and Peter's.

When her father had first phoned, two weeks ago, and asked her to take her mother in, Peter had called the docks and arranged for a leave of absence, citing an unspecified "family emergency." He'd done it almost eagerly, glad that fate had given him leave to spend some time in the country, alone, writing all day long. An hour later, Peter was gone, driving jauntily down the street in his old GMC pickup, with Pepper sitting in the seat beside him. Returning to the apartment, with two hours remaining before her mother's arrival, she'd considered taking Peter's things to her basement storage locker. Peter had always had his own apartment, just two blocks away. So he'd never kept more than a few things at her place. Yet, whenever she saw his clothes hanging beside hers in the closet, and when she went to the bureau and found his socks and underwear, neatly folded, sharing the same drawer with her things, she felt reassured, less alone.

Standing in the bedroom, two weeks ago, she'd realized that the price she would pay for hiding his clothes would come too high.

So, instead, she'd taken a long, luxurious shower and changed into a skirt and sweater, in deference to her mother. Then she'd brushed her hair and tied it up with a bit of ribbon.

It was the same hair style she'd worn when she'd lived at home, years before.

Then she'd gone into the living room, poured a large glass of red wine and played a Simon and Garfunkle record. When she'd been living at home, Simon and Garfunkle's measured melancholy had been her constant boon companion—her only salvation, she sometimes thought.

For two weeks, she'd waited for her mother to ask about Peter—or, at least, about his clothes, hanging in the closet. Not once did her mother even suggest the subject.

As she picked up the two suitcases, one in either hand, she heard the soft, furtive sound of a door closing. It was the kitchen door. At the doorway of the bedroom she paused, giving her mother a chance to settle herself in the living room. Then she stepped out into the hallway, with the two big suitcases banging awkwardly into her legs.

For two weeks, they'd both kept up their separate little charades. While her mother hadn't acknowledged the presence of Peter's clothes in the apartment, she hadn't acknowledged the presence of the gin bottle in the kitchen cabinet.

Which of them was more guilty?

She placed the suitcases on the floor beside the door, and turned to face her mother, sitting in the precise center of the sofa, still holding the handbag in her lap. Still with her feet placed primly together. Still smiling—too brightly.

In an hour or two, her father and brother would arrive. Between her and her mother, time was running out. Two weeks had come down to two hours, no more. Twenty-eight years had come and gone. Twenty-eight years for her, fifty-six for her mother. All gone.

She sat down on a ladderback chair that faced the sofa. "I'm sorry that you can't stay longer, Mother."

But it was a lie. Yet another lie. After twenty-eight years, with only hours left to them, she was still doing it. Still lying.

So, speaking slowly and deliberately, staring into her mother's faded, wounded eyes, she said, "What I mean is, I'm sorry that it—it hasn't worked out, for you to stay longer. I mean—" She gestured: a small, helpless wave of her hand. Signifying the futility she felt as she began again: "I mean, we—you and I—we have our own lives. And they—they're different. So it's just as well, for both of us, that you're going home."

Like a child trying to learn a difficult lesson, her mother frowned, as if she were deeply puzzled. But, still, the meticulously painted lips remained upcurved, clinging to the small, fixed smile. Now, slowly, her mother nervously nodded. Saying softly: "Yes, I know it is, Denise. I know it's better. I realize that. You've got your work. And your—your life, too."

It was as close as she would ever get—as good an opening as she would ever have. So, drawing a deep breath, she said, "One problem—the biggest problem, really—is that, most of the time, I live with a man. His name is Peter, and he's a writer. Peter Giannini. He's very nice—very kind. And—well—I've missed him, the past two weeks. I've missed him very much."

As she'd said it, her mother had dropped her eyes to her lap, where her hands still held the purse in a white-knuckled grip. Finally, still with her head bowed, eyes averted, she said, "How long have you—" A long, painful pause. Then: "How long have you—known each other?"

"I've known him ever since I came to San Francisco. Five years, almost. But he—" She hesitated, then said, "But he was married, then. So we didn't go out together until two years ago, when he was divorced. And it's just been about a year, that we've been living together. Except that, really, he still has his own place. It's—you know—it's insurance, I guess you'd say."

"Insurance?" With an obvious effort, her mother raised her head, to meet her eyes. The artificial smile was gone. But the look of almost childlike puzzlement remained. Was her mother trying to understand? Or was she too stunned to react?

Tentatively, she smiled. "Insurance against his feeling trapped, I guess you'd say. See, Peter took his divorce very hard. So he's not about to commit himself to another marriage. Not for a while, anyhow. He's a very serious man. He takes marriage seriously. Very seriously."

Now her mother was slowly shaking her head. Saying: "I don't know what to say, Denise. I—I just can't understand it."

Searching her mother's face, she let a long, heavy moment of silence pass. During the silence, she saw sadness cross her mother's face like a shadow of death. Behind her mother's carefully applied makeup, she saw a deep, mute agony of the spirit revealed, as if the makeup was a mask that was disintegrating before her eyes. In silent, desperate confirmation, she saw her mother's eyes stray toward the kitchen door.

Then, obviously with great effort, her mother's haunted

eyes returned, meeting her own. Speaking in a soft, almost furtive voice, her mother said, "I won't tell your father, Denise."

"Mother, I don't care whether you tell him or not. Don't you see that? It's not something I'm ashamed of. I'm—Christ—I'm proud of it. Peter is—he's the first good thing that's happened to me. Ever."

"But, still, I won't tell your father, Denise. It wouldn't be right."

"Listen, Mother—" Once more, she drew a long, deep breath. "Forget about Dad. What about you?"

"Me?"

"Yes, Mother. *You.* How do you feel about my living with someone without benefit of marriage?"

"Well, I—" The puzzled frown returned, lending the innocence of confusion to the sad, tortured eyes. "Well, Denise, I—I wish that you hadn't told me." She spoke softly, regretfully.

"But why? Why do you wish I hadn't told you? So you wouldn't have to face it?"

Unable to respond, her mother dropped her eyes. Now, with her shoulders slumped, her head began moving in a slow, stricken arc, shaking sadly from side to side. It wasn't a denial of the question. Rather, it was an admission that, yes, she couldn't face it.

Involuntarily, Denise stretched out a hand, as if to touch her mother, as she said, "I'm not trying to—to give you a hard time, Mother. I'm not trying to rub your nose in it. All I'm trying to do is make you realize that there's a real world out there. It's not the world that Dad preaches about—not the world he's created with a few homilies and a couple of talented set designers. It's not just sinners and saints, Mother. It's people who're just trying to get through, the best way they can. They're lonely, and they're scared. And they're desperate, too. They're imperfect. Very, very imperfect. But at least they *know* they're imperfect. They have some idea of who they are and what they want. Not much of an idea, but some idea. They—they're like me. They're confused, and they're scared. But they aren't so scared that they're not willing to take a few chances with their lives."

Still shaking her head in the same slow, sad arc, her mother spoke in a low, indistinct voice: "You don't have to do it, Denise. You don't have to be scared. You don't have to take chances. Your father would have taken care of you. He—

he's always taken care of Elton. And me, too. Don't you see that?"

"Taken *care* of you? Of *Elton?*" She realized that her voice had suddenly, unpredictably risen: a stranger's voice, shrill and derisive. "How? By giving Elton a house and a sports car and all the money he wants? By giving you pretty clothes, and your daily—" She stopped short, stricken by what she'd almost said.

Once more, her mother's head came up: slowly, reluctantly, as if the effort was overwhelming. Her mouth was trembling, barely able to form the whispered words: "My bottle of gin."

Denise realized that she couldn't speak, couldn't respond. Suddenly her throat closed. Her eyes were filled with tears. It was as if she'd done something shameful—as if she were a little girl again, and had been caught lying, or stealing, or swearing.

And it was true. She'd done something shameful. She'd stripped her mother naked—left her defenseless, without the illusions that were her only protection, her only way out.

With her head lowered, to hide the tears, she heard her mother clear her throat, then speak in a low, exhausted voice: "You're twenty-eight years old, Denise. And you're strong—a lot stronger than I was, at your age. I—I'd already started to drink, when I was twenty-eight. And I never stopped. And I never *will* stop. Not now. But I—"

"Mother, I—" She raised her head, blinked her eyes, tried desperately to focus on her mother's face. "I'm sorry. I didn't mean to—"

"But I'm not hurting anyone, Denise," she went on, still speaking in the same low, toneless voice. "Except for that—that little girl, I've never hurt anyone. Not deliberately. I know that I'm—I'm a weak person. I think I've always known that, about myself. Even when I was a little girl, I was afraid of things. Everything, I remember, frightened me. I always felt very—very small, inside myself, even when I wasn't small anymore. And to make it worse, I was pretty. I was always pretty. Beautiful, some said, when I got to be twelve or thirteen, and I started to—to develop. Which meant that boys were always after me—telling me how wonderful I was, and how much they loved me. For a long time—for years—I thought I was very fortunate, to be so pretty. I—I seemed to be getting everything I wanted. But really, of course, I was still afraid of things—everything. Inside, I was still a little

160

girl. I'd never gotten over it, you see. I'd just been able to—to ignore it, for a while, because I was so pretty.

"But then—I guess it was when I was about thirty—things started to go wrong. You were still just a little baby, I remember. And Elton was still very small. And suddenly—" Momentarily her voice caught. But, doggedly, she cleared her throat, shook her head sharply, and went on: "Suddenly nobody around me was happy. That was in the early fifties, your father wasn't succeeding in his work. Or, at least, he didn't think he was succeeding. And Elton seemed to hate everything—especially me. And you—you cried, all the time. All day long—and all night, too. It—it was all something that I—I just wasn't prepared for. I remember that I used to lie in bed at night, thinking about myself, and what was happening to me. And that's when they started to come back: all those terrible fears I used to feel, when I was a little girl. And there wasn't anyone I could talk to, about it. No one at all. Your father was too busy. And I didn't have any friends, not really. That's—" The mouth twitched again, trying vainly to smile. The wounded eyes were glistening now: tears brimmed over, streaking the Elizabeth Arden makeup. "That's the trouble, you see, with being pretty. No one likes you. Not really. Sometimes the men seem to hate you, because you make them feel—" She broke off and shook her head, unable to find the phrase. Then, sadly: "And the women hate you because you're pretty. It—" Once more, she shook her head. "It can hurt, Denise. It can hurt very much." With her eyes streaming now, her mother lowered her head and began fumbling at her purse, for a handkerchief. Her story was finished.

Denise got to her feet, crossed to her mother, bent down and reached out a timid hand to touch her mother's shoulder—just as the downstairs buzzer rang. Startled, she straightened. Involuntarily muttering, "Shit. It's them."

"Oh, dear. *No*." With her hands to her face, covering the ruined makeup, her mother was scrambling to her feet, turning desperately toward the hallway, and the bathroom. Escaping. Still escaping.

Twenty

"WELL—" Across the room, her father was levering himself forward in the room's only easy chair, ready to rise to his feet. "I think we'd better be going, Denise. Our plane leaves in an hour and forty minutes. How long does it take to get to the airport from here?"

"About a half hour, at this time of the day." She looked at her father, asking, "I thought you had an airplane—a company airplane."

Elton answered the question: "We do. But it's in the shop. Every hundred hours, it has to be checked. It's the law."

"So we came courtesy of United," Holloway said, speaking in his deep, rich voice, falsely hearty. In reply, she nodded and smiled, realizing that, yes, her nod and her smile were as false as her father's. During the past half hour, ever since her mother emerged from the bathroom, makeup restored, the four of them had been sitting like strangers in a public waiting room, exchanging small talk.

"We probably should have chartered an airplane," Elton said. "But at least Hertz had a limo for us, and a driver. So the hassle could have been worse."

Typically, Elton would want words like "chartered airplane" and "limo" on the record. Just as typically, he would use a with-it word like "hassle." Demonstrating that, even though he existed in a world elevated from that of his peers, he nevertheless still retained the common touch—still spoke the language of the masses. On The Hour, it was Elton's job to appeal to the young—despite his banker's jowls and a paunch of middle-aged proportions.

Hopeful that her distaste showed, she deliberately looked away from her brother—to find her mother looking at her directly. Her mother was trying to smile as she said, "Thank you, Denise. Thank you for everything, these past two weeks. Will you come and see us? Soon?"

"I—I'll try, Mother. I really will."

"Christmas," Holloway pronounced, as he braced his hands on the arms of his chair and heaved himself to his feet. For a moment he stood unsteadily, like a groggy fighter trying to get his legs under him. His face was gray and drawn, his eyes lusterless, his lips bloodless. Since she'd seen him last, he'd lost weight. The bones of his head and face had become more prominent: a dead man's skull, showing through thin, sallow skin.

But the voice was the same—his eternal stock in trade, the foundation of the family fortune:

"Christmas," he repeated, smiling at her now. Intoning: "She'll come for Christmas, and stay through New Year's."

She knew it was unnecessary to reply. No one really expected her to do it. Yet her father's mellifluous pronouncement created the momentary illusion that, yes, the family would be united over Christmas.

The artful evangelist could make the moment's illusion seem eternal—at least until the collection plate was passed.

Also on his feet, Elton spoke heartily: "Definitely. Christmas. Do you realize, Denise—" He turned to face her, dropping his voice to a deeper, more unctuous note—a fair imitation of his father's style. "Do you realize that Amy, my youngest, has only seen you twice in her entire life?"

"You can always come up here, Elton," she answered quietly. "Take a trip. Visit San Francisco. Bring the family. Ride the cable car."

Elton's heavy, overfed face sagged into an expression of pious reproach. "It's not the same, Denise. You should know that."

Also on her feet, arms folded as she faced her brother, she stared at him in silence. Could he see the contempt that she knew must show in her face?

Probably not. Because, after only a brief glance at her, following the delivery of his homily, he was turning to face her mother, who was also struggling to get to her feet.

"Are you ready, Mother?" Advancing a measured stride, Elton was gravely extending his arm, crooked to dancing-school perfection. "Shall we go?"

Silently she watched her mother take his arm. Both turned away, to the apartment door. Ahead of them, her father was opening the door, gesturing for the anonymous blue-suited bodyguard who waited in the hallway outside to take the suitcases. The bodyguard nodded stolidly to her, picked up the suitcases and murmured to Holloway that he would be downstairs, in the car. As the bodyguard disappeared, her father, mother and brother turned in unison to face her. Speaking for all of them, Holloway raised his hand to her, unconsciously striking his pastor's pose. "Goodbye, Denise, for now. We will be seeing you soon, I hope. At Christmas, as I said. And, meanwhile, thank you, Denise. I would be less than honest if I didn't admit that, in the past, our paths have separated. But I want to tell you, Denise—I want you to know—that the help you've given, these last two weeks, has shown me that, when it really matters, I can count on you. Just as you can count on me." As he said it, his eyes were slightly raised, suggesting heavenly sanction for the speech. Now he was smiling at her: his famous smile, beloved by millions.

"Yeah, Denise," Elton was saying, mock-heartily, "You really came through for the home team."

Without replying to either of them, she turned to face her mother. Reaching out to touch her mother's cheek, gently, with the tips of her fingers, she said softly, "Goodbye, Mother. God bless you."

She opened the Toyota's hatchback, put the canvas bag inside and slammed the hatchback shut. Across the street, standing behind his cash register, Mr. Byrnes was handing a brown paper bag across the counter to a short, stocky, middle-aged man dressed in a scuffed leather jacket and wearing a blue watch cap pulled low around his ears. She waited for a pickup truck and a green Porsche to pass, then crossed the street to the grocery store. Still at the counter, the man in the leather jacket was speaking in a loud, truculent voice:

"Okay, Harry. You go ahead. You hope for the best. But I'm telling you—I'm *promising* you—that this country is going down the tubes. And I'm also telling you, in no uncertain terms, that it all started in 1954, when the Supreme Court wrote it out on a slip of paper that the blacks was just as good as the whites. Which is just another way of saying that the whites aren't any better than the blacks. Which, sure enough, is just what happened. Look at football. Look at baseball. Christ, just look *anywhere*. And then think about it—" He raised a short, grimy forefinger, pointing across the counter.

"You're full of crap, Roger," Byrnes said amiably. "For as long as I've known you, you've been full of crap." As the stocky man grabbed up his sack of groceries and stalked indignantly out of the store, Mr. Byrnes turned to her, smiling.

"Hello, Denise. I saw you throwing your duffle bag in the car. You going somewhere?"

"I'm going up to Mendocino, Mr. Byrnes. I'm going to go get Peter, and bring him home."

Mr. Byrnes nodded decisively, saying, "Good. It's about time, I imagine."

She smiled. In a few words, Mr. Byrnes had always been able to suggest that, yes, he was interested in her life with Peter—and, yes, he understood its particular rewards and also its problems. All of this he was able to convey without once stepping over the line of impropriety. Just as, now, he was intimating that he realized how much her body must ache for Peter, after the last two weeks alone.

So, nodding agreement, still smiling, she repeated drily, "I imagine."

"Did I see your mother leaving a little while ago?" he asked.

"Yes. She's going back to Los Angeles. That's why I came over. Will you pick up our newspapers and things? We should be back in two or three days. Or, at least, I will. I've got to get back to work."

He nodded. "Glad to. Anytime—" He let a moment of silence pass, then said, "That's some car your mother left in. With a chauffeur, and everything."

She let a beat pass, deciding how to react. Finally, pitching her voice to a light, quizzical note—still smiling—she said, "My family's rich. Didn't I ever tell you?"

"Well—" He waved a deprecatory hand. "Not in so many words. But I remember Peter saying, once, that your father was Austin Holloway. I can't honestly say I've ever seen him preach, being that I'm not a religious man myself. But, of course, I've heard of him. So I imagine that was him, huh—with your mother? The older man?"

She nodded. "That was my father, and my brother, too, in the gray sports jacket. The other man, in the blue suit—" She hesitated, somehow unwilling to say it. But, dropping her eyes and speaking in a lower voice, she said, "He's Dad's bodyguard."

Mr. Byrnes nodded in return, then asked, "What about the other one—a relative," he said. "How come he didn't leave with them?"

About to turn away, giving a signal that she was anxious to leave, she frowned. "My relative?"

"Yeah. Fella about twenty-five, I'd say. Slim, with real dark brown hair. He was asking about you. An hour ago, maybe."

"My relative?" she repeated again, now looking him full in the face, searching for some clue to the riddle. "But I don't have any more relatives. I mean—" Impatiently, she waved away what she'd just said. "I mean, the only relatives I have are my father and mother and brother. Except for a sister-in-law and three nieces."

"Huh—" Thoughtfully, Mr. Byrnes turned toward the plate-glass show window to look across the street. "Come to think about it, the fella didn't exactly add up. Or, at least, he doesn't add up now, knowing what I do about your folks' visit."

"How do you mean, 'knowing what you know now'?"

"Well, I guess your folks must've arrived while I was in back, trying to locate some wine I'd ordered. Because, when I got back to the front, here, I noticed that Cadillac sitting in front of your place. I mean, I couldn't hardly miss it, with the chauffeur, and all. But, naturally, I didn't connect it with you, especially.

"So then, a few minutes later, I noticed this young fella go up to the entryway of your building, and check the names on the mailboxes, like he's looking for someone. Which, of course, wasn't suspicious, or anything. And then I saw him ring a bell, and wait, and ring again. He acted like he was trying to find either you or the people downstairs, but couldn't. I saw him shake his head, and leave. Or, rather, he looked around the neighborhood, and then came across the street, here. He came in, and asked me if I knew you. I said I did. I mean, I didn't see any harm in it. Then, as if he was making absolutely sure he had the right party, he said, 'She's Austin Holloway's daughter.' And I said that, yes, you were. 'You're positive?' he said. Well—" With his jaw set pugnaciously, Mr. Byrnes stroked his gleaming bald head with a chunky, muscular hand. "Well, something about the way he said it—like he was trying to pin me to the wall—it ruffled me, a little. But then he said that he was a relative of yours. Which, of course, cooled me down. So I said that, yes, you're his daughter, for sure." Scowling now, Mr. Byrnes said, "Turns out, my first hunch was right, I guess. I should've kept my mouth shut."

She raised a hand, to reassure him. "Don't worry about it, Mr. Byrnes. This happens all the time, believe me. After all, my father's in the business of catering to some very strange people. Which means that they're constantly turning up at odd times, in odd places. That's why he had a bodyguard with him. He needs protection from his fans. Or, at least, he needs a buffer. Down in Los Angeles, he has a whole security staff, just to keep the nuts away."

"Yeah, but this guy wasn't asking about your father. He was asking about you. And, besides, I didn't much like his looks."

Involuntarily, she looked out into the street. "Has he been back? Have you seen him since my folks left?"

"No. I just saw him that once. But that doesn't mean he isn't still around."

"Yes it does, Mr. Byrnes. I promise you." She smiled, thanked him and turned toward the door.

Twenty-One

TAKING HIS RIGHT HAND from the steering wheel, he switched off the country music station. For the first hours of the trip, driving through the darkness with his eyes fixed on the two twin points of red light ahead, the music had helped. First he'd listened to rock, but the beat had been too hard, too heavy. Next he'd tried a few minutes of the golden oldies— until the sappy, syrupy lyrics began to echo and re-echo from memories of his childhood, distorting the words and the music. Finally he'd found the country music. The easy, familiar rhythms had helped to calm him, as they always did. But now, only silence could help.

Silence, and some answers—some urgent, essential answers. Some life or death answers:

Where were they going? *Where?* He had to know, had to find out. Because, suddenly, the strain of following the Toyota's taillights down the dark, two-lane country road had become almost unbearable. For minutes at a time, no other headlights were visible. It was as if his car and the Toyota were the only cars in the world—as if he was helplessly attached to one end of a string, being hauled through the endless night like some child's toy, pulled by an invisible monster. He had no control over where he was going, or when he would get there. Suddenly this drive through the night had become an abbreviation of his whole life: unplanned, uncontrolled. Unresolved.

Ahead, the two circles of red light suddenly glowed brighter. Stoplights. She was braking. Her right turn indicator was flashing.

Both in front and in back, except for the two of them, the road was deserted. The road they traveled was only two lanes: a narrow, uneven road, in bad repair. A blacktop road, far from any town. A county road.

So, certainly, she would turn off on a smaller access road:

another blacktop road, or a gravel road. Because, to the right, there was nothing. No lights. No sign of life. Only a vast, empty darkness between the county road and a low range of hills, dark against the night sky.

Her car was slowing, turning slightly to the left, then swinging sharply to the right, passing between two white posts, briefly illuminated by the glare of her headlights. Beyond the two white posts, he saw three mailboxes. A dust plume drifted in a cloud behind her car. It was a gravel road, then—probably a private road, that served three houses located-somewhere in the darkness that stretched beyond the gently bouncing swath of her headlights.

So, therefore, he must bypass the two white posts. He must continue on the county road beyond the first curve, until he found a concealed place to stop and turn around. Then, cautiously, he would drive back the way he'd come. He would park where he could watch the private road, guarding against the possibility that she had only come for a few hours' visit. When he was satisfied that she'd come to stay—and when he'd copied down the names on the mailboxes, to identify the turnoff—he'd drive to the nearest town, where he'd sleep. He wouldn't sleep in his car beside the road. He wouldn't risk certain questioning by state troopers the second time they passed on patrol, and saw his car still parked as they'd seen it before.

Then, at first light tomorrow, he would return. He would find the Toyota, and so discover where she was staying. Then he would make his plans.

Twenty-Two

AHEAD, in her headlights, she saw the enormous redwood stump that marked the last sharp curve in the road before Peter's cabin would come into view. Beyond the curve, she would see the soft glow of kerosene lamplight in the cabin windows. She would see Peter's pickup, parked beside the porch. She would stop at the gate, to unfasten it. Pepper would begin barking. Until, as she drove up the driveway, Pepper would recognize the sound of her engine. Peter would let Pepper out of the cabin. Bounding and frisking, Pepper would come to meet her, leaping beside her car as she drove to the cabin.

Steering carefully between the ruts in the road, she gripped the wheel, turned—

—and saw nothing but darkness. He'd gone. Either that, or he was asleep—at eight o'clock.

But, when she stopped the Toyota with its headlights on the gate, she saw a padlock. He was gone, then. For the day? Or gone for good—back to San Francisco? She got out of the car, unlocked the gate, swung it back and hooked it to a small stump, so the gate wouldn't close before she'd driven through— as it used to do before Peter installed the hook. She drove through, unhooked the gate, swung it shut. After a moment's thought she snapped the padlock. Tonight, she would stay here. Tomorrow, she would return to the city.

She drove up the driveway and parked beside the cabin, clear of the driveway. Because, even though he'd snapped the padlock, it was still possible that Peter might return. He could have taken Pepper and gone into town for groceries. He could have met friends, and stayed for dinner and drinks. For tonight's story—for the occasional erotic fantasies with which she'd titillated herself during the long drive—there might still be a happy ending.

The porch creaked under her weight as she fitted her key

in the lock, opened the front door and stepped into the small living room. The room was warm; embers glowed in the massive fieldstone fireplace, Peter's pride and joy—the fruit of an entire summer's work.

So he hadn't gone. Not permanently. He'd only gone into town, as she'd suspected. He would be back. If he came back soon—within the next two or three hours—she would be waiting up for him. It would be a surprise for him, seeing the lampglow in the window, and her car in the driveway.

Or, better yet, she would wait for him in bed.

She was cautiously groping her way across the living room. Outside, the night was moonless; inside, the room was pitch black, with almost no light coming through the windows. But the glowing embers guided her to the fireplace. She could see the dim shapes of the two kerosene lamps that always stood at either end of the thick, hand-hewn redwood mantel. Beside one of the lamps, her fumbling fingers found the old tin matchbox—the one she'd discovered in a junk shop in Santa Cruz. She found a match and lit the closest lamp. In the center of the mantel, she saw a piece of ordinary typing paper that had been folded into quarters and propped against a stack of books. He'd left her a note.

She lit the second lamp, then held the note up to the warm amber glow, reading:

> Dear Denise,
> I hope you're not reading this without me, or, at least, not without having heard about it from me.
> *Because*, you lovely creature with the body I crave so urgently (and, yes, with wit and whimsy, too), if you're reading this alone, it will mean that we've missed each other.
> *Because*, at approximately 6 P.M. on Tuesday, my faithful dog Pepper and I left for Jeff and Shelley's. They're adding a spur-of-the-moment room, and I promised to help them raise the roof. Or, more precisely, the roof beam (from the short story of the same name).
> Yes, Denise, darling. We will be raising the roof without you. It'll only take a day, maybe not even that. Then, tomorrow I'm going back to San Francisco. Where, I have to admit, I hope to find you alone. Very, very alone. Everyone should have a mother. But not for *this* long.
> I should have gone into town and called you, on

the off chance that you might drive up to try and find me. But I just heard about all this an hour ago. And Shelley and Jeff live in the opposite direction from a phone, as you probably remember.

And, besides, it's a spur-of-the-moment room, like I said.

I've had a wonderful, crazy, very productive week. Which I'll tell you about when I see you.

I miss everything about you.

Your admiring roommate,
Peter

Written in Peter's small, precise script, the letter covered the entire sheet of paper. Still holding the letter up to the light, she read it again, slowly. Then she carefully refolded it, and put it into her shoulder bag.

This letter, she would keep.

She slipped off the bag, put it beside the fireplace and began feeding the fire. Tonight, she would sleep in the cabin, alone. Tomorrow, she would return to San Francisco—where Peter would be waiting for her.

Yawning, she glanced at her watch as she opened the closet door. The time was almost ten o'clock; she'd slept longer than she'd intended. A glance out the window revealed the reason. During the night, a cold ocean fog had come in. The fog was so thick that treetops just across the clearing from the cabin were obscured. The bedroom was damp and chilly. Even wearing her sweater and jeans, with two pairs of wool socks on her feet, she was shivering.

As she took one of Peter's old wool shirts from a hook in the closet and slipped it over her sweater, her foot touched the stock of the shotgun that Peter kept in the closet, loaded. She frowned. Whenever Peter left, he always hid the shotgun in the loft, concealed behind a board that looked like part of the paneling. During the past year, the cabin had been broken into twice. The first time, a transistor radio and a sleeping bag had been stolen. The second time, having removed everything that thieves might find attractive—and hidden the shotgun—they'd lost only a few cans of food and a towel.

The gun had always made her uneasy. Even though Peter had taught her to use it, she never liked to handle the big, double-barreled shotgun. Secretly, she was always afraid that it might go off accidentally while she was holding it. But, before she left, she would put it behind the loose board, where it belonged.

She closed the closet door, tugged on her heavy-soled shoes, and went into the kitchen. Probably because he'd left in a hurry, Peter had also forgotten to lay a fire in the big, black iron cookstove that was their most efficient source of heat, especially since the tiny kitchen could be heated so quickly. But at least there was plenty of newspaper and kindling in the woodbox. First shaking down yesterday's ashes, as Peter had taught her, she crumpled up some paper, put the paper in the bottom of the firebox, and began breaking twigs into manageable lengths. She laid the twigs crisscross, not too close together. Then she struck a wooden match and dropped it down among the papers. The match flamed, faltered and finally died. She sighed, and struck another match—and another. If Peter were there, he would be amused.

After flickering uncertainly for a moment, the fourth match ignited an edge of the newspaper. Because of the dampness, the fire caught slowly. But, at last, flames were licking at the wood.

Smiling, she levered the round, iron cookstove cover into place, and took a pail from the counter. After she drew water from the pump, and after the stove top got hot enough to boil the water, she would make a cup of coffee. Elapsed time, at least a half hour.

At home, a flick of the thermostat dial would already have taken the chill off her apartment. A turn of the water tap and a twist of a knob on the stove would have produced boiling water.

She opened the door and walked behind the cabin to the old-fashioned iron pump that stood next to a small storage shed. Hooking the handle of the pail to the iron spout, she grasped the handle and began to pump. The sound of the mechanism was dry and squeaky: iron against iron, unlubricated, unpromising. But, finally, a dribble of water was beginning, spattering the bottom of the pail. It was magic—her own private miracle, a Wednesday morning spectacular. As she threw her weight against the rusty iron handle, the stream thickened: a rushing, foaming cascade.

Coffee was coming: another Wednesday morning miracle. Denise Holloway, the sorceress.

With the bucket half full, she lifted it from the hook and began carrying it to the kitchen door, leaning against the

173

weight of the water. Was the fire still burning high enough to—

At the end of the driveway, opposite the gate, a car was slowing, stopping. Where she stood, half concealed by the corner of the cabin and partially hidden by a big blueberry bush, she probably wasn't visible to the driver. Flexing her knees, she lowered the bucket to the ground, then straightened. Unconsciously, she'd stepped closer to the house, concealing more of her body from view. The car was an orange sedan, unlike any car she'd ever seen either the Andersons or the Taylors drive, the two families that shared the private access road with Peter. Yet the car was going toward the county road, not away from it. Which meant that the driver was coming from the Taylor place, a quarter of a mile farther up the access road.

Of course, the explanation was obvious. Either someone was visiting the Taylors, or else a stranger was lost. Or, possibly, the Taylors had gotten another car.

The driver's door was swinging open. A slim, dark-haired stranger was getting out of the car. He was standing in the road, looking up toward the Taylors, then down toward the county road, in the direction of the Andersons' place. He was plainly puzzled. The stranger was dressed in brown slacks and a tan poplin jacket, both of them new. Now he was turning toward her, walking across the road to the gate.

Fella about twenty-five, Mr. Byrnes had said. *Slim, with dark-colored hair.*

And, later: *This fella didn't exactly add up.*

But that had been in San Francisco, yesterday. This was Mendocino—today.

Could he see her? Only her head and half her upper body were visible around the corner of the cabin, with the blueberry bush concealing her body from the waist down. The distance from where she stood to the gate was perhaps a hundred yards, and the low-lying fog limited visibility. If she stood still, she probably wouldn't be noticed.

Now he was standing before the gate. He was looking down, possibly at the padlock.

A relative, Mr. Byrnes had said.

As she thought about it, she sharply shook her head. She was taking a coincidence and distorting it into something mysterious—something ominous. The incident at Mr. Byrnes' store couldn't be easily explained—not without questioning the stranger. But this incident—this young, neatly dressed

174

man driving a shiny new car—this could be explained. At least once a day, a strange car wandered off the county road and up their access road, despite the warning sign. Their trespassers' explanations varied, but were almost always innocuous—at least during daytime hours.

This car—this man—was undoubtedly harmless: a stranger, wondering how to get to a nearby ranch, or the nearest town. The fact that he was slim, with dark brown hair, was mere coincidence.

But, still, it would be better if he returned to his car and asked his directions of someone else. She'd never before been here alone. There'd always been Pepper, at least. And she'd always known that, in the next hour or two, Peter would return.

Unconsciously, she'd shrunk away from the corner of the house, furtively peeking around the corner now. It was like a childhood game of hide and seek. When she saw her chance, she would run for the goal—home.

Yes, home. She would go inside and fix her cup of coffee, and hide the shotgun and close up the cabin—and leave for San Francisco. Without Peter—without even Pepper—the cabin was suddenly a stranger's house, alien and empty.

She backed away from the corner, picked up the water pail and went into the kitchen. The fire had burned beyond the point of no return: nothing but glowing red embers and a few blazing twigs remained at the bottom of the firebox. She put the bucket on the floor, reached hastily for a handful of twigs, scattered the twigs on the meager fire. Now she must replace the iron cover—and hope.

With the cover in place, she walked into the front room and looked out the window. The stranger had returned to his orange car. As she watched, the car moved forward, disappearing behind the screen of pines that bordered the driveway. Turning back to the kitchen, she was aware that the relief she felt was strangely disproportionate to the significance of the incident.

Twenty-Three

AS SHE LOCKED the cabin door and tested the lock, she glanced at her watch. The hour was almost noon. She'd spent the entire morning trying to stay even. First, she'd had to build the fire hot enough for her coffee. Then she'd had to replenish the fire to make it hot enough to cook bacon and eggs. After breakfast, she built up the fire again, this time to boil enough water to wash dishes. After doing the dishes, she decided on an after-breakfast cup of coffee, which meant another trip to the pump—and a trip to the woodbox, followed by another wait, while the fire got hot enough to boil water. By the time she'd done everything, it was time for lunch.

She unlocked the Toyota, tossed her canvas bag in the back seat and started the engine. Overhead, the fog was thicker; an oppressive blanket of heavy, leaden gray. The air was damper now, laden with the smell of imminent rain.

With the Toyota's engine idling, giving it time to warm up, she drove slowly down the driveway and stopped short of the gate, leaving enough room to swing it open and drive through. If they were in Peter's truck, it would be her job to jump down, open the gate, then wait for Peter to drive through before she closed the gate and locked it. It was, Peter said, the driver's prerogative that the passenger must serve as gatekeeper.

Leaving the car's door open, with the engine running, she walked to the gate and reached through the redwood slats to unlock the padlock. Now she must walk the gate back to the side of the narrow driveway, and hook it open. Otherwise, a gust of wind could send the gate crashing into the side of the car. It had happened once, to Peter's truck. Except that, to Peter, one more dent didn't matter. On the docks, he'd once said, undented pickups were viewed with some suspicion.

Bending down to hook the gate, she heard a car coming up the access road, from the county road. The car was coming slowly, its engine idling. Could it be Peter? Could he have called her in town, and missed her, and decided that—

Through the trees that bordered the road, she caught a glimpse of bright orange, moving toward the gate. It was the car she'd seen earlier. The stranger was coming back.

Instinctively, she quickened her steps, seeking the security of the Toyota. With the door closed and locked, with the engine running, she could—

Emerging from the screen of thick-growing pines that grew beside the driveway, the orange car—a Chevrolet—was pulling across the entrance to the driveway, blocking it. The car stopped; its engine died. Inside the car, she could see the driver moving, opening the driver's door, on the far side of the car. The dark-haired man was getting out of the Chevrolet. He was rounding the front of the car, smiling easily at her as he came closer. His features were regular, and his smile was pleasant. He moved gracefully, carrying his slim body with an easy assurance. Or was it arrogance?

Uncertain what to do, she simply stood in the driveway facing him. Why was her heart hammering? Why had her throat suddenly gone dry?

"Hello—" He lifted his hand, half waving. His smile remained fixed, but she could see his eyes moving beyond her, narrowing slightly as he scanned the clearing, and the cabin. Did he know that she'd been alone in the cabin? With only one car visible—her car—it would be easy for him to guess the truth.

Now his eyes returned to her. His smile widened as he asked, "Are you Denise Holloway?"

"Why—yes." Surprised, she turned to face him fully. "Who're you?"

"My name is James Carson." Within an arm's length of her now, he stopped. "I came up on the plane with your father. Did he tell you?"

"Why, I, ah—" Why was she stammering? Why was she involuntarily backing away? "No, he didn't."

If the stranger—James Carson—had come to San Francisco with her father, then he must have stayed in the limousine during her father's visit.

"Do you work for my father?"

Amused at the question, he genially shook his head. Speaking with an easy, informal familiarity, he said, "No, Denise. I don't work for your father."

"But you—you said you came up on the plane with him. And you know me."

He stood silently for a moment before he said, "I've known about you for a long while. A long, long while." As he said it, she saw the easy smile fade. With the smile gone, the face changed. The brown, muddy eyes, fixed now on her face, seemed to grow smaller, more intense. The mouth was distorting, twisted into a corruption of the smile. It was a deceptive, unpredictable face—a dangerous face.

She realized that, involuntarily, she'd moved toward the Toyota, still standing with its door open, its engine idling.

But he was moving with her—now ahead of her. He moved swiftly, smoothly—with a precise, practiced purposefulness. He slid into the Toyota, switched off the engine, took the keys from the ignition.

"*Hey!* What're you *doing?*" As if she were listening from outside herself, she realized that her outraged exclamation was fugitive from her childhood—from all the terrible fights she'd had with Elton. Was it possible that, from then until now, she'd never been threatened?

Was she threatened?

In danger?

Yes. This man—this stranger—threatened her. But why couldn't she run? What perverse stubbornness kept her fixed where she stood, facing him as she'd faced Elton, so long ago?

Getting out of the Toyota and turning to confront her, he moved with the same smooth, lithe economy of motion that, already, she identified with him. He used his left hand to drop her keys into the pocket of his jacket. His right hand had disappeared under the jacket—and now reappeared, holding a knife. It was a hunting knife, with a thick, strong blade: the same kind of knife that Peter sometimes used. He held the knife low, with a thumb on top of the blade.

Now the corrupted, distorted smile returned: a diabolical twisting of his mouth. A kind of manic glee tore at his face, leaving only the brown eyes strangely dead. He was smiling because of the fear he could certainly see in her eyes—the fear that was suddenly choking her, suffocating her, immobilizing her.

The fear that was, plainly, his purpose for being there.

Your relative, Mr. Byrnes had said.

Her relative? With his face twisted into this sadistic leer? Holding the knife as if it were a holy relic, something to be delicately, lovingly caressed?

"What're you doing?" she said again. But, this time, she could hardly manage the words. Where had the bluster gone—the echo of her childhood bravado? "Wh—" Her throat closed. But, somehow, she must get it out: "Who are you?"

"I'm James Carson," he said, his voice low and soft, silkily malicious. "I've already told you."

"But—"

From her left, from the direction of the county road, she heard the sound of an engine. As if the sound triggered the instinct, she was moving sharply away from him, toward the sound—toward help, and surely safety. But, instantly, she felt his hand clamped on her wrist—felt a pain low in her back, above the waist. It was the knife.

The knife.

He was close behind her, twisting her arm behind her back. She could feel his breath on her neck as he said, "Get in the car. Your car. *Now.*"

Pain shot through her shoulder as he levered her toward the car—off balance, stumbling, almost falling.

"Get *in.*" He hurled her into the front seat, behind the steering wheel. "Slide over. *Quick.*"

Sobbing now, fighting the steering wheel, the shift lever, the brake handle, she was obeying him. Everything was blurred, because of the tears that stung her eyes. She felt him beside her now—felt something hard on her upper thigh. It was the knife blade, shimmering through the tears. The knife was pressed flat on her thigh, its point touching the cleft of her pubes. He held the knife with his left hand, across his body. With his right hand, also crossing his body, he was awkwardly groping for her keys, in his jacket pocket.

"If they stop," he hissed, "you better fucking well wave, and smile at them. Or I'm going to run this knife all the way in. *All* the way in. You hear?"

She couldn't answer—couldn't take her eyes from the bright, obscene knife.

The sound of the car engine was coming closer. Was it Peter? Please God, was it Peter? Could he have—

A dusty white van was visible through the trees, bouncing along the rutted road at a faster-than-safe speed. The single passenger—the driver—didn't look aside, didn't wave. It was another stranger. The van was drawing even with the orange Chevrolet—quickly gone, now only as real as the sound of its engine, diminishing as the driver continued on his way, up the hill toward the Taylor place. Something had been lettered on the side of the van. Meaning that the driver was probably a repairman, or a delivery man. Not a friend. Not someone who would help her, or recognize her.

The Toyota's starter was whirring; the engine caught, roared. Using his right hand, Carson was putting the car in reverse, backing it expertly up the driveway, swinging it into the parking place she'd just left. Carson switched off the engine, and returned the keys to his pocket.

"Now," he said, "we do it all over again, except with my car. Then we close the gate, and we lock it. And then we go inside—" He nodded to the cabin. "And we talk. Right?" The last word was almost a whisper. It was a lover's question, spoken as a lover might speak: intimately, softly. As he said it, she felt the point of the knife touch her cleft.

It was a lover's touch: gentle and delicate—yet knowing, probing, promising.

"And so," he was saying, "that's the whole story. Everything. Now you've got the whole picture. You and me together, we're going to make me a million dollars. Cash and carry." Smiling as he spoke, he looked at his wristwatch. He sat in the big old overstuffed easy chair that they'd found in a Mendocino flea market—the chair Peter always sat in. Carson had taken a small suitcase and a rifle from the trunk of the Chevrolet and brought them inside. Both the suitcase and the rifle were obviously new, doubtless bought in Mendocino, earlier in the day. Ordering her to sit on the dilapidated couch, he'd put the suitcase beside the easy chair, then sat down. From the suitcase, he'd taken a box of cartridges—caliber .30–.30, she'd read on the box. With maddening smugness, smiling, he'd explained that it was illegal to carry loaded firearms in an automobile. He'd also said, regretfully, that he couldn't get a pistol—not in less than a week's time. Then, with slow, deliberate fingers, he'd loaded the rifle: five cartridges, each thrust into a small, hinged receptacle on the side of the rifle. It was a frontier-style rifle, the kind she remembered from Western movies. When he'd finished loading the rifle, he'd worked the lever and then raised the gun, aiming it directly at her chest, between her breasts. He'd laughed as he'd done it—a high, unsteady laugh, terrifying for its tremor of latent hysteria. Finally, he'd lowered the gun, then eased off the hammer. Now he sat with the rifle across his knees. At his belt, the bone handle of the hunting knife protruded from its leather sheath.

Stealing a glance at her watch, she saw that the time was two twenty-five. For more than two hours, she'd sat immobile on the couch, listening to him talk. It had been an incredible monologue—an eerie, rambling, often inchoherent account of one man's hell on earth. Yet, in the beginning, he'd been crisp and concise, describing his plan in short, terse sentences. First, he'd said, he would chain her up, here in the cabin. As he'd said it, he'd opened the suitcase again, this time producing two long lengths of chain, and three padlocks. He'd dangled the chains before her, leering like some grotesque puppeteer, displaying the strings that would make her dance and shuffle to his command.

Then, he'd said, he would drive to a nearby gas station, where he would phone her father. He would take her driver's license, and her social security card. To prove that she was his captive, he would read the cards' numbers to her father. Then he would spell out his demands, and his instructions for delivery of the ransom. The delivery, he'd said, would be somewhere in San Francisco. She would be left here, in the cabin, still in chains. When he had the money, he said, he would make another call, telling her father where to find her.

That much, he'd told her quickly, briskly. But then he'd begun telling her why he was doing it. Austin Holloway, he'd said, had schemed against him—schemed to have him jailed, conspired to have him killed. Then, as if to justify his actions, he'd begun to ramble, describing how her father had worked against him and his mother, all their lives. As he'd talked, he'd become more agitated. His voice had risen; his mouth had begun twisting and writhing—slowly going wild. Even his eyes, at first so strangely expressionless, had kindled at the memory of his past life, snapping sparks of hatred. As he continued regressing into his childhood, the focus of his fury directed itself against his mother—and, striking an occasional glancing blow, at his uncle.

And, sometimes, his anger had focused on her—on her privileges, and her manners, and even on the clothes she wore: the blue jeans and the wool plaid shirt. She was, he'd said, pretending to be something she wasn't: a "poor girl," instead of a "rich bitch."

Every time he'd said it—rich bitch—his voice had risen, his mouth had contorted. As his story rambled on and his focus veered from childhood to prison, from all the wrongs he'd suffered to all his fantasies for the future, she'd seen sweat begin to glisten on his forehead. Clamped on the rifle, his hands had been white-knuckled. His breath had come faster, rattling in his throat.

Until, finally, he'd spewed out the essence: Austin Holloway was his father, and she was his half sister. And he hated both of them "for what they'd done to him."

Having said it—accused her and her father of ruining his life—he'd fallen silent, staring at her with his strange, dulled eyes, as flat and lusterless as two pieces of dark brown lava.

"Are you—" Her throat closed. She shook her head, coughing. She had to talk—had to get him talking. Dealing with psychopaths, she'd read, it was essential to get them talking—*keep* them talking.

"Are you sure that my—my father and your mother—" Suddenly aware that she'd made a mistake, she broke off. Saying instead: "Are you sure that my father—" It was another false start. Finally: "Are you sure—positive—that he's your father?"

"I'm sure," he answered, his voice deadly calm now. "I've seen the papers. Everything."

"Were they—they married? Before he married my mother?"

For a moment he didn't respond. Gripping the gun barrel, his finger tightened. Then, speaking softly, venomously sibilant, he said: "No, they weren't married. My mother was his whore. And it drove her crazy. That's where she is now—in an asylum. And he's going to pay for it. And you'll pay, too."

"But why me?"

"Because," he answered, "you're both guilty."

"Both guilty? Of what?"

"Of driving my mother insane."

"But that's cra—that's unfair. Completely unfair. How could I have done anything to her?"

He didn't answer—didn't stir. He only stared.

"Have you ever considered the possibility of just asking him—for help—for money? If what you say is true—if you can prove it—then my father will help you. I know he will. If he owes you something, he'll pay. I—I'll help you, if you like. I'll talk to him."

"You'd talk to the police. That's who you'd talk to—the police. I can see it in your face."

"No, you're wrong. I promise you, I'll—"

"Besides, I've already asked him. That's why we're here. Because I tried to see him. And I couldn't see him. So now, he'll pay. And you'll pay, too."

"But, Christ, you—"

Suddenly he rose to his feet, angrily gesturing with the rifle barrel. "Get up, and get into the goddamn kitchen. Let's see how you like being chained to that goddamn stove, in there, while I make a couple of phone calls."

Twenty-Four

"HERE IT COMES," Flournoy said, "as advertised."

On the TV screen, Merv Griffin was looking straight into the lens as the camera came in for a closeup.

"And now," Griffin said, "I think, ladies and gentlemen, that you're going to be very interested in what our next guest is going to say. Because he's someone who's known, literally, to millions of you. His name is Austin Holloway, and he's one of the handful of people—TV pastors—who has, literally, changed the face of religion in America.

"But first, before we talk to Mr. Holloway, and learn about the truly revolutionary project that he's working on—the crusade that, in the last week or so, has created interest throughout the entire world—let me show you a couple of film clips."

Exactly on cue, Griffin's face dissolved, replaced by an animated shot of the Temple. It was a night shot, with a perfect camera angle. In the foreground, magnified by the perspective, the Eternal Fountain was a graceful, frothing plume of multicolored irridescence, lit by floodlights from below. In the background, the broad steps and soaring columns of the Temple had never looked more dramatic. To himself, Holloway nodded. Cowperthwaite, he knew, had worked closely with the NBC camera crew. So, as soon as the segment was finished, he would call Cowperthwaite and—

Beside him, on the end table, his telephone buzzed. Annoyed, he glanced down at the row of buttons. Surprisingly, the button for his private line was glowing. Or, as Flournoy had once said, his "private, private" line. His hot line.

Flournoy had seen it too. He was gesturing toward the phone, offering to take the call. But, on the screen, the picture of the Temple of Today was fading away, replaced by a hairspray commercial. Holloway lifted the phone.

"It's Mitchell." His voice conveyed a sense of urgency—of trouble.

James Carson had called. The other shoe had dropped. Hard. Glancing at Flournoy, he saw his own misgivings instantly reflected in his manager's eyes.

"What is it?" he asked, speaking softly into the phone.

"I'm sorry to interrupt you. But I thought I should. I'm afraid I've got some bad news."

Still with his eyes on Flournoy, he repeated: "Bad news?"

"He's got Denise. I'm sorry."

"He's *what?*"

As he said it, he felt his stomach heave. And—yes—a sudden pain shot through his chest. Alarmed, Flournoy was on his feet, standing over him. Protectively. Possessively.

"He's got Denise. Up in San Francisco, I think. He just called."

It was Katherine's fault, then. Like so many others, this problem had started with Katherine. His nemesis. His ancient, eternal cross. How could he have done it? How could he have married her, so many years ago?

And now, the final straw, she'd jeopardized them all: Denise, the new crusade. Everything. It could all come tumbling down. Police—publicity—pictures in the papers, on TV. It was all there, implicit in the tone of Mitchell's voice—in the stark words the headlines would shriek: HOLLOWAY DAUGHTER KIDNAPPED.

On the TV screen, the commercial was fading. Merv Griffin was on his feet, smiling, turning toward the wings—

—as he materialized, advancing across the stage, hand outstretched. Smiling. Nodding. Walking with a firm, sure stride.

"Shall I come in?" Mitchell was asking.

"In ten minutes," he answered. "Wait ten minutes, then come in."

"So that's all I know," Mitchell said, spreading his big hands and shaking his head. "That's everything."

Flournoy was on his feet, pacing the small sitting room that opened off Holloway's office. "Are you positive—absolutely positive—that the driver's license and the social security numbers were hers?"

Plainly contemptuous of the question, Mitchell simply shrugged. "The numbers checked. Or, at least, the driver's license checked. I won't know about the social security number until tomorrow."

"But—" Flournoy gestured angrily. "He could've broken in. He could've stolen her purse. Did you ever think of that?"

"I did," Mitchell answered. "And it's possible, I suppose. Anything's possible. Still, two things are for sure. He's got her wallet, and he's called long distance. So he's probably in San Francisco. He couldn't be anywhere else."

"A million dollars," Flournoy fumed. "It's crazy. Insane."

Aware that his arms and legs felt heavy and useless, Holloway pushed himself to a more erect posture in the leather armchair. The heaviness, he knew, was a delayed reaction. It was shock. And fear. And infirmity, too—a faltering of the heart, depriving his limbs of their essential flow of blood. Resulting, therefore, in this heaviness—this strange, improbable lassitude in the face of crisis. Yet, somehow, he must take charge—take command.

"How long ago did he call?"

It was, he knew, an ineffectual beginning. He could hear uncertainty in the question. Uncertainty, and fear.

Mitchell glanced at his watch. "About forty-five minutes ago. I called Denise, of course. When I didn't get an answer, I called the DMV—called a friend, there. Then I called you."

"When is Carson going to phone again?"

"He didn't say. But I'd guess tomorrow."

"Did you tape the conversation?" Asking the question, Flournoy's voice was sharp. His eyes were hard, coldly calculating the odds. As always.

Mitchell nodded. "Naturally."

"And you're sure it was him. You recognized the voice."

Once more, Mitchell nodded. "I'm sure."

"If he's got Denise," Holloway said slowly, "then we've got to call the police."

"*If* he's got Denise," Flournoy snapped, adding angrily: "That's still not for certain."

"But Mitchell tried to call her," Holloway said. It was, he knew, another ineffectual-sounding comment—a mild-mannered protest, nothing more. Somehow it was all he could manage—all his body would allow. But he must say something more. Anything: "She wasn't home," he said finally.

"That doesn't mean she's kidnapped, though," Flournoy said shortly. Peremptorily, he turned to Mitchell. "Do you know people in San Francisco? People we can trust?" Rapping out the questions, pacing the sitting room as if it were a quarterdeck, Flournoy was taking command—an irresistible force in a pinstriped suit.

"I know a couple of people," Mitchell answered thoughtfully. "I can trust them to keep quiet. But I don't know how good they are. In an emergency, I mean."

"Do they have organizations?"

"Yes. Both of them do. They each have three or four employees."

"Is there anyone in the police department? Anyone who won't talk?"

Regretfully, Mitchell shook his head. "There're people here. Several people. But no one in San Francisco."

Still pacing, Flournoy stopped at the far end of the room. Standing with his back to a bank of bookcases, the manager stared at both of them in turn. "The first thing we've got to do is get up to San Francisco." Then, speaking directly to Holloway: "I think Mitchell and I should go. Immediately. We'll take one of his men. We'll get help, up there, if we need it—private help. The first thing we'll do is verify that she's really been kidnapped. For that, we don't need the police. Meanwhile—" He frowned, considering. Once more, he began pacing, talking as he walked—gesticulating as he talked. "Meanwhile, Austin, I think you should put Elton in the picture. Tell him what's happened—and what *might* happen. Or, if you like—" Flournoy hesitated again, plainly to emphasize what he intended to say next: "Or, if you like, I can talk to him. That might be better. I'll tell him to stick with you—stay at home with you, tonight, and stay with you, tomorrow, to intercept another call. And, of course, I'll be in touch with him, when I find out anything. And, of course—" Another pause, this time fatuous. "Of course, I'll be in touch with you, too."

With an effort, Holloway nodded. "Of course," he repeated.

Twenty-Five

HE SHIFTED the pickup into reverse, glanced back at the traffic, then leaned across the big poodle sitting on the seat beside him to look up at their front window. The window was only dimly lit, with faint light coming from the hallway.

She was out, then. Still out.

With her mother?

Not with her mother?

He waited for one car to pass, then another. Beside him, Pepper was whining anxiously, pawing at the door. Across the street, Harry Byrnes was closing his store, switching off the lights. Meaning that the time was eight o'clock. Rolling down the window, he called, "Hi, Harry. How's it going?"

"Fine." Harry Byrnes rattled the door of his store, then raised a hand, indicating that he wanted to talk. Watching the other man come across the street, dressed in his blue pea coat and walking like a squat, bandy-legged sailor just coming off ship, Peter smiled. Harry Byrnes was an original: rough-cut and honest. He stepped from the street to the sidewalk, waiting for the other man beside the pickup.

"How've you been, Harry? Seems like it's been a year since I've seen you."

"Yeah, me too," Byrnes admitted, offering a stubby, callused hand. His grip, as always, was hard and contentious. Harry was a competitive man.

Byrnes looked inside the truck. "Where's Denise?"

"I don't know." He looked at the other man more closely. "Why?"

"Well, she left for Mendocino—your cabin. Isn't that where you were?"

"Oh—Christ." Exasperated, he shook his head.

"Why Christ? What's wrong?"

"I spent yesterday evening and most of today with friends.

They live about twenty miles from the cabin. Then, this evening, I came down here. I missed her, then."

"Yeah, I see—" Reflectively, Byrnes looked up at their living room window. Something, plainly, was bothering him. Some puzzle. Some problem.

"What is it, Harry? What's up?"

"Well—" Byrnes frowned, passing a reflective hand over his bald head. "Well, I got to tell you, there's been a lot happening around here the past couple of days."

Aware that his viscera had suddenly tightened, he said, "How do you mean?"

"Well, first, Denise's mother left. That was yesterday, just before noon. Her father and her brother came in a big black limousine, with a chauffeur and everything. So then, while all that was going on, there was another guy showed up—a young fella, maybe twenty-five or so, who said he was related to Denise."

"Related to her?"

"Yeah."

"A cousin, probably. Something like that."

Harry Byrnes shrugged. "Who knows? All I know, he seemed a little peculiar to me. I mean, I got the feeling he was conning me. You know—like he wasn't stating his real business."

"What'd he want?"

Byrnes shrugged again. "I guess he just wanted to find out about her—where she lived, I guess. Because, when Denise came over before she left for Mendocino, to ask me if I'd look after your papers, and everything—which I did—it turned out this guy hadn't even rung her bell."

"What time did Denise leave?"

"About four o'clock yesterday afternoon."

"Christ. I probably just missed her."

"You want to hear the rest?" Byrnes asked truculently.

"There's more?"

Byrnes nodded. "There's more. That's what I been *telling* you."

"Well—tell me." To himself, Peter smiled. Harry Byrnes hadn't mellowed during the past two weeks.

"Well," Byrnes said, "about an hour ago, some other guys showed up, for God's sake, asking about Denise, and everything. And these guys, they've got a private eye with them, if you can believe that."

"A private eye?"

Byrnes nodded again. "Definitely. He showed me his credentials, and everything."

"What'd he want?"

"He just wanted to know where Denise was. Just like the other guy. The cousin, or whoever he was."

"Did you tell the private eye where she was?"

"No," Byrnes said, "I didn't."

"Why'd they ask you? Did they know that you knew where she'd gone?"

"I don't think so. They were just asking around, it looked like to me—just winging it. There were three guys, besides this private eye. The three, they stayed in the car, while the private eye, he asked the questions. At least, that's how it looked."

"Did he go inside our building, do you know?"

"I'm not sure. I had customers, see, and I—*Hey.*" Byrnes suddenly pointed down the block. "There they are again, parking behind that sports car, there. That big blue car."

Turning, hands propped on his hips, he watched the blue sedan's lights go out. The car was a half block away. In the glow of the streetlamp, he could see four figures inside. Three of the men wore hats, an unusual sight in San Francisco.

"Well," Byrnes said, "You can take it from here. Me, I'm going home. There's an old Bogart movie on channel forty-four. *They Drive by Night.* Ever see it?"

He nodded. "Yes, it's a good movie—a good, sound story."

"How'd the writing go up in Mendocino?"

"Fine, thanks. Just fine."

"Good. Well, I'll see you tomorrow. Let me know what those fellas want, will you?"

"I will. And thanks, Harry."

"You're welcome." Byrnes waved, and walked away, going in the opposite direction from the parked car. Inside the pickup, Pepper was whining.

"Just a minute, boy. Just hold it a few more minutes, if that's the problem." He stepped to the side of the pickup bed, and lifted out his chain saw and toolbox. Since Denise's mother was gone, he could take the tools inside. Tomorrow, in daylight, he would take the tools down the outside staircase, to their large storage locker.

Eyeing the blue sedan, he walked to the entrance of their building, put down the tools and opened the mailbox. Four letters were inside, three for Denise and one for him—from Los Angeles. He turned the letter over, frowning at the return address, strange to him. Using his key to open the outside door, he shoved his toolbox into the opening, to keep the door from swinging shut. He would—

"Excuse me." It was a man's voice, behind him. The private eye, undoubtedly.

This was the one without a hat: a tall, stooped, gaunt man wearing a corduroy jacket, a wrinkled tie and nondescript trousers, baggy at the knees. His long, sad face was sallow, drawn at the mouth and nostrils. His eyes were hollow and haggard.

"You live in the building, here." It was a statement, not a question.

He let a moment pass, silently eyeing the other man. Then, quietly, he said, "And you're looking for Denise Holloway."

Impassively, the other man nodded. "That's right. You found out from the storekeeper."

"Correct."

The stranger took a step forward, at the same time reaching inside his jacket. Peter raised a hand. "Don't bother. I already know that you're a private detective. What's it all about, anyhow?"

Speaking quietly, in a low, tired-sounding voice, the detective said, "You know Denise, then. Miss Holloway." Once again, he hadn't asked a question. He'd stated a fact.

"That's right. I know her."

"Have you seen her today, by any chance?"

"Look—" He stepped closer to the other man: a taut, purposeful movement. "Look, it just so happens that I'm a friend of Denise's. A *good* friend. So I'd like to know—right now—why you're looking for her. And I'd also like to know who your friends are, and what interest they have in Denise's whereabouts."

Utterly unintimidated, the detective was calmly staring him straight in the eye. Finally, moving his chin toward the blue sedan and speaking in the same low, tired voice, he said, "Those men—the three of them—they work for Austin Holloway. Denise's father. They're—concerned about Denise. They want to know where she is, so they can tell her father. The three of them, they've flown up here, just today, to see about it. So you can see it's important."

"I can see they *think* it's important."

The detective shrugged his bony shoulders.

"Who're you, anyhow?"

"I'm Harold Granbeck. Lloyd Mitchell—he's in charge of security for Austin Holloway—he retained me."

"Why?"

"Because I know the territory." Once more, the thin shoulders lifted. "It's the usual thing to do. It saves time and trouble."

"Why is this Mitchell concerned about Denise? What's happened, anyhow?"

"Listen, mister, I don't have the answers. I'm just a hired hand. And, even if I had the answers—which I don't—it wouldn't be my place to give them to you. Now—" He lifted a long, scarecrow arm. "Now, why don't you go inside, and I'll ask them to come inside and fill you in. You can decide for yourself how much you want to tell them. What do you say?"

For a long, hard moment he stared at the other man. Then, gracelessly, he nodded abrupt agreement.

He looked at the three men sitting side by side on the couch: three blue-suited clones by Hart Schaffner and Marx, out of IBM, each one dressed alike—yet with differences, as befitted their rank and station. Flournoy, the leader—Holloway's hatchet man, apparently—was dressed like a Wall Street broker. With his narrow, cruel face and his cold, calculating eyes, Flournoy could have been a reincarnation of Iago, or Machiavelli, or Himmler.

With his dark, dead eyes, his implacable mouth and his strangler's hands—with his big, burly plowman's body stuffed into a blue suit with padded shoulders—Mitchell could have been a medieval hangman. Or, in later years, a dark, ominous presence in the back halls of Hoover's FBI—or Nixon's White House. Mitchell was a true believer. Whatever he was told to do, he would do.

The third man, named Calloway, was the least of the lot: a mere look-alike, along to provide ballast, to give an appearance of substance to the mission. Calloway was a lightweight—a hanger-on.

Of the four men—the four intruders into what should have been his tender, passionate homecoming—only Harold Granbeck was credible. Sitting slumped in his chair, occasionally scratching reflectively at his crotch, Harold Granbeck was doing a job—earning his hourly wage.

Flournoy was speaking again. His voice, like his persona, was both calculating and thinly abrasive:

"The first thing we've got to do, Mr. Giannini, is find her. That is, we've got to determine whether, in fact, James Carson has her. That, I'd think, should be obvious. And it also should be obvious, I'd think, that the sooner we get to it, the better."

"I agree. Which is exactly—" He pointed to the phone, beside his chair. "Which is exactly why I say we should call the police. We should call the Mendocino sheriff's department. Now. Right now."

Flournoy's thin lips drew together in an expression of pained disapproval. "I've already tried to explain to you, Mr. Giannini, that Mr. Holloway—her father—doesn't want it handled like that." He, too, pointed to the phone. "You heard me call Mr. Holloway, just now. You heard the conversation. I purposely repeated his instructions, so you'd understand."

"But—Christ—we're talking about her *safety*. Her *life*. You—Christ—what you're proposing would take *hours*. She could *die*, in the time it'll take us to get up there."

"Mr. Holloway doesn't think so."

"Oh. I see. Well, Mr. Flournoy, frankly I find Mr. Holloway's attitude very hard to understand. It seems to me that he's more concerned about his reputation—his image—than he is about his daughter's well-being. Christ, if this—this creep has her, which seems likely, there's no telling *what* he could be doing to her, right this minute. And, more to the point, there's no telling what he could be doing in the next four hours, which is the time it'll take us to get up there."

Flournoy consulted a wafer-thin gold watch. "We've already been here for a half hour, Mr. Giannini."

"That's true. But—"

"Why don't we get in the car, and drive to your cabin? It's the logical first step. Let's find out whether he's there. As you describe it, we should be able to determine that without any risk whatever—to anyone. Without doing more than driving past the cabin. If we see a car—or two cars—we'll know where we stand."

"And then what? Suppose they *are* there. Then we've still got to call the police."

"Agreed. The point is, Mr. Holloway doesn't want to call the police until it's absolutely necessary. For reasons I've already explained to you."

"And which reasons I find—incredible."

Sighing, Flournoy didn't reply, but instead glanced pointedly at his watch.

"Well—" He gestured again to the phone. "There's nothing to prevent me calling the police. Which is precisely what I intend to do."

Harold Granbeck cleared his throat, speaking for the first time: "It won't do you any good, Mr. Giannini. What we've got here is essentially a missing-person situation. The police get thousands every month. Which is the reason they don't even act on a complaint for forty-eight hours. That's because, ninety-nine times out of a hundred, the cases are domestic beefs that ended with someone running off. And, when the police *do* act, they only do it on information supplied by next of kin."

"Bullshit."

Granbeck shrugged. "It's not bullshit, Mr. Giannini. If you were the young lady's husband, that's something else. But the way it is now, when you tell them the situation, the first thing they'd want to do is talk to Mr. Holloway. So you're right back to where you started. Except that, in the process, you'd've gone against Mr. Holloway's wishes. And, after all, he's got some rights here. You might not agree with the way he wants to handle the situation. But, still, he *is* her father."

As if speaking on cue, counterpointing Granbeck's slurred, slovenly style, Flournoy spoke quietly, in his dry, precise voice: "If Mr. Holloway weren't deeply concerned for his daughter, Mr. Giannini, we wouldn't be here. Would we?"

"He doesn't give a damn about Denise. He's worried about his own skin. Period."

Flournoy didn't reply—only stared, reproachfully.

"Oh, *shit*." He got to his feet, and reached for his jacket. Lying beside him, startled, Pepper barked.

Twenty-Six

SHE WATCHED HIM get up from the room's only arm-chair—Peter's chair—and cross to the fireplace. Inexorably, her eyes moved to the hunting rifle, propped in a far corner of the room. Twice during the last hours he'd gone to a position in the room that put them at equal distances from the gun. It had been, almost certainly, a ruse to test her—or to tempt her. Did he hope that she would make a try for the gun, giving him an excuse to begin struggling with her? Rapists, she'd heard, got their kicks from the fight women put up, not from the actual sex act.

At the fireplace, he raised the hunting knife and drove it down into the redwood mantel. Then he took an oak log and threw it carelessly on the fire. A shower of sparks erupted, some of them falling on the rug beside the stone hearth. Smiling slightly, he looked at her—then looked down at the rug, already smouldering. Finally—languidly—he stepped on the rug, grinding out the sparks.

"When we leave," he said, "maybe I'll set it on fire. But not now. Not tonight. We need a place to sleep. Right?"

She didn't answer.

"Right?"

In reply, she sighed. It was, she hoped a bored-sounding sigh, projecting long-suffering impatience, rather than the sick, empty fear she felt, almost a physical sensation centered in the pit of her stomach.

He levered the hunting knife from the mantel. Holding the knife loosely in his right hand, delicately balanced, he came toward her.

"You're not talking much." He stood over her, still toying idly with the broad-bladed knife. He'd told her how he'd gotten the knife and the rifle. Last night, he said, hidden in the undergrowth beside the road, he'd seen her lights go out. He'd let another hour pass, making sure she'd gone to sleep. Then he'd gone into town, and gotten a room. This morning, he'd bought the gun and the knife and the chains, then returned to resume his vigil, this time parked in his car on the county road close beside the turnoff to the access road. He'd told his story in great detail, plainly for the purpose of impressing her with his planning, his prowess. His whole life had come down to a sharp, single focus: the humiliation and destruction of Austin Holloway. With that done—with the million dollars to prove it—he would be transformed. Austin Holloway's power would become his power. He would be invincible: a superior being, capable of anything. Nietzsche's superman.

All of it calculated, subconsciously, to conceal from himself the terrible truth: that he was just another strutting, posturing punk who fondled his gun and his knife as if they were phallic extensions of himself—and who cowered among his own fantasies, too frightened to come out and face reality.

"I said, you're not talking much." He spoke softly, insinuatingly, with a different, more sensual inflection. His expression was different, too: suggestive, subtly lascivious. He was thinking of bed—thinking of her. During all their time together—from noon until now, eleven o'clock—he hadn't touched her, hadn't spoken of sex. Instead, he'd talked of his megalomaniacal plans. But she'd seen him watching her—seen him run his eyes over her body—slowly, deliberately, speculatively.

How would it begin? Would he hold the knife to her throat while he forced her to undress?

Would she do it?

Could she do it?

Should she do it?

He took one last step. Sitting on a straightback chair, she was forced to look up at an uncomfortably sharp angle to see his face. The point of the knife was less than a foot from her face. He meant for her to look at the knife—meant for her to tremble at the sight, to mutely beg him for mercy.

So she mustn't look at the knife.

She must continue to look up into the face, staring straight into his dull, deadman's eyes. She mustn't let him see that, yes, she was terrified of the knife gleaming like burnished silver in the soft light from the two kerosene lamps.

"What're you thinking about?" he asked softly.

What should she say? How should she say it? Words were her only weapons—her only hope. She must try to manipulate him, confuse him, keep him off balance—all without antagonizing him.

But how? With which words?

"I was just thinking," she said, "that I wish I was home."

Why had she said it. *Why?* To what purpose—what possible advantage?

"So you can go to sleep in your own little bed. Is that it?"

"It's something like that."

"With your man. With Peter." He spoke in a flat, hostile voice, as if he were pronouncing an obscenity. Earlier in the day, when he'd asked her whether she was married, she'd told him about Peter. She'd done it without thinking, without calculating the consequences.

Now, watching him and listening to him, she realized that Peter had become yet another focus for his hatred.

"Where is he now?" he asked finally. "Right now?"

"He's in—" She broke off. *Where?* "He's in Los Angeles," she finished. "He writes movie scripts, and he's down there talking about one. It's a TV script, actually."

Mincingly—furiously—he mimicked her: "'It's a TV script, actually.'" Saying it, his mouth twisted into a savage rictus. "Is that what they taught you in your college?"

"I—I don't know what you mean."

"'It's a TV script, actually,'" he repeated. "Is that how you talk when you're raised in Beverly Hills? They tell you to use words like 'actually,' that don't mean a goddamn thing. Right?"

"It's—it's just a manner of speech."

"Oh. I see." Wickedly mocking, he nodded. Once more mimicking: "'Just a manner of speech.' Oh, how fancy it all is. How terribly, terribly fancy."

"It's not fancy. It's just—" She spread her hands. "It's just the way I talk."

"Does Peter talk like that, too?"

She hesitated, and then decided to say, "No. Peter talks more plainly than I do, I guess you'd say."

"How long have you lived together?"

"Not quite two years."

"How many times a week do you and Peter screw?"

She didn't answer. But, still, she must keep her eyes fixed on his. She mustn't cower—mustn't turn away. She mustn't show uneasiness, or fear.

"How does Peter's cock feel inside you? Is it big? Is it hard?"

Still desperately holding his gaze, she didn't reply. Now

197

she saw his expression go blank, as if he was listening to some small, obscene inner voice. He still held the knife in his right hand, as before. But now his left hand was straying across his thigh. Slowly—perhaps unconsciously—he was stroking the bulge of his genitals. Momentarily his eyes lost focus. When he finally spoke, his voice was husky: "Are you getting sleepy?" Asking the question, he moved the knife in the direction of the bedroom, invitingly.

"No."

"I am." His voice was still husky—still slightly slurred.

"Then go to sleep."

"What would you do?" he asked lazily, "If I went to sleep?" As he said it, he continued the slow, erotic caress of his swelling genitalia.

"I'd run," she said suddenly.

His mouth twisted into a slow, smug smile. "You're afraid of me, then."

But his eyes had sharpened. Momentarily, the rhythm of his erotic caress was suspended. Her answer had surprised him, taken him off balance.

She looked down at the knife, then up again into his eyes. "As long as you have that knife, I'm afraid of you." She paused, then decided to say, "Is that what you want to hear?"

He looked at the knife, holding it up before his eyes, pantomiming a pretense that he was seeing it for the first time. Then, looking at her, he said, "What if I gave it to you? Do you think it would change anything?" He spoke softly, speculatively.

"Yes," she answered. "Yes, I think it would. I think it would change everything."

His left hand had resumed its slow, obscene stroking. Very seriously and deliberately, as if he were rendering a decision on some matter of great importance, he slowly shook his head. "No," he said softly, "it wouldn't change anything. It wouldn't change a thing. I could give you this knife—" Tentatively, he extended it toward her with his right hand while he pointed to a nearby wooden chair with his left hand. "And then I could pick up that chair. And I guarantee you that I'd be the winner." He let a beat pass, staring at her intently. Behind his eyes, something shifted—something primitive, and predatory. Something more profound than sex, and infinitely more dangerous. Then, once more, he held out the knife. "You want to try it?"

"No," she answered. "No, I don't." Then without forethought, she added: "And you want to know why?"

For a long, silent moment he continued to stare at her while the atavistic light still guttered behind his dull, dead eyes. He didn't want to answer the question—didn't want to be jolted out of the mood he'd created for himself. But, still, he wanted to know the answer. So, finally, he said, "Why?"

"Because I don't want to hurt you," she said. "I don't want you to hurt me. But I don't want to hurt you, either."

As if to fling the sense of her answer away from him, he sharply gestured. "That's bullshit. That's fucking bullshit. You'd hurt me, if you could. You'd fucking *kill* me, if you could."

"No," she answered. "No, I wouldn't. I don't want to hurt you." She let a long, decisive beat pass. Then, holding his eye steadily with hers, she spoke in a slow, measured voice. Saying quietly: "You're my half brother. Don't you see that?"

Suddenly—wildly—he laughed. "That's clever. That's really clever."

She didn't respond.

"You think you'll protect yourself, by saying that."

In reply, she slowly, silently shook her head.

"Half brother," he spat out. "Shit. I'm just—just what happened when Austin Holloway decided to have a little fun for himself. I grew up in a smelly little house with leaks in the roof and rats in the walls. And you—" Savagely, he slashed the space between them with the knife. "I've seen where you grew up. So don't talk to me about being your brother. You hear?" He broke off. Then, shrilly: *"You hear?"*

She'd scored on him—deflected his obscene intentions, at least for the moment. Words—her chosen weapon—were working.

But she'd also roused his rage, another danger.

"You said your mother—" She hesitated. "You said she's in an asylum. You said that my father keeps her there, just like he kept her all her life. Well, my mother—" Once more, she hesitated. It was an obscenity, to use her mother's affliction to save herself from harm.

But she must do it—must try.

"My mother," she said, "is an alcoholic. She's a hopeless alcoholic. So they're both victims, you see—both your mother and my mother, too."

"You're lying. I've seen her on TV."

"She doesn't get a bottle Saturday night," she muttered.

"She deosn't get one until Sunday, after she finishes doing The Hour. It's been like that for—for almost as long as I can remember." As she said it, she was compelled to drop her eyes before the sudden intensity of his gaze.

Suddenly he stooped over her, furious. Hissing: "You're a liar. You're a fucking liar."

She'd scored again—struck through his defenses again.

"No, I'm not lying." Her voice, she knew, was calm. Convincing.

With the knife held loosely at his side, forgotten, he still bent over her, searching her face with a taut, terrible intensity. Then, slowly, his mouth twisted. This time, his smile was real. Grotesque, but real.

"Your mother's a drunk," he said softly. "And my mother's crazy. What'd they say about something like that? What is it? Poetic justice? Is that what they call it?"

Hesitantly, she nodded. "Yes. Th-that's what they call it. Poetic justice."

"Or maybe it isn't poetic justice. Maybe there's another name for it. Maybe you're just agreeing with me, because of this—" He raised the knife again, holding it toward her, as if to tantalize her with its beauty and power, just beyond her reach.

Trying to hold her gaze steady with his, she didn't answer. She saw his eyes fall to the knife, which he now raised before him until its point came in line between his eyes and hers. Slowly, lovingly, he rotated the blade as it reflected the pale glow of the lamplight across his face. It was a light show— a diabolical light show.

"When I was in prison," he said, "I used to lie in bed and think about knives. I used to think about how important they are." His voice was soft and dreamy. His eyes were pensive, fixed on the knife point. "Do you know how important they are?"

"N–" Her throat closed. "No, I don't. I mean, I—I've never had—" She realized that she was helplessly shaking her head. What did he want her to say? How should she say it? Subserviently? Was that what he wanted from her: subservience? A show of palpable terror?

"If you have a knife," he said, "and the other person doesn't, then you're the master. Whatever you order, the other person's got to do it. And I used to lie in bed, and think about that. I used to think about how a knife is better than a gun. You pull the trigger, and that's it, with a gun. But with a knife, you've got a special edge. With a knife, you can make someone your slave. But, of course, you have to be delicate. You have to use imagination. You have to understand a knife. And you have to make the other person understand. That's probably the most important part, you see." As he said it, his dreamy gaze left the knife, and wandered to her.

"Do you understand?" he asked.

"I—" Helplessly, she shook her head. "I'm not sure. I—" She was aware that she was still futilely shaking her head.

"Stand up," he said softly. "Stand up, and I'll give you a lesson. I'll make you understand."

With her eyes fixed on the blade, she drew her feet beneath her, braced her hands against the arms of the chair, levered herself slowly, heavily to her feet. Would her legs support her? Did he realize that, suddenly, her knees were shaking— that she was hollow at the core, trembling with terror?

"Now—" He lowered the knife until its point was inches from her torso. "Now, first, unfasten your shirt. But do it one button at a time. And when you do it, I don't want you to look down. I want you to look at the knife. Right at the knife."

With numb fingers, she found the top button. The knife followed the task, its sparkling point attentive to her hands. The first button came free. The second button was between her breasts. As if to guide her, the knife moved delicately lower. With the second button unfastened, she heard him softly sigh.

"Two more," he said, lowering the knife to the third button. "Just two more."

Suddenly her eyes filled with tears. She blinked, raised her hand to wipe at her eyes.

"Please," she whispered. "Please."

Beneath the point of her chin, she felt pressure, then pain. It was the knife, forcing her head up.

"The lesson is just beginning, Denise. Just beginning. You don't want to stop now, do you?"

She couldn't speak, couldn't move her head without risking more pain. Was she cut? Did she feel a trickle of warm blood running down her throat?

"Now—" As he spoke, she felt the pressure lessen. "Now, the last two buttons, please."

The knife was in front of her now, offering a sadistic reprieve from the pain. Fiercely she used both hands to clear her eyes of tears, then tore defiantly at the remaining buttons, freeing them.

"Ah—" It was another soft, crooning exhalation. "Ah. Yes—" Deftly, one side at a time, the knife flicked her shirt open. Approvingly, he nodded down at her breasts. "Yes. Very nice, Denise." He nodded again. Repeating: "Very nice."

Involuntarily, she stepped back from his obscene stare. Instantly, the knife came up before here eyes. "No, no," he whispered, as if he were chiding a misbehaving child. "No, no, you can't do that. Don't you see, every time you do something your master doesn't like, you feel the knife? I thought you understood that, Denise."

"No." She realized that her voice was dangerously loud, incoherently protesting. She was vehemently shaking her head. Sudden anger rose in her throat, bitter as bile. *"No."*

"Yes," he crooned, moving closer. "Oh, yes." She saw his manic face move close behind the knife. Then she saw the knife slowly lower between them, disappearing as his eyes held hers.

"Stand still, Denise," he whispered. "Stand very still. Do just as I tell you. Because that's the game, you see. The better you behave—the better you obey—the less I have to hurt you. Do you understand?"

She couldn't answer. Suddenly the trembling returned. She felt her knees shaking. The room was tilting away from her, sliding off into darkness. In her ears, a distant roar was beginning, like faraway surf. At the edge of the darkness, tiny lights were dancing.

"I—I've got to sit down."

"No, no—" Once more, the knife point pricked beneath her chin, them moved toward her throat, under her jaw. "No, Denise, don't faint. Because, if you faint, you could really hurt yourself when you fall. You see?"

To stop the room from spinning, she closed her eyes, surrendering to a sudden void of blackness, and to the strange, eerie roaring. Was this how it felt to die? Was this how it began?

He was whispering something. She could feel his breath on her face. And now, a miracle, the pain was gone. Her master had granted another reprieve from the knife.

"...over here, now," he was saying. "Come over here." As he spoke, she felt him moving away. She opened her eyes, blinked against the tears. He was moving toward the chair, and gesturing for her to follow. He sat in the chair, his legs wide apart. "You sit here," he said, gesturing to the floor at his feet. "You sit between my legs, here, facing me. And we'll play another game, Denise." As he spoke, he suddenly drove the knife into the table beside the chair. The blow was so violent that the table top split.

Twenty-Seven

"IT'S UP THERE—" He pointed. "It's just beyond the next curve. You'd better slow down."

Calloway, the third man from Los Angeles, took his foot from the accelerator as he eased the car smoothly into the curve. He was a good, steady driver. Snatches of conversation during the past hours had suggested that Calloway was Holloway's driver *cum* bodyguard. And a chance remark from Granbeck had revealed that, years ago, Calloway had been in prison. Not once, but twice.

"Right there. See those three mailboxes, set back from the road? That's the turnoff."

Nodding, Calloway braked, swung the big car deftly into the narrow access road. Perhaps Calloway had been a wheelman: the one who waited in the high-powered car outside the bank, engine purring.

"You'll see a big redwood stump on the right side of the road," he said. "My driveway is just on the other side of the stump, about three hundred feet farther up the road. So, when you see the stump, you'd better switch off the lights."

"And let it idle," Mitchell said quietly. "Take it slow and easy."

"Slow and easy. Right." Obediently, Calloway slowed the car. Obviously, Calloway took his orders from Mitchell. Just as obviously, from now on, Mitchell would be in charge. Flournoy, the strategist, had tacitly turned over field command to the big man with the dark, inscrutable eyes. The warrior's time had come. Seated in the front seat beside Calloway, Peter was aware of a visceral tightness, a dryness of the throat, a quickening of the heartbeat. What would they find, around the next curve? For the past several miles, driving in silence through the night, he'd fallen into a curious apathy—almost a surrender of the will. Whatever would happen had probably already happened—or hadn't happened.

Yet, for the first hour, driving across the Golden Gate Bridge and through southern Marin County with these four strangers, his hopes and his fears had swung wildly from a kind of tremulous optimism to a dark, brooding pessimism. At first he'd been sure that nothing could happen to her. Violence was something that happened to strangers—something to read about over morning coffee.

Then he'd lapsed into a terrified certainty that, yes, the worst could happen—and had happened. Meaning that, yes, she could have died. "The worst" was a cop-out phrase, a glib, bland euphemism for disaster.

But, just as certainly, she could be alive, safe in the cabin where they'd spent so many wonderful days—and nights. She could merely have lost her purse, or had it stolen. Nothing more.

Up ahead, the headlights shown on the giant redwood stump, a relic of some long-forgotten, nineteenth century logging operation. A click, and the lights died. Had Calloway done it soon enough? Had the lights been visible from the cabin, warning Carson? He didn't know, couldn't decide. Because, once more, that curious indifference had overtaken him—that strange, frightening apathy.

With the headlights off, the familiar roadside landmarks emerged from the darkness: an ancient, split-rail fence, covered with moss and overgrown with wild grapevines. Now he saw a pile of boulders, crusted with moss and lichen.

They were drawing even with the stump—creeping past it. Exposed.

Through the trees, in the direction of his cabin, he saw a soft glow of golden light—lamplight, shining through the cabin's front windows.

"There it is—" He was whispering as he pointed toward the light. "That's the cabin. She's there." As he said it, he was aware of a sudden, trembling mix of emotion: an unsteady rush of joy, and gratitude, and wild, wanton hope.

And, yes, love.

From the back seat, he heard Mitchell's voice: "Someone's there."

Triggering, instantly, another rush of emotion: a cold, frozen fear. What had been given, could so easily be taken away. Hope was a sucker's game. He'd always known it. Even though he constantly fell for the bait, he'd always known that the celestial odds-makers played on the down side.

Yes, someone was there. It could be Denise—or someone else.

Straining to see through the trees, he felt a hand on his shoulder: a big, heavy hand. Mitchell's.

"Should we go on?" Mitchell asked. "Or should we stop. Can we be seen?"

"I—" He was forced to break off, clear his thorat. "I don't think we can be seen. It's about a hundred yards, from the cabin. Through trees." And then, hearing the uncertainty in his voice, he said, "But maybe we should stop, anyhow. Just to make sure."

At a single word from Mitchell, Calloway braked to a stop, killing the engine. With the engine off, a moment of complete silence followed, broken only by the sound of breathing, and the rustle of clothing as each of them shifted in his seat, straining for a view through the windows.

"Let's get out," Mitchell said quietly. "Three of us. You, Mr. Giannini, and Calloway and me. We want to see about a car—whether there's one car, or two."

As he reached for the door handle, he heard Mitchell say, "Quietly, remember. Very quietly." He swung the door open, stepped out onto the graveled shoulder of the road, eased the door closed until the latch clicked. On the opposite side of the car, Mitchell and Calloway were standing together, whispering. Now Mitchell bent down, said something to Flournoy, then straightened. Raising his hand, he gestured for Peter to come to the front of the car.

"Is that your gate?" Mitchell asked, pointing.

"Yes. But it squeaks. Here—this way." Moving through the waist-high underbrush, he forced his way to the barbed-wire fence. "Climb over here. Hold on to the post." He put a foot on the lowest wire, swung a leg over and dropped to the ground on the other side. To the right, a rushing sound came from the brush; they'd startled a deer. Behind him, Calloway was groping his way awkwardly over the fence.

"Just a minute," Mitchell whispered. In the dim light from a half moon, he saw Mitchell move around to the rear of the car, out of sight. The trunk lid came up, then gently down. Reappearing, Mitchell held something long and narrow in his hands—a rifle, or a shotgun. "Here—" Across the fence, Mitchell handed the gun to Calloway. It was a shotgun, single-barreled, slide action—the kind the police carried in their squad cars.

Quickly, with surprising agility, Mitchell climbed over the

fence, then extended his hand for the shotgun. Calloway handed over the weapon, then reached inside his jacket, withdrawing a pistol.

"Listen—" Peter gestured to the weapons. "Take it easy with those."

"If he's in there," Mitchell said, "then he's probably armed." The big man gestured toward the cabin, with its two lighted living-room windows facing the road. "Let's go. You lead. Let's look for her car."

"All right. But I'm telling you—no shooting. Not with Denise inside."

Instead of replying, Mitchell simply gestured impassively toward the cabin. He held the shotgun across his chest. It was a military posture, evoking a verity as old as the race: that, yes, might made right. Mitchell personified the warrior—the centurion—the enforcer.

"I mean it, goddammit. No shooting."

In response, Mitchell suddenly slid the shotgun's walnut forestock backward and forward, jacking a shell into the chamber. Then, carefully, he used his right thumb to lower the hammer. As—still—he simply stared, impassively waiting for him to lead the way.

Wordlessly, Peter turned away and began picking his way through the brambles and saplings, angling toward the cabin. Behind him, he heard one of the two men trip and fall, heard a voice muttering angrily. Now the tress were thinning. He stopped, turned back, whispered: "The driveway's just ahead. We can see her car from there. But we can be seen from the cabin, too."

"You go ahead," Mitchell answered. "We'll stay back."

"All right."

Holding his breath, he stepped out into the narrow driveway.

Parked close beside the house, he saw two cars—Denise's Toyota and another car: a small, domestic two-door sedan. A Chevrolet, or perhaps an Oldsmobile. A General Motors car.

An intruder's car.

As he stood motionless, he saw a figure move between the lamplight and the right front window, throwing a shadow across the curtains. The shadow was indistinct, indecipherable.

Yet, almost certainly, the shadow wasn't Denise's. He would know it, if the shadow were hers. He would sense it— *feel* it.

Involuntarily, he'd stepped back into the shelter of the trees that lined the driveway, out of sight.

"Someone's in there," he said. "Someone besides her—besides Denise."

"Are you sure?" Mitchell asked. "Absolutely sure?"

"There're two cars—hers, and another one that doesn't belong to either of our neighbors. And, just now, I saw a shadow in the window. It wasn't hers. I'm almost sure."

Mitchell nodded, a slow, grave inclination of his head, saying softly: "The next thing we've got to do is make absolutely sure it's him." His voice was steady, his manner firm and measured. "Is there any way I can see inside, without being seen?"

"Not unless there's a gap in the front-room curtains—or unless he goes into the kitchen. There's no curtain in the kitchen. It's in the rear."

"Here—" Mitchell handed him the shotgun, then drew a pistol from a shoulder holster. "Take this. Wait here."

"What're you going to do?"

"I'm going to take a look."

"No. I—I want to do it. You stay here—the two of you. I know the ground. You don't. You might make noise."

"No. I don't want you to—"

"*Yes*, goddammit." He thrust the shotgun against the other man's chest, hard. Hissing: "If you screw up, it's Denise's neck. I won't risk it."

"Mr. Giannini—we already told you, in your apartment, that Mr. Holloway doesn't want—"

"Screw Holloway. He doesn't care anything about Denise. And neither do you—either one of you. You're just—just hired thugs. And I'm tired of taking orders from you." He pointed down at the ground. "This is my property we're on. And that—" He pointed to the cabin. "That's my lady, in there. You understand?"

Taking the shotgun with his right hand, Mitchell hesitated, then returned the pistol to its shoulder holster. For a long moment they stood silently, toe to toe. Finally—reluctantly—the other man nodded.

"All right, Mr. Giannini. Maybe you're right. But don't come back until you've seen him, and can describe him to me. I want to know his age, and his height, and his weight, and the color of his hair and eyes. I don't care whether it takes an hour. I don't care whether it takes all night. But I want

208

to know who's in there—whether it's Carson. Do you understand?"

He nodded. "I understand."

"All right. Good." A short, appraising pause followed. Then Mitchell asked quietly, "Are you scared?"

"Scared?" He realized that, unaccountably, he was smiling at the big man. "Not now, I'm not. That'll come later."

If he mounted the steps to the porch, the ancient floorboards would creak. But unless he were on the porch, he couldn't hope to see inside, or hear voices from inside. Crouching low beneath the level of the porch, he circled to his right, where the porch railing was attached to the cabin. He gripped the chest-high railing, testing it. The railing was solid. He looked back down the driveway, to the place where he knew that Mitchell and Calloway waited. The darkness revealed nothing: no movement, no gleam of moonlight on metal. He took a deep breath. With one foot on the porch, he gripped the railing and heaved. He was standing erect, both feet placed precariously on the few inches of porch that bordered the spokes of the railing. Nothing had creaked, or groaned, or shifted. Slowly, he raised one leg over the railing, then the other leg. He was standing on the porch, his back pressed to the cabin's wall.

He realized that his breath was coming in short, shallow gasps. He was hyperventilating. Because he was frightened. If Carson was inside, and was armed, the intruder could open the front door and find him defenseless, unable to do anything but try to vault the railing and escape into the trees.

It would be better—safer—to return to Mitchell, and demand that they go to Mendocino, and call the sheriff, and ask for help. As a property owner, he could do it.

But not without Mitchell's help—not without the car. He was nothing more than Mitchell's tool, his toady. Because Mitchell had the weapons. And Mitchell had the remorseless, implacable will. Mitchell was an irresistible force, the elemental man.

The window was an arm's length away. One cautious, soundless step—and another—and another. Close beside the window now, he inched his head around the frame—

—and could see nothing but the curtain, thick, brown burlap, impenetrable.

But, from inside, he heard the faint sound of voices. If he

pressed his ear to the glass, risking discovery, he might be able to hear more clearly—might be able to learn what he must know. It was either that, or a walk across the porch to the other window, hoping for a look inside—and risking discovery with each step, because of the porch's rickety floorboards.

Taking one final step, he pressed his ear to the glass. With startling clarity, he could suddenly hear Denise's voice—and then a man's voice. The actual words were still inaudible, but their sense was unmistakable. Speaking in a low, venomous voice, the intruder was taunting her—threatening her—abusing her. Denise's responses were short and faltering, stifled by uncertainty and fear.

It was enough; he'd learned enough. Whoever was inside, whether Carson or someone else, he was an enemy.

He was moving back along the shingled side of the cabin, toward the railing. He would get back to Mitchell. He would—

Beneath his foot, he felt a floorboard give under his weight. The sound of a creak followed, as loud as a shriek in the silence.

From inside the cabin, he heard a sharp, startled exclamation.

Twenty-Eight

"THIS IS A NEW GAME, Denise." As he said it, he moved his legs until both thighs pressed close against her shoulders. "Do you know how it goes? It's called 'head.' Have you ever heard of it?"

She knelt with her eyes fixed on his waist, at the belt buckle. How long had she been kneeling before him, watching him fondle himself, listening to his obscene ramblings? She didn't know, was helpless to decide. Time had become truncated by terror. Terror, and the bulge of his genitals—and the knife, still stuck in the split table top, within easy reach.

"Before we start playing, though," he said, "I have to make sure you know the rules." He spoke in a slow, sensuously mocking voice. His eyes were half closed; his head lay back against the chair. "Did they teach you the rules in college, Denise? Or in Beverly Hills? Did you ever go out in the bushes behind your father's mansion? Or maybe Peter taught you." As he said it he nodded, satisfied with the last possibility. "Yeah, maybe Peter taught you. But, see, this is more than just a game of head. This is a game of chicken, too. Do you know how to play chicken?"

With her eyes fixed on the knife, she didn't answer. When he began unbuckling his belt, she would have her chance. She could—

"*Do* you?" he hissed, his voice suddenly venomous. "Answer me, when I talk to you."

"I—no, I don't."

"That's better." He nodded, pleased that she'd spoken so obsequiously. "You can't very well play, if you don't know the rules. Can you?"

"I—no, I can't."

"The way the game goes," he said, "is that you have a choice. You can either play head, or you can play chicken. And the way you play chicken, you have to take a chance on

211

the knife. You have to make a grab for the knife. But if you miss, then you have to pay a penalty. You have to—"

From outside she heard the sound of a floorboard creaking. It was the front porch. Someone was on the front porch.

"What's that?" He pushed her aside, got quickly to his feet, turned toward the front door.

Also on her feet, pretending surprise, she said, "What?" Then, to cover the sound of more movement, she said, "What're you talking about?"

But, instantly, he'd whirled toward his rifle, snatched it from the corner. Crouched over the rifle, he faced the two front windows, listening intently.

"I don't think—"

"Shut up," he hissed, turning the rifle on her. "Shut up." The rifle's muzzle, a dark, terrible, circular void, was aimed directly at her chest: instant death, a glimpse of eternity. Involuntarily she raised a hand against the rifle—against death.

Now, as stealthy and deadly as a jungle predator, he was moving toward the door, his whole body coiled tight. Just short of the door, he stopped, standing motionless, listening. Holding the rifle with his right hand, he slowly reached out with his left hand for the knob. But, inches short of the knob, the hand drew back. He looked over his shoulder—first at her, then at the two kerosene lamps on either end of the redwood mantel.

"Blow them out," he whispered. "Blow out the lamps. *Now.*"

On her feet, she felt herself sag as her legs momentarily failed her. Recovering, she moved to the first lamp, reaching for the small knob that lowered the wick. As she turned the knob, she looked up at the half loft that extended above the far end of the living room. A ladder was fixed to the wall, offering access to the loft through a square cut in the loft floor. The shotgun was up there, concealed behind the loose board. In the darkness, she could—

"Hurry."

A final twist of the knob, and the flame inside the lamp's glass chimney guttered and died. She moved down the mantel, toward the other lamp.

Could he see her, in the darkness?

Could she get to the ladder, climb it, get the shotgun? Peter had showed her how to use it—made her learn. With her thumb she must push the safety catch forward. The gun was then ready to fire, one barrel at a time. But could she do it? Could she pull the trigger, and watch him die?

As the lamp went out, she heard his footsteps coming closer in the sudden darkness. Now she felt him beside her—felt his hand grip her shoulder. Suddenly he began shaking her, like a cat shaking a rat.

"Get to the door," he said. "Open it. Then do what I tell you." He hurled her toward the door. She stumbled, fell to one knee. Pain seared her back, between the shoulder blades. It was the rifle barrel: a hard, cruel blow. She stifled a scream. Damn him, she wouldn't give him the pleasure of hearing her scream.

At the door, she felt him come close beside her, once more felt his brutal grip on her shoulder.

"Open the door," he whispered. "Open the door, and then get out on the porch—and stand there. I want you to pretend that you heard something, and you're looking around, to see what it was. Leave the door open. I'll be right behind you, with this gun in your back. So don't do anything silly. You understand?" As he said it, the fingers sunk into her shoulder. Involuntarily, she tried to pull away. She felt him release her shoulder—

—then felt a crash against her head. Ears ringing, suddenly sick, she was struggling to stand straight. He'd hit her with his fist, high on her head.

"Understand?"

With great effort she nodded. Braced against the doorframe, she was shaking her head numbly from side to side.

"Then *do* it. And remember, leave the door open."

She was turning the knob, pulling the door toward her. The night air was sharp and cold. Over the ridge beyond the road, a half moon was sharp and bright in a cloudless night sky. With the moon framed by two pine trees that grew close to the cabin, it was a picture-postcard vista.

"Outside. Go out on the porch. But don't go near the stairs. There. That's far enough. Remember, this rifle's aimed right at your back. Now stand still. Pretend you're looking around."

Straight ahead, the graveled driveway ran down toward the gate, invisible in the darkness. But if there were a car in the driveway—or even on the access road beyond the gate—she would see it, reflecting the moonlight.

What—who—had made the sound she heard? If Peter were here—somewhere—she would see his truck.

Could it be the police? The FBI?

During the long, terrible time she'd spent chained to the stove, she'd constructed a best-case scenario. When her father got Carson's call, he would have instructed Flournoy to call the FBI. Agents in San Francisco would go to her apartment, and find the note she'd left Peter, saying that she'd gone to the cabin, looking for him. They would discover the cabin's location—somehow. They would phone other agents in Mendocino, who would come to the cabin and surround it. They would call out for Carson to surrender.

Or else they would wait for their chance, hidden in the woods nearby. They would—

"All right. Come back inside." Carson was whispering. "Act natural, now," he warned. "Don't do anything silly."

She turned back to face the open doorway. Inside the room, invisible to anyone looking at them from concealment, he was crouched behind the rifle, aimed full at her torso.

"Come inside. Close the door."

Slowly, with infinite reluctance, she closed the door. As the latch clicked, she realized that she should have run— *could* have run. She'd been less than two feet from the three stairs that led down from the porch to the ground. She could have thrown herself down the stairs, rolled under the porch, found protection from his rifle's bullets. And then she could have waited.

Waited for what?

For her phantom rescuers?

"Who's out there?" In the darkness, he was standing close beside her. The faint light from the windows revealed the dull gleam of his rifle barrel, inches from her midsection.

"There's no one out there. It was probably a raccoon that you heard."

"That was no raccoon. Not to make a sound that loud."

"The porch is old. The boards are rotten."

"It was no raccoon."

She didn't reply.

"We're getting out of here. Now. Right now. Come here. Come over here, goddammit."

With her eyes accustomed to the darkness, she saw him lay the rifle across the armchair, saw him draw the hunting knife, gesturing with the knife toward the table, where he'd thrown the chains.

"Get over here."

Moving slowly and warily toward the table, she saw him step to her left side, then behind her.

"Now hold still. Don't move, or I'll cut you."

She felt him gather the collar of her shirt, in back, then heard a rip of cloth.

"Wh—?"

"Shut up. Stand *still*." With his hand twisted in the collar, he jerked her first to the right, then to the left. With the collar tight across her throat, she choked.

"Then stand still," he breathed.

Obediently she let her body go slack. Looking aside, she saw him take a long length of chain from the table, then felt him insert the chain into the rip he'd made in her shirt, just beneath the collar, in back. Now he moved close to her, crushing the full length of his body against hers. His left arm circled her body across the breasts, drawing her crudely closer. She heard him chuckle: a thick sound, deep in his throat, obscenely intimate.

"Feel that?" He breathed. "*Feel* it?"

In the cleft of her buttocks, she felt the pressure of his penis: a hard, brutal thrust—one thrust, two thrusts, three.

"You like that, don't you?"

"No," she answered. "No, I don't."

As she spoke, she felt him release her with his left hand—felt him working at her throat, circling her neck with the chain, reinserting the end of the chain through the tear in her shirt. Now he heard a click. The padlock had snapped shut, making a loop of steel chain around her neck.

"It's like a dancing bear," he whispered, at the same time jerking the chain. "I pull—you dance. And if you don't behave, I keep jerking until you do. See?"

"Wh-what's the—the reason for all this?"

"The reason for it," he said, "is that we're leaving. We're going to lock the front door, and then we're going to get in the car. My car, not yours. You're going to drive. I'll be in the back seat, with the rifle and the knife. I'll be down between the seats, where nobody'll be able to see me. And that's how we're getting out of here—with you driving, and me holding on to your chain. But nobody'll know about the chain, because they won't be able to see it."

"You've forgotten the gate. One of us has to get out of the car to unlock the gate."

"I haven't forgotten the gate," he whispered. He sheathed the knife, picked up the rifle and took hold of the chain. "You'll open the gate, and I'll be inside the car with the rifle aimed right at your head. Then you'll get back inside the car, like a good girl. Otherwise, you'll be shot. *Right?*" He jerked at the chain: a cruel, sudden slash at her throat, momentarily choking her.

"And then" he said, his voice dropping once more to a low, obscene note. "And then, when we get where we're going, we'll get down to some serious business, you and me. I think I'll let you take your clothes off, but I'll leave the chain around your neck. How do you think you'll like that?"

She realized that, if she tried to answer, she would lose control of her voice. If he forced her to answer, damn him, she would break down in tears.

So, silently, she turned toward the door, as if to cooperate. Anything was better than crying.

Twenty-Nine

CROUCHED DOWN on his haunches, Mitchell was staring up the driveway toward the darkened house. "All right," he said finally, "I'll tell Flournoy to drive into town, and call the sheriff. But, dammit, I wish you'd seen him, not just heard him."

"Jesus Christ—" Angrily, he shook his head. "I was lucky to get out with my ass. Don't you *see* that?"

"All right," Mitchell repeated stolidly. "You and Calloway stay here. I'll get back over the fence, and tell Flournoy. Here—" He handed over the shotgun. "Hold that."

"Is it on safety?"

"There's no safety. But the hammer is down. There's a shell in the chamber, though. So be careful. Don't pull the hammer back."

"Right." Sitting on his heels, he took the shotgun, resting the butt on the ground between his legs, with the muzzle pointing up at the sky. Waywardly, the feel of the gun in his hands evoked memories of childhood hunting trips, with his father. The feeling was the same—the gun between his hunkered-down thighs, the long, silent waiting in the woods, listening to the small, mysterious sounds of the animals. Over the years since his father's death, he'd come to realize that the memory of the times they'd spent together in the woods was the most poignant, the most profound of all his father-and-son recollections. His father had taken a deep, quiet pride in his talent for shooting, and tracking, and reading animal signs. Yet, in his late teens, when he'd told his father that he couldn't kill any more, his father had understood.

A few feet away, Mitchell was whispering to Calloway. Nodding, Calloway looked toward the cabin. Now Mitchell turned and began walking slowly toward the fence, and the sedan. Carefully placing each foot lightly on the ground before he committed his full weight, Mitchell moved soundlessly among the trees. Gone.

"*Hssst.*"

It was Calloway, urgently gesturing toward the cabin. The cabin door was swinging open. Denise was coming through the door, closely followed by another figure—a man. An antagonist. An enemy.

James Carson.

It was true, then. She'd been kidnapped. She was in danger—mortal danger. He could see fear—mortal fear—in every rigid, limb-locked line of her body.

As the two stood motionless on the porch, he saw moonlight glinting on a long, ominous shape that swung at Carson's side: a rifle, or a shotgun.

Calloway was close beside him. Whispering: "There they are. You see them?"

"You'd better go tell Mitchell. Tell him to get back here. Tell him it's Carson—with a gun."

"You tell Mitchell. I'm staying here."

"No, goddammit. You go. Tell him to put his car across the road, before he comes back. There's only one way out of here. If you block the road, they can't leave. Then the two of you come back."

"But, Christ, he'll still *have* her," Calloway protested, "even if the road's blocked. And, besides, it doesn't look to me like they're going anywhere. They're just standing there, like she did before, when she came out alone. Just looking around."

"He's with her now, though. This is different. They're going to get in the car and leave."

"How'd you know?" Calloway asked truculently.

"I just know. I feel it."

"Bullshit."

"You're wasting time. If Flournoy leaves with the car, we're screwed. We won't be able to stop them."

"But—"

"*Do* it—" He shoved at the other man's shoulder, hard. "*Do* it, before Flournoy leaves for Mendocino."

Angrily, Calloway turned away, following Mitchell's path through the dark, silent trees. Unlike Mitchell, Calloway moved noisily, clumsily.

Would Mitchell do it—block the road? Or had Flournoy already left for town? If he'd already left, then—

On the cabin porch, the two figures were moving. Slowly,

infinitely reluctant, Denise was descending the three stairs from the porch to the ground. Carson was close behind her. And—yes—they were going to the cars—to the strange car, Carson's. He was opening the door of the Chevrolet, getting into the car—in back. Now Denise was slipping into the driver's seat. The car's interior light revealed her face, pale and frightened. The driver's door thudded shut; the light went off. The engine's starter began to grind. Finally, reluctantly, the engine caught.

He looked at the gate. Had they snapped the lock? He couldn't see. But, whether or not the gate was locked, it would still be necessary for either Denise or Carson to get out of the car, swing the gate open, hook the gate to the stump beside the driveway and then get back into the car and drive out onto the access road. The stump to which the gate must be hooked was less than ten feet from where he now crouched, still holding the shotgun.

If Carson got out of the car, he would have his chance.

But if Denise got out of the car—what could he do?

Alone—without help—what could he do?

Quickly, he glanced back over his shoulder, in the direction of Mitchell's car. Did Mitchell know that they'd gotten in the car—that they'd started the engine? No, he couldn't know. Not unless he'd heard the engine start.

Had Mitchell heard it start?

He didn't know—couldn't be sure. And, now—suddenly—there was no time to warn him.

On the wooden stock of the shotgun, his hands were trembling. At the pit of his stomach, a sudden sick, empty trembling had begun.

Now the Chevrolet was backing away from the small graveled parking area—moving forward—backing up again. With two cars parked in the cramped space, it was always difficult to get out. Finally, on the third pass, the Chevrolet was in position, ready to come down the driveway to the gate.

And—still—he was alone.

The car was coming without headlights, its engine idling, coasting down the gentle incline toward the gate.

The gate—

He must move toward the gate, must take a position close beside the stump that stopped the gate. Quickly. Silently. Holding the shotgun clear of the waist-high brush, bent double, he moved to his left, toward a small stand of manzanita. The manzanita grew a little higher than his head, thick

219

enough to conceal him. The car was closer now, less than twenty-five feet away. If Carson looked carefully, he might be discovered.

But now he was among the manzanita. Standing motionless, he would be invisible. He heard brakes squeak, saw the Chevrolet stop with enough room to swing the gate open. The driver's door was coming open. Denise was swinging her legs out of the car. Inside the car, the overhead light came on. James Carson was crouched in the back seat, with only his head visible above the line of the windows. His hair was dark, his face pale and narrow. He was saying something, but the words were lost in the low, muttering sound of the idling engine. Still sitting motionless behind the wheel, Denise was staring straight ahead—straight toward the stand of manzanita. Now she was out of the car. In the back seat, the rifle barrel came vertically up, then horizontally down, across the front seat—aimed at Denise as she rounded the front of the car, walking slowly, woodenly toward the gate. As she reached the gate, Carson reached across the front seat to close the driver's door, switching off the light inside. Murderers craved the dark.

Denise was leaning over the gate, awkwardly using her key to unlock the padlock. He looked back over his shoulder, searching the dark trees for some sign of Mitchell. Nothing stirred. If Mitchell had the road blocked, he would be holding that position.

With the padlock unlocked, she was unlatching the gate, swinging it open—toward him. She was coming closer—closer. She would bend over and drop the big hook into the eye screwed into the stump, to keep the gate from swinging shut.

She was five feet from the stump. Three feet. She was bending down again, this time feeling for the hook in the darkness.

"Denise," he whispered. "Don't look up. It's me. Peter."

He saw her stiffen, begin to involuntarily straighten. But then, by force of will, she bent down again, her fingers on the hook. As she stooped, he saw a length of chain dangling from her neck. Carson had chained her up, like an animal.

"When you go back to the car—when you get close to the door—drop down to the ground and roll under the car. He can't get at you. Not with a rifle. And I've got a shotgun. Stay under the car. And remember, he can't swing the rifle enough

220

to get at you. He's got to get out of the car first—out of the back seat. Do you understand?"

"Yes," she whispered, dropping the hook in the eye.

"I've got help. Your father sent help. It'll be all right. Do you believe me?"

"Yes."

"All right—" He drew a deep, unsteady breath as he pulled back the shotgun's hammer. "All right—do it."

He watched her straighten, watched her turn toward the car, watched her begin to walk—one pace—two paces—three. With every step, the chain tinkled musically. Inside the darkened car, the rifle barrel was moving, its muzzle tracking her.

She could die. In the next instant, following his orders, she could die.

Slowly, she reached out for the door handle—

—and then dropped to the ground.

Instantly, the door swung open.

He aimed at the driver's window—squeezed the trigger—felt the shock of the shotgun's recoil—heard the blast. Momentarily blinded by the muzzle flash, he jacked another shell into the chamber, lowering the barrel. The window was blown out; only fragments of shattered glass remained around its edges. From behind him came the sound of shouting, of help coming, crashing through the underbrush. On the far side of the car, the passenger's door was swinging open. Carson would escape from the far side, drop to the ground, kill Denise where she lay.

"Stop. Don't move."

Inside the car, the rifle was swinging toward him. A flash—the sharp, staccato sound of a shot.

He fired, worked the shotgun's slide, fired again—and again. Through the blinding flashes from the muzzle and the deafening sound of crashing shots, he heard himself shouting—

—and, still, working the slide, frantically firing—

—until, finally, only a metallic click came from the shotgun.

"Quit." It was a scream from inside the car: a high, hysterical scream. "Quit. Jesus Christ."

From beside him, he heard another voice, deep and calm. "Throw the gun out." As he spoke, Mitchell was reaching for the shotgun. A measured, methodical series of metallic clacks followed. Mitchell was reloading the shotgun.

"Here it is. It's coming." As, from inside the car, the rifle came cartwheeling through the window, falling to the ground. Mitchell worked the shotgun's slide—ready to fire. Saying: "Get out of the car, on this side. Put your hands on the roof. Now. Right now."

Slowly, the shot-blasted door swung open—wider, still wider. Awkwardly, the man inside was pushing the driver's seat forward. Now he was clambering cautiously out of the car. Raised high in the air, his hands were shaking violently.

"Don't shoot. Jesus Christ, don't shoot."

"Turn around. Put your hands on the roof."

As Carson obeyed, Mitchell asked calmly, "Are you all right, Giannini?"

Not replying, he stepped clear of the manzanita. "Denise. *Denise.*"

From under the car, he heard the small, timid sound of her voice: a thin, half-hysterical sound, infinitely grateful. Infinitely precious.

Thirty

SITTING ON THE ARM of her chair with his arm around her, he stroked her hair, kissed her once on top of the head and said softly, "How're you doing?"

She moved her shoulder close against him, snuggling up. "I've still got the shakes. But the wine helped. I'd forgotten we had it."

"My only regret is that we offered it around. I'll bet anything Granbeck is an alcoholic."

"I'll bet you're right." Still with her body close to him, she whispered. "I'm never going to forget all that—that shooting. I felt like the world was ending. The whole world. Right then. Right there."

"I know. I felt the same way. I felt—I *knew*—that I was going crazy. Really crazy." He hesitated, then said, "Maybe that's the only way you get through something like that—to go a little crazy. Maybe that's what war is all about."

"You saved my life." As she said it, she seemed to shiver, as if the memory frightened her. Then, solemnly: "You really did, Peter. You saved my life."

He tightened his arm around her shoulder, wordlessly drawing her closer, whispering, "I'm just glad I didn't kill him. Because that's what I was trying to do. I was trying to kill him."

"Yes."

The single monosyllable, spoken so softly, confirmed that she shared his sense of horror—and of deliverance. Because nothing but the most capricious chance had saved him from a murderer's guilt. Nothing but luck. The flying glass had cut Carson superficially around the face and head, but he hadn't been seriously wounded. Yet the blood—his blood—had panicked him.

As they sat silently, content with what they'd said—and felt—he looked around the room. It was a strangely improbable tableau, somehow suspended in both time and space. Because none of these men belonged here—not Carson, sitting crouched down on the hearth with his bloodied head resting on his folded arms—not Calloway, dressed in his neat blue suit and holding the shotgun trained on Carson—not Granbeck, sprawled in the broken chair, eyes closed, gently snoring. And, certainly, not Mitchell or Flournoy, whispering together in a far corner of the room: Rosencrantz and Guildenstern, in impeccable modern dress, conspiratorily sweeping the room with their shrewd, measuring eyes.

"This is like *The Iceman Cometh*," he murmured.

"I want to go home," she said. "Why don't we just get in my car, and go?"

"No. I'm not leaving them here."

"Why not?"

"Because—" He hesitated. Then: "Because I don't trust them. Any of them."

She didn't reply.

And now, as if their inaudible remarks had roused the two plotters to some decision, he saw Flournoy suddenly look toward him. Inclining his head, as if to confirm some unspoken agreement between them, Flournoy raised his voice to say, "Can we talk for a few minutes, Mr. Giannini?"

He gave her shoulder a final squeeze, kissed her again on top of her head and rose to his feet. "Sure."

"In there, then—" Flournoy pointed to the kitchen, where an oil lamp had been lit.

Crossing the living room, he followed the two men into the kitchen. Taking up a position leaning against the sink, arms folded across his elegantly cut topcoat, Flournoy said, "I'm wondering why your neighbors haven't come by, after all that shooting." He spoke softly, covertly. This, then, was a private conversation—their secret, even from Denise. Men's business.

Leaning against the wall, also with his arms folded, he said, "First of all, the nearest neighbor is a quarter mile away."

"Still, they'd have heard the shots."

"True. But, unfortunately, shooting at night isn't all that uncommon. There's a lot of shining around here."

"Shining?"

"Deer. It's illegal. You catch a deer with a strong light, and he won't move. You shoot him. Actually, most of the offenders are the natives, which is another reason no one asks questions. It's a good way to fill the freezer, especially with the price of beef so high. They all do it."

Flournoy glanced quickly, speculatively at Mitchell. Then, probing, he said, "You fired five shots. Carson fired one. A deer hunter wouldn't fire that many shots."

He shrugged. "Deer travel in families, very often."

Another moment of speculative silence followed, while Flournoy and Mitchell exchanged another quick, meaningful look. Then Flournoy said, "You have two neighbors. Is that right?"

"Yes. The Taylors and the Andersons."

"And neither of them have phones."

"That's right."

Flournoy nodded: one slow, measured inclination of his beautifully barbered head.

Watching the two men as they each fell silent, staring off in different directions as they obviously calculated some secret odds, he decided to say: "Why all the questions?"

For a moment Flournoy didn't reply, but instead simply stared at him, obviously still preoccupied by his calculations. Then, quietly, he said, "I'm trying to decide what to do next."

"What's the problem? We take him into town, and we turn him over to the sheriff. They charge him with kidnap and attempted murder."

Flournoy's answering stare was impassive, signifying neither agreement nor dissent.

"What's the problem?" he repeated impatiently, this time including both men in his questioning stare.

"The problem," Flournoy answered, "is that we don't want this made public. Not if we can help it."

"But—" Incredulously, he looked at each of the two men in turn. "But it—it's *already* public. It happened, for Christ's sake. The *law's* been broken."

Still with his arms folded, Flournoy merely nodded—conceding the point, but nothing more.

"And there's one very shot-up car. Which, I assume, doesn't belong to Carson. How're you going to explain that?"

"We were just talking about that, in the living room," Mitchell said. "There're several things we could do."

"But—Christ—" He flung out an impatient hand. "But there's Carson. Arresting someone is a matter of public record, not to mention putting him on trial."

"That," Flournoy said, "is the problem. We can insure Granbeck's silence—with enough money. And I assume that both you and Denise want what's best for Mr. Holloway—which would be no publicity. But then, as you point out, we've still got Carson to—"

"Wait a minute." He raised an abrupt hand. "Correct me if I'm wrong, but I thought that Austin Holloway thrived on publicity. So I'd think that, with a little adroit manipulation of the media, you could make the whole thing turn out to your advantage. Holloway could become a saint. He could ask forgiveness for Carson. He could pray for his soul—on nationwide TV."

"Very funny," Flournoy said coldly.

He shrugged, at the same time glancing into the living room. Denise still sat as before, her eyes haunted. Another long moment of silence followed while Flournoy and Mitchell exchanged a last long, decisive stare. Finally Flournoy sighed. The exclamation seemed to express genuine regret.

"What you don't understand," Flournoy said quietly, "is that James Carson is actually Austin Holloway's illegitimate son."

Involuntarily, his eyes fled to the crouched figure of James Carson—then slowly returned to Flournoy. "Are you sure?"

"I'm positive. Absolutely positive."

"Does Denise know?"

"I haven't asked her," Flournoy answered. "But I assume that, during all the time they spent together, Carson probably told her. And, anyhow, it's irrelevant, now, whether she knows or not. The point is that, as soon as Carson's arrested, it's bound to come out that he's Holloway's bastard son."

"Christ." Incredulously, he shook his head. "Jesus Christ." Then, suddenly, he smiled. "The old bastard. He's human, then, just like everyone else. He probably even craps, once in a while. Just to prove he's mortal."

Flournoy's answering stare was cold and pained. Finally: "It's not a laughing matter, Mr. Giannini. Not to us. And not to Mr. Holloway, either. Incidentally—" He paused, for emphasis, before he said, "Incidentally, Mr. Holloway is in very bad health. He has a bad heart—a very bad heart. That's another factor."

"But—" Once more, he shook his head. "But you've only got two choices—either have Carson arrested, or else turn him loose. And, sure as hell, you can't turn him loose. He'd just do it all over again."

"We're aware of that," Flournoy answered. "That's what

we've been talking about. We're aware that it's a risk either way. But we—Mitchell and I—we're inclined to think there's less risk to us—to Mr. Holloway—if we let him go."

"Let him go?"

Quickly, Flournoy raised a hand. "Please. Keep your voice down. We're taking you into our confidence, Mr. Giannini. I hope you appreciate that."

"But—Christ—" Stepping closer to the other man, he spoke in a low, fervent voice. "He could have killed Denise. And me, too. Both of us. He—he's a goddamn criminal. He belongs in jail."

"That may be," Flournoy answered calmly. "But I've already tried to explain to you about our problem, if he goes to jail."

"But—"

"We're trying to decide whether he'll be apt to go after Mr. Holloway again, if we let him go. That's the decision we have to make."

"But you're taking the law into your own hands."

"I remember reading," Flournoy said, "that someone who's been beaten—badly, systematically beaten—is never quite the same again. And I'm wondering whether that would apply to Carson." He spoke quietly, abstractedly—as if he were speculating on the efficacy of some obscure mathematical formula. "After all," he said, "he'll realize that, if we caught him once, we could catch him again. And, if that happened—" Eloquently, he shrugged.

Peter let a long, hostile beat pass before he said, "I'm waiting. What would happen, if you caught him again?"

"He'd get another beating," Mitchell said. As he spoke, the big man's face was impassive, his eyes inscrutable.

"I think," he said, looking from one man to the other, "that you're both crazy. You're—Christ—you're sociopaths. *Both* of you. You're—Christ—you're not much different from Carson, when it comes right down to it."

"It's obvious," Flournoy said softly, "that you don't share our opinion about the importance of Mr. Holloway's work. Which is the reason we're here—and the reason we're talking to you like this, taking you into our confidence."

"You're right," he answered angrily. "You're absolutely right. I happen to think Austin Holloway is a charlatan. And I also happen to think that what he preaches is pure, unadulterated blasphemy."

Calmly—contemptuously—Flournoy shrugged, plainly

227

indifferent to the criticism. Now he glanced at his watch. "It's one thirty in the morning," he said. "We've got to make a decision."

"Well, I say we take him to the sheriff." But, as he said it, he realized that his demand sounded weak and ineffectual. Mao had once said that political power came from the muzzle of a rifle. And Mitchell had the guns.

"I don't think so," Flournoy said. "I think we're going to do it our way. We've already decided. Mitchell and I will take him outside. Mitchell will give him a beating, and then let him go."

"But that—that's inhuman. It—it's medieval. You're—Christ—you're treating him like an animal."

"I admire your scruples, Mr. Giannini, especially in view of the fact that, less than an hour ago, Carson tried to kill you. And, another time, I'd agree with them. But this is a—" Flournoy paused. "It's a special situation. Special measures are required."

Silently, he stared at them. How could he stop it? His only hope would be to climb the ladder to the loft, and get the shotgun, and force a showdown.

But it wouldn't work.

Because he couldn't do it—couldn't tolerate even the thought of it. Even now—this moment—his hands were trembling at the thought of taking up a gun, therefore evoking the shattering terror he'd felt, facing Carson.

So there was only one hope remaining:

"If you do it," he said, "I'll tell the sheriff what you did. I'll tell him the whole story. I promise."

"That's a chance we'll have to take."

"You don't think I'll do it. But I will."

Contemptuous again, Flournoy shrugged. Mitchell remained silent, impassively staring.

Pushing himself away from the wall, he stalked out of the kitchen. In the living room, Denise sat as before, making herself small in the big armchair. Her eyes were large and round, still reflecting the shock she'd experienced. With her feet tucked under her, wearing her checked wool shirt and jeans, she could have been a teen-ager, fighting back from some terrible trauma.

She needed him—needed to feel him near, needed to touch him. As he needed her.

"What's wrong?" she asked as he resumed his perch on the arm of her chair. "What's happened? What'd they want?"

"I'll tell you later."

"Peter—" Twisting in the chair, she was anxiously searching his face. "Peter. What is it?"

"Shhh. Be quiet a minute." He caught her gaze, then moved his eyes with slow significance toward the kitchen. Mitchell was coming through the doorway into the living room, followed by Flournoy. Looking straight ahead, Mitchell walked to Calloway, still standing guard. A few inaudible words were exchanged as Mitchell looked intently into Calloway's eyes. Calloway nodded once, twice, then eased off the shotgun's hammer and handed the weapon to Mitchell. As if the hammer click had roused him, Carson suddenly raised his head from his crossed arms. At the same time, Flournoy walked into the room and went directly to Carson's .30–.30 rifle, propped in a corner. He picked up the rifle gingerly, one hand wrapped around the barrel just below the muzzle.

"Don't touch the grip or the forestock," Mitchell cautioned. In response, Flournoy nodded.

"All right," Mitchell said, turning to Carson. "On your feet." He spoke quietly—dispassionately.

Staring defiantly at the big man, Carson didn't move.

"Either get on your feet," Mitchell said, "and walk out the door, or else you'll get this gun barrel across the head, and we'll carry you out. It doesn't matter to me one way or the other."

Carson rose to his feet and turned toward the door. He moved as a convict might: slowly and stolidly, with eyes sullenly downcast—yet watchfully, dangerously. His hair was blood-matted; blood stained his jacket, front and back. He held a wet towel that Denise had given him, to wipe the blood from his face. The towel was pink.

Mitchell fell in behind Carson. Still carrying the rifle by its barrel, Flournoy followed Mitchell.

"Open the door," Mitchell ordered, at the same time drawing back the shotgun's hammer. "Then go outside. Slow and easy. And drop that towel."

Carson tossed the towel to the floor, pulled open the door and stepped outside into the darkness. A moment later, Flournoy drew the door shut. From the porch, Peter could hear the sound of their footsteps—then silence.

They would take their captive away from the house, before they beat him. They would probably take him down to the road. They would administer the beating, give him his warning and turn him loose. They would do it all according to their plan, so coldly concocted.

Yet he'd warned them—he'd promised them—that he would tell the sheriff, if they turned Carson loose.

So they were taking a chance. They were taking a double chance. They were risking the consequences of setting Carson free—of having him return, to try again. And they were also risking the judgement of the law. They could be indicted for obstruction of justice—or worse.

It was stupid—a senseless, stupid risk.

And Flournoy wasn't a stupid man. He was devious, and dangerous. But he wasn't stupid.

"Stay here," he whispered, rising from the arm of Denise's chair. "Something's wrong. I'm going outside."

"Why? What is it?"

"I'll tell you later." Then, in a normal voice, he said, "I'm going outside."

"Outside?" Calloway asked, instantly alert.

He smiled. "That's a euphemism. It means I'm going out in back—to the outhouse. We don't have indoor plumbing here. Or hadn't you noticed?"

Calloway shrugged, yawning as he settled back in his chair.

In the kitchen, he took the outhouse flashlight from its accustomed place above the stove, and opened the back door.

The night was dark and still; the half moon was low in the sky, just above the ridge to the west. The three figures were dimly visible standing to the left of the driveway, close to the small stand of manzanita that had concealed him earlier. The Chevrolet was still parked in the driveway, fifteen feet from the three men.

The clearing surrounding the cabin was bordered by trees and thick-growing underbrush. Moving toward the trees to his left, he began circling the clearing. As he drew closer to the three figures, he heard voices: Mitchell's deep, even voice, counterpointed by another voice, hoarse and rough—Carson's voice. With less than fifty feet separating him from the three men, he stepped among the trees. If he was careful, he could advance through the trees close enough to hear them talking without being seen or heard.

Devious. Dangerous. But not stupid.

As he picked his way through the underbrush, the refrain began to recur: taunting, tantalizing, ominous. It was a warning:

Devious. Dangerous. But not stupid.

But warning him of what?

He was closer now—still undiscovered. Still safe. Standing motionless, he saw Mitchell gesture with the shotgun, heard him speak:

"All right. Turn around. Start walking toward the road—toward the gate."

"But why?" It was Carson's voice. Unsteady. Afraid. Deathly afraid.

But afraid of what?

Warning him of what?

"Just do it. Come on. Move."

"I'm—I'm not going to do it." Terror trembled in Carson's voice.

Mitchell raised the shotgun, took a quick step forward and drove the muzzle into Carson's stomach. Instantly, Carson bent double, sagged to his knees, began retching.

"The next one goes across your head."

"Ah—ah—ah—" It was a helpless, mewling sound. An animal sound.

Like an animal, he'd said, accusing Flournoy. They planned to beat Carson, a human being, as if he were an animal.

Yet, with his victim helpless before him, Mitchell made no move to beat him. Instead, he wanted Carson on his feet, walking away—

—running away.

Running, so he could be killed. Shot in the back, trying to escape.

The plan to beat him had been a lie—a ruse, explaining why they wanted Carson outside, alone. Without witnesses. So they could kill him. The rifle, with its expended shell in the chamber and Carson's fingerprints on the forestock and grip, were part of the plan. They would put the rifle in Carson's dead hands, and claim self-defense.

They wouldn't claim Carson was trying to escape. They were smarter than that. Instead, they would claim that he was shooting at them, and they were firing back, to save themselves.

"Get up," Mitchell was saying. "Get up and start walking."

Slowly, sobbing with the effort, Carson was obeying. Head hanging, knees unsteady, he was on his feet.

"All right, now, walk. Go ahead. Walk toward the gate. When you get to the gate, you can stop. But don't go out in the road."

Carson turned, began to stumble forward: the condemned man, facing eternity. Did he know he was facing death? Yes, he knew. The terrible knowledge was plain in the tremor of his voice, and in his dragging, death-house steps.

As their victim approached the gate, the two executioners turned with him, until all three men were facing the road. Slowly, noiselessly, Peter stepped clear of the trees. He would wait. Watch, and wait.

Twenty feet separated Carson from the road. Fifteen feet. Ten feet. Feet braced, holding the shotgun ready, Mitchell was standing close to Carson's car. Waiting. Coldly, patiently waiting.

Five feet.

Slowly, deliberately, Mitchell was bringing the shotgun up to his shoulder, lowering his cheek to the stock.

"Stop. *Stop*."

The gun barrel jerked up, then pivoted, seeking him. It was a reflex: an assassin's instinct. Exclamations erupted, and shouts: angry, confused voices. As the gun found him, he dropped to the ground. He was shouting now, like the others. Screaming:

"Murderers. Murderers."

Thirty-One

HOLLOWAY OPENED his eyes, turned his head, looked at the bedside clock. The time was eight fifteen. Sunlight filtered through the drawn drapes. Beyond the windows, a lawn mower was buzzing. From the direction of the Hollywood Freeway, he could hear the steady rumble of morning commuter traffic.

Morning...

Last night, at ten o'clock, he'd taken the pill: a large white capsule, administered by Doctor Harris. A good-natured warning had come with the capsule—that they mustn't make this a habit. Followed by a fawning, fatuous laugh.

Last year, the sum total of Harris' services had come to more than twenty-five thousand dollars, the price of eternal vigilance—the fee for being constantly on call, around the clock. "Preferred patient," was the term Harris used.

This year the total would be more. Considerably more. The rates for preferred patients, like everything else, had gone up—despite the fact that Harris probably wasn't very good at his job. Or very conscientious. Or even very honest.

With an effort, he turned on his side and pushed the "kitchen" button: one button of many, part of a console mounted beside the bed.

"Good morning, Reverend."

It was Clarissa's rich, African contralto over the intercom. Of all his servants and all his close employees, it was Clarissa who pleased him most. Because, quite simply, Clarissa didn't give a damn. She didn't kowtow, but rather was impertinent. Clarissa had a very clear perception of herself and her professional status. She was well aware that, within a mile radius, a dozen Beverly Hills families wanted her to cook for them— probably for more money than he paid.

"It's a beautiful morning, Reverend. What would you like for breakfast?"

"I'd like orange juice and toast with orange marmalade. And water—a carafe of water."

"Yessir, Reverend."

"Is Elton still here?"

"Yessir. He stayed all night."

"Ask him to come upstairs, will you?"

"Yessir. Right away. How'd you sleep?"

"I slept fine, Clarissa. Just fine. Thank you."

"You're welcome, Reverend. Your juice and toast will be right up. Maybe I'll send them with Mr. Elton."

"Yes. Thank you." He released the intercom button and sank back against the pillows, closing his eyes. It was time for inventory—for the morning's ritual summation. On the plus side, his heart was quiet, beating evenly. There was no pain, either across his chest or down his arms. His legs, supported, were languidly at ease. Relieved of their burden, his legs were wonderfully light, almost disembodied.

On the minus side, his throat was parched, his nose and mouth incredibly dry. It was, he knew, a function of the pill he'd taken, to let him sleep. And, because he'd slept so soundly, dried mucous clung to his eyelashes, as persistent as glue.

He should get up, go into the bathroom, wash his face. He should urinate, drink a glass of water, comb his hair. He should receive Elton in dressing gown and slippers, sitting in a chair beside the window, with the drapes open.

Yet there was another possibility. Until urination was a necessity, he could simply lie quietly, luxuriantly aware that nothing was required of heart, or limbs, or lungs, or spirit.

He could simply lie in his bed...

And hope.

And pray.

Yes, this morning, he could pray. Because, this morning, demons raged at the gates—demons that had been stalking him all his life. Last night, slipping into his drugged sleep, he'd glimpsed the monsters clearly: Mary, raving at him from the depths of her demented dreams—her demonic son, dispatched from the depths of hell to torment him—

—to torment Denise. To stalk her. To hold her hostage. To abuse her.

Obscene. Monstrous. Murderous.

Could he pray? Here in this room, alone, could he—

At the door, a knock sounded: Elton's knock. Why, God, couldn't it have been Elton, fallen victim to the demon's wrath? He might have returned from his ordeal a better man—if he returned.

"Come in."

Carrying the breakfast tray, an improbable emissary from room service incongruously dressed in a Temple of Today T-shirt and jeans bulging at his midriff, Elton entered the room. His feet were encased in leather thong sandals. His moon face was fatuously smiling. But his eyes, as always, were transparently calculating the effect of the smile.

"Well," he said, emphasizing the single word with a comic-opera verve, "she's safe. Denise is safe."

Safe.

His prayer, unspoken, had been answered. Deliverance was his. One last time.

But there was more. One look at Elton's face revealed that, yes, there was something else—some tribute that fate had exacted for this unexpected boon.

Or was it God, not fate?

"You want this on the nightstand?"

Impatiently, he waved. "Yes—yes. Put it down. But tell me what happened."

Elton placed the tray on the nightstand, drew up a chair and sat close beside the bed. Saying again: "Well—" A pause, for the effect. Then: "Mitchell did it, apparently. He rescued Denise."

Not Flournoy, Elton's rival for the reins of power. But Mitchell, the known quantity.

"But?" He reached for the glass of water.

"But Carson apparently got away. I'm not clear on the details. However—" He glanced at his elaborate digital wrist-watch—the one that he'd been forbidden to wear on The Hour. "However, they should be here, before long. They called at six thirty, from the airport in San Francisco. They were leaving immediately in our airplane. So they should be here any time, now."

"Are they coming here? Directly here?"

Elton nodded. "Yes. I thought you'd want them to come here."

Nodding, he drank the entire glass of water, then held out the empty glass. Dutifully pouring, Elton asked, "How are you feeling?"

He smiled. "I feel better than I have for some time, in the morning. I think I'm going to look into those pills."

"I wouldn't. The doctor says that, all day today, you'll probably feel logy."

"Logy?"

"You know—no energy. You'll—"

Beside the bed, the intercom buzzed. Glancing at the console, he saw the "gatehouse" button illuminated.

"I'll get it—" Elton punched the button. "Yes?"

"Mr. Flournoy and Mr. Mitchell are here."

"Yes. Send them up. We're in my father's bedroom. They can come up here."

Holloway drew back the covers and swung his legs out of the bed. "Get my blue silk robe, will you? I'm going to the bathroom, and wash my face. Then I'll sit there, in the armchair." He gestured to the chair beside the window, at the same time leaning forward, pushing at the bed with his arms.

"Here—" Elton came close, standing over him, extending both hands—like a parent, ready to help a toddler learn to walk. "Here—let me help you."

Impatiently, he shook his head. "No. Never mind. Let me do it."

And, slowly, he was doing it—rising to his feet, swaying only slightly as he found his equilibrium—beginning the walk across the bedroom to the bathroom door.

"So that's the whole story, Austin." Looking tired and frustrated, unshaven and unpressed, Flournoy leaned back heavily in his chair, selecting an English muffin from the breakfast tray that had just arrived from the kitchen. "It's not the best resolution, I'll admit. But it's not the worst, either."

He turned to Mitchell. "How do you feel about it, Lloyd?"

But, before Mitchell could answer, Elton broke in: "This Peter Giannini sounds like a—a hippie. If it weren't for him—" He let it go unfinished. Then, frowning, he turned to Flournoy. "Where'd he get the idea you were going to kill Carson?"

Chewing steadily, Flournoy didn't reply, but instead glanced at Mitchell.

"He was upset," Mitchell answered quietly. "He'd been shot at, after all."

"That's all very well," Elton said, shifting petulantly in his chair. "But that doesn't mean he isn't a hippie. And, for that matter, so is Denise, when you come right down to it. In fact, that's the real problem, here—Denise, and her far-out lifestyle. If she'd only done what she should've done, years ago—if she'd shaped up—this situation wouldn't have come up."

"The problem, though," Mitchell said mildly, "is Carson. Denise was just a target. If it hadn't been her, it would've been someone else." He let a moment pass, then said, "You, for instance. Or your family. Your wife, or children."

Elton's answering expression was first startled, then annoyed. Sighing, Flournoy replaced his coffee cup on the tray, saying flatly, "That's all past history. What we have to do now is decide on our next move."

Our next move. It was an ominous phrase. Signifying that only a skirmish had been won, not even a battle, much less the war. Holloway gestured with his empty cup for more coffee, at the same time asking, "What *is* our next move?"

"I'm afraid," Flournoy said, "that our options are pretty much limited, assuming that we still don't want to call in the police. Lloyd and I have been discussing various alternatives on the plane. Of course, we'll want to increase security. Beyond that, all we can do is sit tight."

"We've got Denise covered," Mitchell said. "She's covered around the clock."

"We should insist that Denise come down here," Elton said, "so we can protect her. Up there, in San Francisco, she's running unnecessary risks. Every kook in the world ends up in San Francisco. And they all have guns. And drugs."

No one replied.

"It might be," Flournoy siad, "that Carson's been scared off. And, also, his options might be limited now—" He took a billfold from his inside pocket. "This is his wallet. He had his uncle's credit cards. He'd been using them for car rental— and probably for lodging, and food. Without them, he'll have a harder time."

"He doesn't have a penny," Mitchell said. "Which means that he'll probably have to steal, just to get food. He won't even be able to get to Los Angeles, unless he hitchhikes."

"If he steals," Holloway mused, "he'll be arrested. Is that good?"

"It's not ideal," Flournoy said. "But it's probably inevitable. And, if the arrest doesn't come in connection with you— with ransom, or extortion—it might be the best resolution we can hope for, under the circumstances. If the crime he's arrested for isn't sensational—if he's arrested for robbing a liquor store, as opposed to being arrested for kidnapping De-

237

nise—there's a good chance we can simply hush up whatever claims he might make, concerning his, ah, parentage."

Holloway nodded over his coffee. "Yes, that's true."

"We can't take any chances, though," Mitchell cautioned. "His freedom of movement might be limited, but he might be even more dangerous—more irrational. Personally, I think that's what will happen. He's off his rocker, that kid—and he's a killer. Or, at least, he's a potential killer. And a sadist, and a lot of other things, too. I wouldn't be surprised, the way he's feeling now, if he walked right up to you and tried to shoot you, even though it would mean getting caught, or even killed." Mitchell allowed a long, somber beat to pass, letting him think about it. Then: "He's also smart. Very, very smart. And very determined, too. In two weeks, he's figured out exactly what you do and when you do it. He knows your schedule down to the last detail.

"Which means," Flournoy said, "that we've got to change your schedule, Austin. Or, at least, we'll change the part that involves any contact with the public."

"But what about The Hour?" Elton asked. Holloway glanced at his son. With his brow elaborately furrowed, Elton was trying to project a sense of concern. But his small, avid eyes betrayed him, revealing a gleam of pure ambition. A year ago, after Holloway's first heart attack, Elton had taken over The Hour for a month, assisted by Sister Teresa and Pastor Bob—with Katherine's silent, diaphanous presence always close. The results had been disastrous. Despite Elton's mawkish pleas to "help Dad through," audience response had been almost halved—and the cashflow, too.

Yet, thanks to his murderous half brother, Elton could once more see himself on center stage, singing his silly songs and preaching his awkward platitudes.

"What about Sunday?" Elton pressed, speaking directly to Flournoy.

Regretfully, Flournoy shook his head. But, plainly, Flournoy's concern was genuine, not contrived. Flournoy, too, was remembering their cashflow problems, a year ago.

"We can't risk it," he answered. "We can't risk Austin—not for a week or two, at least. You'll have to do The Hour, Elton. You and Teresa and Bob."

Holloway raised an imperious hand. "We can't do that, because of the China Crusade. It's impossible. Completely impossible. The next two weeks are crucial. Absolutely crucial."

"I realize they're crucial," Flournoy said quietly. "But we've got to make absolutely certain that—"

"With this publicity snowball rolling," Holloway said, "what you're suggesting is out of the question. Unthinkable."

"We could say that you're—" Elton frowned, searching for the phrase. Then, brightening craftily: "We could say that you're indisposed. Temporarily indisposed."

Suppressing an angry retort, he swept the three of them with a long, hard look. "Forget it. I don't care what security measures you take—so long as they don't appear on camera. But, definitely, I'm doing The Hour this Sunday. And the next Sunday, too—and the next." He turned to face Mitchell. "You can hire an army of security men, I don't care—providing they look like they belong in the congregation. Give them Carson's picture, and station them at every door when the people start arriving. And then you can put them in every other seat, if you like. But The Hour goes on—exactly as scheduled."

"If that's what you want," Mitchell answered, "then that's what we'll do. However, I do think you should give up the altar call."

He shook his head. "I can't do it, Lloyd. I'm aware that it's a risk. But the altar call and the final words are two things that never change. They're—" He raised his hands, gesturing. "They're my trademarks."

"Just once, give it up," Mitchell asked. "Just this once."

Regretfully, he shook his head again. "Sorry, Lloyd. As I said, I can appreciate the risk. And, believe me, I'm not anxious to take a chance with my neck. I'm no hero, believe me. But it just can't be done." He paused, then said, "After all, I'm giving you carte blanche. You should be able to put something together. If the Secret Service can protect the President when he's working the crowds, surely we can do the same thing." Once more sweeping the semicircle of their faces, he saw both disappointment and resignation in their eyes. Mitchell and Flournoy were disappointed because he'd chosen to risk his life, possibly to Flournoy's financial loss—possibly to Mitchell's eternal defeat.

As for Elton, he'd missed yet another chance.

Thirty-Two

ON THE STAGE, dressed in white organdy, Sister Teresa stood with her hands clasped beneath her bosom, eyes raised, holding the spiritual's last long, lingering note. Behind her, in unison, the choir swayed to the rhythm. Standing aside, stage right, smiling and nodding benignly, Austin Holloway was waiting his turn.

Carson looked at his watch. The time was ten fifty-five: forty-five minutes into the program. About thirty minutes remained.

But, for Austin Holloway, less than thirty minutes.

Leaving Holloway, his eyes traveled to the TV cameras, one on each side of the stage. The third camera, high above, was hidden.

These were the cameras that, in minutes, would record the death of Austin Holloway.

In the program he held in his lap, the title of the coming sermon was listed as "Salvation and Sacrifice."

Today—soon—Holloway would teach through example—a do-it-yourself demonstration of human sacrifice, on nation-wide TV. He would give up his life on camera. If the program didn't lie—if Holloway didn't lie—then his salvation would follow. So, on camera, Holloway could give a demonstration of his soul's ascent into heaven. It would be a TV first—a record smasher. Reruns would gross millions.

It was a joke—a magnificently inspired, once-in-a-lifetime joke. His joke. His fame. His fortune. All of it. For ever and ever, all his. Because millions would see it happen. Millions upon millions: reruns forever. All through the world, they would see Austin Holloway raise his hand over the bowed heads, pronouncing his bogus, three-for-a-quarter blessing. Then, all over the world, they would hear the shot. They would see Holloway totter, see him fall. They would see the blood, hear the screams. They would watch Holloway die: a slow, agonizing death. It would be the ultimate movie, made for TV.

And, while Holloway lay dying, he, Carson, would be invisible, just one face among thousands, melting into the wild, milling crowd.

And all thanks to the pamphlet he held in his lap: *Bible Stories for Today*. He'd found it just yesterday, in a religious bookstore: an outsized book with a picture of Jesus on the cover, dressed in a white robe, a golden halo behind his head. He'd taken the book to his room and discovered that, yes, the pamphlet would fold over Uncle Julian's .45, completely concealing both his hand and the gun. He'd bought a Bible, too, its purpose to conceal the pamphlet's subtitle, *Stories for Children*.

Forty-five minutes ago, carrying the Bible and the pamphlet—knowing that, certainly, guards were everywhere, watching for him—he's entered this Temple. He'd even smiled at one of the men who, surely, had been stationed at the door to intercept him. He hadn't been afraid to smile—to dare the man in the blue suit to recognize him. Because he'd known, beyond all doubt, that he would never be recognized. His hair was still dark brown; he couldn't change that. But now he wore glasses—heavy rimmed, dimestore glasses, for reading. He hadn't chosen sun glasses; he'd been too clever for that. And then, remembering *The Godfather*, he'd stuffed cotton in each cheek. The results had been unbelievable. In the mirror, he'd seen a stranger.

So, forty-five minutes ago, piously smiling, he'd taken his seat. Perhaps the man seated beside him was another guard. It was possible. It was even desirable. It was important that they recognize the power he held over them—that they realized how helpless they were to oppose him.

Power. Certainty. Success.

They were all his—in mere minutes, all his. Already he could sense the rush of excitement, of sensation, of the wild, kaleidoscopic lights and screams and the blood spattering everything: the frenzied faces, the stage where Holloway lay dying, the camera lens, pulled in for one last closeup.

And, alone in the carnage—above it all, beyond it all—he would be motionless: seeing, sensing, willing—powerful, masterful. In control.

The master of it all.

Still—always—the master.

It had been so easy—so inevitable. Because never, for even

a single moment, had he doubted himself. Not once had he lost control. Even walking down the driveway from the cabin, feeling the presence of the shotgun at his back as surely as if the gun had been touching him, he'd never doubted that he would escape them. He'd been ready to dive into the underbrush, to run, to elude them in the darkness when—a miracle—the one called Giannini had cried out. The momentary confusion had given him the single second he'd needed to escape. Yet even then, he could have made a mistake—could have paid with his life. He could have run—and run—leaving them a trail of sound, to track him with their guns.

Instead, he'd gone to ground. Calmly, in complete control, he'd lain motionless behind a log, listening to the sounds of their frantic searching. He'd heard their shouts. He'd laughed when they cursed, crashing through the underbrush. He'd watched their single flashlight futilely bob and wink through the trees, farther and farther away.

Until, finally they'd given up. They'd given up. They'd gotten into their cars, and they'd driven away.

They'd left him with a pocketful of change and two keys— the key to the Chevrolet, and the key to the locker, at Los Angeles International.

Realizing that they might be expecting him to try for the Chevrolet, he'd struck off instead through the woods, paralleling the road, walking back the way he'd come the day before, following the girl. With dawn breaking, he'd finally come to a small settlement: a cluster of stores and a gas station. In the weeds behind the gas station, he'd found a rusted screwdriver. He'd used it to pry open a newspaper vending machine, getting sixteen dollars in silver. With the money in his pocket, he'd hitchhiked to Los Angeles. Answering questions about his appearance, he'd said that his car had been wrecked, and he was returning home to his parents. That night, after getting the .45 from the locker, he'd used the gun to rob a grocery store of almost four hundred dollars.

It was all the money he'd needed to bring him here— now—dressed in a blue blazer and white shirt with tie, sitting quietly with his hands clasped across the Bible and the storybook, listening to Austin Holloway's voice rise and fall—exhorting the sinners, fleecing the suckers.

Salvation and Sacrifice....

Yes, Reverend—yes, Father. Preach on. Do the dance your

father taught you. Repeat the lies. Diddle the faithful this one last time. Enjoy these last minutes on earth. Rejoice that you will soon depart, bound for the Pearly Gates and beyond, showing the way for all to follow. Blood-smeared. Twitching. Choking on your own blood. Dying, with your dead eyes rolled up toward heaven.

And toward the camera, seeing it all.

All.

With the moment coming closer, there was a tremor beginning, deep inside. It was the same trembling he'd experienced before—so often before, in so many dark, dangerous rooms, listening to his victims breathing rhythmically in the night, sleeping while he crept close beside them, his life momentarily joined with theirs, both risked on the scrape of a shoe in the dark, or an eye winking open. And all for whatever he could find in the darkness—all for a wallet on the dresser, or jewelry tucked away in a drawer.

But not just for the money, or the jewelry. Not for things— but rather for the feeling, for the power.

The power ...

Life or death, his decision. He could steal, or he could kill. He could control them all—just as Holloway did, on stage. They were the same, he and Holloway. Exactly the same. Both of them took from the unwary and the unsuspecting— for the thrill of it. He with his burglar tools, long ago, and now with the gun. Holloway with his microphone clipped to his lapel, trailing a cord like some obscene umbilicus. Scheming. Lying. And, therefore, stealing.

Yes, stealing. And, therefore, killing. Because it was all the same; murder was merely one more theft. The last theft— the final escape. And it all began in small, dark rooms smelling of sour sleep: he with hands groping blindly for trinkets, Holloway with his penis—probing, thrusting, finally exploding inside her. Sending her straight to hell: a madwoman, with her face grotesquely painted, sitting in front of the TV, watching him preach.

"And so, my friends, we come to the close of this service— to the final words." Holloway lifted his eyes from his father's prayer book, and looked out over the congregation.

Was he out there, somewhere beyond the lights?

Which one among the thousands was he, Mary's bastard?

Where was Mitchell—the guards—the protection he'd been promised? Why, suddenly, did he feel so vulnerable?

Why did he feel so alone—so terribly alone? Had he always been so alone? Was that the message—the real message? Was loneliness the real truth?

Two seconds of silence had passed. Three seconds. Four. He must begin again, must take up the burden that his Daddy had lain upon his young, strong shoulders:

"And today, my friends, I have a very special message for you—a message that comes straight from my heart. It comes straight from my heart, and I pray to God that the message will enter your heart like an arrow shot by the Lord God Almighty, laden with love. Because, my friends, this meeting today is about sacrifice and salvation. And I want to tell you, friends, that there can be no salvation without sacrifice. As we give, so shall we receive. It's a natural law—God's law, and man's law. If we want something—anything—we have to sacrifice to get it. You know that, friends, and so do I. It's a fact of everyday life as real as the price of meat and potatos.

"And so, friends, as you and I begin this great crusade that will roll across mighty oceans and pierce barriers of language and custom and save uncounted millions for Christ among the teeming, benighted hordes of the most populous nation on earth—when we labor together for the salvation of that vast heathen multitude—we realize that we must make sacrifices, if this crusade is to succeed. We must make great, unprecedented sacrifices. Because if we don't sacrifice, we'll fail, friends. It's as simple as that.

"And so—" He raised his hand. "And so, when you leave this Temple of the Lord and return to your homes today, or when you switch off your TV sets, all across this vast country, I would like you to consider your many blessings. I would like you to sit down in your comfortable living room, and I would like you to send us a check, friends, to be used in this great crusade for God. Yes—" He looked up directly into the key camera, solemnly nodding. "Yes, freinds, that's what I said. I would like you to send a check. I would like you to do it now. Today." Still staring into the key camera, he let a long, deliberate beat pass. Then: "This is the first time—the very first time—that I have made such an appeal. And some of you, perhaps, will be shocked, at my directness." He paused again—two seconds, three seconds. Beyond the lights, he could sense the audience shifting.

"But, as I stand here before God, I tell you that I am not ashamed to make this appeal. It is my sacrifice—my sackcloth, if you will, and my ashes. Someone has to do it. Someone has to make this sacrifice, if God's work is to be done. And that person, my friends, is I." He held his eyes steady on the camera for a final moment, then slowly lowered his gaze to the rostrum, and to the rows of seats just beyond the footlights. This time, he saw Mitchell, solid as a rock, nodding. Everything was ready, then. A little prayer, the altar call, and it was a wrap. Home free.

Around him, spectators were shifting in their seats. Some of them were rising. Blinking, he looked toward the stage. Holloway was standing with both arms upraised, head lifted up toward heaven—toward the TV camera, directly above. He was praying for the lost among them, inviting those who had sinned to come forward and confess, and let him pray for them.

It was the altar call.

Throughout the entire audience, people were rising to their feet, moving from their seats to the aisles, beginning to file down the aisle to the stage, where Holloway awaited them, still with his arms raised, still praying for the camera.

All the time had gone. Today—yesterday—tororrow: all of it was gone. Everything.

As he, too, was rising. Answering the call.

In his left hand, as he'd rehearsed it, he carried the storybook. In his right hand he carried the Bible. The .45 was thrust in his belt on the left side, its butt turned to the right. The blue blazer was closely buttoned, concealing the pistol.

He was in the aisle now, moving forward. Ahead, a teenager in a long white dress was smiling at him, urging him forward, lifting her hand to him in a gesture of pious invitation. She was a guide—an "usherette in the service of the Lord."

He was smiling as he passed, gravely exchanging a solemn nod with her. The stage was just ahead, built shoulder high. Already some were kneeling down before the stage, where Holloway still stood with eyes closed, arms raised—praying.

Another guide was smiling at him now, gesturing for him to move to the right. He was obeying her. He would move to the right, find a place in line, join the kneeling figures. He would place the Bible on the floor. With his right hand he would draw the pistol, covering it with the storybook.

And he would wait for Austin Holloway to bless him.

Father, forgive us our sins.

* * *

"The Lord will bless you," Holloway murmured, laying his hand on the woman's white-haired head, elaborately ringleted. The woman was raising a blue-veined hand, reaching for the hem of his jacket as she knelt before him. The hand sparkled with diamonds: big, blazing diamonds. Tens of thousands of dollars, just on the one hand.

"We need you," he added. "The Lord and I, we need you very much."

Upraised to him, her face was a mass of ancient wrinkles. Behind rhinestone-studded glasses, her eyes were streaming tears. She was trying to speak, trying to make him understand. But the camera couldn't wait, or the network, either.

Kneeling, he realized that his movements were automatic, independent of himself. He was seeing everything, feeling nothing. Like twin cameras, his eyes were focused in this new direction, registering everything that came before him: the kneeling figures, the spectators in the first row, smiling encouragement...

...and the big, broad-shouldered man dressed in a blue suit, watching him with his killer's eyes.

Mitchell.

He was conscious of the Bible falling from his hand, striking the floor at his feet. The storybook was falling, too—falling slower, floating down, its pages outspread. The .45 was in his hand as he turned toward the stage. The gun was coming up, almost aligned with the figure standing alone on the stage.

But something had struck him a quick, cruel blow. The sound of explosions was deafening. Now a wild confusion of strangers' faces whirled around him, tilted, fell away. He was falling, too—slowly, gently, like the storybook. A light was blinking bright in his eyes: a spotlight, shining from the wings. But he still held the gun, struggling to lift it higher, higher. On the stage, motion-stopped, Holloway stood with arms upraised: a doomed prophet, his face chalky white, his eyes round and innocent. It was a deadman's face, mortally stricken, with its suprised eyes staring helplessly down at the gun, raised between them.

But the gun was falling away, too heavy to hold. He was on his knees now, struggling to raise the gun. Directly above him, Holloway was kneeling, too—staring down at him with a terrible intensity, trying to make him see—to make him understand. But the lights were fading now. And the sounds were softer. The screaming was no more than a murmur: echoes from the past, almost gone. He lost sight of the stricken face above him. The echoes had faded into silence. He was lying on his back, helplessly looking up into other faces, clustered in a circle above him. They were the same faces that had always pursued him: the strangers' faces...

...haunting him.

Hating him.

But now the faces were following the sounds of their voices, fading away. Finally still. Finally silent. Forever gone.

He saw the figure turn toward him, saw the Bible and the oversized prayer book fall away. Eyes blazed behind horn-rimmed glasses, a disguise. The eyes were a strange, dead brown. Mary's eyes.

Mary, Mary, Mistress Mary. It had been their secret, a pet name.

The pistol was swinging toward him, almost in line. The sound of screaming filled his ears. But not his screaming, not on camera.

Please, God, not on camera.

God.

Yes, he'd done it. He'd called out for God.

A shot sounded. One shot. Two shots: thunderclaps sent down from heaven. Mitchell's thunder, saving him, one last time. Now the murderer's pistol was faltering, falling. The murderer was sinking slowly to his knees, a penitent with all the others, declaring for Christ. Bowed down. Bloody.

Dying.

Dead.

But why, then, was he also on his knees? Was he praying, performing for the sinners? Would the pain in his chest let him pray?

No.

He couldn't pray, couldn't speak. Instead, he was falling. Slowly, gently falling, cradled by some unseen grace, watching over him as he came down. Because he'd fallen on his back. Praise God, he'd fallen on his back...

...so that, directly above the podium, between himself and heaven, the key camera could see his face. It was a good, clear closing shot...

...to final fade.

Thirty-Three

SHE LOOKED to her right. Had she seen the glow of a tiny red light in the offstage darkness?

God, there it was: a ruby glow below a TV camera. Signifying that, yes, that camera was rolling. She turned her head to the left. Yes, that camera was rolling, too.

Recording this record turnout—this final triumph for Austin Holloway, lying in the huge oaken casket, center stage.

She'd come back to where she'd started, many years ago—to this same stage, staring at these same tiny red lights. At first, the lights had totally intimidated her. But, slowly, she'd learned to accept them, to live with them. Yet, throughout her life, the red lights had never released her.

Just as her father had never released her—or her mother, sitting beside her. Or her brother, standing now at center stage, where her father had always stood. With both arms lifted high, eyes raised, trailing the long microphone cord that she'd always associated with her father, Elton stood in the vortex of three golden spotlights. It was a lighting effect that had always been reserved for The Hour's most climactic moments, all stops pulled out. As she listened, Elton's voice began to tremble. Was the tremor calculated, or real? She couldn't decide—just as, in the past, she'd never been able to decide where her father's art left off and his true feelings began.

"...and so I ask You, Lord," Elton was saying, still with his hands raised high, "I ask You to pause for a moment in Your labors, and listen to these last few words—these final words." He paused a moment, to emphasize yet another evocation of his father's ritual incantation. "I ask You to recall, with me, all the sinners that, over the years, my father has turned from the devil's work to Your bright, shining service. I ask You to remember, Lord, that Austin Holloway has always been Your faithful servant and—yes—Your partner, too. I ask You to remember that, literally with his last breath, he was mounting an assault in Your name on the largest country in the world, that haven of heathens, where Your words and Your works are ignored."

Another pause. Slowly, the raised arms came down, the head came level. Then, looking directly into the camera, he lowered his voice to a solemn, intimate note. "He died in Your service, Lord. He died on the firing line—on the field of battle, as so many brave Christian soldiers have died before him. His enemy was a poor, demented youth—someone enlisted by your enemies, and given a gun, and told to kill Austin Holloway, Your servant. And, even though the assassin failed—even though one of Your soldiers killed him, before he could fire his fatal bullet—the shock was too much for my father's poor heart, already weakened in Your service, Lord. And so he died. And, as he lay dying, his last words were spoken to his assassin, forgiving him."

Another pause—the final pause.

"Austin Holloway is gone," Elton intoned. "You have lost a good and faithful servant, Lord—and I have lost a father. We are both losers.

"And yet, Lord, You are not forsaken. Because—with Your permission—I intend to carry on my father's work. I intend to take Your word to every part of this great country—and into every corner of the world. Where my father reached a million souls through Your miracle of television, I promise You that I will reach *tens* of millions, carrying Your message to every sinner who will listen, or watch.

"And so—" At the words, background music began. Sister Teresa stepped forward, ready. "And so, it is time for us to close this service. It is time for us to commend the soul of Austin Holloway to Your eternal care. A-men."

Stepping back, Elton bowed his head, standing with his hands clasped on his grandfather's prayer book. It was the same pose her father had always assumed, after the final words. On cue, Sister Teresa began *Onward, Christian Soldiers*. In the wings, the two cameras were pivoting in opposite directions, one to roam the audience, the other to play across the faces of the choir. Today the cameras would be seeking out the tear-streaked faces—while, above, the key camera remained on Sister Teresa's face. It was written into her contract.

Among the faithful watching on nationwide TV, all rating records were doubtless being broken.

Turning her head, Denise looked at her mother, on her left. Eyes dry, face composed, her mother was staring straight ahead. Her eyes were clear; she was sober. For two days, the bottles of gin delivered to her room had gone unopened. Was it shock? Or was it a miracle? She hadn't dared to ask—and hardly dared to hope. She could only wonder whether the obvious might be true: that the real cause of her mother's alcoholism had been excised.

Last night, her mother had taken her to her bedroom, where they'd looked at old family photographs, some of them ninety years old. Occasionally, she'd seen her mother's eyes wander to the armoire where the gin bottles were kept. But only momentarily, only tentatively.

When she'd left her mother's room, the time had been almost 2 A.M. At the door, they'd held each other close. For the first time since she'd been a girl, she'd felt strength in her mother's embrace. Strength, and something more—hope, or purpose.

On stage, the last strains of *Onward, Christian Soldiers* were drawing to a tremulous close. The audience was stirring. The red lights above the cameras winked out.

It was another wrap.

Except that, today, the usherettes would form the faithful into a long line of mourners, waiting patiently to file past the casket. For this part of the ceremony, the casket would be open.

And she would be gone.

Without speaking to Flournoy, or to Mitchell, or to her brother, she would leave this monstrous place.

Tomorrow, she would go to the funeral. Beside her mother, she would play her assigned role—as she was playing it now. But that would be the end. After tomorrow, the time of the scavengers would begin. Elton, Flournoy, Sister Teresa, even Pastor Bob—all of them would be scrambling for the leftover spoils. And for the camera angles. And the perks. And the contract terms.

Or, rather, they would scramble for what Elton left them. Because, after the sermon just delivered—and telecast—Elton's place at the top of the heap was assured. Elton would keep his bogus bargain with God. What Caesar had done for Mark Antony, her father had done for Elton.

She turned to Peter, on her right, whispering, "Why don't you get the car? Bring it around to the side entrance."

Dressed in his blue suit and white shirt and striped tie,

250

Peter could have been any one of a million men—anyone but Peter. She could see that he was suffering, just as she was suffering. If Peter believed in the devil, the face beneath the horns would be Elton's.

He rose to his feet, reached across her to touch her mother's hand, then walked across the stage, moving awkwardly, stiffly. She never should have asked him to come. After they took her mother home, she would release him. She would spare him tomorrow's obscenity.

She pointed through the windshield. "Get over to the right. You have to get on the Hollywood Freeway."

Glancing over his shoulder, Peter switched on the turn signal and cautiously changed lanes. He was frowning and shaking his head, muttering a mild profanity as a bright red sports car cut sharply in front of them. Driving on Los Angeles freeways was almost the only task that could intimidate Peter.

"Are you sure you don't want me to stay?" he asked, scowling at a careening van painted with polka dots.

"There's no need. It'll just be more of the same, tomorrow."

Looking at her, he asked quietly, "How do you feel?"

"A little numbed, I guess. I'm not sure."

"It'll take time, for you to sort it all out. Maybe a lot of time."

"I know."

For a few moments they drove in silence before Peter said, "I talked to Mitchell. He said that he hadn't recognized Carson. If Carson hadn't panicked, he would've—" Peter hesitated. "He would've been able to do what he'd come to do."

"He did it anyway."

"In a way, yes. But not really. Your father died a natural death. And whether you approve of what he did with his life, the fact is that he probably believed most of what he said. He kept working, too, even with a bad heart. And he died doing his job." He raised a hand in a gesture that signified both approval and resignation. "You have to respect him. You don't have to agree with him. But you've got to respect him."

Eyes straight ahead, she made no reply.

Because she couldn't respect him. Not now. Not so soon. Not remembering the bodies he'd left behind, the dead and the dying.

She felt him looking at her, then heard him say, "What about your mother?"

Still looking ahead, she pointed to the "Los Angeles International" exit. He nodded; he'd seen it, and was once more changing lanes. She let another moment of silence pass. Then: "She hasn't had a drink for two days. I'm taking it one day at a time. I guess she is, too."

"Maybe—" He drew a reluctant breath. "Maybe you should ask her to stay with you for a while."

She shook her head. "No. It wouldn't work."

"I guess not. In fact, I agree with you. But I wanted to—to offer."

She smiled at him. Turning his head, he returned her smile. Then he asked, "Will she go on—performing?"

"We talked about it for a little while last night. I told her she shouldn't do it for a while—for a period of mourning, so called. Hopefully, it could become permanent."

"Did you tell her that you hoped it would be permanent?"

"No."

He nodded. "Good. That's smart. I get the impression that a lot of communication between you and your mother is unspoken. Which is good. Or, at least, probably inevitable. The point is, I imagine she knows how you feel about it, whether or not you've actually said the words." He drove silently for a moment before he said, "I wonder whether it's possible that her drinking might be connected to the fact that she's got to play her part every Sunday?"

"I was wondering the same thing myself."

They were on the airport boulevard now, angling toward the sign marked "United," "American," "P.S.A.," "Braniff." Another moment of silence passed. There was more for them to say—more to share. But somehow the words weren't coming, for either of them. The United loading zone was just ahead. Cars were parked two deep at the curb, while harried passengers unloaded their baggage, bid hasty goodbyes and hurried into the terminal—all under the baleful eyes of airport policemen, blowing their whistles, urgently waving the passengers into the terminal and the cars on their way.

Pulling in behind a slow-moving Mercedes, Peter said, "When do you think you'll come home?"

"Two or three days—just as soon as I can. I'll have to play it by ear."

They were stopped at the curb now. Setting the parking brake, Peter sat silently for a moment, staring straight ahead. Finally he turned to face her squarely. His eyes were serious, his voice somber as he said, "I—ah—I've been thinking, lately, about that time in Mill Valley, after we had dinner with Ann and Cy, and we were talking about—about having children, and everything. Do you remember?"

Slowly—almost reluctantly—she was nodding.

Why reluctantly? And why couldn't she answer him? Why could she only stare straight ahead—silently, helplessly? The next moment could mean everything to her. Why did the prospect numb her?

"I—" He swallowed. But, doggedly, he went on: "I was thinking that you were right, that night. I mean—" He swallowed again. "I mean, I guess I can be pretty one-way about things. I—ah—got burned so badly, getting divorced, and feeling guilty about what the divorce did to my kid, that I never stopped to think about you—about what having children would mean to you. I—" As his voice trailed off, she saw an irate policeman standing squarely in front of the car, urgently gesturing them to pull away from the curb. Peter nodded to the policeman, tried to placate him with a palms-out gesture, then turned again to her. Saying: "I was laying my hang-ups on you. Which isn't fair. In fact, it's a pretty crappy trick, when you come right down to it. So—" He gestured again, this time turning his palms up, eloquently signifying his inability to put it into words. He swallowed again, then doggedly continued: "So I—I was thinking," he said, speaking in a low, husky voice, "I was thinking that, if you want to have kids, it—it's all right with me."

She knew the answer that she must give. She didn't need to search for the words. Quietly, she said, "I wouldn't ever want to have children without being married, Peter."

She saw him nod: a grave, considered inclination of his head. "Yeah," he answered. "Yeah, that too."

As she reached out to touch his hand, a sudden crash made her jump. It was the policeman, hammering with the flats of both hands on the hood of the car—furious.

ABOUT THE AUTHOR

Collin Wilcox was born in Detroit and educated at Antioch College. He has lived in San Francisco since 1950, where he operated a small business before becoming a full-time mystery/suspense novelist. He is a partisan of the mystery/suspense genre because he thinks it offers a framework for serious commentary on contemporary life.

Collin Wilcox likes living in San Francisco because "it is an exciting, vital city that still retains some of its frontier excitement beneath an aura of new world sophistication." Currently, and for the foreseeable future, the most important things in his life are his two sons, his Victorian house, his typewriter, his books, his airplane and his ten-speed bike.

THRILLS * CHILLS * MYSTERY
from FAWCETT BOOKS

CURRENT CREST BESTSELLERS

☐ BORN WITH THE CENTURY   24295 $3.50
by William Kinsolving
A gripping chronicle of a man who creates an empire for his family,
and how they engineer its destruction.

☐ SINS OF THE FATHERS   24417 $3.95
by Susan Howatch
The tale of a family divided from generation to generation by great
wealth and the consequences of a terrible secret.

☐ THE NINJA   24367 $3.50
by Eric Van Lustbader
They were merciless assassins, skilled in the ways of love and the
deadliest of martial arts. An exotic thriller spanning postwar Japan
and present-day New York.

☐ KANE & ABEL   24376 $3.75
by Jeffrey Archer
A saga spanning 60 years, this is the story of two ruthless, powerful
businessmen whose ultimate confrontation rocks the financial com-
munity as well as their own lives.

☐ GREEN MONDAY   24400 $3.50
by Michael M. Thomas
An all-too-plausible thriller in which the clandestine manipulation
of world oil prices results in the most fantastic bull market the
world has ever known.

Buy them at your local bookstore or use this handy coupon for ordering.

COLUMBIA BOOK SERVICE, CBS Publications
32275 Mally Road, P.O. Box FB, Madison Heights, MI 48071

Please send me the books I have checked above. Orders for less than 5 books
must include 75¢ for the first book and 25¢ for each additional book to cover
postage and handling. Orders for 5 books or more postage is FREE. Send check
or money order only. Allow 3–4 weeks for delivery.

Cost $_____   Name _____

Sales tax*_____   Address _____

Postage_____   City _____

Total $_____   State_____ Zip _____

*The government requires us to collect sales tax in all states except AK, DE,
MT, NH and OR.
Prices and availability subject to change without notice.   8215